Guns of the Palmetto Plains

To David LeMoine'
Thanks for being
a friend.
God bless You,
Hope you enjoy
this book

Rick Tonyon
11/30/03

# Guns of the Palmetto Plains

*A Cracker Western*
by
Rick Tonyan

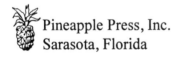

Pineapple Press, Inc.
Sarasota, Florida

Pineapple Press, Inc.
P.O. Box 3899
Sarasota, Florida 34230-3899


LIBRARY OF CONGRESS CATALOGING-IN-PUBLICATION DATA

Tonyan, Rick, 1949-
    Guns of the palmetto plains / by Rick Tonyan
        p.    cm.
    ISBN 1-56164-061-1 (hb). — ISBN 1-56164-070-0 (pb)
    1. United States—History—Civil War, 1861-1865—Fiction.
    I. Title
    PS3570.0533G86      1994
    813' .54—dc20                                        94-28717
                                                              CIP


First Edition   10 9 8 7 6 5 4 3 2

Design by June Cussen
Composition by Cynthia Keenan

Printed and bound by
        Victor Graphics, Baltimore, Maryland

To my wife, Linda,
in thanks for all her encouragement and support
during the writing of this book

# Contents

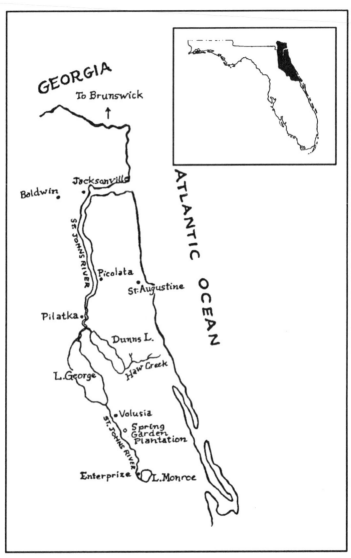

Northeastern Florida, 1863-1865

# Prologue

SOMEWHERE BEHIND THE THICK mass of clouds the sun was setting, but no evening breeze relieved the atmosphere inside the city. Fortifications built around Vicksburg to keep out the enemy seemed to hold the heat captive. Breastworks — 20-foot-high walls of earth — surrounded the heart of the city. Beyond those mounds, fires were beginning to glow in the enemy's campsites. Moist air rising from the brown river near the fortifications drifted over the streets. The humidity seemed to mix with the rotten-egg smell of sulfur to create a choking miasma in the air. Sulfur. It also was called brimstone. The major building block of Hell. It hung in the air after a day in which thousands of pounds of gunpowder had been exploded by those both within and without the city.

The captain believed he could taste the air as he breathed. It was just shy of nauseating. Even worse than the thick, pasty sensation on his tongue was the burning he felt in his feet. Heat radiating off the cobblestones of the streets penetrated the worn soles of his boots. Each step he took further irritated his feet. He tried to get his mind off his discomfort by concentrating on the city as he walked. But there was little to occupy his mind. The brownish red brick homes and shops that lined the street were unlit. Their outlines were becoming indistinguishable in the dusk. The only sounds the captain heard were his own footsteps and the slow clip-clop from the horse he was leading.

After hours of explosions that had shaken the mortar out of brick walls, the silence seemed almost unnatural. The Yankees must have called off the bombardment and gone to supper, the captain thought.

No one else was in the streets, but the captain knew that dozens, perhaps hundreds, of eyes watched him lead the bay gelding. It was rare to see a horse in Vicksburg these days. During the last several weeks, it also was rare to see anything or anybody walking a street without scurrying for shelter from the iron rain of shrapnel. It was easy for the captain to imagine small groups of people huddled inside the buildings. He could sense their dull eyes, vacant holes under their foreheads, following him and the horse. He knew that nobody really had much interest in him, but at least he provided something for their eyes to focus on to break the monotony.

Like those who watched him, the captain was indifferent to where he was going. His orders still were sealed and he would wait until after dawn to read them. All he knew was that he and a sergeant were to get out of the city as best they could by morning. Fine, he decided. Going anywhere and doing anything was better than sitting in Vicksburg and wondering whether he would die by an exploding shell or starvation.

The red cobblestones of the pavement ended abruptly and a dirt path muffled the steps of both the captain and his horse. The line of buildings also ended and the captain saw a small, gently sloping hill topped by a white picket fence. Another horse was tied by its reins to a post of the open gate. A man stood inside a few feet from the gate.

The figure was silhouetted, black against the bit of red light filtering through the clouds. As he approached, the captain could see the head was bowed and the hands were held about waist high, clasping a hat.

"Sergeant Hooker?" the captain spoke in a normal conversational tone, but in the stillness, he felt as if he were shouting.

The head raised and the hands brought up the hat. Turning toward the captain, the man touched the hat brim with his right hand in a salute. "Yes, sir."

Quickly, he slipped the reins from the gate and led the horse halfway down the hill to meet the captain. He briefly turned back to look at the crest. Following his gaze, the captain for the first time realized that the fence surrounded a small graveyard. Tombstones, none of them more than three feet high, stuck out of the ground.

They walked east, through another neighborhood of unlit homes. The captain studied his companion and felt a pang of guilt over the regulation that gave officers more rations than enlisted men. During the last two months, as the Yankee siege tightened, the captain had lost weight until his uniform trousers sagged at the waist. But he felt bloated as he looked at Sergeant Hooker. Ribs showed through the dirty red undershirt the sergeant wore. The trousers hung loosely, needing both suspenders and a belt to hold them. And Hooker was tall, a good six-foot-six, which accentuated his thinness.

The horse also was gaunt, with ribs peeking out from under its saddle blanket. A fan of classic literature, the captain looked at his companion and thought of Don Quixote, but did not smile at the comparison.

Then a light as bright as if someone had taken white-hot metal from a forge and thrust it at their eyes, flashed above the captain and Hooker. They heard the whining of iron fragments flying through the dark before they heard the explosion and felt the street tremble under their feet. The sound was much like a thunderclap, but louder and longer. Each man clung to the reins of his horse as both animals reared.

"Yankees must've finished supper," the captain said. He felt as if he were doing a wild dance with his horse, trying to keep in step while getting next to the animal to shield himself from the shrapnel as it fell. The horse jerked its head, and the reins cut into the captain's hands.

A high-pitched whinny rose above the rest of the noise. The captain looked at his horse. No. The whinny came from the right. The captain looked over and saw the other horse already on the ground, with Hooker standing above it, still holding the reins. The animal got on its front feet, but was unable to make the rear legs obey. The sergeant stared down and dropped his right hand to the holster on his hip. He unbuttoned the flap of leather covering the gun butt. The draw was cavalry style — an awkward-looking motion in which the right hand twisted until the knuckles were against the waist as the gun left the holster.

Then, in one quick, smooth movement, Hooker

twisted his wrist back so that the gun and hand both pointed straight at the horse's head. He fired and the horse collapsed before the sound of the shot faded.

"Damn," the captain said as Hooker knelt by the horse and removed the bridle and saddle.

With a jerk, the sergeant pulled the saddle from the carcass. He looped the bridle around the pommel, put the blanket on top of the saddle and hoisted the bundle to his right shoulder. Reaching over with his left hand, he drew a carbine from a scabbard tied to the pommel.

"Plenty o' Yankees around," he said as he hefted the carbine. "I'll get one to loan me a horse afore sunup."

He and the captain resumed walking. It was now fully dark, but exploding shells lit the sky for them, outlying the man-made hills of the breastworks. The explosions also threw patches of light on the carcass. Behind the shattered windows of the buildings, eyes were fixed on the dead horse. A long dark shape crawled from a hole under a wall of crumbling masonry. When it reached the horse, it stood partially erect over the carcass. Then, other shapes separated from the shadows of the buildings and converged on the horse. Some of them wore baggy trousers, secured at the waists by ropes. Others wore dresses that hung like bags in shapeless folds. All carried long, heavy-bladed knives. The shapes descended and blended into one writhing mass over the carcass.

Three days later, the Union army entered Vicksburg. By that time, the carcass was a jumble of disjointed, pinkish bones without enough meat or entrails about them to attract flies. Thousands of blue-clad men passed the bones without noticing them. The men were busy stepping in time to the tune of "John Brown's Body." Many joined in choruses of "Glory, glory hallelujah." Others were concentrating on keeping in step with the march.

Cavalry regiments entered the city behind the infantry. Major Daniel Greenley was riding in one of these. He was busy thinking about the victory. By the time he reached the bones, Greenley was feeling too tired to join in the singing.

For nearly three months since the siege had begun, Greenley had looked on the city as if it were some fortress out of a Walter Scott novel about the Crusades. It was a dark citadel from which fire would pour out toward anyone who approached too closely. Because that fire was directed at him and his comrades, the city was a place of evil. Then came the day the evil was overthrown and the crusaders entered the castle. The major had half-expected to feel like he had found the Holy Grail, safe at last from the hands of infidels. Instead, he found a dung heap buried within a charnel house. A stench greeted him before he reached the first row of ruins that once had been homes. Even the odor coming from the marching columns, a combination of manure, leather, axle grease, and the sweat of men and horses, was smothered by the smell of the city. From the streets came the smell of open sewers. Above everything else, the air held a strange, almost sweet odor. It was the same smell the major occasionally had noticed when in the sickroom of someone suffering from a fever. Greenley tried breathing deeply. That was a mistake. He tried spitting, but somehow gagged himself. Steeling himself against retching, he swallowed hard and clenched his legs around his horse.

Greenley was several blocks beyond the bones before he noticed any people. After seeing his first Vicksburg resident, he forgot about the smell of the city. The resident was a woman — or a girl; her age could not be determined. She had the flat chest of youth, but her creased face looked at least middle-aged. Her checks were dark indentations in her face, making the cheekbones seem very high and the chin extremely sharp. The eyes sank beneath a corrugated forehead. What would have been very thin hair, had it not been thickened by grime which matted together individual strands, fell down both sides of her head and over her shoulders to hang slightly above her waist. What looked like a pale blue sack draped itself from just below her neck to her ankles. It could have been made from an old bedsheet; or it could have been a once-fashionable dress, now devoid of hoops and petticoats. Two arms, about as thick as the major's wrists, hung down on either side of the sleeveless garment and ended in what seemed like oversized, almost fleshless claws.

The rest of the people — soon there were hundreds of them lining the route of the march — differed from the woman only as much as one charred tree does from another in a fire-ravaged forest. The children, particularly the blacks, were the worst. Some were nearly naked, with arms and legs that looked like broomsticks and bellies that protruded as if they were pregnant. Everyone on either side of the street watched silently as the ranks of blue passed.

Greenley quickly learned to avoid looking at the people. He kept his eyes fixed on the rumps of the horses in the company that preceded his. Eventually, that company turned down a side street and headed for its quarters. The major began scanning buildings to find one for his office. He settled on a single-story wood frame that seemed both vacant and intact. There were smudges from powder burns on its whitewashed walls, but the wood itself was unharmed. He raised his right hand in the command to halt, but he feared that his voice would crack if he tried to shout the word. Fortunately, the sergeant riding at his side yelled out the order for him.

Within minutes, the sergeant had broken the lock on the front door and men were scampering through the house. Some were looking for loot. Others were bringing in supplies and equipment needed to turn a family home into a company headquarters. The sergeant brought in a canvas bag and set it by a desk in the front parlor. He took a pen, an inkwell, and a large book from the bag and looked expectantly at the major. Greenley looked down at the sergeant, who already had written "July 4, 1863" at the head of a page to begin this entry in the company log. But, instead of dictating the entry, the major said, "Find the quartermaster and have him go through the supplies to get some food out to those people."

The sergeant put down the pen. "What people?"

It was then that Greenley felt a burning around his eyes and knew he was in danger of weeping.

# 1

It was perfect weather for a camp meeting on the shore and baptisms in the river. Unfortunately, it also was perfect weather for alligators to swim and feed in the river. If the weather had been warmer, it would have been too hot to stand and listen to the sermon. And the preacher, who could work himself up to a sweat even during a January freeze, would look and feel like an overworked plow horse — a tired, soggy hunk of flesh — by the end of the meeting. But, a hotter day also would have meant that gators would not be swimming through the water a few feet away from the preacher and eyeing the crowd on the riverbank. They would have been been sunning themselves on logs, too contented to bother going after anything in the river. Particularly something as big as a human. It would have taken more effort than it was worth to kill somebody in the midday sun.

If the weather had been very much cooler, both gators and humans would have become uncomfortable. Those who were baptized would have found their clothes turning clammy by the time they got home. But those who went in now would find the water refreshing after two hours in a crowd listening to the sermon. Their clothes would dry off and be pleasantly cool during their trips home. Cooler weather would have made the gators sluggish, encouraging them to stay in their holes along the bank. But the day was warm enough to encourage them to patrol the river. And, with a hint of coolness in the water that foretold of a change in the seasons, they might be tempted to stock their holes with some surplus meat. Humans were the perfect size for storing in a gator's larder.

William Gordon Jr.'s job was to keep his father's flock separated from the gators. It had been his job for the last two years. His father gave it to him. Before a meeting, he gathered up and put in a burlap feed sack about a dozen of the gray, flinty stones that cropped out from the bank. He then stood at the edge of the crowd during the meeting and waited for his father to signal that there were ten minutes left of the sermon.

His father was talking on how the South had to get on the right side of the Lord if it wanted to win the war. It was a variation of a theme that Junior had heard repeatedly over the last two years.

"Think we're more righteous than the Yankees? Think the Lord's gonna fight our battles? Was he fightin' for us at Antietam? At Gettysburg? At Vicksburg?" His father shook his head. Then he made a chopping motion downward with his right hand — the hand that held a Bible. That was the signal.

Junior picked up the sack. He walked to the water's edge 200 yards downstream, away from the flock of 50 listening to the sermon. The people were gathered in a semicircle about the oak under which his father preached. Junior came to a log from what probably had been another large oak.

Years had passed since the tree had died. Maybe it was killed by a bolt of lightning. Or maybe disease got it. Or it simply could have grown too big and heavy for the wet, sandy riverbank to support. However the tree died, the log was weathered black and slick. There were not enough features left in the wood to tell for sure what sort of tree it had been. But, whatever it was, it was large. The log that remained was a good three feet around. Junior kicked at it and swung the sack against the bottom. He hoped to scare out anything that might have crawled under it. Then he lifted the sack and whacked the top of the log. That should get rid of any spiders or scorpions living in the wood. Nothing happened, so he sat down on the log and chucked stones into the water. He lobbed them in a high arch, so that they would come down with a large splash a good 100 yards toward the middle of the half-mile-wide river.

After a few stones had splashed, he saw the results of his labor. Greenish black objects appeared in the water. They were several shades lighter than the water itself, which was stained as dark as black coffee from the silt and decaying plants that filtered into it as the river wound through central Florida. From where Junior sat, the greenish black shapes looked like logs — long, rounded and rough-textured. But, unlike logs, they were not merely floating along in the water. They were swimming against the current. Gators had heard the splashes and were coming to see if whatever hit

19

the water was edible. Junior intended to keep them occupied with the stones while the real edibles entered the water at the baptismal call.

To be truthful, Junior preferred decoying gators to staying with the crowd. A musky odor, something like leather when it mildews, came from the river and the damp vegetation around it. But that smell was preferable to what was coming from 50 sweating farm wives and cow hunters at the meeting. Besides, he was becoming restless and bored listening to the sermon. Not that he objected to his father's preaching. He was rather proud of his father. Sometimes, when a crowd was punctuating each of his father's sentences with screamed amens and hallelujahs, he felt a prickly sensation on his skin. That was the first stirrings of the Spirit moving his body, his father said. But the sermons themselves didn't thrill him. Mostly because each one had been practiced aloud at home and, by the time his father delivered one to a crowd, it had become dull through repetition.

His father had no rectory in which to practice his sermons. Indeed, there was no church. The preaching was done under the live oak, which reached about 60 feet into the air and spread its gray-brown branches to cast at least another 60 feet of shade even at noon. Junior had seen and heard real preachers in real churches. There were a couple as near as two miles away, at Enterprize. That was a town at the edge of Lake Monroe, a body of water that formed out of a wide spot in the river.

In a way, Junior envied the Enterprize preachers and their families. They made most, if not all, of their livelihoods from preaching. His father considered his calling to be more like some sort of spiritual hobby. Never took up a collection. Most of the family income came from farming and cow hunting. If his father was not out plowing, weeding, and harvesting in a field, he was in the forests and swamps gathering cattle. Two or three times a year, he would be gone for months at a time, driving cattle to some market.

Sunday services under the oak stopped during the cattle drives. But, since most of the other men in the flock also were cow hunters and were driving cattle, the crowd would have been drastically cut even if his father had stayed.

His father had returned from a drive two weeks ago and seemed anxious to make up for the missed sermons. He had been practicing this one since Monday. First, he thumbed through his Bible and started reciting passages. As the week progressed, he elaborated on the passages with stories and jokes built around events of the day. By Friday, he had constructed the sermon. Then the rehearsals started in earnest. His father shouted out exhortations while keeping the plow steady as he walked behind a mule, when shoveling manure around rows of vegetables, and when castrating and branding some calves.

Junior had much of the sermon memorized by Sunday. He occasionally caught himself mouthing the words as his father spoke them. His lips began moving involuntarily as he threw another stone into the air. There were five gators in the middle of the river to watch it splash.

He could still hear his father's voice. In fact, from the distance, the deep, roaring bass was softened a little, making it a low rumble that was somewhat more pleasant to the ear. Another reason for preferring to decoy gators.

"Our cause is righteous. But what of us? Look at the Israelites. They were God's chosen. They thought — they knew — they were righteous," the voice said. "God would have to be on their side. Right? Why worry 'bout the Assyrians and the Babylonians — those people in kingdoms to the north and west? Those kingdoms were evil. The Israelites just knew that God would keep them safe from people like that. So, the Israelites lied, cheated, 'n' stole. They were whoremongers 'n' wine bibers 'n' proud o' their sins. What does the Bible say 'bout that kind o' thinkin' 'n' actin'?"

There was a sharp cracking sound, almost like a shot from a small-caliber gun. From his seat on the stump, Junior couldn't see his father, but he knew what had caused the sound. It was his father's leather-bound Bible getting thumped against the side of the wagon that served as a pulpit. Junior felt sorry for that book. He had no idea how old it was, but its brittle pages were stained brown and its black covers were faded until they were streaked with red. Junior didn't know how many more times the book could take being whacked against something every time his father quoted directly from it.

"'Hear this, I pray you, ye heads o' the house o' Jacob and princes o' the house o' Israel, that abhor judgment, 'n' pervert all equity,'" his father bellowed out the quote.

"'They build up Zion with blood, 'n' Jerusalem with iniquity.

"'The heads thereof judge for reward, 'n' the priests

thereof teach for hire, 'n' the prophets thereof divine for money: yet will they lean upon the Lord, and say, Is not the Lord among us? None evil can come upon us.

"'Therefore shall Zion for your sake be plowed as a field 'n' Jerusalem shall become heaps, 'n' the mountain of the house as the high places of the forest.' Micah, three: nine through twelve.

"So what did the Israelites do? They kept on lyin', cheatin', 'n' stealin'. They whoremongered 'n' bibed wine. Right up 'til the day the Assyrians 'n' the Babylonians struck. Israel was turned into a plowed-under field. The temple 'n' all the rest of Jerusalem lay in a heap o' ruins."

The words came out in a rapid tumble amid the amens and hallelujahs from the crowd. Junior knew that his father soon would be calling those who had not yet been baptized to come into the river.

"'N' what about our Southern Confederacy? Can it expect judgment different from ancient Israel? Look at us. See the Richmond politicians grabbing taxes 'n' property with one hand while dolin' out worthless paper money to the poor with the other. See the Atlanta merchants profiteerin' from the war. See them 'n' their plantation-ownin' friends buy their way out o' the military while the poor die in their stead.

"But you don't even have to look as far away as Richmond or Atlanta. Go up to our own capitol in Tallahassee. Watch the sleek, fat politicians 'n' planters live off the public 'n' shirk their duties. Or look two miles east to Enterprize. Watch the county politicians spend our taxes on everythin' from Cuban seegars to lewd women."

The rush of words stopped. Two or three seconds passed silently. Then his father resumed, this time carefully and slowly pronouncing each word.

"But don't go wastin' your bile at politicians. How 'bout ya'll? You men — ever sneak a change o' brand on a steer you hunted up? Ever forgotten 'bout your wife when you got drunk in some bawdy house after a trail drive? Ever sold a blind horse or sick ox? You women — ever smile at some neighbor lady to her face then get with your friends 'n' gossip 'bout her like she was some painted Jezebel? Ever turn away some wanderer from your door without givin' him some chore so's he can earn money 'n' dignity? Ever long for silks 'n' finery out of the fashion plate magazines 'n' disparage your husband for the little he can provide?

"Pride, envy, lust — all the sins that brought judgment on Israel are here in the Confederacy, in Florida, in Volusia County 'n' in the hearts of everybody here who ain't accepted the Lord Jesus Christ as their Savior. 'N' the judgment that came upon Israel will come on us all if we don't cleanse our hearts 'n' welcome Jesus into our lives."

The call was coming. Junior knew his father was taking off his boots and socks and rolling up his trouser legs.

"If we want our cause to be truly righteous, then we have to be righteous in the eyes of the Lord. If you want that, invite Jesus into your heart now. Be cleansed in His Baptism."

His father would be in the water by now. Junior chucked another stone toward the gators. The water would be up to only his father's waist, but up to at least the chests of most of those being baptized. His father was huge — six feet, five inches tall with shoulders at least twice the width of most men.

A sharp, high-pitched cry came from above and behind Junior. He turned in its direction. Off to the east, high overhead, way above the tops of some pines that he knew were at least 100 feet tall, a bird circled in the air — either an eagle or an osprey, it was too far up for him to tell for sure. It was a dark something that changed its shape as it moved against the sky. The sky was so bright and blue that it looked almost white, making the bird stand out against its background. When the wings moved, the bird looked like two small arches. Then it began to glide and it looked like a thin line floating through the sky. Junior waited for it to cry again. Because he was ready for it this time, he was able to pay more attention when it came. It sounded like "Kee-Hi." An osprey, a large hawk that lived along the river and ate only fish. Eagles had a slightly lower-toned cry, which sounded like "Kee-Haw." But, the difference in the cries was lost to anyone who had not spent years along the river and repeatedly heard both ospreys and eagles call. Even then, one had to pay attention to make sure which was which.

The osprey was making wide circles, looking for some food in the river. Its circles also probably were taking it over Enterprize, where Lake Monroe fed into the river. Junior tried to follow the bird's path, but it turned into the sun and he lost it. He lowered his eyes. Live oaks, some as tall and big as the one under which his father preached, stood behind him like huge sentries assigned to guard him. Yards of Spanish moss, colored a brown-gray that was almost the same shade as the oaks' bark, hung down from each branch. The moss swayed in the slight breeze and cast moving shadows across him. He looked through the moss to the pasture beyond the line of oaks. It was like looking through the gauze mosquito netting that covered his bed — impossible to see anything without at least one strand getting into the field of vision.

The pasture stretched between the river and the forest to the east for the full two miles into Enterprize. Indeed, the town was merely a populated spot in the middle of the pasture, which extended for another two or three miles east beyond Enterprize until it ran into the pines.

Junior imagined the pasture looked like the plains that covered the Far West. Featureless, except for a few scattered trees, broad and flat. But God created the plains that covered the nation from the Mississippi River to the Rocky Mountains. Men created this plain. Burned out the pines, oaks, and briar-filled underbrush. A few acres at a time over a span of about 15 years. The burnings came during each January and February, when there was little rainfall and the grass and underbrush became naturally dry tinder. By each May, grass would be growing in the black emptiness of the newly burned section. Two months later, the grass would be more than a foot high and bent over from the weight of its seed heads. Another month would go by and the burned-out section would be ready for grazing cattle.

But the forest did not entirely surrender to the flames, the grass, and the cattle. Even as they burned, some of the pines dropped seeds that would sprout when the grass began growing. After a few years, seed-lings dotted the man-made plains. It was possible to accurately guess how long ago a pasture had been cleared by the height of the seedlings. About a foot per year for the first ten years. Junior remembered seeing this section burned when he was ten. That would have been four years ago and, sure enough, the little pines scattered through the grass were about four feet high.

Patches of palmetto scrub also stood out from the grass. The palmettos came after the underbrush of the forest — tangles of briars and webs of vines grow-ing so thick that nobody could have walked through them — was burned. Some of the palmettos already were about six feet tall. But, unlike the pines, they had reached their full growth. They looked like the large fans that the body servants of plantation ladies used to cool their mistresses. Bright green fronds splayed out from green stalks that grew from blond stumps.

Junior turned back to the river for a moment and tossed in another stone. He looked in the sack. Only three left. Hopefully, not many in the crowd wanted baptism and his father wouldn't spend too much time praying over each one who entered the water.

He glanced back at the pasture and something in the southeast, at the limit of his vision, caught his at-tention. A dot was moving across the grass, seemingly heading for him. As it drew nearer, the dot changed its shape into a triangular speck. A horse and rider. After a few moments, Junior made out details of the horse. A dark, almost black, chestnut, it was no cow pony. Too tall for one thing. For another, its rider obviously knew more about palmetto scrub than it did.

Most brush, palmetto, and tree branches gently bent and gave way to passing animals and people. The one exception was called, for good reason, Spanish bayonet. It looked something like a palmetto bush, except instead of the fanlike fronds, it had thick leaves that grew in spirals. They were no more than four feet tall, but that was high enough to reach the bellies of animals and men. Each leaf tapered to a point. The points were sharp enough to rip through heavy denim jeans and into the flesh. Stampeding cattle sometimes gutted themselves on the plants. Any palmetto scrub-bred horse knew to look out for Spanish bayonet and shied away from it. But the chestnut trotted along directly toward one of the plants until the rider steered it away with a quick pull on the reins.

The horse came on and was about 50 yards away before the rider turned it toward the meeting. Junior studied the rider. From the way he rode, straight up in the saddle, swaying with the movement of the horse instead of bobbing up and down, he obviously was a cow hunter. His hat also looked like a hunter's, a felt slouch-style with a five- or six-inch crown and a wide brim pulled down in front over the eyes. Then Junior saw the trousers — light blue with a yellow stripe running up the middle of the leg. Cavalry style, belonging to somebody who hunted men instead of cattle. Maybe he was on furlough. Or maybe his enlistment was over and he was heading home. Then again, maybe he was a deserter. In palmetto country that was the most likely of the three possibilities.

Deserters by the hundreds had run into the scrubland over the last two years. Some of them were merely frightened youths who wanted nothing except to be left alone. But most, knowing they had put themselves outside the law when they ran from the service, lived by stealing everything from livestock to gold. Many formed into gangs that descended on isolated farms and waylaid trail drives. The worst of them could not even discipline themselves enough to follow the orders of a gang leader and get along with other outlaws. These roamed alone through the scrub, robbing and raping at will.

Fear made Junior's stomach lurch, as if he had just eaten a bad oyster. What would a lone deserter want at one of his father's camp meetings? He doubted that such a man would have an attack of remorse and seek salvation. Junior left the sack leaning against the log and began to follow the rider toward the meeting. Gators at that moment might not be the biggest problem for his father's flock.

People were walking away from the riverbank toward the oaks where horses, mules, and oxen were tethered and munching the grass. The baptisms must have ended. Junior watched the rider thread his horse through the people and around the trees. Some of the people he passed obviously knew him. They would nod their heads toward him and he either would nod back or raise a hand in greeting. As suddenly as it came, the queasy feeling left. Whoever the rider was, some of the flock knew him and were at least inclined to be friendly.

His mother, standing by his father's wagon with his two younger sisters, were among those. "Tree," she called out, the pitch of her voice raised slightly.

As she spoke, Junior also recognized the rider. Tree Hooker. A cow hunter who frequently rode with his father on trail drives and even slept a few nights at his home. Tree had been off in the Army since '61. Junior should have recognized him from the first. Probably would have, except that Tree was much thinner than he had been when he left. The combined efforts of white cotton suspenders and a rope tied around his middle still could not keep the trousers from sagging as he swung one leg over his saddle and dismounted. The black leather gunbelt, which was no aid to the trousers, also sagged despite being cinched as tight as its buckle would allow.

What had started life as a bleached white cotton undershirt, now a shade of tan from stains and wear, hung from his shoulders more like a poncho than the tight-fitting garment it was supposed to be. The sleeves were rolled up to the elbows, revealing arms that looked like they belonged on a mummy. The skin was a dark brown, almost the same shade as a plug of chewing tobacco, and wrapped tightly about the bone, muscles, and sinew. Even from several yards away, Junior could see the veins and arteries running through the arms like mole tunnels lacing a garden.

"Anne," the rider's voice greeted Junior's mother in a low, quiet rumble. The right hand touched the hat brim.

Tree stood beside the horse and leaned against the saddle. The horse, a gelding with "U.S." branded on its flanks, was a good foot taller than most cow ponies. It fit Tree, who came by his nickname by being at least a foot taller than most cow hunters.

A loud splashing came from the river. Junior's

father was wading ashore. He looked at the wagon. The wrinkles of his face deepened as he smiled broadly.

"Praise the Lord!" He sounded as if he still was giving the sermon.

Tree waved his right hand. "Hey, Heavy."

Junior's father also came by that nickname honestly. He was an inch or two shorter than their visitor, but his girth made him the more imposing figure. Even at Tree's fattest, Heavy outweighed him by at least 75 pounds. Now, Hooker's wasted body seemed absorbed by the other man's bulk as they shook hands.

"I thought the Yankees would have marched you off to prison with the rest when they took Vicksburg," Heavy said through his smile.

"No. The Confederacy marched me out two days afore the surrender. Sent me off home with a new job. They call it detached duty."

The smile broadened. "Well, you're late for services. But I can still baptize you. Come on in."

Tree laughed. "Still happy with the baptism my folks gave me when I was born. But I need your help just the same."

Heavy's smile faded. "Glad to do anythin'. What d' you need?"

Another "Kee-Hi" came from above the river. Tree glanced up at the osprey, watching it circle as he talked.

"Need to move cattle to the rest o' the South. Need to talk men into helpin' me when they really ain't got no call to. I can move cattle all right. But I don't know if I can move the men. You're the one who's good with the words. I need you to move men for me."

# 2

WHEN THE DEER CRANED ITS NECK downward to drink from the pond, Skeeter raised the metal frame that held the rear sight of his rifle. Soldered on the barrel near the rifle's breech, the frame was hinged so that it could be raised and lowered. The sight itself was a V-shaped notch cut into a tiny bar within the frame. The bar could be moved along a scale etched into the frame. Aligning the bar with the scale set the range between the shooter and the target. Skeeter estimated it was about 200 yards from the pond to the pine tree under which he knelt. So, he moved the bar up until it was even with the line on the scale for 200 yards. Then he moved the barrel a fraction of an inch until the front sight, a lump of metal near the tip of the barrel, was aligned with the rear. He reached up with his right thumb and pulled back on the spur that stuck out from the rifle's hammer. His right index finger curled around the hindmost of two triggers that were enclosed by a loop of iron beneath the rifle.

All that happened in the time it took Skeeter to fill his lungs and for the deer to take a swallow of water. When the deer raised its head, its muscles rippled and created a small hollow, bordered by its neck, chest, and left shoulder. Skeeter held his breath until he saw the hollow appear just above the tip of the front sight. Then he exhaled and, at the same instant, pulled the rear trigger. That set the front trigger, making it ready for firing the shot. Before he heard the rear trigger's soft click, he moved his finger forward and pulled the front one. The explosion slapped against his ears as the recoil jolted his right shoulder. A black cloud of gunsmoke, filled with the rotten-egg smell of sulfur, blotted out the deer from his sight. When the cloud faded, he saw the deer on its forelegs. Its rump raised into the air and the bright white tail flashed for an instant in the sunlight. Then the animal collapsed into a bit of palmetto scrub.

Skeeter ran from the cover of the woods to the deer, saying a quick prayer that its body would not slip down the slope of the bank into the water. The deer, a young buck with several short prongs sticking out from its 18-inch-long antlers, must have weighed at least 250 pounds. That was 125 pounds more than Skeeter. Handling the body would have been hard enough as was, without the added burden of pulling it out of mud and up the slope.

His prayer was answered. The buck lay still on the palmetto fronds, some of them splattered with blood. The bullet had gone through the heart and, probably, the lungs. Skeeter had put another paper cartridge in the breech of the rifle and had replaced the fired percussion cap under the hammer in case he had to make a second shot. No need for that.

Skeeter walked back into the woods to where his horse was tethered to a pine. He put the rifle into the scabbard tied to his saddle and led the horse over to the body. A coil of rope was strapped to the saddle by two small belts. He unbuckled the belts, took the coil, and tied one end of the rope to the deer's antlers. Holding on to the other end, he mounted the horse and dragged the body into the pines. The deer's weight tugged painfully at his arm and shoulder as he held the rope. His saddle, little more than a triangle of leather with stirrups hanging from it, didn't have a raised pommel in front or a horn on which a rope could be looped or tied. Every time he had to drag something with a rope, Skeeter vowed to find a saddle with a raised pommel and a horn on top of it. He had read about Spanish and Mexican saddles built that way especially for handling ropes. Those saddles were popular among cattlemen west of the Mississippi, but practically no one had them east of the river. They were needed out West, where a rope was the most important tool in the cattle industry. Cattle were caught with a rope, held for branding and castrating with a rope and, when they strayed, brought back into the herd with a rope.

In Florida, all those tasks, with the exception of holding down the cattle, were done with whips. The 12- or 15-foot-long whips were more practical. Throwing a loop of rope around a steer's neck was the easiest, quickest way to control it on the almost treeless Western plains, but not in the forests and swamps of Florida. Anyone trying to catch a steer by throwing a loop of rope around it would be more likely to come up with a palmetto frond or tree branch.

So, when he was cow hunting, Skeeter always had his whip coiled in the belts where his rope had been. He carried the rope only when he knew he would be tying or dragging something. Still, for those times, he wished he had a saddle equipped with something that would help with a rope in situations like dragging the deer carcass.

He did not have to drag it far into the woods before coming upon a pine with a limb that was both thick enough to support the weight of the deer and low enough for Skeeter to reach and loop his end of the rope around it. Finding such a limb quickly was a lucky break. Most of the pines were a good 100 feet tall and were shaped like giant umbrellas. Their limbs didn't start until near the top.

The deer soon was hanging from the limb as if it had been a rustler caught switching brands. Its belly was even with Skeeter's head. That was the best position for field-dressing the body. Field-dressing, the first step of butchering, had to be done quickly before the heat and humidity started working on the carcass. Animals that were not gutted and bled dry within a few hours would start to rot before the meat could be stashed in a smokehouse for preservation.

Skeeter took his Bowie knife out of the sheath in his belt. The knife was his second-most important tool, next to his whip. He kept its 13-inch-long blade sharp enough for shaving. Although he seldom actually shaved with it, he also seldom got through an entire day without using it for something. The tip was double-edged for stabbing, making it handy for picking food up off a plate or for skewering meat over a fire. It was single-edged for most of its length and weighed almost five pounds, making it heavy enough to cut through tree branches. Its blade always held its edge, making it quick and easy to sharpen. That came in handy during calf roundups. A razor-edged blade was constantly in use then, castrating males so that they would grow into fat, tender-meated steers instead of lean, hard-muscled bulls.

Now, Skeeter used it to open the deer's belly. One thrust into the body just below the breastbone and then a quick tear down to just above the pelvis. Entrails and blood spilled out to the ground. In the sunlight, they glistened in a variety of shades of blue and red.

Before his hands got too bloody, Skeeter reached into one of his trousers pockets and took out a thick, dark brown plug of tobacco. He tore off a chunk with his teeth and pushed it with his tongue to a spot between his right cheek and gum. For some reason, the tingling sensation from the tobacco in his mouth seemed to dull his sense of smell. That made the job of field-dressing a little easier. The stench that flowed out of the deer smelled like an old latrine. The tobacco kept it at bay.

Flies were attracted to the blood and began swarming, blocking Skeeter's vision as he worked. He swatted at a fly and batted his own nose, smearing it with the blood that covered his hands. That only made the flies worse. He had to step back from the carcass, take the red bandanna off his neck and use it to wipe his hands and nose.

For Skeeter's 25 years of life, his nose — several long, pointed inches that shadowed his moustache —

had interfered with his activities. When he was a toddler learning to walk, his nose was the first body part to bump into the walls. His nose made an inviting target for bullies' fists when he entered school. It was an obstacle that had to be overcome by twisting his head sideways when he was 12 and first kissed a girl.

The nose also made it impossible for him to turn his size into an asset when courting. Some small men — those with facial features as delicate as the rest of their bodies — seemed to appeal to the mothering instinct in women. They were little boys with the brains, emotions, and sex drives of men. Skeeter's nose made him look anything but boyish. He looked more like Punch, the marionette. Good to laugh at, but nothing a woman wanted around for more than a few hours.

His size and nose also gave him his nickname early in life. He didn't mind that. By the time he was 12, he realized it was useless to kick against a world that was determined to compare him to a mosquito. If the world wanted to consider him a mosquito, he decided to make himself the mosquito with the biggest, most powerful sting. So, when he wasn't at some farm chore or another, he was target shooting. Over the next decade, he developed his sting. Kept developing it until his size no longer mattered. Fifty Goliaths could come at him from 400 yards away and, as long as he didn't run out of ammunition, none of them would reach him.

His horse shied, trying to pull away from the tree trunk to which he had tied the reins. Skeeter looked away from the deer to the horse. "Smell gettin' to you?" he asked.

Then he saw the horse cock its head and turn its

ears away from the deer toward the woods. It was listening to something. From the way its feet shuffled as if it wanted to run, it was listening to something that was moving closer. Skeeter went over to the horse, patting it with one hand in an effort to calm it. With the other hand, he drew the rifle out of its scabbard. He could now hear the noise himself. A rustling among the dead pine needles that covered the ground. Within a couple of seconds, he could distinguish two sets of hooves moving through the needles. Two riders were coming toward him. Skeeter's thumb pulled back the hammer on the rifle.

The riders came out of the shade of the woods. Skeeter instantly recognized them and eased the hammer back to its safety position above the cap. Both riders' heights beat his by more than a foot. One of them also seemed about six feet wide, with shoulders and torso spilling out beyond the width of his horse. The other one was thin, looking like a fence rail glued to his saddle.

"Heavy! Tree!" Skeeter called. The riders spurred their horses into a trot for the last few yards.

"Heard your shot," Heavy's bass voice was accented by a grunt as he swung a leg over his saddle to dismount. "Figured you'd be around here somewheres with somethin' dead."

Skeeter opened his mouth to ask why Tree had returned, but didn't get a chance to speak. "Thank God, tobacco," Tree said, staring at Skeeter's mouth. "Got a chaw for me?"

Tree and Heavy dismounted while Skeeter reached into his pocket and took out the plug. He handed it to Tree, who bit into it and handed it back. Skeeter didn't bother to offer Heavy a chaw. Somewhere along the line, Heavy had decided that tobacco was inherently evil. He would be friendly with those who chewed. But offering him any would trigger a sermon on how tobacco destroyed teeth, gums, stomachs, and — through some demonic process that Skeeter never understood — souls.

"It's been three weeks since I've had enough tobacco to make spit come," Tree said, closing his eyes as he chewed.

"I'd figure you soldier boys got plenty o' stuff like that free," Skeeter said.

Tree shook his head. "Funny. We're fightin' to protect the cotton 'n' tobacco capitals o' the world. First thin' that goes scarce is tobacco. Second thin' is cotton cloth for clothes 'n' socks. Look for a Confederate Army. You'll see lots o' raggedy boys thirsty for tobacco."

He drew his Bowie as he talked. Heavy already had his knife out and was hacking at the deer's innards. With those two helping, the job of dressing the deer, which Skeeter expected to take at least two hours, was done within 30 minutes. Tree and Heavy talked as they worked. After hearing Tree explain that he was back from the Army to raise up a group of cow hunters to work for the Confederacy, Skeeter paid more attention to the deer than the talk.

Skeeter never had much interest in politics. Most of his life was spent in the palmetto scrub, flushing out cattle with his whip or bringing down game animals with his rifle. When he wasn't in the scrub, he was either at his cabin, where he raised a few vegetables and half-wild hogs, or on the trail, driving his cattle to market. He never saw a politician out in the scrub, at his cabin, or on the trail. If they wanted Skeeter's attention, they should show up at those places. If they wanted his support, they should come up with better ways to move cattle, hunt game, or farm. Or they could figure out a way to stretch men and shorten noses. Until politicians accomplished something that directly affected him, Skeeter didn't see the point in even listening to them, much less going off to other states and fighting a war for them.

But Tree and Heavy seemed to care about the war. Skeeter knew that meant he was going to get pulled into the conflict. He always wound up agreeing when Heavy and Tree wanted him to join them on anything, whether it was a cattle drive or a turkey shoot. Maybe he thought that somehow a bit of their size would transfer over to him. Maybe it was the preacher's gift of persuasion, developed from years of sermonizing. Probably it was because, for whatever reason, Skeeter felt more comfortable with Heavy and Tree than he did with any other living creatures.

Except for the disparity in size, Skeeter thought that he, Tree, and Heavy even looked something alike. All three had black hair. Their skins were deep brown and looked as if they should be oiled and glued to saddles. Dark hair and skin were common features in the scrubland. Almost everybody living there worked in the sun, which darkened the skin and turned it leathery. And many had Indians somewhere within their family history.

Skeeter was the youngest of the three, although he believed that Tree was no more than five years older. During the almost two years that he had been gone, some gray had sprouted in Tree's moustache, sideburns, and the stubble on his chin and cheeks. Perversely, Heavy, although at least ten years older than Tree, had almost no gray. His age showed only in the thick wrinkles that made his face look like a piece of crumpled brown paper. He probably could have improved his looks by growing a beard that would hide some of the wrinkles and the two chins that rolled down to his Adam's apple. But Heavy kept himself clean shaven.

After cleaning the body cavity, Skeeter, Heavy, and Tree cut up the deer into four pieces, which they wrapped in sheets of canvas that Skeeter had brought with him. They tied the sheets to Skeeter's saddle and walked through the pines together, leading their horses. Skeeter noticed the saddle on Tree's horse. The saddle was a military style, with a pommel about three inches higher than the seat. It also had a space, about three inches wide, through the middle of the seat. Interesting-looking saddle, Skeeter thought, although he didn't believe its pommel was high enough for a rope to be looped around it.

Skeeter also was interested in Tree's new horse. It was taller at the head and shoulders and broader in the chest and withers than the local ponies. It also was marked with a "U.S." brand. Skeeter hadn't bothered to ask Tree about that. The horse obviously was a war souvenir.

Within an hour, they had reached two narrow ruts of sand that cut through the woods. This was a road that connected Enterprize with towns to the north. It made traveling easier for the six miles that they walked north. Then they turned off into the woods again for another mile to Skeeter's cabin. Along the way, Heavy talked about Northern aggression. "You think just because they ain't got here yet that those Yankees are gonna leave us alone? If we let 'em get finished in the rest o' the South, they'll be here quick enough. 'A fire devoureth before 'em; 'n' behind 'em a flame burneth: the land is as the garden o' Eden before 'em, 'n' behind 'em a desolate wilderness; yea 'n' nothing shall escape 'em.' Joel, two: three."

He got on the subject of starving women, children, and patriots in areas hit by the war. "'Woe be to the shepherds o' Israel that do not feed themselves! Should not the shepherds feed the flocks?' Ezekiel, thirty-four: two."

Skeeter had agreed to join Heavy and Tree long before they reached his place. By the next sunrise, he was off with them, riding out to find cattle and men for the Confederacy.

It was midafternoon when they found cattle and men. Both were in the middle of some acreage that, judging from the height of the saplings, had been burned six or seven years ago. About 50 cattle munched on the grass and chewed their cuds. The cattle were typical of those that lived in the palmetto scrub. They came in a variety of colors, from light tan to black. Many were piebald, with patches of white, black, and brown covering their hides. Most of them were full grown, about five feet tall at the shoulders and weighing a good 600 pounds. All them had horns growing at least three feet out of each side of their heads. Before ending in spearlike dark points, each horn on each animal curved differently; some up, some down, some even turned back toward the animal's face before again twisting outwards.

The men were several hundred yards away from the cattle, near the edge of the pine woods that marked the eastern boundary of the pasture. Two dark piles stood between the men and the woods. One pile, at least twice as tall as the other, was made of wooden posts and stumps cut from the pines. The second pile was a jumble that contained the saddles, guns, and whips of the men.

Their horses grazed near the piles. Each horse walked slowly, as if its forelegs were lame. Skeeter was too far away to tell for sure, but the horses' movements indicated that they were wearing hobbles, leather shackles around the legs that kept the animals from straying but also allowed them to graze. As he got nearer, Skeeter could see five dogs lazing in the grass, alternately watching the horses and the men.

Two of the men were digging with shovels and putting stumps into the holes. The other two were hauling the stumps and much longer poles from the wood pile to the area where their companions were working. They were building a crude corral.

Cow hunters frequently built such corrals when they had gathered a large number of unbranded cattle but had no nearby pens. Sometimes, the makeshift corrals were sturdy enough that hunters would frequent them for years and would even build crude shelters nearby for themselves. Usually, though, the makeshifts fell apart within a few months.

The riders weaved through the cattle, careful to keep their horses out of the range of the horns. There were times when cattle wouldn't abide the passage of men or horses. This was not one of those times. Occasionally one would look up at the riders, and, a few times, one or more would move out of the way of the horses. Still, none seemed ready to bolt or to try goring any of the horses or riders. But the riders startled a covey of quail near the middle of the pasture. The wings made a loud whirring sound as the birds launched into the air and sped toward the woods. Some of the cattle objected to the sudden sound and movement. They bawled and began trotting. That, in turn, started the dogs barking and the men heading for the pile of equipment.

Cradling long guns in their arms, the four walked toward the riders. Skeeter wasn't concerned about the four getting their guns. Those who made sure they were armed when approached by somebody in the palmetto scrub weren't being vicious, just cautious. The four walked slowly toward the riders. As they approached, Skeeter could see that two of them had light reddish brown beards, almost the same shade as sorrel horses and cattle. A third had a gray beard. The fourth was clean shaven.

"The Brocktons," Skeeter said. "It's your in-laws, Heavy. Be on good behavior."

Skeeter meant that as a bitter joke. The youngest Brockton, Eric, the clean-shaven one, was married to Heavy's eldest daughter, Chole. To Skeeter, it was like mixing axle grease with cream. Not much happened to the grease, but the cream went to Hell. Chole, a fixture at most camp meetings and social gatherings since girlhood, married at 16 and then vanished into the plot of land kept by Eric. She never came out in public — at least Skeeter never again saw her. Through Heavy, Skeeter had learned several years ago that she had twin boys. Other than that, any time he asked her father about her, all he could get would be: "Fine, I reckon."

Otto Brockton and his three sons were known to about every cow hunter between Lake Monroe and Jacksonville. Each had a small farm in the scrub about 20 miles north of Enterprize. They had a reputation of not really caring if the cattle they hunted carried other men's brands or ear notches. But the same could be said about dozens, if not most, hunters. Their reputation didn't bother Skeeter. Still, the swaggers in their walk and the loud, profanity-laden way they spoke reminded him of schoolyard bullies. He was as uncomfortable around the Brocktons as he was comfortable around Heavy and Tree.

The four stood side by side watching the horsemen. All were somewhere around the six-foot mark. The shortest, Corley, the middle brother, was about five feet, ten inches, but made up for his lack of height with a barrel chest and big belly that made him the heaviest of the four. Martin, the eldest, was about six foot one. His shoulders were as wide as Corley's but his torso quickly tapered down to a small waist. Eric and Otto were about the same height. The father's stomach was beginning to hang over his belt, but the youngest son looked as fat-free as a rifle barrel.

"What brings ya'll out here?" Otto asked as he held up a hand in greeting.

All the Brocktons nodded at the riders. Martin said, "Tree, I thought you were busy saving us from Yankees."

Skeeter didn't know whether that was meant to bait Tree. If so, Tree didn't take the bait. He merely swung one long leg over the pommel of the saddle and replied: "Sorta. I'm here on what they call detached duty."

Heavy pushed his hat back until his eyes could be seen under its brim. "The government's sent Tree back to huntin' cows with the rest o' us. He's gettin' up a group to drive every beef he can get."

Martin spat some tobacco juice on the ground. "Where to?"

Tree leaned forward in the saddle. "Baldwin, probably. Maybe into Georgia. Maybe as far as Savannah. Anywheres we can find train connections to the rest o' the Confederacy. Government needs our beef. Ready to pay for it. All we worry 'bout is gettin' it to a railhead."

Otto rejoined the conversation. "That's a hell o' an 'all' to worry 'bout. Baldwin? Hell. You're looking at six weeks, two months on the drive. Savannah? The cattle'd drop dead o' old age afore you get 'em there."

Tree's lips curled into something like a grin. "You're also lookin' at eight, maybe ten dollars a head at the end of it. Twice what we got afore the war."

Otto returned the grin. His teeth showed between the gray mass of his moustache and beard. "What'll we get paid with?" he asked.

"Script." Hooker's smile was gone.

All four Brocktons sneered. The value of Confederate script, paper money issued by the government without the gold or silver to back it up, was known to anybody who had dabbled in any kind of business within the last two years. About $500 of it could, if the

46

script holder was lucky, buy a barrel of corn meal.

Otto fished in the right-hand pocket of his trousers and pulled out a coin. He flipped it. It flashed a bright yellow in the sunlight as it somersaulted in the air. "Spanish doubloon. It's good as gold. 'Cause it really is gold. Confederate script. It's paper. Good for lightin' a fire or wipin' your ass. Might as well be a nigger slave than get paid in script. Hell, least slaves get fed."

Skeeter wondered if Tree would take offense. No. Tree didn't even show any hint of irritation in his voice. "It's more than the script. You've got new markets openin' for the beef. There's a grateful government to keep taxmen off your backs. Watch what happens to us once the war's ended 'n' we've got the whole eastern Confederacy as our customer."

Otto again flipped the coin. "'N' what if our new markets have been blown to Hell? What if the government is a bunch of Yankees? Watch what happens to us if the war ends 'n' there ain't no Confederacy, eastern or western."

Another flash of yellow as Otto continued tossing the doubloon into the sunlight. "There're ships waitin' for cattle in Tampa. Those ships get the cattle to Cuba. That means we get these." He held the doubloon toward Tree before pocketing it. "Maybe we'll only see six dollars a head, but we'll see six dollars in gold, not ten dollars in promises."

Martin took a step closer to Tree's horse. "I'd rather even Yankee greenbacks than your Confederate script. Least I know I can spend the Yankee money. There's plenty enough o' them 'round these days who are willin' to buy beef."

That scored some kind of point, if irritating Tree was a game being played by the Brocktons. Tree's voice lowered. His throat made a sound almost like a growl. "Dangerous thinkin'. I ain't 'posed to just get beef to the Confederacy. I'm 'posed to keep it 'way from Yankees."

Heavy reached over and touched the bridle of Tree's horse. "Let it lay." The Preacher almost whispered. "'Answer not a fool according to his folly, lest thou also be like unto him.' Proverbs, twenty-six: four."

Tree's body stiffened in the saddle for an instant. "Ya'll take care," he said, waving his right hand to the Brocktons. All three riders wheeled their mounts and rode back to the woods.

# 3

Early November was a pleasant surprise for Greenley. The Ohio native never before had spent any part of that month without wearing a jacket. But he now stood in his shirtsleeves watching greenish blue waves roll in toward the strip of beige-colored sand on the beach. Each wave crested with white foam just before it broke. The sound of the breakers formed a background to the creaking of the ship's wooden decks and the talk of the crew members. Greenley had grown used to the slightly musky smell of salt water and the prickly sensation of spray on his face during his week at sea. Unlike some of the other passengers, he had also quickly grown used to the constant rocking of the ship. Within two days, he not only had gotten over his seasickness, but found his appetite heartier than it had been in months. All in all, the major had started to wonder if he should have enlisted in the Navy rather than the Army.

Even the thought of soon going ashore and resuming military duties held more promise than dread

for him. The sights, sounds, and smells of battle —
and, more important, of Vicksburg — were almost half
a continent behind him. No more pinched faces to
look accusingly at him. No more friction with what
seemed like the entire Army every time he tried to get
food or clothing to the civilians. No more feeling like
the ogre.

When his superior officers let him know of the
open post in Florida, Greenley immediately applied
for it. He also knew that he would be assigned to it.
His superiors would not have told him of it unless
they saw transferring him about 800 miles to the southeast as a handy way to get rid of a troublesome subor-
dinate. Troublesome because he was beginning to
question authority but had not yet crossed over the
line into actual, punishable, insubordination. They were
not about to court-marshal somebody whose main offense was feeding civilians. But, at the same time, they
did not want somebody running a relief agency instead of drilling troops and enforcing military order
on occupied territory.

Thus, when news came of an open billet for an
experienced cavalry officer at Fort Marion, Greenley
asked for it. He studied his new post through talking
with other officers and reading what history books he
could find in the two months since he had heard about
the possibility of transfer. Everything he had learned
appealed to the Walter Scott reader in him. He was
going to live in St. Augustine, the oldest town in the
States. Spanish conquistadors built the fort in the
mid-1600s to defend against pirates, Indians, and rival
colonial powers. They had called the fort Castillo de
San Marcos. The Castle of Saint Mark. Greenley was

going to get a chance to fight out of a castle.

Shipboard noises became loud enough to drown out the sound of the surf as sails were furled and the steam engine slowed. The ship slowly glided between two sandy points of land. From the way the rolling surf gave way to a steady current in the water, Greenley could tell that the ship had left the Atlantic for a river. Ahead and just to the south of him he could see docks, with dark figures walking on them and up and down gangplanks that led to four other boats. Outlines of several buildings could be seen behind the docks. The fort was slightly north of the docks and buildings, with its eastern wall jutting out toward the river.

Massive gray walls surrounded the fort. Each of the four corners was marked by a tall tower, a cylinder that looked like a giant, upright stone gun barrel. Real barrels of huge, black cannon stuck out at intervals along the walls. Greenley could see little activity at the fort itself. Four small figures, one to each wall, moved slowly back and forth, sentries on patrol.

Greenley swayed on his feet after he left the ship. It was the first time he had walked on land since boarding in Baltimore. He decided to tour the town behind the dock to get used to walking on solid ground. No good looking like a drunk when reporting for duty. Strolling through the town kept his spirits buoyed. At least half of the buildings were constructed of an ancient-looking stone, cut into large blocks, colored the same gray as the fort's walls. As he passed one building, Greenley stopped and rapped on one of the blocks. He expected it to feel smooth, like baked brick. It did not. The stone cut into his knuckles. Looking closer, he saw white flecks of sea shells embedded in the stone. Many of the buildings that were made of the stone had arched doorways, balconies under upper-story windows, and other design features that seemed unusual to Greenley. Evidently heirlooms from the Spanish, the buildings seemed to belong more to the Old World than the log, plank, or brick structures that the major was used to seeing. The buildings helped him feel again as if he were a Crusader, walking though the Holy City.

The streets were sand, but beaten by use into a harder, easier-to-walk-on surface than Greenley would have expected. He first walked west for a few blocks and then took a street heading north. The street led to a plaza of green, well-tended grass bordered by a four-foot-high rail fence. It would make a great place for infantry drills, he thought.

On the north side of the plaza was a large stone church with carved columns flanking a wide, arched doorway. The facade of the church curved up into an arch and was topped by a rounded bell tower, with a cross above and a clock beneath it. Judging by the design, which resembled a Spanish mission, the church was Roman Catholic. Within a few yards of it, across a street from the southwest corner of the plaza, stood a smaller church, built of planks on top of a foundation of the gray stone. As he walked by it, Greenley saw a sign identifying the church as Trinity Episcopal. That also contributed to his sense of well-being. He had grown up in an area where Catholics and Episcopalians spent much of their time cursing each other. Seeing the two churches in such close proximity was refreshing.

A flag fluttered on a pole by the porch of a house

just behind the Episcopal church. Greenley saw that it was the United States national ensign. A new, 1863 flag, it flew 35 stars in defiance of the fact that 13 of those stars also were on a flag of what some considered another nation. Two blue-uniformed sentries, rifles at their sides, stood on the porch. The major went over to the sentries and discovered that this was post headquarters. He had expected to report to the fort, not to what obviously had been somebody's two-story home before the city was occupied. Since he was standing there, Greenley decided to end his walking tour and present his written orders to his commanding officer.

Immediately after he was ushered into the small office of Colonel E. K. Holmes, two weeks' of steadily inflating good spirits began to deflate.

"Gin?" was Holmes' first word after returning the major's salute. Greenley declined. For one thing, he detested even the smell of gin. For another, it was not yet noon. But Homes filled a tin coffee mug with the clear liquid from a decanter on his desk. First he sipped. Then he took a longer swallow and looked at Greenley.

"Why did you get sent he-ah?" Holmes asked. "Pok-een your command-een officer's wife at you-ah last post?"

He spoke rapidly in a Boston-area accent that was hard to follow. Because Greenley had spent all of his life in either the Midwest or South, he seldom heard anybody ever pronounce the g at the end of a word. Holmes' voice seemed to linger on g's, so that "pokin'" became "pok-een." He also transposed r's and a's and added w's to o's. It took several moments for Greenley's mind to decipher what his new commanding officer had said. After the deciphering, Greenley was too startled to be offended. He made no reply.

"Oh, that's all right. You can tell me," Holmes waved the coffee cup. "Must be some reason for you get-een sent he-ah. Don't worry. This is the place to enjoy the wa-ah. Poke any woman you wish. I have no wife."

Greenley stood five-feet, ten-inches tall. He estimated Holmes was a head shorter. The colonel's belly hung out of the unbuttoned uniform jacket and over his sword belt. His face was pinkish, darkening to red at his nose. Sandy-colored hair was thinning on his head. He wore a full beard, the moustache and chin whiskers becoming moist with each swallow from the cup.

The interview lasted about ten minutes. Greenley's orders remained sealed in an envelope that lay unopened by the decanter. Holmes at first did nothing but offer such snippets of information as: "Most of the women here have been poked more times than a dy-een fire on a cold night."

"Ever steal many cows?" The Colonel, abruptly changing subjects from the sex habits of locals, caught Greenley by surprise.

"Huh?"

Holmes went to a nearby desk and took out a long roll of paper. "Cow steal-een. That will be your duty from now on. No jok-een. This is the situation . . ."

The roll of paper was a map of Florida. Holmes spread it out on the table in front of Greenley.

"Now that we control the Mississippi, there's only one place where the eastern Confederacy can get enough beef to supply it's armies. This is the place."

Holmes put his index finger on the map.

The finger traced circles around the Atlantic coast until it found the dot that represented St. Augustine. "We occupy this city." The finger moved north to another dot. "And Jacksonville." The finger moved further north to a small island just offshore near the Georgia state line. "And in Fort Clinch up there. That lets us control the northeastern part of the state."

"But go west," — the finger did so, moving less than an inch across the map — "no more than 40 miles and there's nothing but cattle and poo-ah white trash. Peckerwoods who call themselves cow hunters. Some of them have spent the last couple of years mov-een cattle to the Confederacy. It annoyed us. But noth-een to worry about until now. Now, if we can stop them, we stop every Rebel army east of the Mississippi. The Rebels know that too. And they're worried about it. They want to organize the cattle shipp-een."

Holmes put his finger on another dot, this one slightly west of Jacksonville. "The peckerwoods drive cattle to this town, Baldwin, where there are railroad connections to the rest of the South." The finger moved along the map to a line that curved eastward at Jacksonville to the ocean. "Most of the drives follow this river. The St. Johns. It's about two hundred miles long. It was the main supply route for the local Rebels until our gunboats started patrol-een it. Now the enemy has to stick to the land."

The finger traced along the blue line to the south. "Intelligence sources have told us that the Rebel government has cut loose some regular army men to organize the white trash into a militia unit called the Cattle Guard. Break up the Cattle Guard, starve the damned Confederacy into submission. At least that's the theory."

Holmes stopped his finger on a blue circle marked "Lake Monroe."

"You take out our cavalry detachments and look for cows and the Cattle Guard from this lake north. Detachments from Jacksonville and Fort Clinch will be out too. Keep us well stocked with beef. Enjoy your rides in the woods."

Holmes' entire office smelled of gin, an odor that reminded Greenley of spoiled cabbage. The major was grateful to return to the sea air of the outside. His quarters were in a large, two-story building, almost a block long, to the southeast of the post. Most of the garrison also was housed in the building. Greenley's room was small — a tiny bookcase, chair, desk, cot, and an iron stove were the only furnishings. But it had a window that opened to a view of the river. And, due to his rank, the major's room was private, unlike the large dormitory in which the enlisted men stayed, or the two-man rooms that housed junior officers.

Within a few minutes after arriving in his room, Greenley left to resume his tour, since he could think of nothing else to do. He walked until he was due west of the fort and then was stopped by the combined smells of baking bread, brewing coffee, and a variety of spices. The smells came from a small stone building. A bakery. Greenley's stomach growled to remind him that he hadn't eaten that day. He walked into the bakery and the buoyant spirits returned, raised by a low, soft feminine voice asking, "Can I help you, sir?"

The voice had a Southern accent, but not the deep,

slow drawl of Vicksburg. It was modified by a lilting tone that rolled the "r" in "sir." The accent made the standard shopkeeper's greeting to an unknown customer sound more sincere, as if the speaker was genuinely concerned. Greenley nodded in reply. After walking in the sunlight, it took a few moments to focus his eyes in the shade of the bakery. He smiled once his vision became clear and he saw the speaker. She was young, perhaps in her mid-20s. Her hair was black. Its luster could be seen even in the shade of the bakery and under the net that held her hair back in a tight bun. That hairstyle accentuated her face: a clear complexion with a blush in the cheeks and a tan to the skin as if she worked several hours per day in the sun; cheekbones almost as high as an Indian's; a small, gently rounded chin that gave the head almost a heart shape, and dark eyes crinkled into little more than slits by a wide smile.

She relaxed the smile as Greenley ordered coffee and a meat turnover made of spiced ground pork. Her lips were not quite full enough to assume the perpetual, fashionable pout on women's faces in magazine illustrations.

There were no tables or chairs in the bakery. Customers were to take their food elsewhere to eat. But Greenley had nowhere to go. He leaned back against a wall sipping from the cheap tin cup of coffee, munching on the turnover and watching her as she worked. She was tall for a woman, probably as tall as Colonel Holmes. Her height forced her to bend often when customers asked for something from the pie keepers, which looked like four-foot-tall bookcases with glass doors on them. She could not have done all that bending while wearing a corset. Yet, her figure was comparable to what most women achieved only by squashing their torsos into devices of whalebone and linen. Her shoulders were broad, making the waist seem even smaller than it probably was. The hips were accentuated by the flare of her floor-length skirt, brown but sprinkled with white flour as if it were a pastry from the oven. A white apron tied around her waist covered her front down to her knees. Large breasts swelled against the dress, which was buttoned half-way up her neck. Her petticoats rustled continually, making a backdrop to her brief conversations with customers.

Greenley decided to strike up a conversation when a lull came in her noontime business. The lull came, and he started thinking of how to start a bit of polite small talk. He failed. So, fearing another customer soon would come through the door, he blurted, "Name's Dan Greenley. What's yours?"

He immediately bit into the hairs of his mustache, silently cursing his lack of social graces and waiting either to be snubbed or ordered out of the bakery for being too forward. Instead, the smile returned to her lips as she said, "Doris Brava."

# 4

RAYMOND KEEFER STEPPED through
the swinging doors and onto the veranda of the
Enterprize Inn. He took a deep breath. November was
a good time to do that. The air held only a hint of
woodsmoke, from a steamboat docked on the lake.
Sometimes, the outside of the Enterprize Inn smelled
more like a house of ill repute than the inside. In late
winter and early spring, when the wind blew from the
north or east across the citrus groves, the scent of orange blossoms became almost overpowering, and the
whole town smelled like somebody had spilled orange wine on it. Then, in late spring and summer,
when the wind blew from the south or west across the
wetlands, the heavy, sweet perfume of magnolias clung
to the town.

Keefer yawned, stretched, and headed for his rocking chair on the veranda. The morning was cool enough
for him to be comfortable in the black frock coat and
wool trousers that he was wearing, yet it still was warm
enough for him to enjoy sitting outdoors. It was not

quite 11 A.M., early for someone who had spent the night watching over the bar, bedrooms, and gaming tables of the inn. A squeak came from the hinges of the swinging door behind him. Amazing Grace had followed him onto the veranda. In one hand, she grasped her dress to keep its hem from dragging on the floor. On the palm of the other, she balanced a tray holding an earthenware jug from which steam was rising and two bone-white china cups. Without speaking, she set the tray on a small table near the rocking chair. Then she filled the cups from the jug and handed one to Keefer.

"Thanks," he said as he picked up a cup and took a swallow. Chicory. A drink boiled from the dried, cut, and roasted roots of a weed that grew in the sandy areas around citrus groves and pine woods. It looked like coffee, brewed like coffee, and jarred one awake like coffee. Unfortunately, it didn't taste like coffee. Unless one knew exactly how to fix it, chicory tasted like quinine — so bitter that it instantly made the mouth go dry — more than anything else. And Grace was not somebody who knew how to fix chicory.

Keefer pursed his lips to prevent a grimace. He could only hope that Grace did not notice and would not be offended by the shudder that passed through the rest of his body. It was not her fault that she didn't know how to brew chicory. About the only people on earth who seemed to have that knowledge came from Louisiana, the southern tip of Alabama, and the northern Gulf Coast of Florida. For some reason that Keefer could not fathom, people in those areas always threw a little chicory in their coffee. Through the years, they developed techniques for brewing the weed. Keefer once knew a woman from Pensacola in northwest Florida. She poured a tiny bit of molasses, which took the edge off the bitterness, into the water before she boiled the chicory.

Such skills were becoming increasingly valuable as the Northern blockade of the Confederacy's ports put an ever-firmer stranglehold on the economy. Coffee was one of the first imports to be cut off by the blockade. Chicory became the native-grown coffee substitute of choice in Florida. Still, Keefer did not think that the best cup of chicory he ever had was equal to his worst cup of coffee.

Grace sipped on her own cup while sitting on a brown wooden bench-swing on the other side of the table from the rocker. The swing was suspended on two chains attached to eyelets screwed into the ceiling of the veranda. Squeaks, almost as high-pitched as fingernails running against the slate of a chalkboard, came from the swing as Grace pushed herself back and forth with her feet.

The sounds from the swing did a duet with the squeaks of Keefer's rocker. He took another mouth-puckering sip from the cup and studied Grace. She wore a white cotton dress with blue stripes running its length. It was demure, surprisingly so for Grace, with a collar that ran up half the length of her neck, completely covering her chest. That made her look as if she were trying to hide a watermelon under her top. Usually, she wore dresses with bodices that, for the sake of advertising, showed at least a hint of the breasts. The nickname Amazing came from the size of her breasts, combined with an ability to arch her body in a variety of strange positions while on a bed.

Grace was not quite five feet tall, which made her chest seem all that much larger. The dress appeared to have been made for somebody a bit taller, requiring her to hold its hem above the ground so she could walk. From the rustling that came from underneath the dress, Keefer could tell that she even had bothered to put on several petticoats and a crinoline, the bell-shaped cage of steel hoops wrapped in linen that women used to force their dresses to balloon out from their waists. Since taking the underclothes off and on consumed time and irritated customers who were paying for 15 minutes' worth of the women, few around the Enterprize Inn bothered with petticoats or crinolines.

Grace's hair was pale blonde, just shy of being white; judging from its silken texture, apparently it was her actual color. Many women around the inn had dyed their hair various shades of blonde, but those who did so had strands the texture of moldy hay.

"*Hattie's* at the dock," Grace said as she looked toward the lake and the better parts of town.

Keefer glanced in the same direction. He could see the two smokestacks of the steamboat *Hattie,* wisps of white smoke curling from their tops. The boat was anchored at the end of the long, cypress plank dock that led into the water of Lake Monroe. Two years ago, nobody would have bothered mentioning that the *Hattie* or any other boat was at the dock. There always were boats at that dock, most of them owned by Captain Brock, a Connecticut Yankee who arrived in Enterprize about ten years ago with a fleet of four boats and several thousand dollars.

The boats brought more Yankees willing to pay

to escape the cold of their home states. Much of their money was spent at the 25-foot-tall, 110-foot-long Brock House hotel. It could house more than 60 guests in a town that had less than 600 men, women, and children living within a five-mile radius. The white-washed frame building dwarfed every other building in the area, including the county courthouse, a structure that looked more like the home of a modestly well-to-do merchant than a seat of justice and government. And, the Brock House was the only place within 20 miles that had glass in its windows. Mosquito netting nailed to the sills was the usual window covering.

As the hotel name implied, Brock was the owner. He charged up to $20 per head per day. Hotel guests spent most of what money was left over at the few shops along the narrow dirt street that led to the dock. Since he owned most of the land on which those shops stood, a portion of the money spent there also went into the captain's pockets.

Brock even owned the land on which the county courthouse and jail stood. He donated the use of the land for those buildings in '55, when the state legislature created the county and named the town as the county seat. Keefer always wondered why the legislature called the county Volusia, after a small town on the river about 30 miles to the north, instead of Enterprize. The county covered more than a thousand square miles. It stretched from the St. Johns east to the ocean and from Lake Monroe north for almost 50 miles.

Keefer's inn was to the south of the courthouse, between the town and a mostly deserted small collection of buildings called Old Enterprize. Once the local population center, Old Enterprize faded when Brock arrived and bought his land. His money attracted more investors and the business district forsook Old Enterprize. Brock also popularized using "s" in the name of the town. For the preceding 20 years, locals had been alternating between "Enterprise" and "Enterprize."

Although it was nothing that anybody seemed willing to come to blows about, a feud was developing over the spelling. "Enterprise" was favored by those who believed themselves to be of the gentry, mostly newer arrivals and those in Brock's social circle. "Enterprize" supporters were cow hunters, riverboat men, farmers, and others who had been in the area for years.

The leader of the Enterprize group was Art Ginn, a stocky man with graying hair and a perpetual smile. He settled in the area after the Seminoles were run out in the late '30s. Ginn built a hotel called Enterprize House on what had been the outskirts of Old Enterprize. Ginn's hotel was a two-story building that could hold perhaps 20 guests in its $5-per night rooms. Like most buildings in town, it had a false front of whitewashed planks that came to a peak about five feet above the second story's roof, giving it the appearance of being larger than it was. Most of the building behind the false front was made of rough-cut cypress logs.

Although he had arrived only last year, Keefer felt much more akin to the "Enterprize" people than to Brock's crowd. If for no other reason, cow hunters, farmers, and riverboat crew members patronized his place more frequently than those in the "Enterprise" camp. An occasional tourist came, but Keefer suspected that most of them brought their women along with them on the boats and kept them at Brock House.

There was little or no competition between Keefer and either Brock or Ginn. The only people usually staying overnight at Keefer's were the women who worked in the place. Frequently, one of the inn's customers would slake his thirst and lust and then stumble off into the night to seek a room at one of the hotels. Keefer thought of his place as more of a referral service for than as a competitor with the hotels.

Of the two hotel owners, Ginn seemed to be the more appreciative of Keefer's service. At least Ginn would smile and nod when he passed Keefer or any of the inn's women on the street. Brock, whose full beard and eyes were as black as the frock coat he wore even in midsummer, never so much as looked at Keefer and the girls.

Not that Keefer had a grudge against the captain. If anything, he felt sorry for Brock. Mrs. Brock left for Connecticut a few weeks after Florida seceded in '61. Her husband hadn't heard from her since. Brock apparently stayed out of genuine loyalty for his adopted state. At least greed couldn't have played a part in his decision. Staying did nothing but cost him. His tourist business blew up when the guns fired at Fort Sumter and Yankees stopped coming south for their health. The livestock, citrus, and lumber shipping parts of his business were crippled when he offered the use of his boats to the state and Confederate governments. He used three of the boats part-time. But one, the *Darlington*, the second largest of his fleet, was captured by the Yankees in '62. Brock had a better chance of being reunited with his wife than with that boat.

On top of all that, Brock, like most loyal Southern businessmen, had invested heavily in Confederate war bonds and had accepted script as payments. So, if he ever was going to rebuild his fortune, the South had to win.

Keefer's business was not affected very much by the war. Some of his customers had gone off to fight, but many had stayed. And there always were steamboat men and cow hunters passing through town. As long as men drank, gambled, and consorted with loose women, Keefer knew his income was relatively safe. He always preferred dealing in Spanish gold and silver or in trading for livestock and citrus. So, his wealth was more spendable than Brock's paper script and bonds. And, to be honest, Keefer probably wouldn't suffer very much if the North won and occupied the town for the rest of his life. Yankees would pay just as much for entertainment as Southerners.

After another bitter sip from the cup, Keefer dismissed thoughts about doing business with Yankees. He had spent most of his 25 years in Georgia. Like every other loyal Confederate, he felt that no Northern soldier should be south of the Ohio River. True, he did not feel the need to back up that conviction by putting his own body at risk. He decided to go into business in Florida shortly after news of the Confederacy's Conscription Act of '62 reached his hometown of Dalton. His was not among the professions that the act exempted from the draft. So, Keefer exempted himself by heading for the Florida scrubland. He picked up Grace and three other girls along the way. Eventually, he found Enterprize and a cloth merchant who wanted to sell his two-story house. Keefer bought the home and established the inn.

Since it ran out of what used to be a private home, the inn didn't look like the typical saloon and bordello, or, for that matter, like any other business. It resembled the county courthouse — whitewashed planks for walls and chocolate-brown painted cypress wood shingles on the roof — more than any other building in town. The inn sat on pillars made from the ten-foot-diameter trunks of cypress that had been sunk into the ground. That kept the floor off the usually damp, sandy ground. And, it gave Keefer an edge that he didn't realize he had until several months after he got into business. Cow hunters usually rode into a bar and had at least their first several drinks while sitting in their saddles. Saloon owners throughout the palmetto scrub weekly repaired their horse-damaged front doors and replaced the manure-fouled sawdust on the floors. But horses couldn't make it up the five steps leading to the inn's veranda. The front door of the inn had yet to need repairs, and sawdust had be to replaced only after someone vomited or bled on the floor.

All things considered, Keefer felt he was passing the war years very comfortably. He did his best to support the Southern cause. The few militia or regular Army soldiers who passed through town could get free drinks and cigars at his place.

Dogs yelped in the distance toward the east. Keefer and Grace both drained their cups and looked in the direction of the sounds. Barking dogs were the first signs that a cattle drive was coming. The barks were followed by a sharp crack, not quite as loud as a gunshot. The sound of a cow whip. Yes, it was a cattle drive. Grace got up from the swing and went inside. Keefer heard the clicks of her high heels as she walked up the stairs to the other girls' bedrooms. The arrival of a cattle drive, no matter what the hour was, usually meant it was time for the girls to get ready for work.

But when the cattle and their drovers came into view, Keefer wished Grace hadn't bothered the rest of the girls. There were no more than 75 steers, a small herd by palmetto scrub standards, and only three drovers. Keefer could not see any facial features under the worn, floppy, wide-brim hats. One of the three, who rode at the hind end of the column, seemed to be a short, scrawny youth who wouldn't last very long with any of the girls. The other two looked to be full-grown men. One, who rode at the head of the column, was broader than the other, with a gut that hung over his gun belt. The third rode back and forth along the column, his shoulders hunched forward as he surveyed the cattle. All of the men wore tattered clothing so mud-stained that it was impossible to tell what color it should be. Keefer imagined that the girls who got them would throw a lot of perfume around the room before, during, and after the liaisons.

No matter how they looked, the three knew their business. They used their whips to get the cattle, which were spread out over the field, into a line of two abreast. Keefer didn't see any of the three hit a steer with a whip. Instead, the drovers cracked the whips close enough to the animals to make them jump into line. The only real pain the cattle felt came from the dogs that kept the steers moving by nipping their heels.

There were six dogs, all the same type of mongrel that cow hunters favored. Their muzzles were broad and heavy, like the dogs used in gaming pits to fight bulls or each other. Their bodies also were broad-shouldered and squat, like the pit dogs. But they had the long legs of a coon- or deer-hunting hound.

Men, cattle, and dogs all went down the street toward the pens near the lakeside loading docks. Keefer lost sight of them after they turned a corner toward the pens. Seconds later, the one who had been riding back and forth along the column reappeared, his horse trotting toward the inn. He reined in the horse when he reached the steps of the veranda.

"Your name Keefer?" he asked.

Keefer nodded, slightly apprehensive about someone he never saw before knowing his name. The thought skipped through his head that this might be the husband or brother of some girl he had put into business at some time or another.

The man had a full, black beard. His teeth were a dull, tobacco brown when he smiled. "Amos Mitchell. I'm one o' the partners in the O-Eight brand from the Kissimmee Lake area. Ever hear of us?"

Keefer shook his head. Kissimmee Lake was at least 100 miles to the south and there was no reason for him to have heard of anybody from the area.

"I've driven some cattle for sale to an Otto Brockton. He said to meet him here today. Told me to introduce myself to you. Know him?"

Keefer smiled, relieved to find out how Mitchell knew his name. "Yes sir. Mr. Brockton 'n' his sons are good customers of mine. Come on in. We have at least one lady who is awake."

Mitchell's saddle creaked as he dismounted. He tied his horse's reins to a post supporting the veranda steps. Then he reached into the scabbard that was tied to the saddle and removed a short double-barreled shotgun.

Keefer swallowed hard. "Sorry, but we don't allow any long-arms inside." Concerned for the safety of his customers, his staff, and himself, Keefer knew he had to enforce that rule. Long-arms could be swung into action too quickly. A bullet from a rifle or carbine could easily pass through the intended target and kill somebody else. Shotguns, which sprayed lead over a wide arc, were particularly dangerous to bystanders. The only shotgun in Keefer's place was the one he kept behind the bar.

Mitchell nodded and pushed the shotgun back into the scabbard. He still wore a revolver, a Colt's Army .44 caliber. Instead of being holstered, it was stuck in the wide, black belt that held pouches containing cartridges and percussion caps. The gun rested at an angle across his belly, with the butt pointing toward his right hand. It was a position for a gun that was to be drawn and fired quickly. A sheath holding a Bowie knife was looped into the right side of the belt, where most men carried their gun holsters.

This customer still could be a lot of dangerous trouble, but Keefer knew the impossibility of getting sidearms off cow hunters. They wore their knives and revolvers so constantly that the weapons eventually felt more like parts of their bodies than pieces of steel that could be taken off and put on at will. Trying to get knives and revolvers off a cow hunter was more risky than letting him wear them. And, at least, those weapons seldom were dangerous to innocent bystanders. A knife's blade and a handgun's bullets stayed within their intended targets. Most revolvers usually couldn't be loaded with enough gunpowder to propel their lead through one body into another.

Mitchell didn't seem bothered by the no-long-arm rule. He said nothing about it, only: "Tell your ladies that, for right now, I better just have some whiskey. Won't have the money for any company till I finish my dealin' with the Brocktons."

Keefer opened the door for him. "Our ladies take cattle in trade."

Mitchell shook his head. "Sorry. Want to keep every head we've got now for Brockton. We're already short o' what we promised to deliver."

Grace was downstairs and must have heard the conversation. She went behind the bar and took a bottle of cheap rye from its place on the shelf. The whiskey gurgled into a shot glass as Keefer walked back to the veranda.

He got back to his seat in time to see the pot-bellied man's horse trot up to the veranda. The rider went around to the hitching posts in the side yard and dismounted. After tying the horse's reins to one of the posts, he walked around to the veranda. The man nodded in reply to Keefer's greeting and walked through the door. Keefer sat in the rocker and waited for the third cow hunter.

Voices came from behind the door. One was Grace's. The other was a man's, but not Mitchell's. It must belong to the the pot-bellied one. He apparently had some money and was dickering with Grace over the price. Good. At least Grace will get something for waking up early.

Another round of dog barking came from the east.

Keefer again looked in the direction of the sound. It didn't make sense for another drive to be coming that soon behind the first. One drive would always avoid traveling in the wake of another. Cattle in the first drive would strip most of the grass in their path, leaving little for those in the second one if it followed too closely. Whoever was coming in from the east now must, for some reason, be trailing Mitchell's drive.

Keefer saw three triangle-shaped specks. Horses and riders in the distance always appeared as triangular shapes. There were four or five dots — the dogs — bouncing around the hooves of the horses. The riders came closer and Keefer eventually could make out two of them. One was so broad that he looked wider than the horse. It was Heavy. The one that looked like a small twig sitting on top of the horse was Skeeter. Keefer guessed at the identity of the third — the one that looked no fatter than Skeeter but taller than Heavy. A cow hunter called Tree had taken off for the war before the inn got into business. Still, Keefer had heard about him. Skeeter had talked about his friend during trips to the inn, and several customers over the last month had said that Tree was back in the area.

Keefer doubted that the trio followed Mitchell by coincidence. They probably had been trailing the drive for a while. Exactly why they were trailing it, Keefer really didn't want to know. But, with Mitchell and the second man already in his place, he suspected that he would soon be forced to find out. He felt the chicory slosh around in his stomach. "Trouble's comin'," he muttered as the three riders drew closer.

# 5

"REVEREND," KEEFER SAID as he walked down the veranda steps. "Skeeter. What brings ya'll out here this mornin'?"

"Trackin' down powerful bad sinners. Not surprised their trail leads to your doorstep." Heavy smiled as he talked. But his voice held no trace of mirth.

Skeeter introduced Keefer to Tree. The two shook hands, with Tree leaning over in his saddle to grasp Keefer's hand. "Anybody drive cattle into town today?" Hooker asked before releasing his grip.

Keefer nodded. "Minutes ago. Led by a fella named Mitchell. From the Kissimmee Lake region."

A sound came from Tree's throat. It almost was like a dog growling. Keefer never before had heard that noise come out of a human. It made him walk backwards and up a step, away from Tree.

"Don't know Mitchell or where he's from. But them cattle never been south o' Lake Monroe." Hearing words form out of the growling sound made Keefer take a second step.

He walked down the steps when Heavy began talking. Heavy's voice was a deep bass that probably could be frightening when he was angry, but at least it sounded like it belonged to a person. "Don't reckon any law's come to this place."

Keefer shook his head. Most legal and governmental officials left to join the Army after the war started. Those who didn't enlist with the Confederacy gradually drifted away, taking what public treasury there had been with them. Some took the oath of allegiance to the Union and became scouts for the Yankees. The lack of any type of official to impose regulations upon his business was one of the factors that had made Keefer decide to open shop in the town.

"Well, since we're in a civilized area, we ought to have some kind o' witness for what we're goin' to do," Tree's voice had lost the canine growl. He stared down at Keefer for a moment. "Come along with us."

The riders kept their horses to the same pace as Keefer's short-legged stride down the street. He looked up at the three. Skeeter was the only one he really knew well — a fairly regular customer who drank quietly and properly paid the girls. That was about as good a recommendation as Keefer could give anyone. There was another reason for liking Skeeter. He was one of the few men shorter than Keefer.

Heavy never had been a customer and Keefer never expected him to be one. But the two occasionally crossed paths. Once, the preacher got into a conversation with one of Keefer's girls on the street. Within a month after that, she got baptized, quit the inn and married a cow hunter who lived 20 miles to the north.

Since he knew the others, Keefer spent most of

the walk studying Tree. He wore bits and pieces of a Confederate cavalry uniform — light blue trousers with a yellow stripe down each leg; a light gray, broad-brimmed hat with a five-inch crown and lots of stains from mud, grass, and sweat; black boots that came up to just below his knees, and a black leather gunbelt holding a holstered revolver on the right side and a sheathed Bowie knife on the left. Pouches for bullets, percussion caps, and other tools of a fighting man's trade were spaced around the belt between the holster and sheath.

The rest of the clothes were civilian. Tan suspenders with blue stripes running down them were buttoned into the trousers. A tan shirt had 13 buttons to hold a bib on its front. The bib was folded over and buttoned to the left, showing a red undershirt beneath it.

Tree wore sideburns that dipped below each earlobe and a moustache that ran across his lips, curving down the sides of his mouth. He looked as if he also had started to grow a beard. But the stubble on his cheeks and chin might just be from not bothering to shave while in the scrubland for several days. The moustache and stubble had gray-white flecks scattered throughout them, but Keefer could not tell whether that was from aging or wind-blown sand. The strands of hair that stuck out from under the hat appeared to be solidly black.

Keefer spent most of his walk looking at the hardware in Tree's gunbelt. Here was somebody else who wore a gun — another Colt's Army model — across his belly. He had a carbine in a scabbard on the left side of his saddle. From what Keefer could see of the carbine, its lock plate was on the left side of the gun.

Tree obviously was left-handed and had had the gun made for him.

The flap of the holster hid the second gun from view. But Keefer, who felt that knowledge of firearms was an important part of his business, guessed from the extra length of the holster and the thick bulge in it made by the gun that it was a Walker Colt. Walkers had been around for about 20 years. They were heavy, more than five pounds compared to the slightly less than three pounds of the newer Colt's Army. Their weight and length — nine-inch barrels compared to the seven and a half inches of the Army models — made them awkward to draw and aim. The size of their bullet, .44 caliber, was the same as the newer models, but each chamber in the Walker's fat cylinder could hold about twice as much powder as the newer, sleeker guns. That powder charge made the Walker the most powerful handgun in America, if not the world. Keefer never had heard of anybody surviving a hit from a fully charged Walker. If the bullet struck an arm or a leg, the impact would rip off the appendage and the victim would die before anybody could stop the blood.

The Walker was one of the few handguns that could send its bullets through one body and into another. Still, Keefer wasn't about to try to talk Tree out of wearing it. Besides, if there was going to be trouble from Tree today, Keefer expected the first shots to come from the belt gun. The Walker couldn't be drawn fast enough. Its holster held the gun high on Tree's waist on his right side, with the butt pointing forward. People who spent most of their time on horseback wore their guns in that position. It was more comfortable to sit in a saddle with the holster there than lower down, near the hip, the position favored by townsfolk. Those who wore their holsters nearer the hip also usually had the gun butts pointing to the rear and drew their revolver by simply reaching down and grabbing the weapon. With the gun held higher and the butt pointing forward, the gun had to be drawn with a clumsy-looking twist of the right wrist or with a cross-draw by reaching over with the left hand.

Heavy and Skeeter each had one revolver. Both of them wore their sidearms butts forward in waist-high holsters. Keefer had been around both of them enough to know that, if there was trouble, they first would go for their long-arms. Heavy had an old muzzle-loading .50-caliber rifle in his scabbard and a double-barreled shotgun rolled up in his blankets tied behind the saddle. They were the weapons of someone who occasionally brought down animals for food and, rarely, men for self-protection. Skeeter's rifle was the weapon of someone who cherished guns and was very willing to use them against either animals or men. It was a .52-caliber, breech-loading Sharps that went on the market just before the war began and cost at least $50. Nobody would spend that kind of money on a gun unless he intended to use it often and well.

Keefer and the three horsemen turned the corner and approached the dockside pens. The skinny youngster saw them coming. He watched, sitting in the saddle of his horse, and didn't speak until Tree reached down and opened the gate. "Hey!" The youngster's voice trembled and choked him when he tried to shout. "What ya'll doin' here?"

The growl returned to Tree's voice. "Shut up."

Heavy rode through the gate and was the closest to the youngster. Keefer knew what was coming. He looked around, trying to find some sort of cover. The youngster tried pulling a rifle out of the scabbard of his saddle. Keefer braced himself for the shots he expected to explode around him. But none came. Before the rifle cleared the scabbard, Heavy spurred his horse and it leaped toward the youth. Heavy put out one oak-limb-like arm and grabbed the youngster by a shoulder. He threw the boy into the manure-splattered sand of the pen.

Then Heavy slowly drew his rifle from his scabbard. "Stay put," he said to the youth who was sprawled among the cow pies.

Keefer let his breath out in a long sigh and then followed Tree and Skeeter into the pen and to the nearest steer. Like the others in the pen, its flank was marked by dark, hairless patches in the shapes of an "O" and a figure eight. It was the brand Mitchell had mentioned when he rode up to the inn. Some of the steers also carried other brands. And some of them had ears that were cut and notched by various owners who wanted something besides a brand to mark their stock. But it was a common enough practice to have cattle go through several owners, each of whom would put his own brand or earmark on the stock.

Tree climbed down from his horse and stood beside Keefer. "This is what we brought you for. Want somebody as a witness."

He reached out with his left hand and covered the right side of the "O" on the steer's brand. What was left of the brand formed a "C." Tree's right hand then covered up parts of the both the upper and lower loops of the "8." The parts that were left uncovered formed an "S."

Tree removed his hand. "Look close," he said. Keefer stared at the brand. The parts that had been covered by the hand were slightly pink. Those that he left uncovered were darker. The parts that had been covered were fresher burns than the others. That brand had been created by a running iron, a bar heated and used like a pencil on the hide to alter brands. Originally, the brand had been "CS," the Confederate government.

"Yeah," Keefer said. "They've been stolen. I take it ya'll represent the Confederacy?"

Skeeter leaned over in his saddle and pointed with a thumb to the youth, who had not budged from the ground. "What about him?"

Tree shrugged his shoulders. "Ain't no law to turn him over to. You really feel like killin' him now?"

Both Skeeter and Heavy shook their heads. "Get up 'n' out of here, Boy," Tree growled to the youth. "Get back to wherever the hell you're from."

The youngster scrambled to his feet. "'The merciful man doeth good to his own soul,'" Heavy said as the youth climbed back into the saddle. "Proverbs, eleven: seventeen."

Without speaking, the youth kicked his heels, putting the spurs into the horse's flank. Tree led his horse through the gate. Heavy and Skeeter remained in their saddles and rode out. Keefer followed, latching the gate behind him and trailing the others as they returned to the inn. Tree tied his horse to one of the veranda's rails. The other riders dismounted and began hitching their horses. Keefer sprinted up the veranda steps and through the door behind Tree.

Mitchell was at the bar, his back to the door, sipping from a shot glass. There was no sign of the potbellied man or any of the girls. For a man in boots and spurs, Tree made very little sound as he walked on the sawdust. Light from the doorway shone on Mitchell and cast both his and Tree's shadows across the bar.

Mitchell didn't look up from his glass until he heard a voice growl and then bark out: "Hey you!"

Tree's right hand already was on the butt of the belt gun when he shouted. Mitchell tried to draw, but the Colt's cylinder didn't clear the belt before Tree fired.

In the confines of the room, the shot was painfully loud. Keefer felt as if an angry giant had slapped him about the ears. A thick black cloud of smoke filled the space between Tree and Mitchell. The sulfur in the smoke made the room smell like a chicken coop that had not been cleaned in weeks.

Mitchell's feet went out from under him. He flew backwards. His back smacked against the wall. He stood there for an instant. Then, like a feed sack leaking grain from a hole, he seemed to fold in on himself as he collapsed into a heap on the floor.

Keefer's ears were ringing from the shot. He barely heard a scream from upstairs. The first thing he clearly heard was a thud on the veranda roof. Footsteps pounded on the wooden shingles.

Tree kept the belt gun in his right hand and crossdrew the Walker with his left. He ran for the door.

"The side yard!" Keefer shouted as he ran after Tree. He had quickly decided that he would be safest if he was Tree's ally.

Tree went through the door and ran onto the veranda toward the side yard. Keefer followed and saw the pot-bellied man, clad only in long white underdrawers. He already was aboard his horse and tearing across the open field behind the inn. Tree pointed the Walker toward the horseman. But then he lowered the revolver without firing.

Skeeter was at the edge of the veranda with the Sharps in his hands. He slowly, almost casually, put the stock of the gun to his shoulder, sighted down the barrel, cocked the hammer and pulled the triggers.

Keefer's ears still rang from Tree's shot. Skeeter's didn't bother him nearly as badly.

The pot-bellied man already was only a triangular speck in the distance. A black cloud of foul-smelling smoke obscured the speck for an instant. Then Keefer saw the top part of the triangle — the rider — fall to one side. The bottom part — the horse — kept going.

"Got anybody who can bury 'em?" Tree asked as he holstered the Walker and put the other gun back into his belt.

"Yeah. I'll rent some dockworkers for a couple hours. They can bury 'em after they go to the mill 'n' put down some new sawdust for me," Keefer replied. "But can you at least get the one off my floor?"

Tree nodded. He and Heavy walked through the door and picked up Mitchell's body. The sawdust beneath the body already was turning black from soaking up too much blood.

Grace stood at the edge of the bar and watched Tree and Heavy take the body into the street. She was wearing only a gray silk robe. Her breasts under the silk looked like two young possums squirming in a sack as she tried to control her breathing.

"Didn't give 'em much o' a chance, did they?" She exhaled the words.

"They didn't mean this to be some kind of a duel," Keefer replied. "It was an execution."

After laying Mitchell's body in the sideyard near the hitching posts, Heavy and Tree helped Skeeter put the pot-bellied man across a horse and hauled back that body. They laid it next to Mitchell's. The preacher went to his own horse and removed his Bible from a saddlebag. He read over the bodies as his two companions stood nearby, their hats in their hands. Then Skeeter and Tree went into the inn while Heavy rode back to the cowpens.

Keefer gave them two free shots of Cuban rum. It was the least expensive booze he had, but both seemed to appreciate it. He also opened a humidor, a wooden box with a tight-fitting lid designed to keep the cigars inside moist and fresh. He stowed the humidor behind the bar and usually didn't take it out unless somebody asked to buy a cigar. Keefer, like an Indian offering a peace pipe during a treaty negotiation, thought it would be good to allow the cow hunters a free smoke. Each man took a six-inch-long, almost black cigar. Skeeter bit off both ends of his cigar and spat them into one of the brass cuspidors on the floor. He lit one end. Tree bit off only one end of his cigar and then absently chewed on the other.

Skeeter gulped down his drink, thanked Keefer, and left. Tree, his back hunched so that his elbows could rest on the bar, swirled the liquor around in the glass and sipped it.

Grace leaned over and touched his forearm. "Shootin' bother you? Want me to help you get it off your mind?"

Tree mumbled as he chewed on the cigar. "No thanks. Ain't got that much money anyhow."

Grace moved her hand up and down the forearm, as if she were petting the back of a friendly dog. "You've just gotten your hands on a nice little herd o' steers."

"Ain't mine. They're the government's."

"Hey, I'm good. But I ain't so bold to charge you the whole herd or somethin'. Just a steer."

For the first time, Tree turned his head and looked at her. He seemed to be studying her eyes. His lips curled to the left side of his mouth, stretching out the moustache. "Just killed to keep them steers for the Confederacy. Figure to make sure they all go where they're 'posed to."

Grace sneered in return. Her voice became almost shrill. "When'd Jeff Davis die 'n' leave you in charge of the Confederacy?"

Tree took his eyes off her. He bit into the end of his cigar and spat it into a cuspidor. Grace stalked off, her footsteps thumping heavily as she climbed the stairs.

Early afternoon around the inn was busy. After he watched Tree, Skeeter, and Heavy guide the steers back out of town, Keefer rented two slaves from the overseer at the docks. The slaves buried the bodies and replaced the stained dust on the floor. It was 2 P.M. before Keefer had a chance to sit down and play his daily game of solitaire. His back was turned to the door when he heard three sets of footsteps clump up the veranda. He didn't bother to turn around and see who was coming. He made a bet with himself on the identities.

"Place always smells good after you lay down fresh sawdust." It was Otto Brockton's voice. Keefer won the bet.

"Some friends o' yours caused me to put it down." Keefer, concentrating on the cards in front of him, still hadn't looked at the Brocktons.

"The Kissimmee Lake boys? One o' 'em shoot somebody?" Otto asked. "Hope they're still 'round. Want to see them on some business dealin's."

Keefer looked up from his game and pointed toward the door. "Two of 'em will be here till Judgment Day. You can see 'em over at the cemetery."

Otto frowned, but neither the expression nor his voice belonged to someone who had just lost good friends. His three sons wore the open-mouthed expressions of shock. "God-damn, Daddy," Martin said. "We were countin' on them steers to — "

With a sharp jerk of his head, Otto silenced his son. He kept looking at and talking to Keefer. "Let me guess. Tree?"

Keefer nodded. "Yeah. Just glad he used the Colt's Army. If he'd turned loose that Walker he was carryin', it'd blown a hole through your friend 'n' into my wall. If you tangle with him 'round here, for God's sake, do it outside."

Otto said nothing. He and his sons sat at a table close enough to Keefer for him to hear the conversation.

"Now what?" Corley asked.

"Get us a bottle, Eric," Otto said. His youngest

son pushed away from the table and went over to the bar. Grace was standing there and served him. Otto had resumed talking before Eric returned with a bottle and three glasses.

"So, we've lost some business partners. We'll just have to find some more," Otto shrugged his shoulders as he talked. "Let's hunt up some cattle 'n' trail 'em to St. Augustine. Lots o' chances to find partners along the way."

# 6 🖜

No need for a compass or map. Trees and birds told Greenley he was heading due west of St. Augustine. Among the first things he noticed as he rode west were the different species of birds and trees.

The east side of the city, next to the river and then on the mile-wide stretch of sand between the far bank of the river and the ocean shoreline, sustained only palm trees. The palms were short, no more than 15 feet high, and had rough, light tan bark on the trunks which contrasted with the long, dark green fronds at the top. Many of the trees were bent after years of being blown about by ocean winds. Some of the trunks were corkscrew shaped. Others were shaped like horseshoes and doubled back on themselves.

Seagulls and brown pelicans dominated the sky, while sandpipers ran along the ground. They provided Greenley with much entertainment during his idle hours at the fort. The gulls and pelicans cruised gracefully in the air, often skimming only a few inches above the surface of the water. They suddenly would dive into the water and then emerge with fish in their mouths. Pelicans became Greenley's particular favorites. They were beautiful airborne ballerinas when they flew, and became large, awkward clowns when they landed. They waddled on short, webbed feet when they walked. Their huge beaks, frequently bulging with newly caught fish, fixed permanent, friendly looking grins on their faces. Sandpipers, their tiny white bodies perched on long skinny legs, scurried about the riverbank, poking into the sand with their needlelike beaks.

The gulls were the only sea birds to venture inland, and even they usually didn't fly further than four or five miles to the west. Residential areas of the town were laid out a few hundred feet of the riverbank; and the homes marked an invisible boundary that pelicans and sandpipers feared to cross. Few palms grew by the houses. Most homeowners had magnolias, large trees with long, spearhead-shaped green leaves that gleamed in the sunlight like polished leather. Magnolia branches spread out over the yards and streets, providing canopies of shade. Many homes also had two or three orange trees, which now had fruit hanging from them. Nightingales, mockingbirds, and sparrows lived in the trees, chirping and singing throughout the day and night.

Lowlands, swampy areas dotted with pools of black salty water, began at the western edge of the town. An occasional magnolia grew wild near those areas, but most of the trees were oaks. In the heart of the swamps grew cypress trees, with light-colored bark and visible roots that sometimes arched out of the water. Cypress trunks looked like huge brown celery stalks, 20 feet around and 75 feet tall. The dominant birds in those areas were different species of herons and egrets, all with stiltlike legs and snakelike necks that kept their bodies and heads out of the muck and water while they prowled for fish and insects. The birds ranged in size from small white egrets with bodies no bigger than pigeons to the pipe-smoke-colored blue heron that had a turkey-sized body on top of four-foot-tall legs. When the swamp birds took to the air, Greenley thought they looked eerily like flying dragons.

The land gradually began to rise west of the swamps and the palmetto scrub and pines took over. Another type of long-necked and long-legged bird, the wood crane, searched for insects and small reptiles in the palmetto fronds and the creeks that laced the area. Crows, a variety of songbirds, and the occasional eagle and osprey flew and cried in the skies. The scrub went on for miles until, just before the river, the land again sloped downward and oaks and magnolias reappeared, along with their attendant birds.

Greenley also quickly noticed the constant noise of the birds. The sounds ranged from the high-pitched cries of the gulls, which provided an inarticulate chorus to the pounding of the surf, to the weird, raspy shrieks of the wood cranes, which sounded more like the grinding of unoiled gears than the voices of living creatures.

From the first time he rode west of St. Augustine, the major wished his company included one of the the Northern poets or naturalists who rhapsodized about the silence of the woods.

It was a week before Christmas and Greenley had

decided to take his company of 50 cavalrymen on a quick reconnaissance mission before the post settled down for the holidays. He wanted to ride to the St. Johns River and tour the country that he was supposed to patrol. No local familiar with the area rode with him as a guide. But Greenley had the command's provost marshal, Jason McPherson, who at least knew something about the scrubland.

The first day out, the company had ridden about 15 miles southwest of St. Augustine when Greenley heard the lowing of cattle in the distance. The sound came from a herd of 20, a mixed bag of cows, bulls, and steers. Two ragged men were watching the cattle graze and move slowly through the scrub.

Greenley and his troopers trotted their horses up to the pair of drovers. One of them, a toothless gray-bearded splinter of a man, riding a light, almost cream-colored horse, greeted the company with the question: "Ya'll Yankees, ain't you?"

A quick bob of the head and then the Major said: "You men were headin' west with those cattle, weren't you?"

The second man's hair and beard were about the same dark brown shade as the mare he rode. Both of the mounts were as short and thin for horses as their riders were for men.

"We figure on drivin' 'em to Pilatka," the brown-bearded man said. "We hope to sell 'em there 'n' put 'em on a boat. If nobody there's in a buyin' mood, we'll cross the river."

Here came Greenley's first chance to do the job he was sent out into the palmetto scrub to do. He raised his right hand, which was sheathed in a tight-fitting, military-issue white gauntlet.

"That's Rebel territory," he told the men in his best officer-style imperious tone.

"Well, yes," the older man said. "But we ain't sticklers for The Cause or anythin'. Be happy to sell to Yankees."

Greenley dropped the hand. That was the signal for the troopers to draw their carbines. They did an uncoordinated, but effective, job of getting the carbines out of the scabbards and leveling the guns at the two men. Both had rifles, handguns, knives, and whips, but neither moved toward any weapon.

"Sorry. Those cattle are contraband," Greenley said. "They're now property of the United States government."

The two men backed their horses away for a few feet. Without a word, they then turned and disappeared among the clumps of palmetto.

A bloodless victory. Fantastic way to start his new mission. Greenley couldn't suppress a smile as he ordered the company to turn about and start driving the cattle back to St. Augustine. The company turned about with something that approached military precision. But the cattle dispersed and began munching the stubby grass that grew under the palmettos. They hardly noticed, much less obeyed, the company's efforts to move them.

Greenley, who had grown up in a small Ohio town, had more experience with cows than most of the company, which had been recruited out of New England cities. At least he had helped farmers drive cattle on occasion. But those were docile Holsteins and Jerseys, cattle that had been raised from birth among people, knew man was their master, and placidly went anywhere with the nudge of a stick or shove of a hand. The cattle that Greenley had on his hands now were creatures that had been bred in swamps and briar thickets. They considered man as just one more predator to fight off. Also, Greenley was used to cattle with small horns or none at all, not with sharply pointed curved weapons at least as long as his saber growing out of each side of their heads.

Four or five of the cattle, bulls that snorted and stomped off at the first approach of one of the company, returned to the dense scrub during the hour it took to get the herd moving toward the northeast. That hour also destroyed Greenley's chance of a bloodless victory. Blood flowed freely from long, horn-induced gashes across the sides and down the legs of seven troopers and the major himself. Five others had broken foot bones from being stomped.

The company and its contraband trudged on to the accompaniment of shrill singing from each tree and bush. If nothing else ever came out of his assignment to Florida, Greenley at least had discovered where robins went when they left Ohio in September. Thousands of them lined the way, as if they recognized the blue-coated horsemen as fellow transplants from the North and were greeting them. Greenley tried to stay with the dirt trail, worn into the sand by years of horses' hooves and wagon wheels, that connected St. Augustine with the riverfront town of Pilatka. But the cattle had no intention of staying on the road. They couldn't eat the sand on the trail and wandered off into the underbrush searching for grass. The company followed them and, gradually, lost sight of the trail.

Keeping his back to the afternoon sun, Greenley at least knew he was heading in the general direction of St. Augustine. Still, the closeness of the forest, with pines so densely packed that they stunted each other's growth, made him uneasy and unsure of his sense of direction. He prayed a silent thanksgiving when, as the sky behind him turned pink from the setting sun, he saw a wisp of white smoke rising above the forest pines. The smoke meant that somebody nearby was cooking food. That somebody might be Rebels. But the major preferred a firefight with a chance to capture prisoners who knew where they were to stumbling around with the company and the cattle in the woods after dark.

The smoke turned out to come from the chimney of a small cabin set in the middle of a cleared patch of ground surrounded by the forest. Gray cypress and grayish brown oak logs were used for the sides, with a mixture of mud and straw as mortar between each log. The structure actually was two smaller cabins joined together by a roofed-over porch between them. It was a building style Greenley had never seen until he arrived in Florida, but he had seen hundreds of them since. They were called Cracker homes. The porch served as a cool spot on which to perform most household chores during hot weather. Each of the tiny cabins had a door that faced the porch. During hot nights, those doors would be opened to allow air to circulate around the sleeping quarters.

Floridians called the porches "dog trots." For good reason. Greenley never saw one of them that didn't have at least two long, skinny hounds. From the porch in the clearing before him, four piebald hounds snarled and bayed as the company and the cattle snaked through the trees.

A woman came onto the porch and snapped an order at the hounds. Greenley halted the company and rode up to her, taking off his hat as he approached. Her face had the color and texture of a saddle that had been used for years without getting a neats-foot oil treatment: walnut-brown, dried, and wrinkled. She wore what used to be a blue gingham dress that had faded through use and washings until it was almost white.

There was a flurry from both of the small cabins. Two tiny girls, one from each side of the dog trot, ran out and grabbed hold of the woman's dress. Each of the girls wore gingham identical to the woman's. They seemed to blend into the fabric as they clung to her dress. She put out her arms and held the girls tightly.

Greenley identified himself, throwing in a lot of "ma'ams" and assurances that he meant no harm to the woman or any of her property.

"All we want is to spend the night campin' around here," he said. "First, please let myself and one of my companions inspect your house for weapons. Any that we find will be returned to you when we leave."

He had expected the woman's voice to be cracked and high-pitched with age. It was not.

"Ain't much we can do to stop you, is there?" She spoke clearly and firmly, with the same crispness of a well-drilled soldier saying "Yes, sir!"

Greenley turned in his saddle and called for McPherson, who trotted up to the house and doffed his wide-brimmed black hat to the woman. He wore civilian clothes, a white linen duster-style coat that reached to his ankles over black trousers and a blue shirt. The duster brushed against the few pieces of furniture in the cabin as he and Greenley walked through looking for guns.

The smoke that had caught Greenley's eye was rising from the chimney of the left-hand cabin. Inside, an iron kettle was suspended by a hook over a collection of small logs that burned in the fireplace. Greenley breathed deeply. The aroma coming from the pot was comfortably homey and appetizing, a mixture of chicken and onions. Escaping steam made the lid clatter against the pot.

Business drew his mind away from food. A long-barreled, muzzle-loading rifle rested on pegs on the wall opposite the fireplace. A belt holding a cap box, powder flask, and bullet pouch was looped around it. McPherson picked up the rifle and belt while Greenley ran a hand along a ledge that rimmed three sides of the room. The ledge extended about five feet out from the walls and was about six feet off the floor. It probably was built as a sleeping loft, but now was being used to store the odds and ends of living in a wilderness area. Greenley found hammers, nails, pieces of a weaving loom, molds for making candles and bullets, and various other household goods, but no more firearms.

The two men walked across the dog trot, to the accompaniment of snarls from the hounds, into the other cabin. This apparently was the side used for sleeping. Mattresses, stuffed with Spanish moss, lined the loft. A holstered revolver, a shotgun, and two more gunbelts were stashed under one of the mattresses. What Greenley did not find was any sign, such as pieces of men's clothing or tobacco products, that a man lived in the cabin.

"Where's your husband?" Greenley asked.

The woman shrugged her shoulders. "Somewheres 'tween Richmond 'n' Washington City with Lee's Army. Might as well be 'tween here 'n' hell for all I've heard o' him in the past two years."

"We'll post a guard by the cabin tonight," Greenley said. "Make sure you won't be bothered."

Her lips parted in a sneer. "Well, reckon I should thank you for that. But, if you really want to keep me from bein' bothered, why don't you get every one of ya'll out o' here 'n' go home? Why you're at it, pick up those Yankees in Virginia 'n' take 'em with you. Then my man can get back here 'n' we can make a go at runnin' a proper farm."

There was no good reply to that, so Greenley merely tipped his hat and walked out, carrying the rifle and shotgun. McPherson, carrying the gunbelts and revolver, followed.

During the night, three more cattle wandered off despite guards being posted around the herd. In the morning, Greenley, believing the woman probably knew more about herding cattle in the scrubland than he and the whole company combined, asked her for directions on returning to St. Augustine.

She drew a map in the sand with a stick and told him to keep almost due north for about seven miles and then to start heading east. There was plenty of grass and water for the cattle along the way, so they should not stray too far, she said.

"Thank you, ma'am," Greenley said as he mounted. "Hope we weren't too much of a burden."

The woman waved. "No. Have a good trip. Hope ya'll won't forget me." For the first time, she smiled.

By noon, Greenley knew he would remember the woman for the rest of his life. That was after he was forced to shoot his horse, which had become mired in quicksand. He was able to get another mount only because one of the troopers was no longer able to stay in a saddle. The pain from the trooper's steer-smashed foot had become too great. He lay in a stretcher, tied with linen strips to the carrying poles and towed behind the horse of a companion as the company slogged through a swamp.

Following the woman's instructions, Greenley had led the company into land that kept getting lower and soggier. After about five hours, the horses and cattle were wading through two feet of water. The trooper in the stretcher was covered with water to his knees.

"Want something to think about?" McPherson asked as his horse splashed up next to Greenley's. "This is what the locals call the dry season."

McPherson, or Mac as he was called, was the closest thing to a friend that Greenley had made since arriving in Florida. Their relationship was helped along by Mac's birthplace and accent. He was from Pennsylvania, while almost everyone else in the garrison was from New England. Greenley could understand every word Mac said, while most of what the others said sounded like gibberish. But, as the water deepened and the swamp seemed to stretch on to infinity, Greenley began to wish he couldn't understand the sarcasm that came from Mac's lips.

Most soldiers despised provost marshals. The marshals enforced the law for the military. They brought in everybody from renegades guilty of desertion and murder to halfwits and drunks who forgot to show up for sentry duty. Since the latter class of criminal was much easier to find and safer to arrest, the marshals brought in vastly more halfwits, drunks, and average, run-of-the-mill soldiers who violated some minor rule. Some of the marshals were regular soldiers assigned to provost duty. But many, including Mac, were civilians, appointed to their jobs by political friends in their home states or in the federal government. They were halfbreeds: neither regular Army nor fully civilian. Whether soldier or civilian appointee, the marshals were exempt from the rest of the Army's chain of command; they obeyed no authority but their own, yet they had the power to draft any other soldiers to serve in posses. To top it off, they did not serve in combat. All in all, the rest of the Army found plenty of reasons to dislike the provost marshals.

The major never shared that sentiment and felt it was particularly unfair in the case of the gregarious, witty Mac. At least that was how Greenley felt until Mac's wit led him to say: "The lady was right. Plenty of water."

Even Mac's humor began to fail him by midafternoon. That was when the company was introduced to the feeding habits of alligators.

A calf strayed a few yards away from the other cattle. Greenley started going after it. He saw, but didn't take any notice of, what he was sure was a log, green-black and rough textured, floating toward the calf. He was within a few feet of the calf when the water around the floating object suddenly frothed up. Foam spewed from the water and splashed Greenley. His ears were filled with the panicked bawling of the calf, which sounded frighteningly similar to the wail of an unfed baby. He noticed a pink tinge to the foam. Through the spray, he saw the dark object rolling around in the water. The calf, at the head of the object, spun with it. First the bawling stopped. Then the spray quit flying and water returned to normal. A set of parallel ripples, with the pink tinge between them, ran in a straight line like some sort of watery railroad tracks, heading off from the spot where the calf had been.

"Jesus Christ!" It was Mac's voice, expressing awe more than simply cursing.

Everybody sat in their saddles, staring blankly at the ripples as they faded. That is, everybody except the trooper with the hurt foot. He trashed about in the water-logged stretcher and yelled, "Get me out of here!"

Greenley complied. He had another horse brought directly behind the one that towed the stretcher. Two soldiers then lifted the hind end of the stretcher out of the water and tied it to the saddle of the second horse. It would be difficult riding for the troopers bearing the stretcher. Each would have to keep his horse in step with the other. But that difficulty seemed trivial when compared to the chances of an alligator sampling the stretcher-bound trooper.

While the stretcher was being affixed to the second horse, several in the company talked about going back to the woman's cabin and putting a torch to it. Greenley earlier had mulled over the same idea. He had decided against it and got the others to agree by asking the question: "Anybody really want to double back through this to find her?"

The herd depopulated as the afternoon continued. Although nobody reported seeing an attack, alligators may have gotten some more calves. Adult animals apparently tired of wading and wandered off in search of drier ground and better fodder. Seven cattle, three steers and four cows, remained.

By sundown, the company had waded out of the swamp and onto a ridge of high, grassy land. Greenley was more relieved at finding the dry pasture than he was distressed at losing most of the herd. He posted sentries and bedded down for the night.

The scream came several hours after Greenley had drifted into a dream-plagued sleep. A long, drawn-out wail. High-pitched. So loud that it seemed to vibrate the air. It was as if a woman were lying next to Greenley's bedroll giving birth to a 20-pound baby. He couldn't tell from what direction it came. With one hand, he threw off his blankets while with the other he groped for his gunbelt and holster.

He found the belt and had unholstered his revolver by the time he got to his feet. All the other troopers also were up and armed. They stood in the flickering light of the campfire and peered into the darkness beyond. The night filled with sound —horses whinnying and cattle bawling. Then came the rapid drumbeatlike pounding of hooves. The cattle were stampeding. Men ran for their horses before the rearing animals could snap the ropes that tethered them. Then the scream came again.

Greenley still could not get a fix on the direction. But Mac, who had experience chasing deserters through the scrub, identified the source.

"A panther," he said as he held his horse by its

halter and stroked the animal to quiet its nerves. "Big cat. Like the cougars up in the mountains. They prowl all over the palmetto scrub during the night."

Eventually, the company was able to get the horses calmed down enough to go in search of the cattle. It was nearing noon of the next day before the troopers found any of the herd. Two cows became Greenley's only spoils.

# 7

Greenley's saber hissed as its steel blade left the brass scabbard. He tightened his grip on the handle and swung. There was a slight jarring sensation as the nine-pound blade struck home. Then the round clump of mistletoe flew off into the air and fell to the ground as the company cheered. The major looked down from his perch on the oak limb. A sergeant was picking up the green ball of leaves with its tiny white berries. The clump was at least three feet across, more than enough to provide decorations for both the officers' and enlisted men's Christmas parties and have enough left over for the private celebration to which Greenley had been invited.

He steadied himself by grabbing a branch just above his head. Then he replaced the saber in its scabbard. Cutting the mistletoe was the first time he had drawn the saber since arriving in St. Augustine seven weeks ago.

Tilting the scabbard upwards, to prevent it from getting tangled with any branches and twigs as he descended, Greenly lowered himself from limb to limb until he could swing down from a low-hanging branch and touch his feet to the ground. He had taken off his spurs to make it easier for him to use his heels when he shinnied up the tree. Mac held the spurs out to him as soon as he landed.

"Another mission accomplished," Mac said, smiling through the whiskers that helped hide his slightly bucked teeth.

Greenly knelt down and strapped on the spurs. "What do you mean 'another'? This is the first thing I've accomplished since I've been here."

Mac's grin widened. He pointed to the two cows chewing their cuds as they stood among the company's horses. "How about them?"

The company arrived back in town the day before Christmas Eve. The two cows were turned over to the quartermaster. Greenley divided the mistletoe. A third went to a Massachusetts captain who was coordinating plans for the officer's party. Another third went to a sergeant who was in charge of the enlisted men's celebration, and the rest went to Mac, who boarded in the house where the private party was being held.

It was Mac who got Greenley an invitation to the Christmas Eve party in the boardinghouse. "My landlady's servants fix the best dinners in town. You'll enjoy yourself food-wise, at least."

Greenley, committed to spending Christmas Day at the officers' party, quickly embraced the chance to eat a holiday meal not prepared by disinterested soldiers in the post's mess. And, since it was designed mainly for boarders and friends of the spinster who owned the house, Greenley was not expected to escort a woman to the private party. After less than two months in St. Augustine, Greenley had not had time to find a woman he could escort to anything.

❖               ❖               ❖

He walked a block west and three blocks north from the barracks to the boardinghouse. Before he turned a corner and saw the house, he could smell it. A warm mixture of odors, dominated by cinnamon but with a variety of other spices and cooked meat added, came from a small building hidden behind the boardinghouse. A pair of two-story buildings, one squat and the other elongated, were joined together and formed the two wings of the boardinghouse. The small building in the backyard was the kitchen, built apart from the rest to keep down heat in the summer and fire dangers all year.

The kitchen and the first floors of both wings were built out of the cementlike crushed shell material that Greenley had discovered on his first day in St. Augustine. It was called coquina. Most of the older buildings in town were made out of the stuff, which was mined on an island a few miles offshore. When first chiseled out of the quarry, coquina was soft enough that it could be sawed as easily as wood. Then it dried to rock hardness. Unlike the fort and many of the older coquina buildings, the boardinghouse was both stuccoed and whitewashed. Sometime during the structure's history, wooden second floors had been built above the coquina of the first floors of both buildings.

Greenley followed a small path, laid out in white crushed sea shells, around a corner to the rear of the boardinghouse. The path led through a small garden, where oranges dangled invitingly from several trees. Pungent smoke rose from the kitchen's chimney and hung over the garden. Greenley breathed in the beckoning odors as he followed the path to the back porch, which served as the public entrance to the house.

Sounds of tinkling glasses and chattering voices greeted him as he opened the door. A short, thin serving woman took his hat and coat and, raising her voice to be heard above the noise in the room, announced him to the 25 or so other guests. They crowded a room, a parlor for boarders, designed to hold less than half that many. Most were standing. The furniture consisted of a rocker, seven straight-backed chairs, a sofa, and a few small tables. Except for the motions of their jaws as they talked, the people were as unmoving as the furniture.

Three women, all gray-haired and withered, sat on the sofa. With a rustle of blue silk, the smallest and most wrinkled of the three stood and smoothed her dress.

"Major Greenley, I am Louisa Fatio. Welcome to my house. Enjoy yourself." She held out a hand. It reminded Greenley of a canary's claw: tiny, dry, yellowed, and wrinkled. Following etiquette, he took the hand and brushed his lips against it. A prominent vein ruffled the hairs of his moustache.

He knew Miss Fatio only by reputation. Nearing, if not beyond, 70, she was a leader among the St. Augustine gentry who decided not to join the migration of Southern patriots out of the city when the occupation began. She kept operating her boardinghouse, substituting the wealthier among the occupying forces for the rich invalids who used to escape Northern winters by staying at her place.

Her voice, although thin and cracked with age, was as accentless as any he had ever heard. She spoke very precisely, stopping at the end of each word as if to make sure that her listeners understood. Each "g" was clearly pronounced, but she didn't draw them out and emphasize them like the New Englanders. Greenley knew enough of her history to make a guess about how her speech developed. Miss Fatio was born in Florida, but she was from a family of Swiss immigrants who formed a colony about 30 miles northwest of St. Augustine. Her speech was a combination of the harsh, almost guttural accent of her family's homeland and the slow, soft drawls of her Southern neighbors.

Miss Fatio took Greenley's arm and introduced him to the other guests. Her companions on the sofa were her half-sister and a widowed friend from their church. Another six guests were nephews of his hostess. Seven of the others were officers whom Greenley knew. They and Mac could afford Miss Fatio's $45-per-month charge for rooms and meals. Each officer had a woman, either hooked into his arm or facing him, listening to his talk. Mac also had a woman companion.

The hostess used the introductions to give Greenley a quick lesson about the furniture. Most of the pieces came from a plantation owned by the Fatios during the '30s. "Fortunately, we had these things out and in St. Augustine or they'd have been lost," she said. "Everything would have burned up when the Seminoles struck New Switzerland in '36. The fainting couch is about the only new piece in here. I bought it a few years ago."

The fainting couch was the sofa on which the other two elderly women still sat. Greenley looked at it. Its legs were short and its seat curved so that women could sit or lie on it without having their hoop skirts balloon out from their underclothes. Since it was fashionable for women to tighten their corsets until their lung capacities were near zero, it was a well-named and handy piece of furniture to have about the house.

Greenley nodded and smiled as Miss Fatio talked, but paid little attention. To him, a chair was something to sit on. He didn't care about its age and place of origin as long as it would support his weight. At the moment, he was even more disinterested than usual in furniture. What interested him most was the woman talking to Mac. Greenley knew that Mac had an invalid wife back in Pennsylvania. He didn't think of Mac as a philanderer. Probably he wasn't. The woman was not clinging to him like most of the others were on their escorts.

Mac's companion seemed to glow in the red light that the setting sun threw into the room from the small, square windows. The light reflected off the woman's black hair, most of which was pulled up on her head, with two ringlets spiraling down each side to the neck. The hair was the only feature that Greenley could make out from across the room. She was dressed in a tan gown that hugged her shoulders and waist before flowing outward and down to the floor. It was a relatively simple gown, no lace or ruffles that women used either to draw attention to themselves or to hide stains and patches on old clothes. Maybe it drew his attention because it was almost the same color as the woman's skin. From across the room, it looked as if she were naked to the waist.

Miss Fatio slowly guided him over to Mac and the woman. Greenley was within three feet of her before he could distinguish the satin material of the gown clinging to her back. From that distance, he also could recognize her. She was Doris, the woman from the bakery that he frequented for its meat pies and pastries.

"You of course know Mr. McPherson," Miss Fatio's voice trilled as Greenley and Mac shook hands. "This is Mrs. Brava."

Doris had time to say, "We've met on a business basis," and Greenley was able to bow before Miss Fatio led him back through the guests.

The servant who had taken his hat and coat also circulated through the room, lighting lamps on the tables. A smell of kerosene wafted up from the lamps' glass chimneys and lingered briefly in the room. That odor quickly was absorbed by the fresh, sweetly clean scent of cedar wood shavings, which had been placed strategically near the lamps.

Miss Fatio led Greenley to a second servant who held a tray and stood in the middle of the room. The second servant might have been the daughter of the first one. They both were thin with their skin stretched over sharp chins and high cheekbones. The second one was younger and had a slightly lighter complexion than the first. She thrust the tray toward him. The tray and the six tumblers on it looked as if they were made of silver. Yellow flashes of light from the lamps glinted off them.

"Eggnog?" Miss Fatio asked. "It's cold. Usually I serve hot drinks for this party. But the weather has been much too much warm this year. Don't you think?"

Greenley nodded and took a tumbler.

"The silverware is another heirloom from Mother. Oh, I'm so glad we were able to get it away before the savages came."

No matter what the tumbler was made of or where it came from, the drink inside was good. Its sweetness was tempered with a shot of bitter whiskey and a dash of nutmeg that pricked the tongue. Greenley held the tumbler to his lips and glanced back across the room at Doris. She still talked with Mac, but both of them were looking in his direction.

Miss Fatio suddenly let go of his arm and trotted a few steps over to an officer who was putting a tumbler down on one of the small, round tables. "Captain Howell!" Her thin voice suddenly took on a militarylike tone of command. "Please sir, no glass or silverware on the bare wood. We spend enough time polishing the furniture as is. Ellen! Ellen! Take Captain Howell's tumbler."

The younger of the serving girls weaved her way though the room, carrying the tray with her, and collected the tumbler from Howell. Miss Fatio walked back to the sofa and resumed her seat.

"Well, major, are you enjoying the hospitality of St. Augustine?" The soft, cheerful voice came from behind Greenley. He turned and looked down into Doris's brown eyes. He glanced slightly lower to the cleavage between her breasts. He quickly raised his eyes back toward her face.

"Mrs. Brava. Good to meet you outside of the bakery. Please, just call me Dan."

She brought a small wine glass to her lips. It was

filled with a dark liquid that took on a reddish glow in the lamplight. She took a sip and lowered the glass.

"I'll call you Dan if you call me Doris. 'Mrs.' sounds funny to me any more. 'N' I thoroughly hate the sound of 'Widow Brava.' Makes me sound like I belong on the faintin' couch over there." She gestured with the glass toward Miss Fatio and her companions.

"I take it you lost your husband. I'm so sorry," Greenley said, unsure whether he actually was sorry. He tried to suppress a feeling of relief over the fact that she did not have a husband.

Doris shook her head. The ringlets bounced off each side of her face. "Lost. Don't care for that word. Sounds like I misplaced him in some corner of the storage room. He's dead. And, afore you ask, the war had nothin' to do with it. Yellow fever. A good year afore the war."

Greenley quietly drank his eggnog for a few moments. Doris picked up the slack in the conversation.

"Mac speaks highly of you, considerin' you've only been here little more'n a month," she said.

"I didn't know you two were acquainted," Dan said.

The dark eyes brightened. "He's a customer at the bakery. Doesn't come as frequently as you, though."

"Guess it's a type of professional interest. Always admired pastries and baked goods. I owned a flour mill before the war. Millers and bakers always seem to go together. "

A humming sound came from Doris's throat. "Maybe Mac was thinkin' 'bout millers 'n' bakers goin' together. I've got a good hunch he invited me to this affair more for your benefit than anythin' else."

Greenley looked across the room. Mac was leaning against a wall. His eyes were on Greenley and Doris. A grin split his face. Dan remembered mentioning Doris once or twice during conversations with Mac. The provost marshal apparently read those conversations as hints for a social introduction. Well, so be it.

Miss Fatio's voice piped up above the rest of those in the room. "Ladies and gentlemen, dinner is served."

The younger servant opened a door at one end of the sitting room to reveal a dining room with two large tables. Meats and spices sent their odors out of the room and toward the guests as they filed toward the tables.

Greenley was seated near the end of one table with Doris at his right elbow. Mac was seated next to her and said little throughout the meal. Greenley didn't say very much either. He was too engrossed in the meal, which started off with a fish chowder. White-meated fish, kernels of corn, and pieces of potato swam in a red-tinted broth that tickled his mouth with peppers, ginger, and garlic.

"Minorcan chowder," Miss Fatio announced as the servants passed down the lengths of the tables, ladling the chowder out of a tureen and into each guest's bowl. "It's a specialty of St. Augustine."

Doris had a strange smile on her face. It was almost a sneer. The servants came to her with the tureen. "And how'd a Swiss spinster get the recipe, Helen?" Doris whispered.

The older of the servants smiled and ladled out a portion of the chowder. Doris leaned over to whisper at Greenley. "My recipe. I gave it to Ellen — that's Helen's daughter — once."

Miss Fatio was the only person who talked very much during the meal. After describing the chowder, although leaving out Doris's contribution to it, she went on to talk about the tureen and the bowls. "Ridgway China. From England. They belonged to the former owner of this house. I fell in love with them and insisted that they go along with the building."

For the first time in listening to Miss Fatio lecture on her household goods, Greenley really admired the object of her boasting. The china was as white as polished enamel and decorated with a delicate blue pattern of birds and flowers. He didn't blame Miss Fatio for bragging about the set, particularly the tureen, a large octagon-shaped bowl with dark blue handles contrasting with the lighter shade of the pattern.

And the food itself also lived up to her boasting. The chowder was followed by a salad of mixed greens and boiled eggs with a hot vinegar dressing. Then came meats — a goose and a ham — with candied yams, a vegetable stuffing, and a mixture of peas and onions in a cream sauce. Finally there were pies: mincemeat, pecan, and sweet potato.

After the meal, the guests left by different doors. Women went up a set of stairs to what Greenley had been told was Miss Fatio's private parlor. Apparently, there was some sort of piano up there; within a couple of minutes of the women leaving, tinny renditions of Christmas carols began filtering down from the second story.

A few of the men stayed where they were in the dining room. Others, including Greenley, went back into the guest parlor, where the coffee carafes were joined by a glass decanter of brandy. They also made their way to a table on which sat a cigar-filled humidor. A silver pair of scissorlike cigar snips lay by the humidor. Greenley cut off one end of the black cylinder of tobacco and then poked a hole with the point of the snips in the other end. He lit it with one of several dozen matches from a silver container by the humidor.

The hot smoke in his lungs from the cigar and the warmth in his stomach from the brandy seemed to help him digest the meal. The uncomfortable feeling of being overstuffed and bloated left him as he sipped the liquor and inhaled the smoke. But he also found himself tiring of the company in the parlor and dining rooms. Most of men were talking in New Englandese. The topics ranged from how high the price of gold would become on the New York exchange to whether the former slaves now being enlisted into the Army and sent to Florida would fight well. Greenley didn't know much about any of that.

Notes from the piano kept drifting down, giving the conversation a musical background. A chorus of female voices sang along. True, whoever was playing the piano was not adept at hitting the right notes, and the chorus strayed far from the right key. But Greenley believed that listening to any rendition of "God Rest Ye Merry Gentlemen" was a better way to spend Christmas Eve than arguing over money and war. So, he edged himself to a position just under the doorway to the hall that led to the stairs. From there, the singers drowned out the talkers.

A flickering light fell across him. It was cast from the stairs by a candle in a holder in the hand of a bell-shaped shadow. Greenley turned as the shadow descended the last few steps. It was Doris, coming toward him with a rustle of petticoats.

"What are you doin' down here? Don't you want to join in the singin'?" he asked, keeping his voice to barely above a whisper.

She shook her head. The eyes again shone and the smile returned. "I've got a horrible voice. Out o' respect to the Lord on his birthday, I will refrain from singin'. How 'bout you? Don't you want to join these gentlemen in figurin' how to become rich 'n' win the war all at the same time?"

Greenley started to put the cigar to his lips, but Doris's whisper stopped him. "Go put that thing out. You want that smoke to drift up into Miss Fatio's room 'n' get on her drapes?"

He walked off a few feet to an ashtray by a brandy decanter. In a moment he was back in the doorway, cigarless.

"That's better," she said. "Maybe I can't sing carols, but there's one Christmas tradition I want to participate in tonight."

She stood on her tiptoes and kissed Greenley.

The kiss was unexpected. It also was just a short peck with her lips tightly pursed. A sister could have given a similar kiss to a brother. But it shook Greenley. Her lips were light. He could barely feel them as they touched his. It was what he always imagined kissing a flower would feel like. He braced his back against the door frame to prevent a shudder from passing through his body.

Doris looked at him, her smile broadening. "Don't think I'm bein' too bold. You brought it on yourself."

She pointed a finger up toward the door frame.

His eyes followed the gesture. There, affixed with a tack to the wood at the top of the frame, was a small green ball of mistletoe.

# 8

Even on the brightest day, only dim light filtered down to the road north of Spring Garden Plantation. The oaks on either side of the five-foot-wide path saw to that. Their upper branches, at least 50 feet above the ground, reached over the road and intertwined. During the summer, the trees provided a cool green canopy that kept both heat and rain off travelers. But, on an overcast winter day, the road, particularly for the last two miles before the plantation, was like a dark, clammy tunnel.

Volusia was traveling on just such a day. It was the second day after Christmas. Tree wanted everybody to meet at the plantation that day and to start the drive before New Year's. He told Volusia that he wanted those with families to have time for Christmas at home, but he hoped to have the drive finished by late February or early March.

Volusia had no family, so he didn't care when the drive started. Except he wanted good weather. It didn't appear he would get his wish.

He rode on the seat of the wagon for the last bit of the trip. Throughout the day and a half it took him to travel from home to the plantation, he frequently changed from riding on the seat to walking beside the oxen. Badly healed broken hip and pelvic bones, combined with arthritis in some of his joints and every other bone that had been broken over his lifetime, plagued him. First, the hips would tighten up on him as he walked, forcing him to waddle from side to side until his arthritic knees ached. So, he would climb up on the seat for a while. Then, the jarring of the wagon would irritate his pelvis until he felt like there was a belt of fire around his waist. So, he would get down and walk until the hips again tightened.

The four oxen didn't seem to mind if he was walking or riding. They just kept plodding along, hitched two abreast to the ten-foot-long covered wagon. Volusia had stowed most of what a trail drive would need, from pots for cooking meals and washing clothes to shovels for digging latrines and graves, in the wagon bed. He planned to get the rest of the gear, primarily blacksmithing tools and such foodstuff as grits and corn meal, when he got to the plantation. All told, he expected to haul about three-fourths of a ton in the wagon. The oxen walked in their yokes as if they were pulling a light plow through loose sandy soil. They were as good a team as Volusia ever had raised and trained in his life.

Few people used the road. The oxen occasionally stopped, lowered their heads and munched the grass that grew profusely along the way. Volusia was in no hurry, so he let them take bites. He used the whip, cracking it over the heads of the team, only when an ox strained against the yoke and tried to turn off the road.

The oak canopy stopped and the wagon rolled onto the pastures leading to the plantation. Hundreds of cattle dotted the pastures. The cattle had been flushed out of the palmetto scrub by Tree's recruits. Now, the cow hunters were gathering together their individual collections to make one large herd for the drive.

Several of the hunters rode among the grazing animals and waved at Volusia as he passed. Volusia lifted his whip in reply to each wave.

With a shout of "Gee" and crack of the whip, Volusia turned the team to the right toward the main yard. The plantation looked more like a small town than a private business operated by one family. There were the small cabins of the slaves lining the pine-needle-covered lane that led to the main yard. At the edge of the yard was the whitewashed, one-story frame home of Sims the overseer. The yard was a square of bare, black soil dotted with various buildings.

Sims' house was at the opposite end of the square from the largest building in the yard, the mill. The mill also was the noisiest, with a deep bass groan coming from the incessantly turning water wheel on its side. That wheel was about 30 feet tall. It was slightly shorter than the mill building, which was about 150 feet long. To the groan of the water wheel, machinery inside the building added various clanks, squeaks, clatters, and tomtomlike poundings.

Made of rough, unpainted cypress planks, the mill sat on the edge of what could be called either a large pool or a small lake, a 60-foot-diameter circular basin filled with greenish water. The wheel dipped into the basin and drew its power from the spring that was the source of the pool. About 20 feet below the surface, the spring threw up enough current to move the wheel. Volusia had no idea of how many gallons of water passed through the spring each day, but it was enough to make this place one of the principle sources for the St. Johns.

The plantation owed its life to the spring. Even its black soil, so much denser and richer than the sandy ground of most of central Florida, was created by the silt thrown out from the spring over the centuries. Cotton, sugar cane, and corn, crops that didn't grow well in most local sand, thrived in the plantation's soil. And the spring's power allowed the mill to process the products grown in the soil. Corn was ground by the mill's two six-foot-diameter stones. Cane was reduced to pulp and juice by a series of metal presses. Cotton seeds were removed from the fibers by combs inside three gins.

The spring and its silt had drawn men to the area around the mill ever since humans wandered into central Florida. First were Indians, from tribes whose names were lost to history. Then came, in turns, the Spanish, the Creeks, the English, the Spanish again, the Seminoles, the Americans, the Seminoles again, and the Americans again.

Part of the current mill's foundation had been laid by Spaniards in the late 1500s, after they had cleared away the forest and the Indian village from around the spring. About a century later, Creeks cleared away the Spaniards and kept watch over the spring and the relics of the mill until the mid-1700s.

Then England got Florida as a spoil of war from Spain. British colonists rebuilt the mill, cleared away the Creeks, and restarted the plantation. That lasted 20 years, until Spain retook Florida as a spoil of war from England. Meanwhile, renegades from the Creek nation and other tribes joined together and formed the Seminoles. They helped rid the area of the British and worshiped their gods at the spring.

Eventually, through a combination of financial negotiations and military adventures, the United States got its hands on Florida. Crackers descended from Georgia and South Carolina, took the spring from the Seminoles, again rebuilt the mill, and established the plantation for the third time. That work started in 1828 and ended in 1836, when Seminoles returned. They burned everything that didn't move and shot, clubbed, or stabbed everything that did. For another two years, they worshiped at the spring. Then American soldiers arrived and repaid the Seminoles with another round of burning, shooting, clubbing, and stabbing.

Volusia happened to have been in on that second round, serving as a scout to General Zachary Taylor, who boated up the St. Johns searching out Seminoles. The first of Volusia's badly healed breaks occurred in a battle a little bit north of the spring. Two of his ribs gave way to the butt of a musket swung by a Seminole just before Volusia's tomahawk split the brave's skull.

Several years after that, heirs of the last plantation owner traded the ruins of the mill and their former home to Thomas Starke for 50 slave women. Starke arrived from South Carolina with his remaining slaves, two sons, and their families. They started rebuilding and, within ten years, had a thriving plantation. Most people in the area now referred to it simply as "Starke's place," although the family kept the original name of Spring Garden.

Starke's two-story house was the only brick building Volusia knew of and the closest thing to a mansion he had seen south of Jacksonville. It was about a mile away, on the south side of the pasture, to isolate its inhabitants from the hubbub of the main yard.

Few Starkes actually lived there now. The old man had died two years ago. One son, John, formed a company of volunteers early in the war and left to fight in Virginia. The second son, Tom, was a doctor who spent most of his time going from town to town and treating patients.

In fact, Tom was the doctor who treated Volusia's last badly healed breaks. That was four years ago, when his pelvis and hips gave way to the hooves of 30 or so cattle during a stampede. Tree, Heavy, and several other cow hunters had been out in the scrub with him. One of them went in search of a doctor while the others toted Volusia to Tree's cabin. Tom Starke arrived a couple of days later. He won Volusia's friendship by saying the breaks were in areas that could not be set. So, rather than mess around with Volusia's body, the doctor prescribed large amounts of whiskey for the pain and left.

A popping noise came from his hips as Volusia climbed down off the wagon. Probably nobody else could hear it, but it sounded as loud as a gunshot to him. A hot stab of pain went with the noise. It felt like someone had stubbed out a cigar in the joint where his right leg joined the hip.

He grimaced and groaned through clenched teeth. Then he quickly looked around. Heavy Junior stood a few feet away, near the oxen that drew the wagon. He was the only person who could have heard the groan.

"I'm not old," Volusia said to Junior. "Just my body is."

It was midday, but still cold enough that Volusia could see his breath as he talked. The first really cold day of the winter. Cold enough for him to wear a heavy wool coat and still feel the bite of the air.

Junior wore a brown cotton twill jacket and obviously didn't feel the cold. He smiled broadly.

"If you don't want to make the trip, I'll take the wagon for you. Can't be too tough o' a job. Just ride in the wagon 'n' stop to cook the meals. Pa says the only tough part o' your job is listenin' to ever'body cuss you out three times a day." He looked into Volusia's face.

"Ain't there passages in The Book 'bout children respectin' their elders 'n' keepin' quiet? All the readin' 'n' preachin' your Pa does, why ain't he got 'round to quotin' them scriptures to you?"

At that moment, Volusia actually would have preferred that Junior, or anyone else for that matter, go on the drive. The thought of several hundred miles of travel, either walking beside the wagon or sitting in it, was repugnant. He put a hand at the sore hip joint and tried moving his leg to loosen the stiffness. No good.

He looked up at the sky. It was a gray blanket. The clouds were so thickly packed that they couldn't be distinguished from each other. That meant the cold spell would continue for at least another day. Worst possible weather for his bones. There wouldn't be a really hard rain, but he could expect a cold, nasty drizzle that would seep into every badly healed break and arthritic joint in his body.

Still, he had made a commitment to the drive. Promised Heavy and Tree, two of his best friends, that he would come. No use crying about it. He went to the wagon and, with Junior's help, unhitched the oxen from their yokes and led them to the pasture to graze. After returning to the wagon, Volusia took out a large, black bundle from the canvas-covered bed.

The bundle was made from his poncho, a rectangle of canvas four feet wide and six feet long, with a hole in the center. One side was coated with black rubber. Such ponchos had been on sale for about five years in Florida and had become the closest things to uniforms among cow hunters. No article of clothing was more versatile. During rain, the owner stuck his head through the hole and, with the rubber side worn out, kept dry from shoulders to knees. A rider could keep anything from his rifle to a newborn calf dry by draping the poncho over it while it lay in front of him on the saddle. Meanwhile, the rider's hands were free to hold the reins and use a whip. The hole could be buttoned shut and the poncho turned into a little tent or lean-to. Things that had to be kept warm and dry could be rolled into the poncho, tied securely, and stored until the end of time.

Volusia was using his poncho to keep dry the stalks of chicory he had collected over the last several weeks as he prepared for the drive. He untied the bundle and spread out the poncho. He and Junior sat cross-legged by the poncho and began picking up the three-foot-long stalks, using their Bowie knives to cut off and peel the roots.

"I ought to go along," Junior said.

Volusia looked at the boy. It was easy to tell he was Heavy's son. His waist was not thick like his father's, but, at 14, Junior's shoulders already were broader than most men's. He also stood a shade over six feet.

"You've got the size o' a man. 'N' you can hunt cows good enough," Volusia tried to smile as he talked, but sitting on the cold ground aggravated his pain. The smile faded. "Still your Pa 'n' Tree are right. No sense anybody under sixteen gettin' involved in this drive. 'N' it ain't like we're goin' to be gettin' anythin' but grief outa this. No money. Your family's already donatin' your Pa. You stay home. Get some crops planted. Fatten up some hogs. Hunt some more cows 'n' sell 'em. Let at least one person 'round your house earn a livin'."

Junior didn't reply. He kept his eyes down on the chicory. Volusia stopped work long enough to take a bite out of his plug of tobacco. What he said to the boy made sense. Too much sense. It applied to himself as well as Junior.

At least Junior would be home, doing things that would bring in an income for the family while Heavy spent months on the trail. Volusia had no family. Nobody was going to be home in January, the time to find wild hogs and drive them into pens for fatting, or February, the time to plant the first vegetable crop. Even if everything went perfectly on the drive, Volusia would not be home earlier than the first two weeks of March.

And things seldom went perfectly on trail drives. Rain could bog down the cattle, cutting in half their normal eight-mile-per-day pace. Cold weather could freeze the grass into dry hay, forcing the cattle to slow down because they had to eat more to get the same nourishment out of the hay than they did out of fresh grass. Fires could break out in the dry grass, forcing the drive to detour for miles to stay safely away from the flames. Stampedes could force the drovers to spend days, sometimes more than a week, searching for and rounding back up a herd scattered over miles of scrub.

Volusia thought he had given up going on drives after the stampede four years ago. Since then, he had been unable to sit a horse for any length of time. He devoted most of his time to raising and training mules and oxen for other cow hunters, townspeople, and farmers. It didn't take long until he found himself happier than he had been as a run-of-the-mill cow hunter. The actual cow hunting had been enjoyable. He felt relaxed and free while spending days out in the scrub rounding up cattle. Often his catch dogs and horse were his only company. He would ride through the underbrush and around trees, looking for signs of cattle. During the day, the only sounds he would hear would come from the horse, dogs, bobwhites, and songbirds. At night, there usually would be only the whipoorwills and tree frogs. Hunts became contests between the wild cattle's instincts, size, and strength and his knowledge of the scrub, experience with animals, and skill with the whip. That gave excitement to hunting. But drives usually were dull. They amounted to escorting to some marketplace a bunch of steers that leisurely grazed and moved at their will. At least, that is what drives amounted to until something went wrong.

So Volusia didn't miss the drives. He now traveled to cowpens during roundups to look at the yearlings and calves that other hunters had gathered. Most male yearlings and calves were castrated. The biggest and toughest of the young males were saved and turned loose to become studs for the cows.

Volusia tried to get to the pens and buy the largest of those before they were turned loose. He kept them in pastures near his home until their bodies began to ripple with muscles. Then he castrated them to make them docile and turned them into oxen, training them to pull wagons and plows. Between selling the oxen and breeding horses with donkeys to produce mules, he actually was making more money now than back in his cow-hunting days.

He had no sane reason for promising Tree and Heavy to go along on this drive. Out of 20 who were going, everybody else had some kind of reason. Tree simply was indulging his need to fight for a cause. He had been like that ever since he drifted into the area about 15 years ago. In '56 he joined a militia unit, went a couple hundred miles southwest to Fort Myers and spent two years fighting Seminoles. Those two years were nothing like the wars in the '30s and '40s, when the Indians were at least equal in numbers and weapons to the whites. The fight in the '50s was more like a glorified cow hunt, with whites tracking Seminoles instead of cattle. But it was the closest thing to a crusade that Tree could find at that moment, so he went on it.

Besides the scrapes with Indians, Tree always was the first to ride off into the scrub after rustlers. He got into several knife- and fistfights — and at least one stand-up gun duel — over real or imagined insults to himself or others, usually women. Sometimes, the women were only casual acquaintances. More often than not, the woman was some tired, shop-worn trollop. Volusia wasn't surprised when Tree went into the Confederate service as soon as Florida seceded in '61.

Heavy believed in the righteousness of The Cause. Volusia had heard his friend give enough sermons to realize that. He knew that Heavy had wanted to go off with Tree at the war's start. But Anne, Volusia, and other friends eventually got him to listen to reason. The preacher was knocking on the door of 50, not a good age to go adventuring in an army. And his family needed his services at home more than the Confederacy needed the services of an aging soldier. Still, staying at home galled Heavy. Somehow, he felt his manhood was being questioned by not serving. Considering he had been through an Indian war and various fights with rustlers, it was a silly attitude to have. But it was Heavy's way of thinking. Volusia knew that Heavy leaped at the chance to join the Cow Cavalry.

Skeeter's motive was easy to understand. He'd go anywhere and do anything as long as he was with Tree and Heavy. As for the others, the oldest of them was 20. They all were bred on pro-secession newspapers and political speeches. All of them wanted to hit a lick for The Cause and become heroes in the eyes of whatever girls they could find in the scrubland.

The only man whose motives Volusia couldn't understand was himself. True, like everybody else living anywhere south of Kentucky, he had chafed at Northern interference with his life. He had felt that most keenly when he was cow hunting. Like most hunters, he sold many of his cattle on the Cuban market. That market thrived for years until, in the mid-'50s, Northern politicians began to dominate the U.S. Congress. Congress imposed duty fees on exports that forced cow hunters to either raise their beef prices beyond what the Cuban market could bear or slash their profits. Figuring that little money was better than none at all, hunters took the cuts.

Meanwhile, hunters had to import, from either overseas or the North, everything — from their felt hats to their guns — that they could not grow or make themselves. Congress raised import tariffs and increased the costs on goods from overseas. Northern manufacturers also inflated the prices of the goods they sold to the South, forcing the costs of living to escalate at the same time that profits were decreasing.

Heavy, who, as a family man, felt the Northern-induced depression most keenly, frequently used the word "vampires" when describing Yankee politicians in his sermons. Volusia could sympathize but, as an unmarried man, he didn't feel the same, painfully frustrating pinch of the economic pliers.

The same economic conditions were felt all over the South. If anything, it was worse in areas where cotton and tobacco were the main crops. There, increased tariffs all but closed foreign markets. Planters had to sell their crops for whatever Northerners felt like paying for them.

But Volusia really didn't think any of this would be bettered by Florida seceding from the Union. Graft from excessive taxation and export-import fees now might not flow into the pockets of Northern politicians. Instead, it probably was flowing into the pockets of Southern politicians.

So, Volusia didn't feel like he owed anything to The Cause. He was as old as Heavy, but had no family to make him want to improve the world for the benefit of the next generation. The Seminole wars gave him enough soldiering to last a lifetime. He had nothing to prove to anybody. If the truth were told, all he really wanted to do was to live out the rest of his life as quietly and comfortably as possible. He couldn't even figure out exactly what good he was going to do for the drive. Junior was right. Anybody could cook as well as he. Probably better.

A wind picked up and blew across the spring toward Volusia and Junior, carrying with it the smell of the spring water. It stank of sulfur, the same rotten-egg smell of exploded gunpowder. Evidently, there was a deposit of sulfur somewhere below the surface where the source of the spring was. That source was a river flowing hundreds of feet underground until it burst out of a fissure — the spring itself — in the earth.

Volusia wrinkled his nose. The gesture was not in disgust at the smell — he had been around sulfur water enough to become used to it. The wrinkled nose was an expression of curiosity about something that had been bothering him every time he came to the plantation over the last several years. He could put his hand on the Bible and take an oath that the smell was not as strong as it had been 20 or 30 years ago. Either he was getting too used to sulfur water or the spring was flushing the sulfur out from itself.

If the odor actually was getting less pronounced

as the years went by, God only knew what this place smelled like when the Indians had it. And God only knew why anybody, except people who had the mechanical know-how to use the power of the spring for such things as the mill, would want to keep this place bad enough to fight for it.

But, obviously, people did, even when the only power they could harness from the spring was spiritual. As he began thinking about that, Volusia could swear that the ribs caved in by the Seminole began hurting more than usual.

He thought about the man who had swung the musket butt — short and swarthy, with his hair bundled up inside a turban. All the Seminole knew was that his people wanted to keep the spring, no matter how badly it smelled. They figured they knew how to use it best: farm the soil and use the spring as some sort of outdoor church. Volusia was one of the people who wanted to take it because they felt the spring would best be used for things like the water wheel.

Over the years, Volusia had grown to feel much like the Seminole. Both of them were natives of the area. Volusia's nickname came from a trading post on the St. Johns where he was born. He was one of the first non-Spanish whites born south of Jacksonville between the St. Johns and the ocean. Volusia spent the rest of his life out in the scrub while others, such as the Starkes, moved in with enough money to exploit the land and make it work for them.

The Starkes were the people who really had a stake in this war. They could expect nothing better from the Yankees than the last white owners got from the Seminoles. Or, for that matter, than the Seminoles got from Volusia and the Army.

Maybe the Seminoles were right. Maybe the spring actually belonged to a god. Maybe that god acted like a landlord, renting the spring out to whoever seemed best able to use it and evicting the tenants when they didn't meet the terms of the lease.

Volusia had no idea of what the lease terms were. But, from all indications, Southerners, be they cow hunters like himself or planters like the Starkes, were not doing any better than the Spanish, the English, the Indians, or anybody else.

Maybe that was why he was going on the drive, Volusia thought. He wasn't so much fighting for a cause as he was fighting to keep from being among those evicted from the land.

The chicory roots were cut and peeled. They lay in a pile on the poncho like long, white grubs. Volusia began to stand. More popping sounds came from his hips as he tried to straighten his legs. This time, he knew Junior heard the pops, for the boy extended an arm in an effort to help him rise. Volusia waved off the arm and tried to make his grimace look like a pleasant smile.

# 9

JUNIOR AND VOLUSIA WALKED ACROSS the yard to the mill. Its interior was dark and painfully noisy. About a dozen black men, darker shadows among the dusty gloom, moved about their tasks. One of them looked up as the two whites walked through the doorway.

"Can I help you, sir?" The black had to shout to be heard.

Volusia shouted back, "Mind if we take a feed sack?"

The black stooped down and reached into a corner by a pair of slowly moving, rumbling gears. He stood up, with an empty sack in one hand. "You the boss o' that outfit out there?" he asked as he walked toward the whites, holding the sack out to them. "I understand the boss is a powerful tall man."

"No. Just the cook," Volusia smiled as he replied and took the sack. Before middle age thickened his waist, he and Tree frequently had been mistaken for each other. Even now, people sometimes asked if the two were brothers. Tree was perhaps an inch taller. But their height was close enough that Volusia understood the mistakes. And they both had black hair, although Volusia's hair and beard now were streaked with gray.

The sack was to hold the chicory roots. Volusia and Junior put the roots in it and then walked to the long, low, one-story plank building that served as the cook shack for the mill workers. More blacks, this time women, were inside, doing such kitchen chores as peeling onions and kneading dough. Volusia asked if he could have the use of an oven for the four hours it took to bake the roots. A smiling, wrinkled woman, whose round body showed that she ate too much of her own cooking, ushered him to an oven that wasn't being used. A younger, thinner woman and Junior shoveled burning charcoal into it from an already-hot oven. The old woman and Volusia put the roots on a metal rack and shoved it into the oven.

There was nothing else to do until the roots were baked. Junior and Volusia went back to the wagon and built a fire near it with twigs and pine shavings. Volusia used a fire starter, a small crescent of steel that he held in one hand and struck against a chunk of flint held in the other. The striking motion sent a shower of sparks into the pine shavings, which Junior protected from the drizzle with his hat. Fire spread from the shavings to the twigs. Many people over the last ten years had converted from fire starters to matches. But Volusia stuck with the centuries-old fire starter. It would work in wet weather, when matches wouldn't. And, he could carry the steel, flint, and a little brass box of dry tinder without fear of them accidentally igniting themselves. The phosphorous and sulfur in match heads occasionally would go off on their own in a pocket or cupboard.

Junior took a coffee pot from the wagon and filled it from the spring. He put the pot on the fire and then wandered off, leaving Volusia sitting by the flames. The cook got back to his feet and went to the wagon. He took his rifle and shotgun from under the seat and then unholstered his revolver.

Might as well clean his guns now while there was nothing better to do, Volusia decided. Gun cleaning was one of the duller daily chores, but it had to be done by anyone who wanted his weapons in working order when he needed them. Gunpowder corroded the metal of the guns and stuck inside the barrels. So, each day, gunowners unloaded, flushed out particles of powder from the weapons, and reloaded.

It took Volusia about a half hour to clean his three guns. The revolver, a Colt's Dragoon .44 caliber, was the last. That model was a few years younger and several ounces lighter than Tree's Walker, but it had almost the same firepower. Volusia carried a spare cylinder for it in one of the pouches of his gunbelt. The spare gave him an edge in fights. He could reload simply by switching cylinders. Without a spare, anyone who had fired all his shots had to take several minutes to laboriously reload each chamber in a cylinder. It took only a few seconds to pull down the loading lever — a hinged piece of metal that ran under the barrel and held the cylinder in place — remove one cylinder, and replace it with another.

Volusia finished his chore by reloading the spare and the revolver cylinder. He worked the loading lever to wedge the pistol ball and gunpowder tightly into each chamber. The lever made a tip-tap sound as it struck the lead balls. Then, the beat of horse hoofs trotting toward him drew Volusia's attention away from the revolver.

He saw Tree riding the large, dark chestnut. The tall, skinny hunter reined in the horse and dismounted.

"Saw your fire. Got any chicory?"

Volusia shook his head. "Not brewed. Just heatin' water for gun cleanin'. Just wait. You'll get plenty enough o' my chicory once we get on the trail."

Tree wore a coat that looked as if it belonged on a toy soldier. It was patterned after a civilian style that was called, for good reason, a swallowtail. The coat forked at the tail, like its namesake bird, with either side of the fork reaching below the knees. Its color was the same gray as the cloudy sky. The collar stood up against Tree's neck. Yellow piping ran around the edge of the collar and down the double-breasted front. The bright color of the piping, of the chevron — the sleeve decoration that denoted Tree's rank, and of the two rows of brass buttons on the front gleamed against the dull color of the heavy wool fabric.

"What'd you do?" Volusia asked sarcastically. "Raid some general's closet on your way here?"

Tree stared at the ground, embarrassed. "Yeah. I know how it looks. It was given me in Vicksburg. First time I've worn it. Weather ain't been cold 'nuff for it till today."

Volusia changed the subject to something that had intrigued him since Tree first returned. "That saddle you brought back. It must make your rump feel like its covered with piles inside and out," he said as he walked over to the horse. He ran his hand along the split in the middle of the seat.

"Not really. Takes some gettin' used to. Gotta sit just right on it," Tree replied, this time looking Volusia in the eye. "Good thing about it is ridin' in hot weather. Air circulates 'round the saddle. Doesn't chafe either the horse's back or your tail like a regular saddle does when its hot 'n' humid. Yankee cavalry uses 'em all the time. We'd pick one up whenever we could."

Tree mounted the horse. "Reckon I'll get back to the job. Take care." He rode out toward the pasture.

Eventually it was time to get the chicory out of the oven. The roots were baked to black, crispy bits. Borrowing the kitchen's red-painted, cast-iron coffee mill, Volusia ground what was left of the roots into fine, dirtlike granules. He wound up with about 20 pounds of the stuff, slightly more than he figured he'd need to complete the drive, in the sack.

Because he had cleaned his guns in the afternoon, Volusia that evening was able to lean back and rest his head against the wheel of his wagon while the others did that chore. His lips curved up into a satisfied smile as he watched the hunters gather in small clumps around six fires — five plus the one he had started and kept going throughout the afternoon. The yard filled with the smell of woodsmoke.

Volusia took a thick quilt out of the wagon bed. The quilt was made of red and blue patches of cloth, stuffed with cotton fibers. It had been sewn together and given him by a woman he almost married 20 years ago. He wrapped it around himself and moved from the wagon toward the fire. The night was cold. Although it didn't seem like it'd get down to freezing, the air was much cooler than the water of the spring, which stayed at a constant temperature. Steam came off the spring, creating a fog that spread over the yard and out toward the pastures.

The fog prevented seeing more than a few feet in any direction. But, for sounds, it acted like a low ceiling in a room. Noises that usually would have risen and dispersed into the air bounced back to the ground. The lowing of the cattle joined the constant groaning from the water wheel to become background noises for everything else. And, although Volusia couldn't see horses tethered at the edge of the yard less than 100 feet from his wagon, he could hear voices laughing and muttering from the slave cabins a good half-mile away.

Singing — low, harmonious, and sad — replaced the other sounds from the cabins. Volusia heard the singing about the same time that the hunters began wrapping themselves in their blankets. At least most of them did. Tree and a young hunter from near Spring Garden were taking the first watch.

That meant they would spend the next two hours nightherding, riding in circles around the cattle and singing. For some reason, cattle were soothed by the sound of a voice. Any voice. So, night herders sang continuously, whether or not they had voices that any human would want to hear.

Over the decades, Volusia thought he had become accustomed to the nightherders' singing. But not tonight. For one thing, Tree and the boy out with him, a skinny youngster called Lonesome, had incredibly bad voices. For another, they competed with the snatches of song coming from the cabins. Having Lonesome and Tree drown out that singing was the musical equivalent to burying fresh, ripe oranges in horse manure.

Tree and Lonesome rode in opposite directions around the herd, which had the effect of their taking turns covering the slaves' singing. First came Lonesome. He had the vestiges of an adolescent squeak. Exactly the wrong sort of voice for the love song "Lorena."

"The years creep slowly by, Lorenaaaa. . . ." The boy squawked as if he actually was a tenor who could hold the last notes. "The snow is on the grass againnnn . . . ."

Volusia gave Lonesome credit for at least picking the right sort of song. The whole point to a night herder's singing was to give the cattle a lullaby. Slow, quiet songs, like "Lorena" or the hymns and spirituals being sung in the cabins, were best suited for that. But, for some obscure reason, Tree sang "The Bonnie Blue Flag," a patriotic song that was supposed to be a blood-stirring, quick-tempoed march. Tree's version of it slowed the tempo. And he tried to get something of a lullaby rhythm in it. But all he managed to do was to make it sound as if he had been singing it so long that he was tired of hearing it himself.

"We are a band o' brothers. 'N' native to the soil," Tree rasped in a voice that sounded like a cross between a frog and a dog. "Fightin' for our liberty, with treasure, blood 'n' toil."

A shape that seemed to be an oak tree came out of the fog. It was no more than five feet away before Volusia realized it was Heavy.

The preacher squatted down by the fire. He was

finishing up his gun cleaning. His revolver still was in his right hand. The left hand moved the loading lever up and down while the right turned the cylinder after the lever finished with each chamber.

"Chicory?" Volusia held out a cup. "Might as well get used to how I fix it now, 'cause in a few days you ain't goin' to get nothin' else till the drive's done."

Heavy smiled and nodded. "Thanks. Let me go ahead 'n' finish this first," He put his head down toward the revolver. It was a Remington Army model. Volusia thought it was more attractive than the Colt. It had a frame that went entirely around the cylinder, giving it a more balanced look than any model of the Colt, none of which had frames on top of their cylinders. The Remington's octagonal barrel also sloped downward slightly from the frame, making it look graceful. But it gave fits to somebody who tried to aim it after being trained with Colts, which had their barrels lined up straight from the top.

Still, from all Volusia had heard about it, once a person got used to aiming the Remington, its .44 caliber bullet hit as hard and true as the Colts or any other gun ever made. And the Remington's frame gave it a little more strength, making the gun less damage-prone if it was dropped. For cow hunters, it was a plus to have a gun that could take falling out of a holster while its owner was being thrown by a horse.

Heavy was one of the few hunters to own the gun. He had bought it in early '61, shortly after it went on the market. Then it was no longer available. The Remington people were Yankees who stopped selling in the South once the war got going.

Volusia again offered a cup of chicory. Heavy took

the cup with his left hand as he holstered the revolver with his right. Then, from out in the fog, came Lonesome's voice. "Lorenaaaa. . . ."

Heavy shuddered as he swallowed. "The chicory or the singin'?" Volusia asked.

"Both, I reckon," Heavy replied. "Maybe I can get used to 'em by the time we get to Baldwin."

Lonesome's voice faded and the singing from the cabins welled out of the fog. Volusia couldn't make out any of the words, but he believed they formed some sort of musical prayer.

Heavy cocked his head toward the singing. He sighed. "Well, at least we can always thank God we can't afford slaves."

"What?" Volusia always found himself taken aback by things that came out of the preacher's mouth. Things that had no relation to what was being talked about at the time. Things that bounced around his mind and then bounded out, instantly changing whatever the subject of the conversation had been.

"Ownin' slaves. It's a burden we don't have."

Volusia tried not to sneer at his friend. He had heard about slavery being a burden to whites since he was a child. Preachers sermonized on it. Newspaper owners editorialized on it. Politicians speechified on it. Supposedly, slave owners carried the burden of bringing white civilization to blacks.

"Oh, don't give me that 'white man's burden' crap," he told Heavy. "Rich folks been workin' up a sweat 'bout that all my life. But that's the only thing I've seen that works them into sweat. Most of the real sweat still comes from the slaves. They're the ones bearin' the burdens."

Heavy shook his head until the flesh that hung from his jowls wiggled back and forth. "No. No. That ain't what I'm talkin' 'bout. It's a burden on the soul. Think of what happens if you can afford slaves. Here you go through life controllin' other people's lives. Livin' off their work. Then you come afore the Judgment seat. 'N' you're goin' to have to answer for every one of those lives you had under your thumb. 'Masters, give unto your servants that which is just 'n' equal. Knowin' that ye also have a master in Heaven.' Colossians, four: one."

Another sigh. "Not havin' the money, it's a temptation that we're spared facin'."

The sun was up for several hours the next morning before anyone saw it. During the night, smoke from the campfires and chimneys mixed with the fog and wrapped everything on the plantation in the gray mist. Volusia awoke at what should have been dawn and walked to the kitchen. The kitchen help served him and the other hunters a breakfast of grits, biscuits, and gravy.

By the time he finished eating, the machinery within the mill had begun its racket. The bawling of cattle could be heard faintly above the noise of the mill. Volusia walked toward the animal sounds. He hoped the walk would both stave off boredom and loosen up his stiff joints.

It was past 8 A.M. and the sun had yet to burn off the fog. Volusia walked through the mist toward a cowpen at the edge of the pasture. The pen was made of rough cypress logs, divided in the middle by an inner gate, which was closed. A fire, with four men standing around it, glowed on the far side of the inner gate. Volusia took a few more steps and recognized the four as Tree, Heavy, Skeeter, and Junior.

A fifth man stood by the open outer gate that served as the main entrance to the pens. He was only slightly taller than Skeeter and about as thin. Volusia recognized him as Sims, the plantation overseer. They nodded to each other as Volusia walked through the outer gate. Heavy pulled back the inner gate and Volusia walked up to the fire. Three-foot-long handles of four branding irons stuck out of the coals of the fire.

Whips cracked out in the fog. About a dozen steers trotted out from the gray curtain, urged on by three mounted hunters. Sims stepped back from the open gate, watched the steers walk through, and then closed it behind them. The horsemen went back into the fog.

This was the beginning of a day of throwing and branding steers, the hardest and most dangerous part of cow hunting. It was not too bad when dealing with young calves, weighing no more than 150 pounds. But this time the hunters were working with steers no younger than a year old and no lighter than 600 pounds.

Volusia decided to watch the show, at least for an hour or two. He propped a foot on a cypress rail as Tree walked through the inner gate, closing it behind him. Tree strode toward the steers, cracking the whip as he came. He crowded the steers into one corner of the pen and then, with a few more cracks, scared one of them into separating from the rest. Tree stood behind that one and urged it through the inner gate.

The steer was barely through when Heavy, lunging with a speed that was startling for someone his size, grabbed its horns. Junior reached out with both arms and, standing to one side to avoid a kick, grabbed its tail. Heavy used the horns to twist the head in one direction while Junior twisted the tail in the other. The steer fell to the ground and Heavy laid his body across the neck. "Iron!" he shouted.

Skeeter, wearing heavy leather gauntlets, pulled one of the branding irons from the fire. He walked, quickly but cautiously, to the steer and pressed the iron against the flank. There was a sizzling sound, followed by a bellow from the steer. For a second, the stench of singed hair and burned meat overpowered the smell of the fire's woodsmoke. Then Heavy got up from the steer's neck and pointed the animal's head toward the gate. Tree used his whip to urge the steer back through both gates and out to the pasture.

If the steer had been a calf, Heavy would have held it down for a few more seconds to give Skeeter time to use his knife and cut off the testicles. But that operation had been performed on these animals when they first were rounded up from the scrub. Now, all the hunters needed to do was put the "CS" brand on grown steers to mark them as government property.

After four steers, the hunters took a break to give the irons time to reheat. The quickest, deepest, and best brands were made when the edge of the iron turned white and the rest of it glowed a dark red. Sims walked over and chatted with the hunters. The conversation got around to techniques for steer throwing. Tree began talking about heading-up, wrestling a steer to the ground single-handed by twisting its head.

"I've heard ya'll talk about that," Sims said, a slight smile on his face. "Never seen one do it."

Tree pointed to Heavy. "He's done it dozens o'

times. With his size, he can do it quicker'n anyone I've ever seen. I ain't so fast, but I can get the job done."

Sims took off his hat. He was bald, with a scalp blotched by the red spots that come from a hairless man spending too many hours in the sun. He reached in his trousers' left pocket, took out two silver pieces of eight, and threw them into the hat. "Spanish silver says neither o' you can do it."

Heavy stood up and shook his head. "You're probably right. I ain't done it since the roundup o' sixty-one. Tree, you ain't tried it since then either. You've been off soldierin' 'n' ain't even been near a steer till a few months ago."

Tree also stood. He was wearing his light blue cavalry trousers that had no pockets. But he had a leather pouch looped into his gunbelt. He opened the pouch and took out two silver pieces. "You're on," he said as he threw the coins into Sims's hat.

"You're also a good fifty, seventy-five pounds lighter since the last time you tried this," Heavy said.

Tree stood by the inner gate. "Somebody cut out a steer."

Junior picked up a whip from the ground and, smiling broadly, went into the other pen. He began cracking the whip. One steer, large and muscled enough that Volusia wished he could have it for an ox, jumped like a bucking horse to get away from the whip. Junior singled out that steer, getting between it and the others.

Heavy shouted to his son: "Come on now. Don't go deliberately pickin' out the biggest for him."

One side of Tree's mouth curved up in a sneer.

"Let him keep on. Bet didn't say anythin' 'bout size. I'll take what he gives me."

Heavy shrugged his shoulders and opened the inner gate. Junior, his smile widening, again cracked the whip. But this time, it wasn't only for the noise. The leather tip smacked the steer on the rump.

The steer bellowed as if it were being branded. It ran, head down and horns pointing toward the gate. Heavy swung the gate wide and wedged himself between it and one side of the fence. Volusia, Sims, and Skeeter ran for the opposite side. Tree stood in the open gateway, his arms spread.

He was quick enough to grab the horns. But when he tried to twist, the steer's neck jerked upward, not sideways. The jerk took Tree off his feet. He clung to the horns, carried along between them like a child in a mother's arms.

Volusia heard Tree say "Ohhh. . . ." as the steer carried him past and to the far side of the fence. Anything else Tree said was lost among the sounds of the splintering fence rails. The wood came apart in a series of small, gunshotlike explosions.

As the fence dissolved, Volusia saw something gray and light blue catapult into the sky. It was Tree. He landed just behind the steer as it continued its head-down charge. An oak stood about 100 feet away from the pen. The steer rammed into the trunk as if it expected the oak to give way as easily as the fence. Some of the branches trembled and the oak gave out a sound like a bass drum, but it easily withstood the charge. The steer fell at the base of the trunk.

Cattle have an uncanny instinct for identifying weak spots and breaks in fences. The other steers in the pen used that instinct to run through the inner gate, out the gaping hole in the far side, and over and around Tree. They did not repeat the mistake of their liberator. They ran around the oak and disappeared into the fog.

The hunters followed the steers out the fence. Sims picked up his hat and pocketed the silver before joining them. Tree sat up before the hunters reached him. His eyes had the wide, but glazed and unseeing, stare of a drunk just before he vomits.

Tree shook his head. The glaze began to clear from his eyes.

"There must be something appropriate for this moment," Heavy said. "How 'bout 'Even so the tongue is a little member, 'n' boasteth great things. Behold, how great a matter a little fire kindleth.' James, three: five."

Tree seemed not to hear. He stopped shaking his head. "Well," he said, pointing to the steer, which still was stretched out by the oak. "He's down."

# 10

STEAM CLOUDED THE MIRROR as Green-
ley poured water from the hissing teakettle into the
tin basin. He looked at his image, fogged and dis-
torted in the glass. Stick with the moustache, he decided. Shave the beard, but leave some of the sideburns. So, he sharpened his razor on the leather strop
that he kept next to the basin. Repeatedly dipping his
shaving brush into the almost-boiling water, he then
lathered his chin and cheek with the soap he kept in a
dish near the strop.

He had lost count of the number of times he had
pondered what facial hair to shave and what to keep.
And he couldn't remember how many times he changed
styles. Sometimes, he would grow a full beard. Other
times, just the moustache. Once, he tried letting his
sideburns grow down to his jaw and out across his
cheek to his moustache, a style made popular by General Ambrose Burnside. It took only three weeks for
Greenley to decide the style was not for him.

His biggest problem was in deciding whether to

grow a full beard. This time, he had started one while he was out on patrol. But, faced with the prickly look of his chin and cheeks, he decided to shave it before Doris saw him again. She had asked him over for a New Year's dinner. Two weeks worth of stubble would not look proper at the table.

There was one good thing about his continual indecision: few people realized that he suffered from it. Years of riding in the sun had turned his skin the same brown shade as his hair. Unless someone was very close to his face, it was hard to tell whether he was trying to grow a beard.

After he shaved, he poured the used water into the porcelain chamber pot that usually was stored under his bed. An orderly soon would be by to empty it and the other officers' pots. Since he had the ability to sleep through the night without needing to relieve himself until morning, when he went to the latrines, he seldom used the chamber pot for anything but wastewater from cleaning or shaving. He believed he deserved the gratitude of every orderly that ever served with him, but he never had one talk to him on the subject of chamber pots.

The stove that heated the water for him also kept the room warm. He felt comfortable shaving while dressed only in the light nightshirt that he used for sleeping. Now he took off that shirt and dressed in the newer and better-looking of his two uniforms. Nine-tenths of post would be recovering from New Year's Eve hangovers. He doubted that anyone would give him a job that would dirty his good uniform before he went to Doris's at 1 P.M.

He was right. A surly cook who served him breakfast in the mess and a few sullen sentries who came to attention when he walked by were the only soldiers he saw that morning. He decided to tour the stables and make sure the horses were fed despite the holiday. They were. Then he wandered east from the stable to the fort. His footsteps sounded like drumbeats as he walked across the planks of the drawbridge leading to the main gate.

The planks had to be fairly new. They were sturdy enough to bear the weight of horses pulling a wagon. But the moat beneath the planks was one of the oldest man-made structures in the city. The moat's history went back almost 250 years to the beginning of the fort. It was not very broad, only about 100 feet across. Still, it was a good 25 feet deep and had steeply sloping banks. The moat really was a small channel of the Matanzas River, which ran by the fort's east wall. Spanish engineers diverted the dark, brackish water to run in a semicircle around the rest of the fort.

After returning a sentry's salute, Greenley walked through the archway of the main entrance and onto the fort's grounds. Being a holiday, only the one sentry was on duty. Even during the busiest of duty days, few soldiers spent much time in the fort, except for artillerymen who maintained and occasionally practiced with the cannon.

Its time as a military post was gone. The fort was built to withstand invasions by 17th- and 18th-century enemies from sea or land. It was built in a square, with a bastion — a high triangular wall topped by a watchtower—at each corner. The apexes of the triangles jutted outward toward the river and the town, like spearpoints held out to threaten potential invaders.

Throughout its life, the fort performed its job brilliantly. Nobody had ever breached its walls. English armies in the 1700s pillaged throughout the area and laid siege to the fort. The walls held and kept safe everyone within them.

But that all was before the invention of rifled cannon and other artillery that could lob explosive shells for more than a mile into a fort. Beginning with Sumter in '61, this war was showing that all a fort did any more was give artillery condensed, easy-to-hit mass targets.

Everybody assigned to Fort Marion lived and did most of their work within the city. The fort itself was supposed to be used mostly for housing military prisoners. At the moment, and for most of the time the fort had been in Union hands, there were no such prisoners.

The only noises inside the fort's walls came from the cries of soaring gulls and the rhythmic beat of Greenley's footsteps. He climbed the steps leading to the northeastern bastion. It was not easy. Wind-blown spray from the river coated the stairway like the slime on a frog's back. He had to mince his steps to keep his boots from slipping.

Greenley pulled up the collar of his greatcoat to keep the spray from going down the back of his neck. The doubled-breasted coat was made of heavy wool, and reached below his knees. It weighed a good ten pounds. In Ohio, such a coat would keep him warm when the snow was so thoroughly frozen that it would crunch when someone walked on it. Here, the air was not cold enough to freeze water. But Greenley was more uncomfortably cold than he remembered being in the depths of a winter back home. Maybe it was because of the chill spray, which covered the city and hung in the air like a misty rain. The water soaked through the wool of his coat, making it feel like a cold, wet blanket.

When he reached the bastion's top, he turned toward the river and the spray slapped his face. The wind blew with enough force to make the water droplets sting as they hit. He buried his head further into the upturned collar of the coat. Holding onto his hat, he pulled the brim further down toward his eyes.

Greenley turned his head to the southeast. Nothing showed on the horizon but gulls and the gray tower of a lighthouse perched a few miles away on a sand bar. He looked down toward the riverfront docks. A merchant ship was moored to the pier. No smoke came from its stack. Its flag was furled, so he couldn't tell its nationality. It probably was either American, going to northern ports, or Spanish, destined for Cuba. St. Augustine's port had been closed to most shipping, but Holmes had the authority to grant docking privileges.

Cattle milled around a pen near the ship. They were the first stock Greenley had seen in the pen. He thought cattle were contraband and their trade forbidden in the area. But Holmes apparently also had the authority to reopen the port to cattle shipments.

Actually, the colonel had the authority to do pretty much anything he wanted. Because of the isolation of the St. Augustine forces, he might as well be an absolute dictator. His nearest superior officer was in Jacksonville, 30 miles — more than a day's ride — to the north. The next closest Union outpost to that was Fort Clinch on Amelia Island, another 30 miles north of Jacksonville.

All of that was Holmes's worry. Greenley's only concern at the moment was getting to Doris's on time. His right hand dug through the layers of his greatcoat and uniform jacket and removed the watch from his vest pocket. A little more than a half hour to go. Might as well arrive early. He walked down from the bastion and out of the fort.

Her house was just behind her bakery. It was typical of the more recent buildings in the city, with its whitewashed wood frame and peaked roof. The roof was covered with gray-brown wood shingles. Its two stories made the building seem about as tall as it was wide. The one-story bakery was typical of older buildings. It was made of coquina, possibly by Spaniards who built much of what would become St. Augustine's business district with the stone left over from constructing the fort.

Doris used the bakery as her kitchen. She walked out the back door, carrying a large, black iron pot, as Greenley passed. He took one of the handles, using his gauntlet instead of the hot-pot holder that Doris offered him. They brought the pot through the front door of the home and set it on an iron stove that warmed the dining room.

A strange, but not unpleasant, earthy odor rose with the steam from the pot. Dan looked inside. Several fatty pieces of pork rested on top of sand-colored, kidney-shaped beans. Each bean had a black spot in its middle.

"Hog jowls and black-eyed peas," Doris said as she put two bowls beside the pot. "Today, you've got to eat at least 365 of them peas. One for each day. Gives you luck for the year. Wish you'd waited till I told you to show up, though. I figured on changin' into somethin' better. "

Greenley smiled. "You look fine."

He wasn't merely being polite. Doris was dressed in working clothes: a blue, high-collared heavy cotton blouse, a faded black wool dress, and a white apron. The clothes were strictly utilitarian. She didn't even have a crinoline under the dress. Still, she looked neat and trim.

Doris spooned the beans and pork into the bowls and set them on the table. Greenley held a chair out for her and then moved to the other place that was set at the table. He was in the process of sitting when something gray leaped down from a nearby stairway and landed in the chair just ahead of Greenley's rump.

Startled, Dan jumped back into a standing position and looked at the chair. Two yellow eyes stared back at him. A cat, gray with black stripes ringing its back and tail and with a gleaming white throat and chest, sat on its haunches and laid claim to the chair.

"Coacoochee!" Doris' voice approached a scream. "Get away!"

The cat turned its head toward Doris. Then the head snapped back to Greenley and the unblinking stare resumed.

"Nice-lookin' cat," Dan reached out a hand toward the head. "What's the name again?"

"Coacoochee. Spelled C-o-a-c-o-o-c-h-e-e. Lots of people pronounce it COH-a-coo-chee, like its spelled. Actually, it's pronounced Coh-WAH-cu-jee," Doris spoke very slowly. "It's the name of a Seminole chief who used to live in these parts. Gave it to this cat when I found him outside the bakery door. Means wildcat."

A paw, as white as the throat and chest, flashed out from beneath the body and slapped Greenley's hand before it touched the head. Greenley was thankful that he had not yet removed his gauntlets. The slap sounded like a whiplash when the paw hit the leather. Dan heard a tearing noise as he jerked back his hand. He looked at the gauntlet. Zig-zagged lines tore across it where the claws had hit the leather.

"Good name," Greenley said as he and the cat went back to staring at each other.

Doris ended the stalemate by getting up from her chair and tipping over the one claimed by Coacoochee. The cat dug his claws into the flowered upholstery on the seat, but eventually surrendered. He bounded a few feet behind Greenley and then leaped back to the stairway. He sat on one of the steps and glared through the posts of the banister.

Greenley blamed that stare for the prickly sensation he felt throughout the meal. Hairs on the back of his neck bristled as he ate.

"Most of the Yankees 'round here are from New England. You ain't, are you?" Doris said, eyes fixed on his face. The brown irises darkened. If it wasn't for the tiny golden highlights within them, it would be hard to tell where the irises ended and the pupils began. "From Indiana, right?"

Dan shook his head. "Ohio."

"Well, some place to the west," Doris's face was impassive, but her eyes gleamed, betraying the fact she was teasing. "The really bad Yankees — Sherman,

Grant — all the ones who seem to be winnin' — are from there. You a really bad Yankee?"

"Depends on your definition of bad. I sure intend to be one of the winners, if that's what you mean."

He had expected the beans to be rather tasteless and mushy. Instead, they were spiced with some type of pepper that tingled his lips and tongue much like the fish chowder did during the Christmas Eve supper. They had a meaty texture that complimented and contrasted with the soft, chewy pork.

"You're awfully cheerful around us, considerin' we're occupyin' your city." Greenley kept watching the lights dance in her eyes. They formed golden flecks on the dark irises.

"There were folks 'round here who really hated your guts. But they're gone now." Doris shrugged her shoulders. "The hard-line Confederates left when the Yankees arrived. A lot o' 'em headed west 'cross the St. Johns. Either that or they went upriver to Volusia County."

Greenley doubted if he ever would get used to the way people in north-central Florida used words like "upriver." Volusia County was to the south. It would be logical to think of going down, not up, to there from St. Augustine. But the St. Johns flowed north; that meant upstream was to the south and downstream was to the north.

"I wish you people would just say north or south," he said. "Your ideas of up and down river just get confusin'."

Doris didn't reply to the tease. A smile wrinkled her nose. "The rest of us are used to Yankees. This was a big health resort afore the war. 'Specially durin' the winter. Yankees were all over the town. Seems our climate was 'posed to be good for consumption 'n' lung fever. Got used to dealing' with 'em. Ya'll ain't that much different. Just wear blue all the time 'n' cough less."

Feeling self-conscious, Greenley stopped looking into Doris's eyes and concentrated on his bowl. Then he felt compelled to look back up at her. The golden flecks were gone from the eyes. So was the smile from her lips. Doris stared out a window, at clouds drifting over the river, heading east to the ocean.

"There's somethin' else. Ain't talked about it much. Hard to put into words," she said. "I'm a Minorcan. Know what that means?"

"That you're from Minorca, I guess." He had seen many people in the city with the same dark hair and eyes and creamy, tanned complexion as Doris. He assumed they were all of the same ethnic group. But he didn't see what relevance that had to her sympathies in the war.

"Maybe. Don't really know for sure. My people are from some island in the Mediterranean," she said. "Since Minorca is one o' the biggest islands 'round there, folks just call all o' us Minorcan. But, the point is, my people came over here as indentured servants. They might as well been slaves."

Greenley stopped eating and watched her face grow more serious as she talked.

"British land speculators swept through the Mediterranean islands durin' the 1700s, when Florida was an English colony. They picked up a lot of people. Promised 'em land, money, 'n' God-knows-what-else. All they had to do was work on this Englishman's big plantation for a few years. My great-grandparents came over with about fourteen hundred others. They get put on this plantation a hundred miles south o' here. None o' the promises held true. Their contracts expired 'n' the plantation owner still wouldn't let 'em go. Anybody who complained got beaten 'n' starved."

"Some o' the folks escaped to St. Augustine. The British governor here pitched in on their side. He got the Minorcans released 'n' threw the plantation owner in jail."

"If it weren't for the governor, I'd be cuttin' sugarcane on that plantation today. I got to thinkin' 'bout that in late '62, after your Mister Lincoln signed that Emancipation Proclamation. Sorta the same thing that governor did for my people. I decided I didn't want to side with the plantation owner."

"I could have used you in '60 when I was helpin' in the Republican campaign," Dan said. "No. I take that back. The last thing we needed was somebody else to talk about the morality of emancipation. Too many folks in southwest Ohio already were 'fraid of that."

Doris' eyes held his. "You weren't?" she asked.

"No. But then, the Democrats said that was because I owned a mill and wanted to free slaves for cheap labor."

Greenley could feel the corners of his lips pulling into a sneer. "Hundreds of thousands of immigrants comin' into the country each year. Thousands of 'em headin' into Ohio. And I supposedly have to raid plantations in order to find mill labor. But, if you don't think folks believe such things in the North, just come up to Ohio for a spell. Hell, Lincoln still hasn't done as much for emancipation as he could've. All he's done is tell the slaves in the Confederacy that they're free. Tellin' isn't freein'. The slaves are slaves until we occupy the piece of the Confederacy that they're sittin' on. Meanwhile, we haven't touched the slaves in the states that stayed in the Union.

"Still, Lincoln's done more than I feared he might when the electioneerin' started in '60. About all I got out of the campaign was a reputation among the Republicans. They started recognizin' my name. When the war started and a regiment formed in my area, my name was well enough known that I got elected captain. Got promoted to major just before Vicksburg fell."

Doris ladled out some more beans into the bowls. "Didn't think you seemed like a professional soldier. But then, you don't seem like a politician, either."

Greenley exhaled heavily. "Never intended to be one. All it amounted to was that I couldn't see any moral justification for one person ownin' another. I didn't start out to be an abolitionist. Way too many crazies, the John Browns and the like, were in the abolition movement. Trouble was, I tried to keep my head durin' a time when insanity was in fashion. In some of my neighbors' minds, me just takin' a dislike to slavery put me in the same sack with Brown.

"Whether I wanted to or not, I got pulled into politics. Found myself organizin' the Republicans in my neck of the woods. Started out supportin' one of our Ohio senators, Salmon Chase. He seemed to feel about the same way I did on slavery. But then it seemed like everybody was scared of goin' to bed one night and wakin' up the next mornin' to find an emancipated slave workin' his job.

"We backed off full emancipation and I wound up supportin' Lincoln. He wasn't an abolitionist, but he would keep slavery from expandin' into new territories. Still, people beat us over the head with the 'slaves'll-get-your-jobs' fear. If the Democrats hadn't been crazier than us and split into three warrin' factions, Lincoln never would've been elected. "

A flash of white teeth interrupted as Doris smiled gaily. "'N' you never would've been here to taste black-eyed peas."

Greenley returned to his meal. He didn't bother to count the beans, but he was sure that, by the time he was finished, he had eaten at least 365.

# 11 🖤

As for the luck in black-eyed peas, all Greenley discovered in the meal was a bad case of gas the next morning. If anything, he believed his luck soured. He still was belching and feeling bloated when an orderly arrived with a message summoning Greenley to Holmes's office.

The office smelled even more strongly of gin than usual. But, for a change, Holmes wasn't drinking alone. Four other men sat in the room. Each held a glass in one hand and the wide brim of a hat in the other. All were dressed in the rough, dirty clothes of people who'd been in the scrub for a long time. One was about Greenley's height. The others were several inches taller. They all had square shoulders and ruddy complexions. Only one of them was beardless. He also was the slimmest. His hair was the same sorrel color as two of the bearded men. The fourth's hair and beard were almost the same shade of gray as Spanish moss.

"Major Greenley, this is Otto Brockton," Holmes pointed to the gray-haired man. "And his sons. They have volunteered to be scouts. We need such men."

By the end of the week, Greenley was joking that, if the black-eyed peas hadn't brought him luck, they at least brought him the Brocktons. And the Brocktons at least brought him success on the job. The week ended with Greenley's company bringing in more than 200 head of cattle, thanks to the scouts guiding the troopers to a herd close to the banks of the St. Johns. About a dozen cow hunters guided the herd and they put up a short, futile struggle. Nobody in the company was hurt in the exchange of shots. The major saw several of the hunters fall from their saddles. He couldn't tell if they were killed or, if they were alive, how seriously they were wounded. The gunfire stampeded the cattle, so he was busy riding after the herd.

Greenley also found time for revenge on his return to St. Augustine. With the Brocktons' help, he made his way back to the woman's cabin in the clearing. This time, he didn't intend to stay the night. He sat in his saddle and watched several privates go through her smokehouse. They took out two hams, a chicken, and a turkey. Other members of the company pulled up the green leafy plants that were growing in a nearby acre of plowed ground.

There were no cattle on the place, but there were more than a dozen pigs of various ages and sexes. The oldest of the Brockton boys — Greenley had discovered his name was Martin — and several of the company used the pigs for target practice. Those bodies that they could not butcher and carry off they dragged into the woods.

"Sorry about all this, ma'am," Greenley had to shout to be heard about the gunfire and laughter. "I'm doin' it to teach you somethin'. You do not mock representatives of the United States. If I ever hear of you interferin' with, or even bein' disrespectful to any of us again, I'll be back. Next time I'll burn your house and everythin' else you own to the ground."

The woman stood on her porch, arms again around both of the girls, and glared. But not at Greenley. Despite what he was saying, she ignored him.

"I know you, Otto Brockton," she called out. "Laugh all you want now. See how funny you think it is when Tree hears 'bout this."

Hours later, when the company and the herd were back on the trail to St. Augustine, Greenley began feeling sick. Yes, he felt he had to do that to the woman. Directing him into the swamp was not some child's Halloween prank. The calf was an example of what could have happened to anybody in the company. That woman was a dangerous enemy sympathizer living in an area he was to secure for the Union. He would have been within his rights to arrest her, burn down her house and throw her into a cell in Fort Marion and her children into the nearest orphans' asylum. Many, if not most, officers he knew had served out such punishment to openly hostile women in Vicksburg after the occupation. And few of those women had actually jeopardized anybody's life. The worst most of them did was dump chamber pots on passing federal soldiers.

During the time the company was raiding the woman's property, the major felt no remorse. The woman's hard, unblinking eyes didn't solicit pity and he saw no reason to give any. But now, he had time to think. When he first joined the Army, he never imagined taking revenge against a woman and small children. He decided the less he thought about it, the better. So he turned his horse around and trotted back along the column.

The Brocktons were at the rear. They watched over the cattle that leisurely grazed and moved in a pasture bordering the road. Greenley pulled up his horse next to Otto's and asked a question that had been bothering him since the raid on the cabin.

"What'd that woman mean by 'a tree hears about this?'"

Otto swung a leg over the pommel and sat sidesaddle, facing Greenley. "Not 'a tree.' Just Tree. He's a cow hunter who's called that. Used to live a ways east o' Enterprize. He rode off to the Army. Now he's back. Roustin' out hunters who feel for the Confederacy. He's drivin' a big herd up to the Rebels."

Greenley looked beyond the herd to the west. "Well, let's go after him."

Otto shook his head. "Not now. He's somewheres 'tween here 'n' Baldwin with 'bout 20 good gunhands. We've got green Yankees. The only reason we got these cattle was that we outnumbered those boys by a good three to one. 'N' none o' 'em seemed to know much 'bout fightin'. When we go after Tree, we better plan real good. We gotta pick the place 'n' the time.

"We'll get Tree, but it ain't gonna be today. It ain't gonna be tomorrow. Probably ain't gonna be next month or the month after that. But, long as there's a war, Tree'll be drivin' cattle north. Sooner or later, we'll get him."

Otto's tone of voice was as casual as if he were

discussing a quail hunt. Greenley was surprised by the lack of emotion shown by all the Brocktons ever since he met them. After all, what they were doing was considered treason by Florida's government. And not simply the treason-of-conscience of such Union sympathizers as Doris. The Brocktons had calmly thrown themselves into actual warfare against the Confederacy.

"We just shot up some people that might be your neighbors. We raided the farm of people who know you. This Tree is somebody else you know," Greenley said. "Doesn't it worry you that we're tanglin' with your people?"

A noise that combined a chuckle with a snort exploded from Otto's mouth. "Hell. Ain't none o' 'em my people. Only people I've got are my boys. To me, there's family 'n' everybody else. Don't care how long I've known 'em, these Crackers still are just somebody else."

He swung his leg back across the saddle and resumed a normal riding position. "Tree sure ain't nothin' to me but somebody else who might get in my way. He was stupid afore he went off to the Army. Lots o' time mixin' into things when he didn't have a call to. From what I've seen of him since, he's even stupider now. Take this Cow Cavalry. Cow huntin's a hard life. Idiotic to do it for no money. But Tree's doin' that like it's a better pastime than whorin'. The hell of it is, he's found others at least as stupid as he is 'n' they're all out there now huntin' cows for Jeff Davis."

Greenley spoke without thinking: "But you're out here huntin' cattle for us."

Otto didn't take offense. He simply shook his

head. "Way different thing. This is business for me. I need places to ship out my cattle 'n' people to buy 'em. Nearest port for me is St. Augustine. Ya'll got it in your pocket. You've also got the most people with the most money who're willin' to buy cattle. 'N' I sure don't mind comin' out to help ya'll collect some more cattle, long as I get the money from 'em."

His eyes stared straight ahead and his mouth worked on a quid of tobacco. "Maybe if I was some planter with a hundred slaves or so 'n' a thousand-odd acres of cotton, I'd care 'bout the war. But I ain't. Hell, I don't even know that many slaveholders. This is the palmetto scrub. No good for slaves. Too much space for 'em to run in 'n' too many places for 'em to hide."

He turned his head toward Greenley. "For all I care, Yankees 'n' Rebels can go on killin' each other from now till the end o' time. Just as long as they leave me alone to hunt cattle."

Then he leaned over his saddle, away from the major, and spat. He turned back, reached into a vest pocket and pulled out a linen handkerchief wrapped into a small square bundle. "Chaw?" he unwrapped the bundle and held out a dark square of tobacco to Greenley.

"No thanks. I'll stay with cigars."

Otto smiled. A sliver of tobacco came out of his mouth and lay on his lower lip. "Wait till summer. Air gets too damp to light up when you're outside. If you want tobacco, you chew."

As he watched Otto lick his lip and draw the sliver back into his mouth, Greenley silently vowed to give up tobacco entirely rather than spend the summer chewing and spitting.

When they reached St. Augustine, the Brocktons herded the cattle east to the dockside pens while Greenley led the company north to the stables near the fort. The troopers unsaddled and groomed the horses while Greenley walked to headquarters. He wrote his report at a desk in front of the closed door leading to Holmes's office. The writing was interrupted briefly when the Brocktons walked into the room. Greenley put down his pen to smile and nod at them. They walked into the colonel's office without knocking. It was a half hour before they left, still smiling, and Greenley was able to submit his report.

Greenley left headquarters and went to his room. He took his second uniform and a fresh set of underclothes from his trunk and then walked five blocks north to a barbershop. The shop was a small frame building with one great attraction. It had a room in the back with three copper bathtubs and a furnace that continually heated large pots of water. After paying 25 cents, Greenley stripped off his mud-caked uniform and underclothes and stepped into one of the tubs. He sat in the tub, which looked like a laundry basin with a high back attached to it. A large, silent black man poured buckets of water over him. The man handed Greenley a cake of white soap that smelled of the pork fat and wood-ash lye from which it was made. Greenley felt the soap scrape off some of his skin as he scrubbed the ingrained dirt out of his pores. When he stepped out of the tub, he looked at the water. It was gray. A thin layer of black soil lined the bottom of the tub.

After dressing in his fresh uniform and going to

the front room, he decided to treat himself and paid another 25 cents for a shave. The barber was a small thin man who, judging from his complexion and dark eyes and hair, was a Minorcan like Doris. He had lathered Greenley's face and was beginning to remove the week's growth of whiskers when the front door opened. The Brocktons entered.

"Hey Danny," Otto said. "You again. Don't mean to seem like we're followin' you. Reckon it just happens that we've got business in the same places. We're gonna have to clean up a might afore any tart worth the money will come near us."

Greenley gritted his teeth until his jaw moved and the barber, who was shaving the chin, fussed at him. Nobody had called him "Danny" since his grandmother died in '51. He never liked the diminutive nickname. His distaste for it recently had grown because the Brocktons frequently sang the Irish ballad "Danny Boy" while riding around the cattle at night.

Otto turned his attention to the barber. "Let the boys get cleaned up first. Just give me a hot towel after you finish with Danny."

He spat into a nearby cuspidor and again addressed Greenley. "Spanish ship's come into port. We'll make a good piece o' change from them cattle. Want to come out with us 'n' celebrate with some whiskey 'n' women?"

Greenley had to wait a few seconds, until the barber backed away to wipe lather off the razor, before replying. "No thanks. Have some appointments to keep once I get cleaned up." Actually, he had nothing that he had to do. He merely wanted to get over to Doris's as soon as possible.

"Suit yourself," Otto said. "But I know the colonel would let you off your duty if you want. He's as happy 'bout this trip as we are."

The smile broadened until Greenley could see the tobacco juice squishing out between Otto's teeth. "Colonel's a damned good businessman. Wish I could understand more o' what he says to me, though. Maybe I should hire you on as an interpreter when I go see him. I can understand your talk real good."

Greenley smiled through the lather. "Sorry. Can't help you there. I don't understand him that well myself."

The shave ended within a few minutes. Greenley said goodbye to Otto and walked out of the shop. He dropped off his dirty clothes at a laundry and went to Doris's bakery. There, he had a beef pie — ground, spiced meat wrapped in pastry — and a cup of coffee. He talked about his patrol as he ate.

"Ridin' with the Brocktons, are you?" Doris broke into his discourse.

Dan was taken aback by the sarcasm-tinged, high pitch of her voice. "Take it you know them. Don't sound very fond of them."

"Sure, I know 'em. Otto Brockton's been in 'n' out of this town for as long as I can remember. His kids have tagged along with him since they've been able to sit a horse. I know 'em well enough. Enough not to want to go galavantin' 'cross the country with 'em. "

Greenley laughed. "I wouldn't want you to ride out with them either. I'm the one ridin' with them. Maybe I wouldn't take them with me to high tea with Queen Victoria, but they're mighty handy out in this country. Believe me, they're good at their job. I couldn't have run that patrol without them."

"Well, I reckon if your job's cow stealin' you couldn't pick better company," she said.

He let the subject of the Brocktons die and didn't resurrect it. Over the next week, he ate most of his meals at either the bakery or Doris's home. The two of them occasionally walked the streets together. Mostly, they simply talked. They talked about politics and the course of the war; about novels and stage plays; about which breeds of horses were best for riding; and whether Florida or Ohio had the better overall climate. But Dan never again talked about the Brocktons.

At the end of the week, Otto appeared at the bakery door while Greenley was having lunch. "Hi Danny," he said as he entered. "One of your soldier boys told me I'd find you here." He nodded towards Doris. "Hey, sugar. Ain't seen you for a good while."

Doris's eyes narrowed to dark slits. "Why should we see each other? I don't sell booze or myself. You ever buy anythin' else but liquor 'n' easy women in this town?"

If Otto took offense, he didn't show it. "Sugar, if this war keeps up, I'll have enough money to buy the whole damned town. Your friend here —" he nodded toward Greenley "— is helpin' me with that. 'N' that's why I'm here. Me 'n' the boys ran into some Crackers pushin' a herd a little ways to the west. Come along, Danny, 'n' help us get it."

Greenley's company caught the herd, about 100 cattle and an equal number of hogs, just as it crossed to the west bank of the St. Johns. This time, the five drovers with the herd didn't even attempt to fight. They scattered before the company got across the river. Nobody fired a shot.

The Brocktons, with the help of some of the troopers who were learning how to handle animals, rounded up the herd within a few hours and started moving east. By sunset, they were about ten miles from St. Augustine. Otto led them to a sandy rise in the ground near a creek. The creek's water looked black and smelled of sulfur, but the elder Brockton guaranteed that the water was drinkable.

"Water 'round here always picks up the color o' the roots 'n' leaves 'n' such that fall into it," he told Greenley. "Most water picks up sulfur. Learn to live with it. Not all that bad once you get used to the smell."

He and Greenley walked to an ambulance, a wagon with a square, unbleached canvas cover. Ambulances, unlike most wagons, had springs on the axles that supposedly provided smoother rides for passengers. They usually were used to transport either severely wounded soldiers or high-ranking officers in some degree of comfort. Greenley pressed one into service for his company at the insistence of Otto, who wanted a wagon for carrying various supplies and tools of cow hunting.

Otto went into the ambulance and emerged with a coffee pot. "Least now that I'm a Yankee I can get the real stuff," he said, scooping some coffee out of a sack and into the pot. "Ya'll's blockade stuck us with nothin' but chicory for the last couple o' years."

He turned toward Greenley, a smile forming between the moustache and beard. "Hey, why don't we set up a trade? Ship me the coffee 'n' I can guarantee you'll see three dollars back for every dollar you spend."

Greenley shook his head. "I'll bring it up to the colonel," Otto said, his smile fading.

The two walked down to the creek. "Folks in St. Augustine got real coffee?" Otto asked.

"That's one of the first things to follow our armies. It's an advantage of bein' occupied," Greenley said.

"Thought I smelled the real stuff when I went into the Widow Brava's place," Otto removed the coffee-filled metal basket from the pot. He bent down at the edge of the creek. "Ya'll got plenty o' coffee, though. So I reckon the coffee ain't the only reason you spend your time there, is it?"

Maybe Otto thought his smile was friendly, but it looked too much like a leer to suit Greenley. He couldn't stop the irritation from infecting his voice as he replied: "I don't talk about my off-duty activities."

The pot was filled with water. Otto unbent his body. "I can respect that. Didn't mean no offense."

Footsteps crunched through the tall, dry grass behind the major. He turned in the direction of the noise. The shortest, stockiest of the Brocktons, Corley, stomped toward the creek, a limp piece of cloth in one hand. Nodding to Otto and Greenley, he took off the heavy canvas jacket he wore. His movements were stiff, like those of an arthritic old man.

Despite the chill of the evening, he also took off his shirt. Greenley saw a dark, jagged line slashed across Corley's ribcage.

"Got hooked," Corley said to nobody in particular. "God-damned steer caught me when I was off my horse adjustin' the cinch."

He dipped the piece of cloth in the water and wiped it across the gash.

Greenley and Otto walked back to one of several fires in the camp. Otto rested the coffee pot on a smoldering log as Greenley sat on the ground. Corley came up behind them, wearing the jacket over his bare torso. His shirt was tied around his chest, holding the cloth over the wound. Reaching into one of a pair of saddlebags, he drew out another shirt. He came close to the fire, took off the jacket, and put on the shirt.

Corley's back was toward Greenley. In the few seconds between taking off the jacket and putting on the shirt, the major could see a lacework of scars across the back. The yellow glow of the firelight made the scars look like white worms, each one no wider than Greenley's little finger.

Corley put on his shirt and jacket and walked off into the dark.

"Christ, what happened to his back?" Greenley asked.

Otto starred back silently, uncomprehending.

"I mean the scars," Greenley continued.

"Oh, those," Otto nodded. "Rough life out here. Kids gotta get used to that early. My boys got used to it real early."

The elder Brockton's right hand reached across his body and patted his left hip. His whip was coiled there, held against his gunbelt by his knife sheath.

"Their ma died young. Couldn't take our kind o' life. I saw to it that the boys could. Learned 'em good." His fingers absently drummed against the whip handle. "Made damned sure they grew up quick 'n' right."

# 12 🌿

As the drive neared its end, Tree spent more time as an outrider, a scout for the drive. He rode several hours ahead of the cook wagon looking for water and campsites. Also, he stayed alert for trouble, particularly Yankee patrols. It was late February. The day began cool enough that Hooker wore the swallow-tailed coat when he left camp just as the sun was turning the eastern horizon pink. By the time the sun was overhead, the day had warmed up and he could take off both the coat and his shirt. He rode in a red undershirt, with the sleeves rolled up to his elbows. That afternoon he was searching for a lake called Ocean Pond. Tree knew the cattle could find water there and, although most of the land was swampy, there was enough dry ground for camping. It would take about two more days of driving east from the lake to reach Baldwin.

Tree was riding near the Florida, Atlantic, and Gulf Central Railroad tracks that ran into Baldwin and that soon would be taking the cattle to the rest of the

Confederacy. He found the tracks and began following them west, figuring that if he didn't find Ocean Pond he would come to the little town of Olustee, a few miles west of the water hole.

Then he saw a sight he thought he had left behind in Vicksburg. An entire Confederate infantry regiment marched along the road that paralleled the tracks. Hundreds of soldiers held their rifles at their right sides and kept more or less in step with each other. Drummers tapped out a beat for the march. Officers rode horses that seemed to prance in time to the beat. Sunlight bounced off the gleaming bayonets and created a halo effect around the regiment. Tree almost hated to interrupt the parade-ground-like perfection of the march. But, his duty required him to identify himself to the commanding officer, and his curiosity spurred him to find out what the regiment was doing. So, he rode across the tracks and stopped in front of the advancing column. The leader, a colonel, halted the regiment. Hooker saluted and identified himself. In return, he got a salute and found out that he was facing the 28th Georgia Infantry.

"How many are with you?" the colonel asked. "Better get 'em 'n' fall in with me."

"There are twenty of us. Most of 'em are 'bout five miles behind," Tree replied. "But we've got twelve hundred head of cattle with us. They ain't gonna drive themselves. Sorry colonel. Our duty is to stick with the herd. Least till Baldwin."

The colonel shook his head. "Only if you want to give the Yankees beef on their table. That's who's waitin' for you in Baldwin. Ya'll have been on the trail too long. We've been chasin' or bein' chased by Yankees 'cross north Florida for the last week. Right now, some of 'em are in Baldwin and the rest are headin' toward us. Big doin's are at hand. Better get what men you can 'n' catch up with us."

Hooker replied to that by saluting again and turning his horse to the southeast. He rode through a pine forest at a brisk trot, the fastest pace he felt the horse could stand for the trip back to the herd. The horse was a sorrel mare he picked out of the herd accompanying the drive. She was small and not very strong, but she responded well to the reins and stepped nimbly over fallen logs and branches in the forest. The horse was what Tree called "woods smart."

Another battle was coming. This time in his home state. He should have felt excitement. But he didn't. All he could feel was a slight nausea. The same feeling always gripped his stomach before a firefight. After about half a dozen brushes with Indians in his youth and various pitched battles over the last three years, Tree had grown used to the sickly feeling.

It usually kept getting worse until the first shot was fired. After that, the job of staying alive crowded out anything else and the nausea disappeared, at least until the fighting ended. Then, often, the nausea returned, along with a weakness in his legs and arms that kept him from moving for hours. Sometimes, he crawled off into the brush and vomited repeatedly until he felt able to stand. And, for all those times, only once did the excitement and rewards of a fight make up for the sickness.

Strangely, that didn't happen during the actual battle itself. Nor did it happen during the flush of a major victory. It came after one of the dozens of small, bloody affairs near Vicksburg. One of them occurred around a town called Bovina, a tiny Mississippi hamlet that wouldn't have concerned anybody in the either army, except that it had the last undamaged railroad bridge across the Big Black River. And the Big Black was the last obstacle between the Yankees and Vicksburg. So, Bovina suddenly became a major concern to everybody in both armies.

Tree was among the cavalrymen who set fire to the bridge after the Yankees broke through the Confederate defenses. Then, he and the rest joined the thousands of others running west toward Vicksburg. For most of the 12 miles between Bovina and the city, the closest to heroics that Hooker came was to stop occasionally and fire a shot toward blue-clad cavalrymen who were a few hundred yards behind him. Mostly, he just spurred his horse onward, at least until he caught up with a team of six fear-crazed horses. The horses pulled a limber — a two-wheeled cart used to carry ammunition for artillery — and a cannon. Tree never found out what happened to the driver who should have been sitting on the limber or to the gunners who should have been riding on the horses. At the time, all he thought of was that somebody ought to take control of the team and get the cannon to Vicksburg where it belonged.

Jumping from a running horse to another moving animal or object was fairly easy for Tree. He had done it several times while hunting cattle. He sometimes had jumped on a steer when there was nobody around to help him bring it down for branding. Instinct took over as he drew his horse alongside the limber. He slowed the gallop of his horse to the same speed as the limber's team. He reached out and put his carbine on the limber's seat, knowing that if he didn't keep that gun near him he would never see another left-handed lock plate, at least until he returned home. He unhooked the saber sheath from his belt to avoid getting tangled in the spinning wheels. He swung his right leg out from the stirrup and toward the limber seat and brought his left leg up until the knee rested on the saddle seat. Then he jumped.

Fear did not strike until after he landed on the ammunition chest. Then he realized that the reins to control the two lead horses were dangling from their harnesses and dragging along the dirt. He had no control over the horses. Meanwhile, his own horse, carrying his saber, shotgun, and most of his other possessions, had veered away and probably would become the property of the U.S. government within a few minutes. Trapped and unable to think of anything else to do, Tree jumped again, this time onto the pole that extended out from the limber and to which the horses were harnessed. He sat on the narrow, rough wood of the pole and scooped up the reins. Leaning back so that his shoulders rested on the front of the limber, Tree gradually slowed the pace of the horses.

As he pulled on the reins, Hooker began to feel his temples throb in time to the rhythm of his heartbeat. His muscles tightened. Somehow, he seemed to be able to breathe more deeply and smell the air about him more clearly. There should have been pain from the bumping and scraping of the pole against his rump and the front of the limber against his back. But there wasn't. The thrill drove out almost any other sensation from his body. It lasted for at least an hour, until he brought the team to a stop along the riverfront of Vicksburg.

A dozen pairs of hands helped him get up from the pole while others held the team. Several soldiers helped him walk from the limber to the boardwalk fronting the shops, warehouses, and saloons across from the docks.

Hooker pulled his mind away from the memories. He always did that at this point. Beyond getting the team to Vicksburg, the memories either led to melancholy or rage. But the monotony of riding through the woods at a steady pace began to overtake him. Unbidden, the memories began to push themselves through his mind.

As he sat on the Vicksburg boardwalk and his breathing returned to normal, Tree was seized by thirst. His mouth felt as if it were gagged by a cotton boll, complete with seeds and husk. Nothing sounded as welcomed as the feminine voice that asked "Would you like something to drink?"

Tree was unable to speak, but he nodded and held out a hand, expecting that some chippy from a nearby saloon was going to give him a shot glass or a beer stein. Instead, he found himself holding a glass tumbler. He took a sip, still expecting to feel the burn of some alcoholic beverage. Instead, he swallowed cool, but not uncomfortably icy, water, with a slight hint of ginger in its taste. The ginger, a trick long practiced in Southern homes, allowed the drinker to pour large amounts of water on an empty, overheated stomach without getting cramps. Tree gulped the contents of the tumbler.

He gasped out "Thanks," and turned to his right to look at his benefactress as he held out the tumbler. Two large blue eyes looked into his. Light blue. Very light blue, something like the color of his uniform trousers. But lighter and more brilliant. He had seen that shade of blue once before, but not in a pair of eyes. It was in the Gulf of Mexico, near Pensacola. Sandbars about 100 yards offshore lightened the color of the water to that shade just before the surf began to foam and roll onto the beach.

"More?" she asked.

Tree nodded and she refilled the tumbler. But he did not bring the tumbler to his lips. He kept looking at her eyes, still holding the glass toward her. "Is something the matter?" Her voice broke through his reverie.

"No ma'am," he replied before downing the water. "Thanks again." His hand touched hers as he returned the tumbler to her. Her hand was cool, almost chill, from holding a water jug. Tree forced his gaze away from her eyes. A few strands of hair, the color and thickness of corn silk, escaped from the bun in which she had tied her hair with a red ribbon. The wisps of hair brushed her brown eyebrows and eyelashes and lay along her cheek. They dangled below her jaw and rested on the ruffled collar of her white blouse.

The scent of lilacs came to him from her hair and skin. Sweet, but not the cloying, heavy scent of flowers like magnolias or orange blossoms. Tree was fond of the smell and regretted that lilacs didn't grow around his home area. Occasionally, he would run across a woman who used lilac oil in her soap or shampoo. But, since most of the women he knew were trollops who needed a heavy perfume to combat the smell of the cow hunters with whom they dealt, that happened very seldom.

She had been kneeling beside him as he sat on the boardwalk. With a rustle of petticoats, she stood. Tree also got to his feet. He automatically reached to the top of his head to take off his hat, but discovered that it had blown off sometime during his ride. As he stood beside the girl, he realized that the top of her head came to the middle of his chest. The width of her shoulders was no more than the length of his forearm. Tree suddenly felt freakishly large and boyishly awkward. He almost felt relieved when the girl nodded, smiled, and went down the boardwalk. Her skirt was pink — or maybe it was faded red — with white polka dots. Its hem brushed the planks of the walkway.

He watched her until she disappeared around a corner. She stopped several times and poured out water for other soldiers. Some of the others kept her in conversation for several minutes. Always, the conversations would end with her smiling and nodding.

Tree sat back down at the edge of the boardwalk and decided to wait until somebody gave him an order to move and do something. Within a few minutes, he was shaded by the shadow of someone standing behind him. He expected to hear an officer give him an order. Instead, he again heard her voice, "I keep runnin' out o' water with this pitcher. Would you mind helpin' me fetch a bucket from home 'n' carry it for me?"

They walked for several blocks without talking. Then, they merely exchanged names. Hers was Laura Mason. They were within sight of her house before Tree said: "Thirty thousand-odd men 'round here. Why'd you pick me?"

She smiled. "I've been waitin' for a chance to walk with a real hero. They say you're one."

Tree shrugged. "I ran."

Laura's smile broadened. Her walk became more brisk, almost a skip. "Oh, but you were 'bout the last to run. 'N' you brought in that cannon. Everybody's talkin' 'bout your ride."

Her voice was muffled by the noise of the milling animals, troops, spectators, and other civilians fetching drinks and food for the soldiers. The streets and boardwalks teemed. Tree had to stoop over to hear her. He should have taken more notice of the scene around him. But he was too busy with her. Smelling the scent of lilacs. Watching the sway of her hips as she stepped. From the time she asked him to walk with her until they parted at sundown, he would not have noticed if the Confederacy had won the war. If Jeff Davis had resigned and had appointed him as successor, Tree's only concern would have been that he would be forced to leave Vicksburg.

# 13 ✺

WHEN HOOKER FOUND THE COOK WAGON, Volusia had stopped and was preparing lunch for the drive. He was brewing chicory and putting slices of salt pork between biscuits that he had baked the night before. Tree told him of the Yankees in Baldwin and sat down under a pine to wait for the rest of the herd.

The memories returned as he munched on a biscuit. Once something triggered them they were hard to quell. Almost anything, ranging from the chance of a fight to a cool sip of water, could act as a trigger. Details of Vicksburg in general and Laura in particular then would fill his mind and crowd out any thoughts of the here and now. Sitting under the shade of the pine, he could smell the heavy perfume that came from a magnolia tree on the side of her house, near the well where she first brought him. The house itself was two stories of red brick sitting on a hilltop and enclosed by a white picket fence. A whitewashed roof sheltered the rope and pulley atop the red brick well housing. Tree never found out exactly how deep the well was, but it took several minutes of hard pulling on the rope before he brought a bucket to the surface.

"See why I needed a man along for this?" Laura asked brightly as Tree felt sweat running down his back.

He sweated much during the next several hours as he helped Laura. And he never enjoyed himself more. For her part, Laura seemed to grow more energetic despite the increasing heat as the afternoon sun hung over the streets. She never seemed to walk. Instead, she had a bouncy sort of skip-step that allowed her to keep up with Tree's long-legged walk. Although his normal stride was at least twice hers, he sometimes found himself lagging behind her when he was weighted down by a full bucket.

The excitement of the battle and his ride faded as he tried to sort out the new emotions he was feeling. Desire? Maybe. Probably. But not the desire he had felt around other women. As he walked beside Laura, Tree began thinking of sex as a mechanical, almost animalistic act. Something like scratching an itch. That was not what he wanted with this small, airy girl. He wanted to hold her, pet her, keep between her and the sorrows of life.

Crowds in the street thinned over the next several hours as the soldiers found their regiments, reorganized themselves, and established camps. Tree knew that he also should find whatever was left of his regiment. But he couldn't bear to part from Laura. Eventually, she solved his problem for him on a return trip to her house. Instead of going to the well, she took the empty bucket from his hand, said goodbye, walked onto her porch, and went through the front doors. He turned around, trudged down the hill from her house to the streets, and began searching for familiar faces.

Usually, he enjoyed walking the streets of Vicksburg. He became fond of the city during almost a year of being stationed in and around it. Vicksburg was enough like home to make him feel comfortable. There were the same swamps and pasture lands in rural areas. The same types of trees, particularly oaks and magnolias, were abundant. Although the Mississippi winter had been the coldest of his life — he never before had seen ice on ponds — most of the year had been almost as warm and moist as Florida. God seemed to have decreed a limit on heat and humidity in areas where people live. Both Mississippi and Florida reached that limit in July and August and went no further. There even were some alligators in the Vicksburg area, although they were puny and effeminate compared to the ones Tree knew from home.

At the same time, there was enough that was different about Vicksburg to give it an exotic air. Much of the city sat atop 300-foot hills and bluffs that overlooked the Mississippi River. Tree never had seen hills that high. After spending all his life either in the pinewood flatlands of west Florida or the palmetto scrub plains of the east and central parts of the state, it was a thrill to stand on a cliff and look down at the river traffic. Huge steamboats and the barges they towed looked like toys. Sometimes, he would gaze across the mile-wide river and watch troops or civilians go about their work on the Louisiana shore. In Florida, he usually would have to climb a tree to see more than a few hundred yards. At least some, although not most, Vicksburg streets were paved with brick or stone.

Before enlisting, Tree had never seen anything other than clay or sand streets. Most Vicksburg homes were made of brick. Practically every building in rural Florida, from outhouse to courthouse, was made of either rough logs or cut lumber

Vicksburg also held fleshier attractions. Dozens, if not hundreds, of saloons lined the boardwalk next to the river. Hundreds, if not thousands, of women worked those saloons. Tree had been used to traveling 20 miles or more of forest and scrubland to find either a drink or a woman. Having both readily at hand was a novelty when he first arrived. But he soon tired of nightly bouts of drinking. Within a few months, he also tired of encounters with women who gave him about as much thought as he did his cattle.

And now, the thought of embracing some perfumed-soaked, chubby woman in an upstairs loft of a saloon almost sickened him. But he also knew that probably would happen within the next few days as the loneliness and boredom of camp defeated common sense.

The sun was setting by the time he found the regimental flags that announced the camp of his company. Considering that he was returning late, without a horse, clothing, or equipment, Tree never expected the reception he got upon reporting. Officers — from a full colonel, whom he had never seen before, much less touched, to his lieutenant, whom he frequently saluted but seldom talked with — came out of tents to shake his hand. A huge crowd of enlisted men gathered around him and gave three cheers. He was offered places around dozens of campfires, complete with food he did not gather served on plates he did not own. As he settled down by a campfire for the night, wrapped in blankets a stranger gave him, Tree smiled to himself and thought of Laura's use of the word "hero."

Victorious armies don't need many heroes. Winning a battle gives its own rewards. Everyone in an army feels like his own hero among the clapping hands, shouts of thanksgiving, and all-around elation that, once the battle fatigue is over, follows a victory. At the same time, glory might come to the commanders, but the battlefield medals and promotions don't filter down into the ranks. There is no need to raise morale. An Army will search diligently for heroes only after a defeat. It is then that somebody is needed to act as the silk purse that is fashioned out of the sow's ear.

After mulling over such thoughts as he drifted asleep, he was not surprised the next morning when his lieutenant told him that Sergeant First Class Hooker now would be Sergeant Major Hooker. That should have meant added responsibilities and more money.

But, Tree quickly discovered, nobody in a cavalry regiment has many responsibilities of any kind in a city under siege. Cavalry troopers are supposed to roam the countryside, scouting for the rest of the army and foraging for food. They search for enemy troops and unnerve opponents by charging into their midst with guns blazing and sabers slashing.

During the siege, there was nothing for which to scout. No river crossings to find. No roads to check for hazards. No woods to search through for paths. For the few short weeks in which supplies lasted, foraging simply meant everybody sat around and waited for the quartermaster to pass out rations. There was no need to search for the enemy. Everybody knew where the Yankees were — at the city limits, lobbing cannon shells into the heart of downtown. And with tens of thousands of Yankees busy building fortifications of their own, nobody was going to be stupid enough to try a cavalry charge.

So, about all Tree and every other cavalryman in the city could do was to hunker down, dodge the cannon balls, and hope that somebody in the rest of the Confederacy would rescue Vicksburg.

As for the increased pay that went along with his promotion, he had not seen any money out of the Army for nearly six months. Even if the pay arrived, it would come to no more than $25 of Confederate script. At that time, it took $200 in script to buy a pair of boots. Tree was one the luckier enlisted men. He could live off money from home — in his case, Spanish doubloons saved up from years of selling cattle to Cuba.

So, about all the promotion really meant was that Tree could sew a semi-circle above the three V-shaped stripes on the chevrons decorating the sleeves of his uniform jacket. At least he could have if it weren't for the fact that his uniform jacket was someplace between Bovina and Vicksburg, tied with the rest of his belongings behind his saddle on his horse.

The horse had been more or less replaced the same morning that he learned of his promotion. A colonel, not the one who had shaken his hand but another whom Tree had never seen before, gave him a horse. Thinner and not as strong as the one that probably now was carrying a Yankee across the Mississippi countryside, the gift was still more than a good-enough mount with the cavalry penned inside the city limits. The jacket problem was not solved for three days. Then, a short, narrow-shouldered man, wearing a white linen suit and carrying a bundle wrapped in paper, arrived in camp. He came to the corral where Tree and several other cavalrymen were brushing down their horses, and asked for Sergeant Hooker. Tree identified himself.

The civilian announced, "I am Joseph Mason, father of Laura. She has told me about you."

Worry, approaching fear, flashed through Tree. She told him what? Did an afternoon of carrying a bucket escalate in the retelling to some passionate encounter? Did he violate some obscure Mississippi code of conduct about escorting young women on the streets? Was he going to find himself in a duel with this little civilian? Those questions were quickly answered by Mason holding out his right hand to shake Tree's.

"Thank you for your kindness 'n' consideration in escortin' her that day," Mason said, as he dropped his hand to the bundle and began unwrapping. "We want to show you our gratitude."

The bundle was a bolt of wool cloth, dyed gray. True Confederate gray, like those of the best uniforms early in the war, before the Yankee blockade made dye expensive and hard to get. By '63, almost all new uniforms were colored butternut, a yellowish-brown dye made from local plants.

"I've had this set aside for two years, waitin' for a special occasion," Mason said, holding an end of the bolt against Tree's chest. "My family 'n' I decided you're the occasion."

He gave Hooker the address of his mercantile-tailor shop and left. A few hours later, after scrubbing off the dirt and scent of the horse he had been grooming, Tree was in the shop getting measured. Before leaving, he offered to pay out of his horde of doubloons. Mason refused, but accepted a doubloon and gave Tree $19 in script as change for a light gray, high-crowned, broad-brimmed hat to replace the one that blew off during the ride.

Tree left the shop with an invitation to the Mason home for supper. The family consisted of Mason, Laura, and her mother, Susan. The mother would have been a double for her daughter, except for slight crow's feet and a few other wrinkles in the face and a slightly darker shade to the eyes. Tree glumly reflected on the fact that he was nearer the mother's age than the daughter's. The family lived in their home without servants. Susan and Laura took turns throughout the meal announcing which one of them had cooked what dish. Tree, engrossed in the first meal in a year that had not come either from army rations or foraging, quickly lost track.

Three days after that supper, he had the swallow-tailed coat. In reality, it was too warm to wear except for a few months out of the year, and its design was too extravagant for anyone below the rank of brigadier general. But Tree was never more grateful for anything in his life. Indeed he wore it that evening to the Mason home for another supper. If any of them noticed that he was sweating profusely, nobody mentioned it.

They were sipping on their after-dinner chicory when the house began to shake. A chandelier over the dining room table swayed, and the glass beads that dangled from it clanked noisily together. Cups vibrated until the chicory sloshed from them and spilled over the saucers onto the white linen tablecloth. A yellow-white light, almost as painfully brilliant as the sun, flashed outside the west windows. Then came a rumbling noise, something like thunder except magnified several times. The noise had to have come less than a second after the house began to shake, but it seemed like several minutes. Laura and Susan, almost in unison, put their fists to their mouths and stifled screams. Mason gasped and looked toward the west. Tree got to his feet. He took a few deep breaths, to make sure his voice would sound steady.

"Guess we all should've expected this," he said. "Sound's like Yankee artillery'll be knockin' at our doors for a while."

# 14 ⚝

Yelping dogs announced the arrival of the drive and called Tree's mind back to the present. He stood up and left the shade of the pine. Heavy, who was riding near the front of the herd, spurred his horse into a gallop and pulled up in front of Hooker. "What're you doin' here?"

Instead of replying, Tree waved his right arm in a circle above his head, a signal for the rest of the cow hunters to gather around him. Once everyone was near, most of them eating the biscuits and pork, he spoke. "We're 'posed to supply cattle 'n' protect Florida," he said. "So far, all we've been doin' is the first part of the job. Time's come to do the second."

Most of the hunters had spent the last three years questioning their manhood because they were not yet shooting Yankees. They all but clapped their hands at the news. Even Heavy, despite years of Indian fighting, got caught up in the excitement. His voice came close to a whine when Tree told him, Volusia, and five others to stay with the herd while the rest trav-

GUNS OF THE PALMETTO PLAINS

eled to Ocean Pond. "I'm the oldest. I've got the experience. Why should I stay?" Heavy asked.

Tree held out his right hand and began ticking off reasons with his fingers. "One. If the Yankees win, there's a chance they'll come this way 'n' hit the herd. Two. If I'm killed, you 'n' Volusia are the only two who have ever taken a herd this way afore. Three. If we don't chase the Yankees out o' Baldwin, you've got know-how to get the herd through to Georgia."

Tree thought of, but didn't say, "Four. You're the only one with a wife, kids, 'n' grandkids. More people would miss you."

He did say, and managed to smile while he said it: "You're needed more here. Out there, you'll just be another target for the Yankees. 'N' a mighty big, easy-to-hit one at that."

It was the right thing to say. Heavy nodded his head and leaned back in the saddle. Nobody else of those who were staying behind even began to grumble. Hooker went to the horse herd and saddled his Yankee cavalry gelding. If something does go wrong, might as well see that he gets back to his rightful owners, Tree thought. The rest of those who were riding with him also changed horses.

As he wheeled his horse toward the north, Tree shouted at Heavy: "If you don't hear from us in four days, start the herd north 'n' west. Keep away from anythin' that ain't flyin' a Confederate flag."

Tree spurred the horse into a trot and the others followed. They weaved their way through the pines. Most of the riders chattered happily about what they would do when they caught the Yankees. The talk aggravated Hooker. But no sense telling them to shut up. They soon would find out what it means to catch Yankees. Tree cut himself off from the talk by letting his mind return to Vicksburg.

❖　　　　　❖　　　　　❖

Everyone in Vicksburg had seen and heard artillery fire periodically for over a year. Yankee gunboats frequently would ply the river and lob shells at the city and surrounding fortifications. Until the after-dinner shell burst somewhere near the Mason's lawn, most of the fire had hit either military camps, where everybody was expecting it and had built protections against it, or the riverside area, where mostly unoccupied shacks and vacant wharfs had been damaged. But, as the siege tightened, every building in the city was equally liable to be hit from either a Yankee boat or gun emplacement. So, everyone, from the newborn baby of a slave to the great-grandfather of the millionaire who owned the slave, was an equal target.

Knowledge of that led to about two weeks of mass digging into the sides of Vicksburg's hills. Tree would look east from the camp and see the hills almost covered with Vicksburg residents throwing up mounds of yellow clay as they dug bomb shelters. The shelters ranged from simple holes to elaborate multiroom caves. Tree helped Laura's father dig a sort of halfway point between the extremes of shelter construction. Mason's shelter had one large room with four smaller ones, one for each member of the family and one for a chamber pot. Bedspreads were used as doors, both at the entrance and to separate the rooms from each other. The yellow clay walls were lined with old copies of the *Vicksburg Whig* newspaper. It took three days to build, with Mason and Tree doing the work in between bouts of shelling from the Yankee positions.

On the first day, as they lay in the depression that was the beginning of the cave, Mason blurted out: "She's growin' fond of you." He shouted to be heard over the screams of the flying shells.

Tree felt his cheeks burn. Mason continued to shout. "It's Laura. She's fond of you."

The burning grew more severe. "Are you askin' me what my intentions are?" he shouted back to Mason.

"No need for that." Mason shook his head. "I know you. Or, at least your type. You wouldn't have been invited here if I had any doubts 'bout you. I've got friends in headquarters. Had them check you out after Laura told me 'bout you the first day. That's why it took three days for you to get an invite."

Tree cocked an arm and rested his head on his elbow, watching the little merchant. "Exactly how old is she?"

"Nineteen."

"Do you or she know that I'm on the far side o' thirty?" Tree looked for a reaction and saw only a slight shrug of the shoulders.

"She was betrothed once to somebody closer her age," Mason said. "I think she has sworn off young men now."

"What happened?"

Mason again shrugged his shoulders. "The war."

"Dead?"

"No. Worse. At least by Laura's reckonin'. He went off in July of sixty-one. Was captured by September. Signed a pledge to the Union by October. Last she heard, he was living in Pennsylvania 'n' engaged to a Quaker girl."

The shelling came to such an abrupt halt that the words "Quaker girl" echoed in the silence around the hilltop. The two men got back to their feet and resumed digging. "How'd you stay single?" Mason suddenly asked.

"Just happens. Never even asked a girl. Guess it's livin' where I do. Think I've seen 'n' talked to more eligible females since I joined the Army than I did the whole rest o' my life. Make your livin' out in the scrub 'n' you never see anythin' but cattle, horses, 'n' dogs. Time goes by differently. One day you're seventeen 'n' not even thinkin' 'bout settlin' down. Next day you're thirty."

Mason leaned on his shovel and looked at Tree as if he were a bolt of cloth being offered by a salesman. "'N' you think thirty is too late?"

Tree kept his head down and dug his spade into the hillside. It was not until the next day, during another break in the work brought on by shelling, that he thought of an adequate reply. The reply came out as another question: "Are you givin' me permission to court your daughter afore I ask for it?"

Laura's father seemed to be trying to smile, but his lips twisted into something that was closer to a grimace. "Court her. Propose to her. Get her to an altar. Can I be more clear than that? I want to know that somebody else is ready to care for her. 'N' quick."

A shell, trailing a wisp of gray smoke from a sputtering fuse, arched into the blue sky. It exploded hundreds of feet above Tree and Mason as they huddled in the hole. Bits of shrapnel made pock marks in the clay outside the hole and tore away the few remaining tufts of grass on the hillside.

"Those ain't autumn leaves fallin'," Mason shouted. "The world I built for my family is bein' blown apart. If Susan 'n' I don't make it, I want somebody to be here for Laura. You're the kind of somebody I want. Thank God, Laura does too."

That evening, in the stillness created by Yankee gunners eating their supper, Laura sat beside Tree outside of the newly completed cave. They watched the sun go down, turning the brown thread of the river a deep, angry red.

"Poppa told me what he told you," Laura said in a calm voice that was barely above a whisper. "Forget what he said."

Tree had been reclining on the hillside. He sat up straight and looked at her, his mouth working, but no words came.

Laura smiled. "Yes. I think I love you. Yes. I think I want you as a husband. But I will not make promises until this war ends. I'm not going to marry you 'n' then watch you march off to Lord-knows-where. If we marry, I will go with you to anywhere and do anythin' with you. But I will not sit here readin' your letters 'n' wonderin' if I'm your wife or widow."

Tree had been holding his breath. He exhaled as he said: "Fair enough. More than fair. Didn't mean to seem like I was in that much of a rush."

A wind came out of the north and brought Hooker back to the present. The wind brushed the pine boughs against each other, making a sound like hundreds of brooms sweeping wooden floors. Tree looked around and realized that they had almost reached Ocean Pond. Smoke from dozens of campfires already rose above the trees, showing the riders where to go. It was the largest camp he had seen since leaving Mississippi. Thousands of troops hunkered down among the pines. Hooker led his men through the camp for about an hour before finding the guidon of the 28th Georgia and reporting to the colonel. The hunters were told to go to the southern fringe of the camp, across the railroad tracks, and wait. They rode across the tracks, built their campfires, and cooked what chicory and pork they had brought with them. Night fell without anyone in the Confederate camp moving. Apparently, everybody had decided to sit and wait for the Yankees.

Tree slept fitfully during the night. When he was not anticipating the prospect of fighting Yankees with a group of youths who had never been in an organized battle, he was reliving the worst of Vicksburg. The memories tangled up in his dreams when he drifted asleep and then stayed with him, making him grit his teeth until they ached, when he awoke.

Vicksburg's horrors only slowly dawned on him. For the first several weeks, he and Laura had all their emotions and senses tied up in each other. It took a while for them to realize that everything around them was disintegrating. The first thing Tree noticed was that he and Laura almost never whispered endearments into each other's ear. They couldn't. The sound of the guns forced them to shout even as they held hands with each other. Frequently, instead of gently embracing her, Tree found himself covering Laura's body with his own to shield her from shrapnel.

There were no quiet walks in gardens, parks, or streets. No pleasant trips to shops or restaurants. Simply finding someone willing to sell vegetables and flour became increasingly difficult. Even those with something to sell, usually blackmarketeers who stole from the military or speculators who hoarded supplies waiting for a chance to sell at killingly high prices, seldom appeared on the streets. The shelling kept almost everybody in the dugout caves. Those who did venture out walked in the middle of the streets. That safeguarded them against being buried under the rubble when a building was blown apart beside them. Piles of masonry and brick blocked many streets. It would have been impossible to drive a team of mules or horses through the city, if anyone beside the Army even still had mules or horses.

Civilians' draft animals were the first to go as Vicksburg looked for meat. Then the stray cats and dogs that used to roam the streets disappeared. About the only animals one would see on the streets were rats. And even they became fair game. Several weeks into the siege, a corporal in Hooker's company offered him a piece of meat on a biscuit. The meat was tough and somewhat sweet. Tree assumed it was squirrel and asked where the corporal found it. It was a rat that had been trying to steal grain from the corral. Rat hunting soon became a major pastime among most of the Army. Tree frequently would bring some to the Masons, telling them it was squirrel. He neither knew nor cared if they suspected the truth.

Despite everything, the siege was more than a month old before Tree considered it more than an inconvenience. Laura consumed too much of him for anything else to intrude. During the heaviest of the shelling, he would try to be with the Masons in their cave, with his arms around her shoulders. He even got something of a thrill out of the way she would tremble as the earth shook around them. The best times were the interludes between the shellings, when they sat beside each other by the wellhouse in her yard. Neither of them talked much. They merely sat, being comforted by the warmth radiating off each other's bodies.

Laura was a presence that was always with him, even when he was on duty. Lying in his bedroll at night, he could feel her skin against his. Delicate, like a small, young frond plucked from a fern, it seemed to brush across his arms and down his chest. Her scent, the trace of lilac water, stayed with him. It somehow overcame the combined stench of burned gunpowder, sweat, and manure — both animal and human — that hung over the camp. His lower lip and the hairs of his moustache continually tingled from the massage of her kisses.

Tree was so ensnared by Laura that, unlike almost everyone else in the city, he did not worry about being trapped by the enemy. Rations grew shorter, but he seldom had an appetite. It was not until Laura's parents complained of food shortages that he even noticed what was being issued to him. And then he paid attention only because he smuggled much of his food to the Masons. More of his time began to be taken up by guard duty, protecting the company's horses from being slaughtered by meat-hungry civilians and soldiers. He found himself worried more about not being able to spend time with Laura than about the rest of Vicksburg wanting the horses.

Gradually, he noticed a change in Laura's skin. It had felt something like silk, except soft and warm. The skin, tanned and spotted with darker brown freckles, was taut above the muscles of her arms. But, over the weeks, Tree could feel the skin loosen, until it hung like a poorly wrapped bandage. He could feel each bone of her arm when he caressed it. Her color began to lighten until he could see blue veins running through her hands and arms.

The cheekbones had formed something like a delicate frame under her eyes. Gradually, they seemed to push up, as if they were going to break through her skin. Her eyes became watery. Then they seemed to shrink, hiding behind the cheekbones. Dark half-moons developed beneath her lower lids.

More than her appearance changed. She had spent hours each day bringing food and drink to military hospitals around the city. Gradually, she stopped making the rounds of hospitals. By late May, she would not leave the house except to go into the cave. Tree would spend hours sitting with her in the parlor, reading Dickens' or Scott's novels to her.

It was as if Laura's soul was made up of the brick and mortar of the city. She crumbled along with Vicksburg. Tree tried to find something to shore up her spirits. He changed the reading material from novels to farcical short stories. She occasionally smiled, but spent most of the time merely nodding her head as he read. He tried to take her for walks during lulls in the shelling. She would lean on him and limp along for a few minutes, but soon would beg to be brought home. Food, even when it was wholesome, didn't interest her. And she began to dread trips to the cave. Perhaps it was the stories — some true but many not — of people being buried alive when a shell hit their caves. Or, perhaps, self-protection was becoming less and less desirable. Maybe the thought of being blown apart was less painful than the prospect of living under the siege guns.

Tree gave up trying to sleep with Vicksburg haunting him and decided to assign himself as an extra sentry. He unrolled from his blanket, picked up his carbine, and and walked past the tethered horses to the edge of camp. There, he leaned against a pine trunk and stared off toward the east. The night was cool, but he was comfortable enough in his coat. The sky was cloudless and the moon was nearly full. Shadows from the tree trunks striped the ground, much like the shadows cast by bars on a jail cell's floor. Whippoorwills called to each other from the scrub. Occasionally, an owl would hoot from the top of a pine. But, after weeks of hearing the constant lowing of cattle, Tree thought the night was strangely quiet. His mind wandered back to Vicksburg.

"Not the rat hole today," Laura told him, using the slang for the caves that Vicksburg residents had adopted early in the siege. "Too hot. Too stuffy. Please, let's just sit here in the breeze."

They were on the porch of the Masons' home. A stiff wind was blowing out of the east, bringing relief from the heat and a trace of the perfume from the magnolia near the wellhouse. Tree couldn't blame her for not wanting to leave. Her parents were in the cave, but Laura wanted to stay in the porch swing. She lay across the swing seat, facing the magnolia. A white sheet with pink flowers along its border covered her white cotton dress down from the knees and over the feet. Two pillows propped up her back and cushioned it from the swing chain. Tree sat on the plank floor of the porch, his back resting on one of the masonry pillars that held up the roof. He was enjoying the fact that, for the first time in a week, Laura was smiling. The smile rounded out the sharp points of her facial bones and added dimples that filled in the pinched look in her cheeks. A glow seemed to come from her eyes again. At least for that day, she had lost the brooding, gloomy expression that had settled around her face. The breeze tousled some of the bright, freshly washed strands that peeked out from under a broad-brimmed straw hat, colored almost the same pale yellow as her hair. She breathed deeply, swelling the bosom that had seemed to shrink over the weeks. "Smell those magnolias," she sighed out the words.

He nodded. Magnolias seemed to bloom later in Mississippi than Florida, but they also seemed to be more fragrant.

"Pick me one?" she asked. Tree didn't bother to reply. He stood up and walked toward the magnolia. He was under the tree branches, reaching up for a white bloom that was larger around than his hand when he heard the hellish scream of a shell in the air. He stopped reaching for the flower and looked up. The shell exploded above him, leaving a dirty gray cloud of powder hanging in the sky.

It didn't bother him. One exploding almost directly overhead like that wasn't dangerous. All its shell fragments would be blown away from the Masons' house. "The one you see isn't the one that kills you." He muttered the old battlefield proverb and again reached for the flower.

A light, as bright as a lightning bolt, flashed around him. Something rammed into his back, picked up his body, and hurled it through the limbs of the tree. Heat enveloped him. He felt as if he were a piece of coal on a blacksmith's forge that had just been hit by a blast from the bellows. He heard nothing, but his ears rang as if someone had slapped the side of his head with a fence rail. A swarm of multicolored lights blotted everything else from his vision.

Without yet being able to see, he picked himself up from the ground and ran toward the house. The lights faded within his first few steps and his vision cleared. A column of smoke rose up from the home. There were only a few flames playing around blackened stumps where the porch columns had been. The front half of the house was gone. The back portion stood open to the daylight, as if it were a dollhouse. Beds stood in their rooms on the second story. Tree even saw a glint of sunlight off a mirror, its glass untouched, in the dresser by one of the beds. He heard screams from behind the house and knew they were coming from James and Susan Mason. By the time they reached where the porch had been, Tree already was throwing pieces of smoldering timber aside. He shouted Laura's name as if he actually expected an answer.

❖ ❖ ❖

The night sky over Ocean Pond lightened to a

shade of gray before a pink streak appeared between the trees on the eastern horizon. From other parts of the camp, bugle calls blared reveille. Tree pushed himself away from the pine and walked back to the rest of the cow hunters. Throughout the morning, a variety of officers from other units rode over and gave orders to Hooker. The upshot of the orders was that the Yankees were coming and the cow hunters would be deployed with the rest of the army to meet them.

Tree's group was among the units guarding the southwestern edge of the army. It was as far as possible from where the worst of the fighting was supposed to be, a good place to put a small group of young men who never had been in battle. Hooker decided that the forest was no place for fighting on horseback. The pines were barely far enough apart to ride through on a horse. Anybody galloping through the trees would have to spend more time looking out for low-hanging branches than fighting. He had the horses tied several yards behind the stand of pines which sheltered the hunters.

They stood in a group and waited, seldom talking. Hours passed. By noon, they could hear cannon fire echoing to the east. Nobody ate lunch, to Tree's relief. He was expecting the nausea to come upon him at any moment and didn't want to hurry it along by the sight or smell of food. A bugle called somewhere to the east. Tree looked over to Skeeter, who was sitting hunched over beneath a pine, cradling the Sharps rifle in his arms. Skeeter's shooting ability was a weapon that Hooker intended to put to good use.

"Come here," Tree, deliberately keeping his voice as calm and low as possible, said to Skeeter. "We may be gettin' visitors 'n' I want you to be the first to greet them."

He had his friend put down the rifle and get a coil of rope. Then Tree and another hunter lifted the smaller man about six feet above them to the first limb of a pine. Skeeter climbed about 50 feet further to almost the top bough and then let down the rope. Tree tied the Sharps to the rope and Skeeter hauled it up to the bough on which he sat. The little hunter perched in the pine, cradling the rifle in his arms and staring off to the east.

"If anythin' happens," Tree shouted to the rest of the group, "Nobody fire till Skeeter does."

Gun and cannon fire could be heard throughout most of the afternoon. The horses behind the cow hunters whinnied and stamped their feet in response to the explosions. Tree and the rest sat under the pines and listened to the shots getting closer. The sun sank almost to the tops of the trees in the west before a group of figures on horseback appeared, riding four abreast down the road and the cleared shoulder of the railroad tracks. Tree could not tell how far back the column of riders stretched, but there were at least 200 of them. The column stopped as the cow hunters spread out among the pines. A bugle call came from somewhere near the head of the column.

Could they really be stupid enough to charge in that formation down an open road? Tree asked himself. A bugle from the column blew "Charge." Yes, they were that stupid, Tree answered himself.

He stood against a pine and watched them come. The setting sun cast a golden light around the galloping horses. About a dozen small egrets had been poking around a clump of palmettos in front of the charging column. The pounding of the hooves flushed the birds and they flew off, parting before the horses like a wave breaking before the prow of a boat.

"Easy, easy," Tree said to the group scattered among the pines.

Then a small explosion came from above and behind him. Skeeter had fired the Sharps. Tree saw one of the figures on the horses careen in the saddle. He sighted on another rider and squeezed the trigger at the same time that the guns of the others fired around him. The galloping column disappeared behind a foul-smelling dark cloud. By the time the cloud lifted, Tree had another ball and more gunpowder loaded in the carbine.

He brought the gun stock to his shoulder and aimed. Unmoving blue figures, looking like stick men drawn by a child, lay in the road. Anything in blue that was moving was running away, either on horseback or afoot. Tree got a figure on horseback in the middle of the carbine's front sight. He squeezed the trigger and the rider disappeared behind another black cloud. Other gunshots came from all around him. When the second cloud cleared, there were dozens more unmoving figures littering the road.

Suddenly, Tree realized that he didn't feel the nausea. He felt only an emptiness, almost like hunger, in the pit of his stomach. But there were no cramps, like he would expect with hunger. He heard Skeeter clamber down from the pine. The rest of the group were making noises ranging from cheers to retches. They could hear distant gunfire all around them, although no bullets whizzed past. Tree paid no attention to any of the noise. He stared at the figures on the road.

Then he felt something brush against his arm. It was somewhat like silk, except it was warm. And then he smelled a faint trace of lilacs.

# 15 🌾

Most of the Confederates in the Battle of Olustee had no more trouble than Hooker's group. When fighting ended at nightfall, about 5,500 Yankees ran back to Jacksonville. They left behind almost 2,000 corpses in blue. Less than half that many Confederates died in breaking up the largest attempt ever made by the North to invade the interior of Florida.

The immediate result of the victory for the cow hunters was the largest after-drive party of their lives. They arrived in Baldwin five days after the battle. The town had been liberated and the victory celebration had ended. Yet, the euphoria seemed to linger. Soldiers and civilians were ready to seize on any excuse to restart the party. The arrival of Tree's herd, the first since the battle, provided that excuse. Cheering started before the first steer drew even with the little pine log cabins that marked the town limits.

Women waved handkerchiefs and men threw their hats into the air. The women were dressed in everything from demure calico to gaudy silks with low-cut bodices. Some of the men were in Confederate uniforms, but most were dressed in a variety of civilian clothes, from brocaded vests to bib overalls. A piano behind the doors of one of the saloons began playing "The Bonnie Blue Flag." The tune was picked up by pianos and banjos in other bars. An old man, dressed in a faded top hat and a suit with a frock coat, stood in the street, his white-bearded chin resting on a fiddle. He sawed away with the bow, squawking out the song while swaying from side to side.

The street itself was broader than most, as it had been designed to allow herds to pass along it to the holding pens by the railroad tracks. Those tracks formed a crossroad in the heart of town, with one set running east and west and the other north and south. Baldwin owed its existence to the crossroads. It was the handiest shipping center for cattle, citrus, lumber, and turpentine. Before the tracks were laid in the late '50s, two stagecoach roads intersected at the town.

Because it always played host to tired, hungry, thirsty, and lustful cattle hunters, farmers, and lumberjacks, Baldwin grew up with a reputation for wild partying. It started life in the '40s as one building. The building was a combination saloon and inn run by a man named Thigpen. Others seeking various types of profit — legal and moral or otherwise — became attracted to the crossroads. The town was called Thigpen until '60, when residents, tired of hundreds of swinish puns, named the place after a local politician.

Several in the crowd handed pint bottles of whiskey to the hunters as they guided the cattle into the pens. Five uniformed Confederates, led by a small, red-haired, smooth-faced lieutenant, stood by the pens and watched. As soon as he rode up, Tree saluted. He then quietly sat on his horse until the last of the herd was penned.

The lieutenant pointed toward a single-story saloon a few yards up the street. It had no doors on its wide entrance way. "Tell the bartender to charge the first round on the Confederate Commissary Department," the lieutenant shouted. He disappeared in the dust cloud as the hunters wheeled their horses about and, shrieking Rebel yells, spurred up the street. They went through the saloon entrance without bothering to dismount.

Heavy came down from his saddle, stood by the pens, and watched the others go. Whoever owned that saloon was smart. He had eliminated the necessity of rebuilding after every drive by simply not having doors in the first place.

The dust returned to its place in the street as Heavy gave the lieutenant a notebook in which Tree had jotted down the head count of the cattle.

"We can check your tally," the lieutenant told Heavy. "Don't you want to go on with the rest of them?"

Heavy shook his head. "'Wine is a mocker, strong drink is ragin': 'n' whosoever is deceived thereby is not wise.' Proverbs, twenty, verse one."

The lieutenant recoiled slightly, as if he had picked up a freshly baked biscuit and found it to be hotter than expected. Then he smiled broadly. "Oh? How 'bout Proverbs, thirty-one: six? 'Give strong drink unto him that is ready to perish 'n' wine unto those that be of heavy hearts'?"

That launched an hour's worth of dueling Biblical interpretations. The lieutenant turned out to be an

Episcopal seminarian from Georgia who left his quest for the priesthood when the war started. Drinking was but one area of life where he pulled out passages for argument's sake. He quoted scripture to back up his beliefs on everything from infant Baptism to weekly Communion. Heavy believed that Baptism meant dunking adults, not sprinkling water over newborns. His worship services were concerned with calling up the Holy Spirit, not serving wafers dipped in wine. Neither his nor the lieutenant's beliefs were swayed after the session of quoting scriptures to each other, but Heavy had not enjoyed himself so much since the drive started.

It was the first time in months that someone kept a pleasant expression on his face while listening to Heavy's quotations. The preacher knew that he sometimes irritated the rest of the hunters. As a matter of fact, he knew he sometimes irritated Anne and the children.

Memorizing scripture was a habit that had started in his childhood in Georgia. The Bible was the only book in his home and school. Once he learned to read, he found little need for another. Bits of chapters and verses began lodging themselves in his mind. They would stay there until he found himself looking for advice or comfort in some situation. At first, he would have to make a conscious effort to call forth a passage to fit the situation. Then, in his early 20s, they started coming unbidden to his mind. He took that as a sign calling him to the ministry.

And that calling meant that he should turn people toward The Word. Hopefully, unsaved people — and he found himself surrounded by them more and more frequently these days — would hear one of his quotes. Sure, the people might be irritated, but at the same time, they might also take a moment to reflect on the quote. Who knew what the moment of reflection might lead to?

That evening, the lieutenant and Heavy ate fried catfish together in the dining room of a hotel near the tracks. Neither of them had seen any of the other hunters since the last steer went into the pens. Heavy paid for a room in the hotel, but slept uneasily. His discomfort was partly due to the night noises of Baldwin. Piano, banjo, fiddle, and other loud music came from a half-dozen saloons. Singing, yelling, and laughing burst from scores of male and female voices. Every once in a while, shots were fired by some carouser who, hopefully, was shooting into the air.

Heavy also was uncomfortable because of the hotel ceiling. It was the first time in two months that he had tried to sleep in a building and it seemed unnatural not to have stars or clouds above his head and not to be wound up in the blanket and mosquito netting of a bedroll. He knew many cow hunters who were plagued by the same discomfort after a drive. Volusia once said the reason most of them got drunk when they finished was that they could pass out on a saloon floor and get several full hours of sleep.

The next morning was cold enough for Heavy to see his breath when he walked outside the hotel, but not cold enough for him to shiver. Walking in the air was almost like bathing in cool water with clothes on. Good weather for sobering up people after a drinking bout. A perfect morning for him to gather up the rest and get headed back home. He was walking past the cowpens when he heard somebody call his name.

The somebody was Volusia. His limp forced him into a skip-step as he hurried toward Heavy with another cow hunter in tow. The other hunter was a couple inches shorter and a good many pounds lighter than Volusia. He was called Dinghy, because he built himself a small sailboat that he frequently used for fishing. Both were smiling happily as they approached. They also were unable to stand still as they talked and swayed back and forth. Even though Heavy was several feet away, he could smell the whiskey on their breath and clothes.

"I'm in love," Volusia said through his smile. "I'm gettin' married. Will you perform the service? I've got the best man here." He put his arm around Dinghy's shoulders.

If Heavy had listed the conversations he ever expected to have with Volusia, this one would have been at the bottom. He couldn't keep the skepticism out of his voice as he asked: "Kinda sudden, ain't it?"

Volusia pointed back toward a two-story hotel several yards up the street. "Met a girl yesterday. Can't stand the thought o' ridin' out o' here 'n' leavin' her behind. She told me she felt the same. We're ready for marriage. How 'bout it? Didn't the Lord say somethin' 'bout it ain't good for man to be alone?"

Heavy felt warmth spreading through his body, as if he had just wrapped himself in a blanket. Maybe his quotations were doing more good than he thought. "Somethin' like that. Look, you two get cleaned up. Change your clothes. Brush your teeth. 'N' then get the rest of the boys together. Everybody'll want to get in on this. First we've got to get a marriage license.

We can pick one up at the courthouse."

Baldwin inherited the circuit courthouse of Duval County from Jacksonville after Yankees invaded the latter city in '62. The courthouse was in a former mercantile store in the center of town. Heavy walked in there and found an elderly, white-haired, black-suited man stoking a fire in a pot-bellied stove. The man was the clerk of the court. He happily trotted about the room, fetching the blank marriage license forms. The other cow hunters began drifting into the room over the next several minutes. Heavy sat at a desk, with the forms, a quill pen, and an ink well, to wait for the groom. Eventually, Volusia and Dinghy, their hair still wet from being scrubbed, entered the room.

"Skeeter's fetchin' the bride from the hotel," Dinghy announced as he took a seat.

Heavy gave the pen to Volusia and shoved the forms in front of him. Volusia picked up the pen and held it unsteadily over the paper, as if he were trying to line up a branding iron on the rump of a struggling calf. He read the form. Then re-read it. Then turned to Dinghy and asked, "Hey, what's her name anyhow?"

The warm feeling evaporated from Heavy. He sighed, took the forms and writing materials away from Volusia, and handed them back to the clerk. Everybody filed out of the room and headed toward the stables.

It took two weeks for the hunters to get back to their homes. Heavy said nothing to Volusia during the course of the trip. He didn't even complain about the food.

Once back, each of the hunters spent a few weeks in their own cabins and then disappeared into the scrub. It was calf roundup time, the busiest season for cow hunting. Most cows gave birth during March and April. Hunters prowled the bush for the calves and their mothers. Each hunter looked for cows that either had his brand or were unbranded. Then the animals were driven to the nearest cowpen, where the calves were separated from the cows. All the calves were branded and most of the males were castrated.

Each calf then was matched up with a cow that, hopefully, was its natural mother. The matching process, called mammying up, was vital to the well-being of both the calf and hunter. A cow usually would only nurse its own calf. Any calf not reunited with its own mother after the roundup starved. Hunters relied on a variety of clues, such as color and markings on the hides, eye shape and size, and the sound of a cow as it lowed at a calf, to guide them in the reunions. Each hunter usually missed one or two. But Heavy almost never missed. Although he tried to keep quiet about it, his skill at mammying up made him popular around cowpens. He could not describe how he did it. Several attempts to teach Eric, Tree, and others over the years all failed.

Heavy also used mammying up to give him a chance to inspect the calves and pick the largest ones with the best potential for strength as oxen. Instead of letting the two or three best prospects run back into the scrub at the end of the roundup, he would drive them and their mothers over to Volusia's place for training. He and Volusia split the money from the sale of the oxen. After the wedding episode, Heavy debated with himself over foregoing a partnership with Volusia this spring. But, after mulling over several dozen passages concerning forgiveness, he decided to swallow his disgust and stay with the practice.

After slightly more than two weeks in the scrub northwest of Enterprize, Heavy had nearly 70 cows, each with a calf. He drove them to some pens just east of a bend in the St. Johns, about halfway between Enterprize and Spring Garden. Tree and Skeeter earlier had agreed to meet him there for branding, castrating, and mammying up. They and perhaps 200 cattle were at the pens when Heavy arrived.

It was at those pens when another consequence of the Olustee victory came upon Heavy. His son-in-law switched sides and joined the Cattle Guard. That happened one morning as Skeeter and Tree rode through the cattle, trying to separate calves and get them into a smaller pen for branding. Heavy was outside the pens heating branding irons. He looked up at the sound of a distant whip crack and saw Eric coming. Tree and Skeeter dismounted and walked over to the fire. They stood with Heavy as Eric's cattle began to plod into the camp. The young Brockton rode over to and then opened the gate of the pens. He began driving in his cattle.

'Reckon Jeff Davis can use these too," he called out above the bawling. Tree and Skeeter picked up their whips and began driving in those of Eric's cattle that were balking at the gate or trying to bolt from the rest.

Heavy stood to one side and watched. "What does Otto say 'bout this?"

"Didn't talk to him. But I can't see where he'd have any call to object. Daddy always wants us to win. From what I see, ya'll are turnin' into the winners. Yankees got beat at Olustee. They ain't stoppin' cattle from gettin' through. Their gunboats keep gettin' sunk on the river."

He turned in his saddle and faced Tree. "Figure you're right 'bout gettin' in good with the Confederates. See myself becomin' somebody big once the war's over. Daddy's too far in with the St. Augustine Yankees to get out now. I ain't. Somebody in the family's got to look out for the future."

Heavy was tempted to cut off his son-in-law's blooming enthusiasm for the Confederacy. Olustee meant little when compared to Vicksburg and Gettysburg last year. One Yankee army was knocking on the door of Atlanta. Another was in the outskirts of Richmond. Most of Tennessee was in Northern hands. Even though he read Southern papers that propagandized for The Cause, playing down defeats and inflating minor victories into major ones, Heavy could tell that destruction was looming. With Eric throwing in his lot with Tree, Chole and the children might become targets of Yankee retribution. Even if that never happened, Heavy didn't like the idea of his daughter and grandchildren being deprived of a share of the money from wherever the Brocktons sold their cattle.

But there was another side. Heavy was a Southern patriot. He knew that every cow in Tree's hands was another chance to fend off the starvation threatening most of the South. On a more personal level, Heavy saw a chance to wean Eric from the rest of the Brocktons. In the long run, that could only help Chole and the children. Probably help them a lot more than the flow of money from illegal cattle sales.

So, Heavy decided to say nothing. He picked up

his whip and helped get the cattle into the pen. "'We may lead a quiet 'n' peaceable life in all godliness 'n' honesty,'" he mumbled, "First Timothy, two: two." The words were lost among the lowing of the cattle.

# 16 🕸

DORIS'S BAKERY WAS CLOSED AT 10 A.M. on a Monday. Greenley began worrying as soon as he tried the door and found it locked. His concern increased when he realized there was no smoke coming out of the chimney. That meant the ovens had not been fired. Maybe she would have locked the doors to run an errand. But, unless something was wrong, she would have had fire in those ovens before dawn. He went to her house and knocked on the door. A thin voice, sounding as if it belonged to an old woman, called out from the other side: "It's unlocked."

The voice was Doris's. She lay on her parlor sofa. A white wool blanket was wound around her, covering everything except the heart-shaped face. The face itself seemed to be more deeply lined, as if she had aged 20 years during the 24 hours since Dan last saw her. A tinge of yellow lightened her complexion. Greenley stood in the doorway. He and Doris stared at each other.

"Oh, I thought you were Margaret," she said

through chattering teeth. "I'm sorry."

"What's wrong?" Greenley took a step toward her. She stopped him with the gesture of a hand she drew from under the blanket. "Ague. You shouldn't see me like this. Can you run over to Margaret's for me?"

He nodded. Margaret Woods, the wife of a Confederate officer, was a friend of Doris. He had met her a few times and knew that she lived two houses down the street from Miss Fatio's. He turned back toward the door. Her voice stopped him. "Wait. Before you go, give me a glass of water and a spoonful of that."

She pointed toward the coffee table, on which sat a pitcher, a tumbler, a tablespoon, and a brown glass jar. The jar contained, according to the label that Dan read as he dipped the spoon into the white powder that was within, "Bark of Quinine." He put the spoonful in Doris's mouth and held her hand, which was almost painfully hot, as she sipped the water.

That was his introduction to ague, also called malaria or intermitting fever. He had heard of the disease in Ohio. There, it affected mostly old-timers who had come into the state when it was still wild or who had spent time in the Far West. He never thought of it hitting a young woman in the middle of a town on the Eastern Seaboard.

But, as Margaret explained as she trotted along with Greenley back to Doris's, "We all have it. Comes from livin' 'round all the swamps. Get it when you're a kid 'n', if you live through it, you know it probably ain't ever goin' to kill you. But it comes back for a visit now 'n' then. Sometimes, it makes you wish it'd kill you. Since Doris's man is dead 'n' mine's gone, we've got a deal. We check on each other every day. If the ague's got one o' us, the other sticks around 'n' does the nursin'."

Greenley visited Doris on each of the five days she was ill. She steadily improved with regular doses of quinine. The lines smoothed out of her face. Her voice strengthened. For most of the time, she wore cotton wrappers, floor-length, long-sleeved dressing gowns that buttoned at the neck. But on the fifth day she was wearing her green-checked dress. That day, she also put her hair back into a bun. Before, she had let it fall in a black curtain, which parted at her shoulders. Some of it hung to near the small of her back and some cascaded down her bosom. As soon as he got over his initial fear for her health, Dan found himself slightly aroused at the sight of her hair hanging loose. He also felt a small pang of guilt over the arousal.

Most of his visits were taken up by reading to her out of magazines or novels. He noticed that she was beginning to fix her eyes on his for longer and longer periods. The coy glances and slight smiles that marked their first months together were gone. Alone in his room at night, Greenley began thinking that she might be longing for him as much as he did for her.

He had plenty of time to devote to her. There were few military duties that spring. Nobody from the St. Augustine garrison was involved in the Olustee debacle. Holmes merely told about the defeat at an officers' call one morning and pointed out that about half of the Union troops were black.

"I knew this was go-een to happen when they enlisted all those niggahs. See what happens when you fight with niggahs?" Several of the officers, including two who were in command of black companies, nodded. "I won't let that happen. We'll fight with whites."

Otto Brockton arrived in late March to ship out some cattle and told about Eric's defection. The news wasn't particularly surprising. Greenley knew dozens of families with brothers, fathers, and sons in opposing armies. Otto seemed more annoyed than angry, talking as if Eric were a teenager rebelling at doing his chores around the house.

"Sooner or later, Eric'll come around," he said as he sat with Greenley in Holmes' office. "If we bide our time 'n' let him go on his way, it'll probably work out better for us in the long run. Like when a freeze wipes out your oranges. Sure, you can't ship 'em out 'n' make money right away. But you pick what you have, grind it all up 'n' make a hell of a lot of wine. After a while, that wine brings in the same money you'd make out o' shippin' the oranges. 'N' you've got enough left over to get drunk on."

Otto shifted topics. "Tree's fellas are movin' cattle. They'll want to try gettin' in a drive before the rainy season hits 'n' slows 'em down. Now's the time ya'll oughta do somethin' to slow 'em down yourselves."

Greenley leaned forward in his chair. "Such as?"

"There's a place in Volusia County, 'bout twenty, twenty-five miles north o' Enterprize. A plantation owned by folks called Starke. Ol' Man Starke's gone on to a pine bed. But his people still are Rebels. Cow Cavalry gets everythin' from sugar to horseshoes from 'em. Get rid o' Starkes 'n' ya'll tie a knot in Tree's tail."

Holmes quickly endorsed the plan. The major's company and the three remaining Brocktons were riding southwest the next day. They intended to camp their first night by a lean-to and cowpens a little less than 20 miles from St. Augustine. Otto had led Greenley there on their first expedition together. The shanty and pens were on a sandy ridge that ran between two swampy areas. As they approached, Greenley at first thought someone had attacked the place. The lean-to, a collection of split cypress logs held together with wooden pins, was gone. The gate to the pens, which was perhaps 50 feet from one of the lean-to walls, had also vanished. Only a huge crater was left in the ground. It was as if somebody had hit the place with either a large exploding artillery shell or had blown it up with several tons of gunpowder. But there were none of the signs that would have put blame for the destruction on man. Whatever hit the place, it didn't use explosives or fire. No charring on the grass or the few logs that remained scattered on the ground. Nor was the destruction caused by a storm. A storm would have left a huge tangle of logs and would not have created the hole.

Greenley climbed off his horse. He heard the Brocktons coming up from behind. "God damn," Otto said. "I've heard o' 'em takin' houses 'n' such. Just never seen it happen afore."

The Major walked to the edge of the crater and peered down. It was about 30 feet deep, with sides that slanted like a funnel. Three pieces of gray log stuck up from a pile of clay and sand at the bottom.

"Sinkhole," Otto said as he came up behind Greenley. "They're all over these sand ridge areas. Lots o' 'em have water in the bottom. Good many of the lakes 'round here are old sinkholes."

Greenley nodded. He had noticed that the grass and scrub lands were dotted with almost perfectly round lakes. It was as if the ground was dough and a giant had punched out the lakes with a cookie cutter. "What causes them?" he asked.

"Don't know for sure. They seem to happen durin' the dry season, when the underground water runs low. Reckon the water level supports part o' the ground. Kinda like a beam supportin' the roof o' a house. When the water gets low, its like a beam getting eaten by termites. The ground the water was holdin' up just caves in. I've heard tell o' a horse 'n' rider gettin' sucked down by a sinkhole. Don't really believe that. Usually the hole opens too slow for it to catch a body, let alone a horse."

Although they had to hobble the horses instead of corralling them in the pens as they originally planned, Greenley's company and the Brocktons still camped that night by the ruins of the lean-to. Their camp the next night was much more pleasant. Otto led the company to a cypress log cabin along a stream called Haw Creek. The cabin was a typical Cracker affair with two rooms, each about 100 feet square, connected by a roofed-over dog trot. It sat on a hammock where branches of the creek forked to the north and south. The main body of the creek was within a few yards of the cabin's west walls. Like most of the water in the area, the creek was almost black. But, unlike most other water, it didn't stink of sulfur. The creek itself was about 75 yards wide and each branch about 50 yards. There was little current in the water. It flowed silently through stands of cypress and thin water oak that cast shadows over the cabin. Trees and underbrush were cleared for at least 100 yards to the east. Grass had grown into the thick brown and green tangles, indicating that it had been months since any animal had grazed in the clearing. A forest of pines was to the east of the clearing. Greenley's company wound its way around the trunks to reach the cabin.

Otto pulled on the right-hand room's door. It swung outward to the accompaniment of screeching rusty hinges. Dust fell from the top of the doorframe like dry rain. The Brocktons walked inside, followed by Greenley. He could smell the dust that accumulated from months, if not years, of wind-blown sand coming through the chinks in the walls. Guided by the light of the open door, Otto went to each of four windows and opened the shutters. That threw in enough light to reveal such details as the hard-packed sand and clay floor and the sleeping loft built into the west wall about six feet above the ground. Something scurried along the east wall. Greenley turned. It was a slender, brown lizard getting out of the light.

"Not bad at all. Let's get this place cleaned up a bit. Clear out any bugs or snakes," Greenley said. "How'd you know this was out here?"

He called for some of the enlisted men to come in and start the cleaning. The Brocktons and he walked back outside before Otto answered the question.

"Used to belong to a cow hunter I knew a few years back. It's a handy place to know 'bout. Good for stoppin' off if you're drivin' to St. Augustine."

"What happened to the owner?" Greenley asked.

"Took his whole family out on a drive once 'n' didn't come back. They won't be needin' it."

Corley joined in the conversation. "They're stayin'

in a swamp near Baldwin." He smiled and glanced at his father. The left side of Otto's mouth curved into a sneer. The son walked off toward his horse.

"We're 'bout fifteen miles due north o' Starkes'," Otto said. "We'll hit 'em afore the next sundown."

The sound of Greenley's heartbeat drowned out the pounding of his horse's hooves as the company rode full gallop into the plantation. He was expecting a fight, but he didn't find one. There was no resistance. Only a running, screaming crowd, mostly black women and children. The major halted the company in the yard and dismounted. Everybody in the company carried matches and, in case of wet weather, many also had flint-and-steel firestarters. But they didn't need those any more than they did their guns. There was a large fire going in the blacksmith's forge. And there were enough jugs of coal oil about the place to soak rags and bits of cotton, which then were tied to tree branches to make torches. By sunset, the glow from burning cabins and outbuildings was a deeper and brighter red than the western sky.

Only one white man, short and thin with a bald head, was on the plantation. There were three white women: one of them ancient and withered, another pudgy and middle-aged with pepper-and-salt hair, and the third young and slender with dark brown hair. The man trundled the women into an ox cart and took off toward the west as the fires started. Greenley had the blacks herded into a pasture and put a guard around them.

The biggest problem the next day was figuring out how to destroy the machinery in the mill. Greenley, drawing on his experiences with repairing his own water-powered mill back home, formed a detail to search the plantation for wrenches and other tools. After breakfasting on confiscated ham and eggs, the detail set to work on the gears and driveshafts within the mill. By noon, the guts of the machinery had been sunk into the pond. But nobody in the company was enough of a mechanic to remove the huge water wheel. Greenley eventually decided to leave it in place. By noon, the company was on the road north, with the plantation's cattle, hogs, and 30 blacks. Women and children rode in mule- and ox-drawn wagons that the company gathered from around the plantation. Although some had saddled mules or horses, most of the men walked.

Hymns from the blacks and chatter from Otto accompanied the major for most of the way back. Although he could not recognize many of the songs, Greenley enjoyed the singing. Meanwhile, he became increasingly suspicious of Otto's conversation. The scout argued to be allowed to continue with the cattle and blacks beyond St. Augustine. The company was at the Haw Creek cabin when Otto modified the proposal and offered to let the cattle stay with the company if he and his sons could go on with the blacks. Otto never really said what he intended to do, but Greenley believed he knew the plan. Keep traveling north, probably to Savannah, and sell the slaves. Greenley felt seriously ill by the time the company reached St. Augustine. Otto undoubtedly would make some sort of offer to Holmes. After that, Greenley expected to stand by helplessly and watch the Brocktons guide the blacks out of town.

He was wrong. Greenley was standing on the veranda of the headquarters, preparing to go in and make his report, when he heard Holmes' voice coming from the parlor. "Your deal is to keep four-legged stock. If they walk on two legs, they stay."

Otto came out of the headquarters' door as Greenley entered. The knowledge that his commanding officer had some sort of scruples worked a cure on the major's stomach.

After the formalities of his report, Greenley brought a change of uniform with him to the barbershop, where he bathed and shaved. Then he went to the bakery, thinking that he would help Doris close shop for the day. The shop was already closed. Thoughts of another bout with ague shadowed what had been cheerful spirits. But the shadow vanished when he heard the rustle of petticoats coming around the corner of the building.

"Heard you were back, so I locked up early," Doris said as she approached. She extended a hand and hooked it under Greenley's arm. "I decided to fix dinner at home."

She was in a green suit, made out of a shiny silk that she must have had before the blockade cut off the overseas textile trade. The skirt flared out from her hips down to the ground. It was topped by a jacket that buttoned from her neck to her waist.

"At your home? Good. I'm way too tired to travel any more," Dan said, a smile widening as he talked. "The way you're dressed, I thought we had an invitation to dinner at the White House."

Doris's grip tightened on his arm. "You saw me shufflin' 'round for too long in my dressin' gown 'n' all those sloppy things. Figured it was time to sparkle a mite. Just put a chicken in the oven 'n' got some soup 'n' greens simmerin' on the stove. We might as well walk 'round a bit 'n' work up a hunger."

They went east to the riverfront. Nobody was along the bank. No ships or stevedores were on the docks. To avoid the smell of the cattle in the pens, Greenley and Doris turned back when they reached the docks. The lowing of the cattle, cries of the gulls, and slaps when ripples in the water came up against the bank were the only noises.

Doris broke several minutes of silence. "You were sweet. Very, very sweet, to care for me like you did. You took off on that mission afore I really had a chance to thank you. Then, while you were gone, I got to thinkin'."

The sun was beginning to lower. Shadows from trees and buildings to the west fell across the the bank and turned Doris's tan several shades darker. Enough heat was left in the day to make her perfume radiate off her body. It was a mildly sweet scent that didn't smell like any one flower in particular but reminded Dan of several.

"Maybe I've been thinkin' too much." Tears began to glaze her eyes and spill out over the corners. "Kept turnin' over in my mind 'bout you ridin' out o' here every whip-stitch to fight. Maybe someday you won't ride back."

Greenley pulled her closer to him until he had trouble walking without stepping on the hem of her dress. He swallowed hard and tried to sound cheerful. "You sure as hell didn't have to worry about that this time. Maybe I could have set myself on fire. But there wasn't anybody with a gun to give me trouble."

Doris leaned over and rested her head on his upper arm. The tears were gone, but the voice trembled. "I had one man die on me. Don't figure to have it happen agin."

Greenley stepped on the dress and nearly lost his balance. Despite his attraction to her and their relationship, he had never thought of himself in a way that Doris apparently was thinking of him. He never considered describing her as "his woman." But she apparently was ready to consider him "her man."

"'N' maybe you won't get killed. Maybe the war is just goin' to peter out 'n' someday you'll leave here for Illinois . . . . "

"Ohio." Greenley hoped that throwing in the correction would make her pause and change the course that her conversation was taking. The hope was false.

"Wherever. Fact is, I aim to keep you around as long as I can."

"Doris, look, I. . ." Dan struggled with the words. He was trying to verbalize something that he didn't know enough about to put into words. Emotions were racing through him. His body was reacting in various ways. His heartbeat increased until he could feel pain in his chest. His breathing became heavy, ragged gasps. None of this ever happened to him in years of squiring women around back home. He could not explain what was happening to himself, let alone try to tell Doris about it.

She put up a hand to stop his efforts at speech. "Don't worry. I think I know what you want to say. You don't have to say anythin'. What's going to happen between us, be it tonight or fifty years from now, will happen. Talkin' 'bout it won't change a thing."

Her head raised slightly and Greenley bent over to meet her. Their lips touched and their mouths opened. He could see nothing, only feel her lips caressing his and then brushing his moustache. Both of them were sweating by the time the kiss ended.

The hoop skirt pressed against him. It settled back around her as she withdrew slightly from the embrace. Dan relaxed his hold on her. They walked back to the bakery. The food was done. He helped Doris take the loaded pots and pans into the house. She put the chicken on a platter and the vegetables and soup into bowls. He helped her set the dining room table. As they were putting spoons by the soup bowls, their hands touched. Doris put down her spoon.

"I'm not all that hungry. Are you?"

He shook his head. "Depends on what you mean by hungry. For food? No."

They left the food on the table and went upstairs. Neither of them got around to eating that night.

But the chicken wasn't wasted. It's aroma drew Coacoochee's attention. He sat on his haunches looking up at the table for several minutes. When nobody came around to tell him any differently, he jumped up and took a few bites from the bird. Still no reprimands. So, digging his forepaws into the chicken to steady it, Coacoochee began eating in earnest. His feast had ended hours before he heard footsteps coming down the stairs.

# 17 ⚡

Wᴵʟᴅꜰʟᴏᴡᴇʀꜱ ᴀɴᴅ ʀᴀɪɴ ᴍᴀʀᴋᴇᴅ the passing of the seasons on the trail. It was spring when the grass was laced with a reddish purple flower whose petals were shaped like the rowels of spurs with four rounded ends. They seemed to glow, something like the coals of a campfire on a moonless night, but their color was deeper and darker. This flower thrived on the light, misty rain that occasionally fell between February and April. Those also were the months when both cultivated and wild orange trees bloomed. Their tiny flowers, as white as bleached linen, perfumed acres of land. Whole tracts around the groves smelled like enclosed kitchens in which somebody was peeling oranges. The days usually were warm enough to work outside in shirtsleeves. Still, the nights, particularly during February and early March, were cool enough to make people wrap themselves in blankets and huddle near fires.

April was the tricky month. Usually, it was one of the most pleasant. The light rains of spring would continue. Bright yellow wildflowers, with delicate petals arranged in a ring, would begin crowding out the purple ones. Days would be warm, but not so oppressively hot and humid that clothes would stick to their wearers like gummy, tightly wrapped bandages. Nights would be cool enough that sleepers wouldn't sweat, but not chilly enough to require more than a sheet or a light blanket. It was a month that cow hunters looked forward to and was a favorite time for driving cattle. Sometimes, though, April bushwhacked its admirers.

Frost occasionally struck in April. Then the grass became brown, dry hay. Its stalks withered and stretches of what should have been good pasturage looked as if someone had taken a scythe to the land. Usually, a cold spell in April also meant the dry season would linger, giving the land only sporadic, light showers. The yellow flowers would not appear and, sometimes, even the purple ones would dry up in the drought.

There also were years when the rainy season would begin by mid-March. That would be accompanied by weeks of extreme heat. Within a month, the humidity would be so dense that a cigar left outside for an hour would be too soggy to light. It was if the earth itself were sweating, the perspiration rising from the ground to the sky, where it would condense into evil-looking black clouds. By three or four o'clock in the afternoon, those clouds would tower for miles into the sky. Eventually, they would let loose rain in drenching, waterfall-like downpours. During those Aprils, the purple flowers would disappear quickly, as if drowned in the rain. The others would grow so thick that cattle and horses would have yellow rings around their mouths from munching grass containing the flowers.

Eric thought this was one of the good Aprils. The last two weeks of the month were spent on the trail. The days became hot, but the nights still were cool enough to require at least one blanket. After being baked throughout the daylight hours, the ground and most bodies of water became a good deal warmer than the night air. That created mist, which thickened throughout the night. By dawn, fog wrapped everything in gray. The hunters would stumble through the camp, guided by neighs and whinnies, to find horses that were hobbled only a few yards away. Some mornings, the fog was so thick that hunters used their sense of touch more than sight when saddling. They usually were on the trail for three hours before the fog lifted. As it began to rise into the sky, it created a ceiling under which the herd would walk and graze.

The fog didn't slow the progress of the drive. Even the destruction of Spring Garden added only two days to the schedule. The drive was perhaps 15 miles north of Enterprize when Tree learned that Starke's plantation was gone. A rider on his way to Enterprize from Orange Springs, a town on the west side of the river where the white refugees sought shelter, stopped by the cow hunter's camp and told about the raid. Hooker decided to go to the town of Volusia for supplies. It was at a narrow bend in the river, about ten miles northwest of Spring Garden.

Besides being the hometown of the drive's cook, Volusia was a moderate-sized Confederate outpost. About 50 soldiers were stationed there, living in tents and cabins scattered through the pine woods that bordered the riverbank. The town itself consisted of a blacksmith shop, several stores, a sawmill, and a hide tannery, all built of cypress planks that were gray from weathering.

Those buildings sat on the site of a centuries-old Indian village. The main street was white, from ground shells that had been taken from the Indians' refuse mounds. Before the river trade built up in the south, Volusia was one of the biggest settlements in central Florida. Nobody knew for sure what the name "Volusia" meant. But a trading post at the site had been called that since before Florida was an American territory.

Tree climbed onto the seat of the wagon with the cook and rode into town while the others herded the cattle into a circle in a field about a half mile to the south. Eric and most of the hunters idly drank chicory and watched the cattle graze until the wagon returned. Tree told the others that a cavalry detachment was in town and would help supply the drive. But there were problems.

"Yankees took over Pilatka," he said. "They're all 'round that area. No sense tryin' to cross near there. Since we're here, reckon we might as well go through town 'n' cross. River's no more'n a hundred yards wide. But deep as sin 'n' no sandbars. Gonna have to swim the herd."

Volusia had been rummaging through the back of the wagon for pots and pans. He emerged as Tree stopped talking. "It ain't goin' to be much o' a problem, though," the cook said as he drew the bucket of bacon grease from its cubbyhole. "I've swum cattle, horses, 'n' hogs 'cross there hundreds o' times."

Tree nodded his head. "Probably right. I didn't want to cross this far south 'cause o' the Yankee patrols on the other side. But it's the only sensible thing to do now. So get ready, boys. We'll stock up tomorrow in town. Next day we hit the water."

Volusia reached into the bucket. His hand emerged covered with a gray slime. He wiped off his hand by moving it in a circular motion around a frying pan. Eric never before had seen Volusia prepare a meal. The cook usually was far enough ahead that the meals were ready by the time the hunters brought up the herd. Now, as he watched, Eric wished he had stayed ignorant. Everybody else was a veteran of other drives with Volusia. Most of them watched impassively as the cook reached into the pork barrel at the side of the wagon and began drawing out slabs of pinkish meat. Eric noticed that a few hunters, particularly the younger ones, avoided looking.

Crossing the river took all day, but every head was accounted for on the other side. The drive continued northwest through the fields of grass and purple flowers. The yellow flowers began appearing as the heat increased and the afternoon thunderstorms began.

Driving became more difficult and, potentially, more dangerous as the rainy season progressed. Cattle slowed down as their hooves cut into the soil, stirring it up and creating pools of sticky mud. They frequently became fractious just before and during a storm. When electricity had built up in the air until men felt the hairs on their arms standing up, the cattle's bawling became louder and they would stop grazing. Sometimes, the electricity built up on them until blue sparks danced about the tips of their horns.

The increasing volume of the bawls told the hunters to ride in circles about the herd and sing to keep the cattle as calm as possible. Everybody tried to avoid using their whips, for fear of scaring the herd into a stampede. Eric was somewhat surprised that they were able to get through more than a week of daily storms before the herd bolted. And even that stampede was not as bad as most. The cattle ran through a driving rain for about an hour. Then, seemingly of their own accord because the hunters had not been able to control them, they milled around in a circle for a while before settling down to peacefully graze. Nobody was hurt. No cattle were lost. All the equipment was undamaged.

It seemed as if that one episode convinced the herd that stampeding was a useless exercise. For some reason, the cattle never again ran. They even stayed put during one storm in which lightning struck and set afire a pine within 200 yards of them.

Eric eventually discovered an advantage of the daily storms, provided that one struck early enough to interrupt lunch or late enough that the drive was in camp. Skeeter showed him that, during a storm, it was possible to take the edge off Volusia's chicory by holding the cup out and letting rain pour into it.

A thunderstorm was whipping around Baldwin when the drive ended. That dismayed the portly, middle-aged man who owned the doorless bar nearest to the cowpens. His sawdust floor quickly turned into a foul-smelling mush from water dripping off the hunters. Besides the water, wet mud and manure that had clung to their horses flowed off in little brown rivulets as each animal stamped and shuffled its feet on the floor.

Eric spent most of the next two days in a fog of whiskey. But it still was not like the after-drive sprees that he was used to going on with his father and brothers. Whiskey, yes. Women, no. He noticed that women didn't gather around the Cow Cavalry like they did other hunters. Not enough money. Volusia, who carried some gold from home with him, searched through the first night and finally found a rather plump blond. The other hunters referred to her as "the Bride." Eric asked several of them how she got that name. Each of them told him to ask his father-in-law, but, when he did, Heavy only grunted out "Never mind."

After the drinking session in the first bar, some of Eric's companions cleaned up and, by the next day, were wandering around town with women. Most of them were dressed more demurely — higher necklines and duller clothing colors — than the average working girl. Even those that appeared to be chippies didn't act like them. No forced laughter and bawdy jokes. They didn't seem eager to bed the men and then get rid of them. Maybe the women were patriots who sought the company of Confederates. Maybe they simply loved the individual hunters and wanted them after each drive. Whatever the reason, it was obvious that most of the cow cavalrymen who squired women around Baldwin were involved in some kind of relationship other than a financial deal.

With Chole and the twins at home, Eric wasn't looking for any relationship. All he wanted was release from tension. Tarts were best for that. Offer them money. If they accept, take them. Bruises, broken bones, anything that happens to their bodies are as much a part of their business as getting gored by a steer horn is of cow hunting. Eric seldom had complaints. Usually, all he did with a woman was twist one of her arms around behind her back as he was on top of her. He kept twisting until she cried out in pain. Then the job was done. He just kept a knife and gun close by in case the cry brought on someone to help her. In dozens, if not a hundred or more, such encounters, he had only had to kill one would-be rescuer.

He knew that this time he would have to content himself with drink and hope that his tension would fade. For one thing, he was so used to getting money at the end of a drive that he carried almost none with him. For another, his father-in-law was too close. When he joined the Cattle Guard, Eric didn't think of the potential trouble that he invited by riding with Chole's father. Now, he felt Heavy's presence, even though Eric didn't see his father-in-law anywhere near the saloon. So, Eric gulped shots of rye and tried to block out the sounds of women's laughter and the smell of their perfume.

The hunters formed a quiet, mostly hung-over parade back south after three days in Baldwin. They rode in a group through the yellow flowers and grass, retracing the route of their drive, until they came to the town of Volusia. From then on, the group grew smaller as each hunter struck off for his home.

An afternoon thunderhead was forming into a sooty tower hundreds of feet high when Eric reached home. The twins were on the dog trot, rolling a handleless tin cup back and forth between them. As it rolled over the planks, the cup made a jingling sound. The sound stopped when, in unison, the twins looked up at the bark of one of their father's catch dogs. Both twins stood in the shade of the dog trot and watched their father tether his horse to a gate post.

The twins had the Brocktons' reddish brown hair, but they had their mother's clear green eyes. Their mother's side of the family also showed in their large, ungainly hands and feet and in their height — more than four feet tall and not yet four years old.

They wore unbleached cotton twill breeches that reached to the ankles of their bare feet. Their gingham shirts were different. One had blue checks and the other red.

Eric put a foot on the bottom step to the dog trot and the twins flinched in unison. They frequently greeted him that way and the instinctive gesture always made him smile faintly. He still flinched when his father advanced toward him. In a way, it was a sign of respect.

"Where's your mother?" he asked. The twin to his right pointed toward the east. Neither of the boys spoke. They seldom said anything to anybody, a trait that Eric appreciated.

He walked in the direction of the gesture. That was where he kept about 40 acres of plowed ground for vegetables. A flash of anger struck him like a slap in the face when he got to the field.

Okra plants were pushing through the soil, but by now, they should have been almost a foot high and the first green pods should be sprouting among the leaves. Corn stalks were less than half of the three feet that they should be. Nothing was as fully developed as it should have been a month into the rainy season.

In the far eastern corner of the field, silhouetted against the golden light that was filtering through the clouds, he saw one of his mules pulling his plow. A small figure plodded along behind the plow. Chole. Eric strode through the plants and across the unplanted furrows in the soil until he reached her.

She was wearing a shapeless dress that once had been navy blue but had faded into something like a dull purple. Sweat stains now darkened the dress to almost its original shade. Strands of black hair came out from beneath a wide-brimmed palmetto straw hat. Some fell backward across her shoulders while other strands fell forward and across her face. Except for the hair color, there was almost nothing of Heavy in Chole. She was just slightly more than 5 feet tall and not even the birth of the twins had boosted her weight beyond 100 pounds.

Eric approached her and she brushed a few of the wet strands of hair away from her eyes.

"What the hell's goin' on?" Over the years, he had practiced a snarl that he could put into his voice when he asked a question. But, somehow, he found that he almost never used it except when talking to his wife or the twins.

Chole pulled on the reins to halt the mule. "Doin' all the plowin' 'n' plantin' myself. Goin' lots slower than it should've."

Distant thunder growled in the sky. Eric thought it matched the tone in his voice. "Storm's comin' on now. Don't bother doin' any more. Just go 'n' get food ready. I'll take care of the mule."

He grabbed her about the shoulders and pushed her toward the plowed ground. She caught the heels of her bare feet on the slope of the furrow and tripped backwards. Eric looked at her as she lay across the furrow, her knees bent upwards. Then he let reins fall between the plow and the mule. He unbuttoned his trousers and knelt beside her. With one hand he encircled her left wrist and with the other he pulled at her clothes. Then, he twisted her left arm around until the wrist touched her spine. Her body arched upward toward his as the first cry escaped from her.

The mule stood impassively by the couple for several minutes until the rain came with a loud thunderclap. Then the mule brayed and shuffled its feet. Eric stood up, grabbed the reins to steady the mule and looked down at his wife. The rain already had made it impossible to distinguish the tears on her face.

# 18 🌿

Eric was home for about six weeks. He had time to bring in the okra, plant a few more rows of vegetables, and shoo a few dozen head of cattle out of the scrub. Then Skeeter rode by one afternoon and told him that Hooker was ready for another drive.

"What in hell's Tree doin'?" Eric snapped at Skeeter. "How's he figure anybody's got enough cattle together to make another drive this quick?"

Skeeter's lips turned up in a slight smile. "He went off into the scrub soon as we got back. Me, Heavy, 'n' a few of the others been out most o' the time. We've got a good six hundred head o' steers and a couple hundred o' hogs to boot. Just bring what you've got 'n' join us. Week from today. At them cowpens just east of Crow's Bluff."

Eric nodded. It was as if he had stuck a foot into what he thought was going to be a little mud and then found out he was in quicksand. He was being pulled away and he couldn't figure out how to get out of it. Joining the Cow Cavalry was supposed to get him on the good side of the Confederacy. Fine and dandy. He had done that. It had cost him the money he usually would have made after a calf roundup. He expected that to happen and considered it to be something of an investment for the future. But now, he was being pulled away again before he had a chance to make anything off his crops. He was going to have to spend God-knows-how-long on another drive. And there was no chance of him getting anything out of this drive but more trouble.

The only gesture of defiance he could think of was to put his own brand on about half the cattle he had gathered. He put the "CS" brand on the other half, so he would have at least something to show when he met the others. He drove the ones with his brand to his father's cabin.

"You 'spect me to take these to St. Augustine for you?" Otto asked. "Hell, boy. Do your own goddamn work."

Eric was sitting in his saddle, looking down at his father, who leaned against an oak. A tingling sensation crawled up Eric's back, traveling along the scars of the whip marks. The same sensation happened every time Otto raised his voice.

"Daddy, I've got to go on another drive. But I've got to have at least some money to fall back on. Chole 'n' the kids need it too." Eric knew his voice had a note of whining in it. He was disgusted by it, but there was nothing he could do.

His father smiled and spat. His teeth were a light brown line between his moustache and beard. "Don't cry boy. Make you a deal. I'll take your goddamn cattle to St. Augustine. But I get half the sale price."

Eric nodded, turned his horse around and rode toward his cabin. He was on the trail north a few days later. This drive was almost identical to the last weeks of the first one. Rain practically every day. The only difference was the heat before the thunderstorms. It was worse. Each hunter had at least three horses and changed mounts every few hours to save the animals from heat exhaustion.

Several of the hunters who had been at Olustee rode saddles similar to the one Tree used, military-style with a space in the middle. Eric noticed that the horses of those hunters always seemed to have less foam and sweat on their backs than the others. Also, everybody else had more sweat stains on their trousers than the riders of the split-seat saddles. Eric decided that the military saddles really did have better ventilation. He vowed to get one as soon as the opportunity presented itself.

The cattle also felt the heat and it made them more jittery than their predecessors on the last drive. They bolted repeatedly during thunderstorms. But the stampedes usually were quelled without too much trouble. During one of them early into the drive, Eric was hooked with a horn on his left leg. A burning pain from the gash plagued him for several weeks. Several other hunters also were hurt in the stampedes. Tree was hooked in his right thigh once. But nobody was seriously injured. All told, after at least a dozen quickly squelched stampedes, the drive lost no more than 20 cattle.

About two weeks before the drive arrived in the area, a Confederate captain named J.J. Dickison led the second Florida Cavalry against the federals in

Pilatka. The brief fight convinced the Yankees to leave town, at least long enough for Tree to use his favorite crossing. The herd crossed the St. Johns without trouble.

Eric was looking forward to Baldwin. If nothing else, at least he could spend a couple of days in the shade of a building and out of the saddle. Skeeter was the outrider when the drive neared the town. It was no more than two miles away when Skeeter galloped up and, with two quick cracks of his whip, signaled there was trouble. Eric and the others turned the herd into a circle and let the cattle graze peacefully while Tree and Skeeter sat on their horses and talked.

Eventually, Hooker gathered the rest of the hunters around him. "We may as well go ahead," he told them. "But I want ya'll to know what's up there. We ain't stoppin' in Baldwin."

The rest of the hunters groaned.

"There ain't no Baldwin to stop at," Tree continued. "Yankees hit it a few weeks ago. It's gone."

Lonesome asked aloud the question Eric was thinking. "Now what?"

"We keep headin' north. There's a railhead in Brunswick."

Eric felt his body stiffen. "Christ, that could take another three weeks."

Tree pushed the brim of his hat back until Eric could see the gray eyes. They were staring ahead, but not at anybody or anything in particular. "So? Brunswick's the first place that I know of where there's trains. We're goin'. Might as well camp tonight in Baldwin. Least there'll be plenty o' flat, cleared ground to sleep on."

Not even the railroad tracks were left. For miles in any direction, the tracks and ties had been torn up and brought into town. There, judging from the charred remains that could be seen in some of the blackened rubble that was left, gigantic bonfires had been made of every building. The ties had been thrown into the flames and, when the heat was great enough, the rails had been taken from the fires and twisted around tree trunks. Most of the trees were burned through and lay on the ground beside the black tangles of metal. What was left of the rails looked like gigantic corkscrews. Some of the rails had been thrown into a pile that made Eric think of a writhing mass of huge worms knotting themselves together as they mated. Brick chimneys, most of them charred as black as the rails, stood out amid piles of ashes and timber.

Eric and the others circled the herd in a broad, grassy field. A few minutes later, red light from the setting sun made tiny black silhouettes out of two figures that walked from a patch of nearby woods and approached the herd. Tree spurred his horse toward them. Eric and several others followed.

The two figures were a man and a woman, both in dirty, tattered clothing. Eric rode up in time to hear the man say, "No more'n three weeks ago. They got the people out in the street 'n' marched us away. Then they took buckets of coal oil 'n' threw 'em all over. Whole place went up. It was like somebody opened the front door to hell."

Eric quickly guessed the occupations of both the man and woman. Bordello owner and one of his women. Or, at least that's what they had been until his place and their joint livelihoods went up in flames.

Their clothes, now mottled from sun bleaching and dirt, gave them away. The woman stood no taller than five feet two. She wore what probably had been a purple, low-cut dress. It now was blotched with varying shades of blue. Two or three weeks ago, she probably had the plump, round curves of a woman who did little manual labor. But the bodice of the dress now sagged because her chest was losing its fullness. She wore no crinoline, so the dress hung shapelessly from her hips. Her light brown hair was tied back with a black scarf that might at one time have been a sash for the dress.

Her companion wasn't much taller and had the same appearance of someone whose leisurely lifestyle had suddenly, drastically, gone wrong. The man's hair and beard looked as if they used to be regularly barbered. Now, it was obvious that the whiskers and hair had been growing without a trim for at least two weeks. One side of the beard appeared longer than the other. Hair crept down the back of his neck in an uneven wave that stopped where his shirt collar should have been. The collar was gone from what used to be a bleached linen shirt, now stained to a grayish tan. Any starch in it had been sweated out at least two weeks ago. Over the shirt he wore a vest that had started life with a black, red, and gold brocaded pattern stitched into it. The colors had faded until it was hard to tell the black from the red. The gold looked like a pale, sickly yellow. His trousers appeared to have been black, but they also had faded into a red-tinged gray.

Eric heard hoofbeats behind him. He turned and saw his father-in-law ride up to the group. "Where was the army while all of this was goin' on?" Heavy asked as he reined in his horse.

The man jerked his head in the direction of a corner of the field. Eric followed the motion and saw a cemetery. A row of sandy soil mounds showed that several of the graves were freshly dug.

"There were only five o' 'em here. From the commissary department." The man spoke in a nasal whine. "Reckon they did the best they could."

Heavy dismounted and reached into his saddlebag. "A young lieutenant was in charge, right?"

The man nodded. The preacher withdrew his Bible from the saddlebag and led the horse over to the cemetery. He took off his hat when he reached the freshly dug graves and bowed his head.

"Maybe a dozen o' us left. Scattered in the woods." The man looked up at Tree as he talked. "We're 'bout out o' food. Can you spare us a cow or hog?"

Tree shook his head. "Sorry. They're government property. Can't sell or give 'em away. But —" he said, reaching down with his left hand and drawing his carbine from the scabbard "— government says nothin' 'bout steers that die on the trail."

He snapped the carbine to his shoulder and fired. One steer instantly dropped to its front knees. Then it slowly rolled over on one side. By the time it had fallen, the rest of the cattle were in a mad, bawling rush. The herd plowed through the squealing pack of hogs and out toward the pinewoods.

"'N' I reckon any you recover from a stampede are yours too," Hooker shouted above the racket. He spurred his horse toward the running cattle. The rest of the hunters joined the chase. Several, when they got within earshot of him, cursed Tree. He said nothing in reply. Eventually, they got the herd resettled in a field several miles north of Baldwin.

"In a way, I'm glad this happened," Hooker said as the hunters prepared to eat an hours-late supper. "Ya'll got a chance to see real hunger. Goin' be more as we push north."

The St. Marys River, about 40 miles north of Baldwin, separated Florida and Georgia. It was only half as wide as the St. Johns, but more than twice as deep, and its current, which flowed eastward from the huge Okefenokee Swamp, was swifter. Crossing the St. Marys would have been a problem under the best conditions. But the daily thunderstorms had swollen the river and created more than a mile of marshlands on either side of it. On top of that, nobody in the drive was familiar enough with the river to know a good crossing. As a result, 25 steers and half a dozen hogs drowned before the drive reached firm ground in Georgia. Drowned, but not lost. Residents of the woods and a town near the river saw to that. Ranks of spindly men and boys gathered along the north bank as the herd crossed and hauled in the carcasses with ropes and pulleys.

At least another 25 cattle and several more hogs were lost in the 40 miles between the St. Marys and Brunswick. The losses were Tree's fault. Twice more he started stampedes by shooting cattle. Each time came when the drive neared collections of tents, canvass lean-tos, and rickety shacks. These shantytowns were inhabited by refugees from fighting around the Atlanta area to the north and west. The refugees all reminded Eric of the man and woman in Baldwin. Many of them were clad in the remains of finery — lace, silk, and satin for the women and linen and broadcloth for the men. The clothes were stained, sunbleached, and tattered, although most of the wearers obviously tried to keep them clean. None of the clothes fit; all hung loosely about the shoulders, waists, and hips. The women looked to be of various ages, but Eric didn't see a man younger than his mid-50s. And there were no boys older than 14.

"Rest have gone soldierin'," Tree explained when Eric asked about the age spread among the males.

Eric could feel pity for the inhabitants of the shanties, but he was repulsed by Hooker's shooting stunts. His entire life had been devoted to making as much money as possible from cow hunting and farming with as little risk as possible to himself and his family. There was no need to give beef away and at the same time put all the hunters in jeopardy with the stampedes.

Others seemed to agree. "We're 'posed to deliver these critters somewheres," Lonesome shouted at Tree as they were getting the herd circled after the third shooting-caused stampede. "Not scatterin' 'em all over God's creation."

Tree stood up in his stirrups, casting his shadow over Lonesome, and shouted back loud enough for any hunter within yards to hear: "We're 'posed to be doin' our job. The job's to feed the South. That's what I'm doin'."

His answer satisfied nobody. Hunters grumbled about the stampedes as they built their fires, ate dinner, and even after they rolled up in their blankets for the night. Tree said nothing to anybody. He had the first watch that evening. Ever since Baldwin, he had kept mostly to himself.

Eric lay in his blankets near Heavy at the edge of the camp and, unable to sleep, he listened to Tree singing while riding around the herd.

"We are a band o' brothers 'n' native to the soil. . ." Tree kept singing what was supposed to be a lively march in a strange, slow tempo that made the song seem like a dirge.

Eric sat up in his blankets. The song faded as Tree rode out of earshot. "Heavy?" Eric whispered hoarsely. He wanted to ask aloud a question that had been nagging him for days. His father-in-law would be the best one to answer.

Heavy, looking bleery-eyed, rolled over toward Eric. "Do you think Tree is crazy?" his son-in-law asked.

A trace of a smile, not a mocking smile, but more of a sad, knowing expression of sympathy, turned the edges of Heavy's mouth. "No. Not in the way we think o' crazy. Tree's determined to do his duty. Least his idea o' duty. Maybe devotion to duty after a certain point makes you seem a little crazy. But it's almost a divine kind o' craziness. 'Be ye steadfast, unmovable always aboundin' in the work o' the Lord.' First Corinthians, fifteen: fifty-eight. Reckon Tree's just sorta livin' out that scripture."

Reaching Brunswick did not result in the usual drive's-end celebration, mostly because there was no liquor. In Georgia, corn, sugar, and other ingredients that went into alcohol production had become too valuable as food. There were plenty of cheers from soldiers and civilians who greeted the drive. But that was all. Brunswick itself seemed to be merely a larger version of the shantytowns along the trail. True, there were substantial brick and lumber buildings through-out the city, but they were hidden behind the squalor of the refugee camps.

Every refugee who talked to Eric told of being run out of their homes and seeing their crops, live-stock, and supplies carried off by soldiers. Those who had not fallen victim to marauders of Sherman's Yan-kees had found all their goods impounded by Hood's Confederates. There were two differences: Confeder-ates usually seemed sorry for what they did and they frequently gave their victims handfuls of governmen-tal script as payment. Knowing the value of script, Eric wondered if it might be less hypocritical for Hood's men to simply steal like Sherman's.

At least cattle and crops in Florida stayed with those who raised them, Eric thought. That's the ad-vantage of living in a backwater of the war. Neither side was too interested in the state. A few buildings might be burned and cattle stolen. But, when com-pared to what Eric had seen in even this brief taste of Georgia, Floridians had a good chance of making a living. At least those people who avoided military ser-vice. And Florida's isolation also allowed the people to indulge in fantasies about the rest of the war. From talking to the Georgians, Eric knew that everybody expected Atlanta to fall soon. It might have fallen al-ready and the news not yet reached the Brunswick area. With Atlanta in Yankee hands, the northern and central parts of the state soon would be gone. And the enemy then would march toward Savannah, the state capital. Yankees had toeholds along the east and west coasts of Florida. Yet most of the interior and its capi-tal, Tallahassee, were safe. Olustee had seen to that.

But talking to those who had seen hundreds of thousands of bluecoats swarming around northern Georgia, Eric realized that the battle had stopped an invasion that was only half-hearted at best. If the Yankees took it into their heads to come down to Florida after they finished with Georgia, there was little the Confederacy could do to stop them.

The hunters started on their return trip the morning after they arrived in Brunswick. For hours on end, they rode without talking. The barking of their dogs, bird calls, and the humming of insects in the brush were the only noises for most of the day. Eric was glad for the quiet. It gave him more time to think.

"When you know you've got a losin' hand, fold 'n' get out o' the game soon as possible," his father always said.

But there were almost 20 other players in this game, each one heavily armed. If they didn't want Eric to leave the game, they could easily force him to stay in and keep betting his income — and maybe his life — on whatever Tree might decide to do.

Within a week of leaving Brunswick, Eric began to feel sick. He blamed it on exhaustion. His body seemed to creak like dry saddle leather when he mounted or dismounted. When he walked, he could feel water sloshing around in his knees. A dull, throbbing pain, that seemed to keep pace with the beat of his horse's hooves, entered his head and stayed there through most of the daylight hours. By the time he rode up to his cabin, he didn't even feel like smiling when the twins went through their cowering act. All Chole said was, "Your Pa was here two weeks ago. Says he wants you to look him up soon as you're back."

He nodded, dismounted, shoved his wife and kids away from the door, and went inside the cabin. He lay fully clothed in the sleeping loft and was snoring before Chole had fed the horses and dogs. He slept for almost 24 hours. When he awoke, he remembered his father agreeing to split the sale of the 30 cattle he had saved from going on the drive. Well, at least that would be some money. Eric told Chole to heat some water and pour it in the copper bathtub outside. He bathed, shaved, dressed in some clean clothes and was back in the saddle within a few hours. His father's cabin was empty, so he went on to Martin's, which was a few miles to the south. His brother's wife, a dark-haired women who was as plump as Chole was thin, met him at the door. "Martin tole me you might be by," she said. "He said to tell you they were all goin' to Enterprize for a couple o' days. Said to come on there if you want what's owed you."

Martin was at one of the tables of the Enterprize Inn when Eric walked through the door. Amazing Grace was seated beside him, her left hand dangling limply above his crotch and her right holding a glass filled with light brown liquid. Martin was leaning back in his chair, holding a glass in one hand and a bottle in the other. Both he and Grace obviously had quickly thrown on their clothes in order to come downstairs for drinks, missing some buttons in the process. Tufts of reddish brown hair peeked out from the gap caused by two missed buttons on Martin's shirt. The bleached white of Grace's petticoat showed through the gap caused by a missed button on the side of her skirt.

"Upstairs. Big room on the right." Martin gestured with his glass toward the steps.

Eric walked up and knocked on the door. "Daddy?"

His father's voice was muffled by the door and slurred from drink, but Eric still could detect a note of cheerfulness in it when he heard: "It ain't locked. Come on in."

The room's smell hit him as he opened the door. Perfume, relying heavily on the overpowering sweetness of both magnolias and jasmine, combined with alcohol and sweat. It should have repelled Eric. But, instead, he found his heartbeat increasing and his breathing becoming heavier. Typical bawdy house smells. They triggered old memories.

It was the largest suite in the house. Three alcoves with beds in them branched off from a parlor furnished with two chairs, a short-legged table, and a couch. Corley was lying on the purple upholstery of the couch, sharing it with a blonde, no older than 18, who curled up near his feet. Otto was sitting in one of the chairs, with another girl, perhaps a year or two older than the other, in his lap.

"Look at this," Corley said, barely glancing in Eric's direction. "The prodigal returns."

Corley, his father, and the two girls all were in underclothes. Otto and Corley were in drawers, barechested. The blonde had a blue cotton robe over her shoulders, but its sash was undone, revealing red pantalets — a trouserlike pair of underpants — and a corset with the lacings undone. Pink flesh from her chest spilled out from the top of the corset while her calves and ankles stuck out from the pantalets. The girl in Otto's lap didn't bother with a robe. She wore a white chemise, a sheet of linen held to her shoulders by lacy straps. From the way it clung around her body from her chest to her ankles, Eric could tell that she wore nothing underneath the chemise.

He had known the one in his father's lap, but had forgotten her name. She was thinner than most women who earned their living on their backs. Her hair was so black that it almost seemed purple when the sunlight hit it. The hair parted over her shoulders and fell down either side, brushing against the chair legs. Her eyes were as black as her hair and her skin was a reddish brown. The hair, eyes and skin all betrayed what had to be Seminole blood.

She looked up at Eric and then curled deeper into Otto's lap, burying her head into his shoulder. It was a cringing motion like the twins'. Eric smiled. She must have remembered him.

Otto didn't respond to the gesture. He stood up, letting the girl hold on to him as she slid down his body. Then he took her arms from around his neck and pointed her to one of the alcoves. "We've got man talk to do, sugar." He waved a hand toward the couch. "Both of ya'll. Leave us be for a couple of minutes."

Instead of going into the alcove, the dark-haired girl walked out the door. The blonde followed her and shut the door. The latch was clicking as Otto went to a pile of clothes in a corner of the parlor. He untied the strings of a leather pouch from around his gunbelt. He threw the pouch across the room. It landed on the table with a metallic clunk.

Eric bent down and picked up the pouch. He opened it and spilled 11 doubloons onto the table. It amounted to about $220 in Yankee money. More than twice what Eric had expected. A smile crinkled the corners of his eyes until he could barely see. His father must have given him the full sale price of the cattle. Otto never before had made a gesture like that to him.

"Cuban market's gone wild. We got near fifteen dollars a head." Corley's voice punctured Eric's illusion about their father. "Between the Rebels keepin' what they can to themselves and the Yankees blockadin' the ports, them Spanish are gettin' mighty hungry for beef."

Otto had walked into one of the alcoves. He returned with a bottle and three glasses, which he put beside the doubloons on the table. "Don't mind drinkin' after those hussies, do you?" he asked his youngest son as he poured from the half-empty bottle.

Eric took the glass, which had a red smear on its rim from the touch of rouged lips, and swallowed. Bourbon. Really good, aged bourbon like he had not tasted since the beginning of the war.

"It's hog heaven for us, Boy," Otto smiled after draining his glass. "That share of yours at least'll get ya'll through the winter. Get some more crops goin' 'n' maybe you can join us for some fun next time we hit here."

Eric finished his drink and shook his head. "Tree figures to get in one more drive afore December. Goin' back and start huntin' the cows soon as possible. Sure goin' to cut some more out for ya'll, though. We'll split again."

Both his father and brother snorted. Corley held out an empty glass toward Eric. "You figure us to keep on sellin' your cattle 'n' holdin' onto your money till you finish galavantin' 'cross the countryside? We ain't your goddamn bankers."

Otto took a step toward the center of the room. He held out his arms as if he were the referee in a prize fight separating the boxers. "No need to think like that." His voice was low, soft. "I think there's ways Eric could help us and even earn a full share. Corley, why don't you go find those two girls? Tell Martin to get him 'n' his up here too."

Corley left the room. Otto took Eric's glass and refilled it. "Son, we've got to talk. Let's get started on gettin' you everythin' you want."

# 19 ✹

It had been a relatively quiet, easy drive. There were about 1,000 head of cattle, almost all steers, and about 500 hogs. Tree had been able to keep to his plan of staying east of the St. Johns. Nobody had seen any Yankee patrols or any bands of deserters. For the most part, the drovers merely chaperoned the cattle. They were slightly less than three weeks out of Enterprize and had traveled about 100 miles. Everybody was familiar with the route. They all knew they were approaching their first major river crossing.

The crossing actually would be over one of the many creeks that flowed into the St. Johns. Usually, Tree would have avoided the creek by skirting around its eastern edge until he neared Pilatka. But outriders had again seen Yankees. The Confederates who had been protecting the town had pulled back and the bluecoats filled in the void. Rather than attract the Yankees' attention, Hooker decided to cross the creek and turn to the west. He intended to cross the St. Johns a good 20 miles away from Pilatka.

Although the creek itself, which barely had a current in it even during a flood, was only a few hundred yards wide, crossing it never was easy. The water flowed through the western edge of swamps that stretched about 60 miles, almost to the ocean. Even during a drought, the creek had marshes for at least a mile on either side dotted with patches of quicksand that could suck down animals and men within seconds. Alligators and cottonmouths threatened to take any unwary dog, calf, or hog. After a rain, the marshes flooded and became part of the creek itself, often with water too deep for the animals to wade. At those times, hogs, cattle, horses, and drovers would have to swim for about two miles.

Knowing that the creek was ahead, everybody spent the morning coaxing the herd into a tight column of no more than three cattle abreast. That way, the cattle would be easier to control when they walked through the wetlands and into the water. As they always did, the cattle balked at being herded together. Whips kept cracking and dogs continually nipped at the heels of steers that strayed from the column and headed for the grassy scrub through which the herd was passing.

A gently sloping ridge led to the marshes and the creek. Volusia waited for the herd at the crest of the ridge, leaning against the wagon. His oxen already had been unyoked and were grazing as the herd approached. A rider cantered up from the opposite slope. Eric Brockton had been working as an outrider and was returning after scouting routes across the creek. Tree joined Volusia and Eric at the wagon.

"It's as dry as it's ever gonna be," Brockton said before Tree dismounted.

Hooker looked at the western sky. It was a light gray, just overcast enough to threaten rain sometime during the night or the next day. "Maybe five, six hours o' daylight left. Think we can chance it today?"

Brockton nodded. "Better the chance of finishin' after dark than lettin' the herd spread out durin' the night."

Since he already had searched for the narrowest, shallowest crossing, Brockton led the way. A youth of perhaps 20, called Black Creek, rode with him. All Tree knew of Black Creek was that he was a cousin of Skeeter's. Eric and Black Creek had seemed to become friendly along the course of the drive, and Tree decided that the two worked well together. Black Creek and Brockton rode about six yards apart from each other. Each carried a six-foot-long branch, broken off nearby oaks, to measure the depth of the mud and water. They started into the marshland. Their horses' hooves stirred up the rotting vegetation that was mixed with the mud, and a stench like sewage rose into the air. The rest of the drovers began bunching the cattle up and driving them into the water. Everybody had put their long guns and powder flasks into Volusia's wagon. They wore their holsters and gunbelts around their necks to protect the handguns and powder from the water.

Tree was near the middle of the herd, with the rest strung out for almost a mile both in front and behind him. He rode a young dappled-gray gelding. The horse, like many of the others, went reluctantly through the mud and then reared when the creek water hit his ankles. Although the air was comfortable, the water was cold from several weeks of chilly nights. Tree stood up in the stirrups and leaned over the horse's neck to force its head down and keep it under control. He spurred it into the water and they began to wade across, keeping the cattle in as tight a bunch and as straight a line as possible. He could see Eric and Black Creek on the opposite bank, sitting on their horses at the top of a slight rise. The two were dark silhouettes against the brown trunks of water oaks behind them.

Volusia's wagon was in the rear. A river crossing was the only time the cook rode behind the herd. That way, if the wagon stuck, it would not block the ford for the cattle. Also, after getting the rest of the herd to the opposite bank, the drovers could return and help pull the wagon out of the mire. Tree glanced behind him. The oxen had just stepped into the mud, but they seemed to pull the wagon easily. In front of him, the lead cattle were emerging from the marsh toward the rise where Eric and Black Creek waited. Everything indicated a quick, safe, trouble-free crossing. Tree breathed deeply and cracked his whip to keep two steers from wandering away from the bunch into deeper pools of the black water. The continual whip-cracking from all sides sounded as if an infantry regiment were firing volleys.

Then, another crack, slightly louder and deeper than the rest, came from the far shore.

Hooker jerked his head toward the noise and saw Black Creek falling. A cloud of gunsmoke hovered over his saddle. Eric still pointed a smoking revolver toward the saddle. Other shots and puffs of smoke came from the trees behind Brockton.

A bullet screamed by Tree. Instinctively, he drew the Walker Colt from the holster around his neck. The newer revolver lay in the wagon with the carbine. Everybody else also pulled handguns. But their shooting was useless. Most of them were too far out of range for a handgun to hit the woods — even if they could have aimed accurately amid the milling animals and on their bucking horses. Tree's horse put its legs together and leapt out of the water, coming down with a splash that soaked his revolver. He gave up trying to fire it and tried to spur the horse back through the water to the wagon.

Painfully loud noise surrounded him. Gunshots mixed with curses and shouts from the hunters, panicked bellows from the cattle, barks and howls from the dogs, squeals from the hogs, and screams and whinnies from the horses. A dull roar, the sound of the water being whipped up by the thrashing of the men and animals, underlined all the rest.

Tree's horse bucked again, sending up another wall of water that splashed over him. The horse jumped clear of the water a third time. It twisted its back while in midair, its forelegs going in one direction and its hind legs in another. Hooker couldn't keep his seat on the water-slicked saddle. He began to fall, but his right spur caught in the stirrup strap. His foot twisted in the stirrup as he fell headfirst. As the black water rushed up to meet his face, he felt a stab of pain running up his right leg. He heard a popping noise from somewhere in his leg as the horse jumped again.

Free of control by the spurs and reins, the horse began running through the water, dragging Tree behind it. For a few moments, Hooker felt the water coming into his nostrils and mouth and burning his throat and chest. Then, he felt, heard, and saw nothing. A black emptiness wrapped around him.

Cattle, hogs, and spare horses scattered in four directions. Within a few minutes, most of the hunters had splashed through the water back to the southern edge of the marsh. Volusia turned the oxen and saved the wagon from either sinking or capture. But by the time he got to the south bank, only Heavy was there to greet him. The rest had galloped out of sight.

Firing from the trees petered out and, in groups of twos and threes, 50 men emerged from the woods and stood near the northern edge of the marsh. Greenley was one of the first. The last few shots still were echoing as he walked from the shade. He watched the wagon, with one horseman beside it, begin climbing the slope of the southern ridge. Then he looked at the creek. Five bodies floated in the water. A sixth, the one the youngest Brockton blew away at the start, lay on dry land a few yards away from Greenley's feet. The body was on its right side, any facial features hidden by blood. A few strands of dark hair were visible along a thick, reddish brown trail that stretched at least three feet to where a black, wide-brimmed hat, with blood still slowly dripping from it, was hung up on a piece of Spanish bayonet.

Otto Brockton came up and stood between the major and the body. "You damn sure won this one." Brockton's voice was high-pitched with excitement. Greenley half-expected it to break, like a young boy's as he enters puberty.

The elder Brockton had to shout over the noise

of the animals. Some had become caught either in mud or quicksand, and were struggling vainly. Others had made it to one or the other shore and were escaping on dry land. Still others were plowing through the water like four-legged boats. One horse came through the mud, trying to run but being held back by the muck. Something that looked like blue tube dangled from the right side of the saddle. Greenley watched the horse for a few seconds before he saw a yellow stripe down the side of the blue thing. It was a leg and it was attached to a body dragging through the mud. The major sloshed through the mud toward the horse. Several of the soldiers followed him. The horse, snorting through its nostrils from exhaustion and fear, took a few steps toward Greenley and then stood still. A private held the horse's bridle while Greenley and a corporal took the boot-clad foot and twisted it until it unwound itself from the stirrup straps. The private let go of the horse and helped them lift the long body from the muck. Except for the one leg that had been caught, the rest of the body was covered with the black mud. It was cold and clammy from the water. The private and corporal dragged it by the arms toward dry land while Greenley gave orders to the other soldiers to collect the other bodies and form a burial detail.

Then a gagging sound came from the black body. The two who were dragging it dropped the arms and jumped backwards. "Jesus! It's alive!" the private screamed.

Greenley sprinted over and helped the two soldiers carry the body to the dry sand of the small rise. They let the body rest on its stomach. Water began trickling from the mouth. Greenley picked up the body at the waist and squeezed. More gagging and choking noises came from the mouth. A gush of water followed. Then coughing and finally, after what seemed like minutes but probably was seconds, came normal breathing.

Otto, who had gone back into the woods for his horse, returned, leading the animal by the rein. He stood by Greenley, looking down at the body.

"God damn," Otto said, his voice again tightening. "It's Tree."

The major stared at the mud-covered figure. He sensed, rather than saw, Otto reaching for a holstered gun. To stop the draw, Greenley put out a hand and laid it on top of Brockton's.

"Somethin's goin' to come out of the woods or the water and get him tonight. Might as well finish him now ourselves," Brockton said.

Greenley shook his head. "We'll take him with us. Prisoner of war. Let's get him to the Pilatka doctor."

Brockton snorted, "There're cattle to round up. Me 'n' mine'll be doin' that. Good luck to ya'll."

Ignoring Brockton, Greenley had soldiers carry Tree to the ambulance that was hitched in the woods with the horses. The major followed them.

Otto watched and shouted: "The hell. I'd sooner sleep with gators than have Tree on my hands. If he lives, we won't."

# 20 ✺

Laura, as she always did when she was close to him, spoke in little more than a whisper. "You have to go." She was lying beside him, breathing into his ear.

Tree didn't reply. Instead he encircled her shoulders with his right arm and drew her closer to him. He heard her petticoats rustle and felt the fabric of her dress fold around his side as her body pressed into his. The scent of lilacs filled his lungs with every breath. He looked down and all he could see were her eyes. They glowed like blue-stained panes of glass in a church window after candles had been lit. Then he felt her hands press into his side. Her shoulders squirmed against his rib cage. The petticoats rustled again and the folds of the skirt left him.

"I'm sorry, love." The whisper sounded fainter this time. "But you really have to go."

There was a rumbling sound from above, like thunder in the distance. The rustling of the petticoats, the touch of her dress, and the scent of lilacs all disappeared. Her eyes faded into darkness. Tree stared, trying to find her. But he saw very little. In the blackness of a very dark night, he could make out something rippling about four feet above his head and making the rumbling sound. It was a piece of canvas, moving in a very stiff breeze. He was on his back and could feel a slab of wood beneath him. One brief effort to get up was enough. A hot bolt of pain stabbed upwards from his right knee to the middle of his groin. It was so bad that, for several seconds, he did not even notice the pinching sensation in his wrists. He became aware of the pinching about the same time he realized that neither arm would move more than a few inches. They were shackled on either side of him. It took at least a minute after he woke up before he was aware that that he was in a canvas-topped wagon. He struggled and again brought on the pain in his right leg, this time accompanied by a shock of cold air on his body. He realized that he was naked, covered by a blanket that he had dislodged in the struggle. A jerk of his arms made the shackles clang angrily. The echo from the clanging had not died when he saw a light approach the wagon.

"Easy there. Easy there," a voice, high-pitched but male, called from behind the light. For a moment, Tree thought the voice was talking to a fractious horse instead of himself.

The light was at the end of the wagon nearest his head before Hooker saw the face. A young black man. He looked down at Tree and flashed a smile that was too wide for the circumstances. Again, like training horses. It was the same sort of smile Tree used when he tried to reassure a skittish horse.

"Wall, I win the bet," the young black said. "Ol' Jacob didn't think you were goin' come 'round. I knew Doc Elliston better. He tole me to watch. That you were goin' pull out o' this."

Tree looked up at the black and then down the length of his own body. Bandages and towels were wrapped around his right knee, which looked as if it had a 12-pound cannonball stuck to it. Again looking up, he opened his mouth. The black stopped him from talking by holding up a hand.

"Don't strain your lungs talkin'. You want to know what happened to you. Wall, you nearly drowned. 'Pears like you'll be all right. At least 'cept for that leg. Looks like your hoss took you on some ride without you bein' in the saddle. Doc says somethin's inside your knee there come loose. The only way you'll ever get back together is to keep still." The voice still sounded full of false assurances, but at least the smile had faded.

"You want to know where you're at. It's Pilatka. You want to know who I am. Private Jesse Stowe, U.S. Army, late o' the Thirty-fifth Colored Troops. Now orderly to Doctor Major Elliston o' the Seventh Connecticut Infantry. We're part o' a detachment that's holed up here awhiles."

Stowe produced a canteen from beneath the wagon and began soaking the towels around Tree's knee. "Doc says to keep this as cool 'n' wet as possible. Cut down the swellin' thataway. You want to know where your clothes are. They're in a boilin' pot. Half a swamp was soaked into 'em. You'll get 'em back in the mornin'. Boots too. Trust me on that. I got 'em hid. Like a drink?"

Hooker nodded. Stowe climbed into the wagon and reached over until he could put the canteen to the prisoners' lips. Tree took several gulps and then nodded again when Stowe asked, "Enough?"

Stowe crawled out of the wagon. "I'll bring you 'nother blanket for the night. You also want to know what's goin' to happen to you. But damned if I know that. You belong to some major in a Yankee cavalry outfit passin' through town. Reckon what happens to you is up to him. Get some sleep. See you in the mornin'."

When Tree managed to fall asleep, all he did was subject himself to uneasy dreams that bordered on nightmares. He was grateful when dawn came and he would not be expected to sleep. He was even more grateful when Stowe arrived with a bundle that proved to be his clothes and boots. "Got your boots here, like I promised," the private said, holding the boots, heels first toward Hooker's face. "Sorry. One o' the Yankee cavalry got the spurs. "Didn't promise you nothin' 'bout the spurs."

The right legs in the underdrawers and trousers had been slit, to allow them to be pulled over the swollen knee. Before he was allowed to dress, Tree was taken out of the shackles and led, with a blanket wrapped around him, to an outhouse. Stowe had to help him sit down over the hole and held on to one of his arms to keep him balanced while he used the privy. Tree felt like some calf in a pen, being watched to see if it was old enough to properly eat and digest grass. The private helped him back to the wagon, got him dressed and then fastened the shackles back on the wrists. One end of each shackle was attached to iron supports under the seat of the wagon. There was enough slack in the chains to allow the prisoner to keep his hands at his sides and to move a foot or two in either direction. It was about as comfortable a position as possible in which to be shackled. But, still, shackles were shackles.

"Are these really necessary?" Tree asked as Stowe turned the key in the locks of the iron cuffs. "I'm sure not runnin' anywheres."

Stowe smiled. "Orders. You're a prisoner. 'Member? Look at the bright side. Least ways nobody's fixin' to sell you."

He walked off, returning in a few minutes with two biscuits and a hunk of salt pork on a wooden tray. He put the tray down beside Tree's right hand and watched the prisoner eat. A deep, metallic boom sounded off to one side of the ambulance. It was not a gunshot or thunder. Tree jumped, rattling the chains. Stowe giggled. "That's the bell in the Episcopal Church. Don't ask me why, but when this place was occupied, somebody took the bell down and put it in an aisle. We've been using the church for a stable. The bell makes a pretty good hitchin' post, but ever'time a horse kicks it, it makes that sound."

The clip-clop of a walking horse came from behind the private. He turned and saluted. Tree could see a blue-clad officer leading a horse. The officer returned the salute and Stowe stepped to one side, out of the prisoner's sight.

The officer's blue slouch-hatted head popped into the end of the wagon. "Major Daniel Greenley," he said.

Tree held out his right hand and rattled the chain

of the shackle. "Can't salute."

Greenley nodded. "Don't worry. The doctor tells me you're fit for travel. We're goin' to St. Augustine. Then we'll decide what to do with you."

By then, other soldiers were walking around the yard near the ambulance. Most led horses. Two of them each led two mules and hitched them to the ambulance. Nobody talked to the prisoner, even as some of them entered the wagon and packed supplies around his body. Then, with a rattling jolt that bumped his head against the side of the wagon, the patrol started. Hooker watched out the rear of the ambulance as it went through what was left of Pilatka.

He often drove cattle to the town, but never really felt comfortable in it. It was perched on one of the highest banks along the St. Johns and was a stop for every boat. For some reason, even though it started as just another fort during the Indian wars, Pilatka quickly developed a genteel gloss unlike any place he had been in before Vicksburg. It was part cow-town, part gathering spot for quality people, and part supply depot for plantation owners. The divided nature of the town was reflected in an ongoing feud over how to spell its name. It was similar to the Enterprize-Enterprise argument, except that it did not stem from an honest misspelling. Some Pilatka residents wanted to change the "i" to a third "a" because they feared folks would confuse their town with Picolata. That was another hamlet, which catered to rivermen, cow hunters, and small farmers, a few miles down river.

Tree's attitude toward Pilatka stemmed partially from a wedding he once attended in the town. The wedding was held in what had been St. Marks, the church now being used as a stable. A daughter of a steamboat captain was marrying the son of a plantation owner. The captain frequently had hauled cattle and freight for Hooker and, for some reason, felt compelled to invite him. In fact, invitations were sent to about every Cracker with whom the captain had done business. The result was a guest list that must have given the vapors to the groom's mother. About 20 cow hunters, most of them chaffing from high starched collars and frock coats usually worn only twice a year for Christmas and Easter church services, were squeezed into a smokehouse-sized balcony at the rear of the church, a place usually reserved for slaves. The reception consisted of the captain buying drinks for the cow hunters at a riverfront bar while the rest of the wedding guests were ushered off to the groom's plantation.

Among the guests who went to the plantation was a Yankee from New York who had been a congressman before moving to Florida in the '40s and becoming a judge. He moved to Pilatka about ten years ago and built the largest house in town. But he died a year after that and his widow left town when the war began.

The judge's house on the riverbank was the first building Hooker saw as the patrol began moving. The ambulance must have been parked within a few hundred yards of it. That home had been a monument to the leisure class in central Florida. Two stories of whitewashed planks with concrete columns and iron railings. Now the whitewash was fading. Lead glass windows were tinted yellow after years of not being washed. Tree saw a lone man, Stowe, leaning against a column on the front porch and watching the ambulance. The patrol passed the Episcopal church, also made of whitewashed planks but perhaps a third the size of the judge's house. Its roof peaked gracefully to the bell tower. A blue-uniformed black man stood in the middle of the wide front doorway. He held a shovel and threw manure out into the street a second after the last horse in the patrol passed the church. A few other blue uniforms walked the streets, but no civilian seemed to be in town.

Almost all the soldiers were black. That seemed fitting for Pilatka. At least half the people he usually saw on the streets had been black. The white population of the town had money to buy enough slaves to run errands for them in the heat of the day. It was the only place Tree knew of where half the town could afford to own the other half.

Now, the town was eerily quiet. Even the usual animals — dogs, cats, squirrels, and birds — seemed to have fled. The only sounds Tree heard were creaks from the ambulance springs and clip-clops from the mules' and horses' hooves. The patrol at first moved south, to a place called Horse Landing. It was a shallow stretch of the river, about 500 yards wide but with a huge sandbar in the middle that allowed animals to get their footing in midstream. Tree had often used that crossing, until Yankees came to Pilatka. After Horse Landing, the patrol turned north and the prisoner settled down into the wagon, bracing himself against the bumps that sent waves of pain up his leg from the knee.

Although the sky was blue in the east ahead of the patrol, clouds overhead seemed to stay apace with the riders. A drizzle began falling within a few hours. It gradually increased until, before nightfall, it was a steady, chill rain that hit the canvas of the ambulance with a sound like the tapping out of a march beat on a snare drum. Tree lay in the wagon, listening to the beat and wandering in and out of fitful sleep. The rain slowed the pace of the patrol, turning what should have been a day's journey into a day and a half. Sometime during the night, while the patrol camped at least a dozen miles southwest of St. Augustine, Tree began to feel as if ice water had been injected into the joints of his elbows, fingers, and knees, particularly the injured one. He knew what was coming. Soon, a burning sensation moved into the joints and the cold was crowded out into his muscles. He began shivering, the two blankets doing nothing to warm him.

Greenley was in his bedroll near the ambulance. A sound woke him — the creaking of the ambulance's springs. The wagon was rocking back and forth. He unrolled from his blankets and looked inside. The prisoner was shaking, his face a deep red and shining with sweat. Greenley reached in a hand and felt Tree's forehead. It was as hot as the handle on a tin cup filled with fresh coffee. "Ague?" the Major asked.

Tree was slipping into a fever dream, but he still had enough wits to hear the question and nod his head. He was off into the dream, cuddling Laura and talking about building a home near Enterprize, by the time Greenley said, "Nothin' much we can do here. Hang on. We'll try gettin' you fixed up as soon as we hit St. Augustine."

Fever dreams are something like marriages. They join memories of the distant and recent past and give birth to new realities. At various times over the next several days, Tree was: frantically trying to finish construction of a huge, two-story home on the banks of the St. Johns before his and Laura's wedding in the Pilatka church; being sold at auction to Greenley by Stowe; and trying to swim the St. Johns while a horse danced on his back. Occasionally, a very bitter taste in his mouth intruded on his dreams. The taste became a burning sensation in his throat. It was almost as bad as vomiting bile. But the burning quickly faded and then a comfortable warmth spread through his body.

The worst part of a fever dream is waking. That is when reality has to be sorted out from the fictions that the fever branded into the mind. Tree felt an arm under his head. Laura? He opened his eyes and waited for them to focus. No, not Laura. Brown eyes were looking into his. Stowe? No. The eyelashes were too long and the brows too thin. They belonged to a woman. A liquid went into his mouth, followed by the bitter taste and the burning sensation. Quinine. The woman, the taste, and the sensation then all were reality. He still was lying on his back, but he could not feel the wood of the wagon bed. Instead, he felt something rustle under him as he shifted his weight. It was the straw filling of a mattress. He moved his arms. They were free of shackles.

"Ah. Welcome back." The woman spoke just above a whisper.

"Do I know you?" Tree was trying, without success, to move his head enough to see all of the woman's face.

The woman gradually slipped her hand from under his head, easing it back onto the mattress. "No. I'm Doris Brava. I'm a friend o' Major Greenley. He asked me to check on you a couple times a day 'n' dose you with quinine."

Tree's mind was returning. "Thanks, Ma'am. Reckon this is St. Augustine."

"Yep. The best room in Fort Marion. It's also the only room. Leastwise, the only one with anybody livin' in it. Your hosts fixed it up special for you."

Doris had been kneeling on a cushion by the prisoner's cot. She arose, taking up the cushion with her, and walked to a door, made of thick wooden planks with iron bands. She knocked once and the door swung outward within seconds. Light from outside silhouetted her in the doorway. She nodded toward the cot and stepped through into the light. The door made a thumping sound as it closed. Hooker looked around him. The room was no more than a dozen feet across in either direction and maybe seven feet tall. Light came from a small fireplace in one wall and from a narrow slit of a window directly above his cot. But neither the fireplace nor the window could do much to relieve the shady gloom or the damp coolness that seemed to ooze out of the coquina walls.

Tree sighed, drew the blankets up to his chin and closed his eyes. He knew he should be worried about being a prisoner. But he was too weak and tired to really care.

# 21

AFTER BRINGING IN HIS PRISONER and reporting on his fight, Greenley felt as if he had gone fishing and returned with a 20-pound carp. Nice to brag about. But ugly to look at and foul-tasting to eat. Good for nothing. The problem of getting rid of it was not worth the pleasure of showing off the catch. Nobody in St. Augustine was any more appreciative of the idea of keeping Tree alive than Brockton had been. Even Doris asked, "Why don't you bring in a rattler next time 'n' make a pet of it?"

It was only after he talked her into nursing the prisoner that Greenley began to have his own doubts. After her first trip to the fort with quinine, Doris took too readily to the job for Greenley's taste. She talked too much about Tree's slow improvement and sounded too sympathetic when she complained about the dampness of the cell. But Dan said nothing to her. He knew that to question or complain would only open him up to accusations of jealousy. Totally justifiable accusations, he privately admitted.

Colonel Holmes was downright surly about having an injured prisoner of war on his hands. For a while, Holmes toyed with the idea of hanging Tree as either a spy or an outlaw because he was fighting without a proper uniform. Greenley successfully argued that, with the Southern textile industry in ruins, there were no Confederates in proper uniforms on any field of combat.

Several days after Hooker was brought in, the Brocktons arrived in town with a few hundred of the confiscated cattle. At first, Otto egged on the kill-him-or-keep-him controversy by telling Holmes of the wasted chance to get rid of Tree on the riverbank. Then, he inadvertently mollified the colonel with a share of the cattle sale. Greenley never knew how much these transactions brought either his commanding officer or his scout. But, within hours of the cattle sale, Holmes was talking about taking leave and going back to Boston for the holidays. Before the sale, the colonel had groused that he could not afford to travel to Amelia Island for a planned officers' New Year's Eve party.

The rain that followed Greenley's patrol into St. Augustine brought a taste of real cold. At first, Greenley welcomed the sight of his breath when he stepped outside in the morning and the smell of the woodsmoke from every chimney in town. But his excitement at the approach of winter soon faded. Since last year, he had forgotten how miserable chilly weather, even when it was above freezing, could be when living in a humid climate next to an ocean. Moisture in the air soaked through any coat within a few hours. Greenley went for what should have been a pleasant five-mile ride and returned chilled to the bone. He handed over the horse to a stable orderly and hurried to the stove in his quarters. There, he peeled off the soaked clothes, set them on the stove to dry, and poured a stiff shot of brandy. After the stove did its work on his clothes, he dressed and trotted to the bakery.

Most of the natives stayed huddled in their homes during the cold snap. Except for Doris, who was even more sprightly than usual. When Dan entered the bakery, she was sitting in a rocker in front of the open doors of the ovens. "It's times like these that I'm glad for this job," she said.

The cold lasted less than a week. Greenley again rode patrols and was comfortable in either a light jacket or his shirtsleeves. Doris reported that Tree improved as soon as the weather warmed. Soon, the prisoner was limping about the room. Instead of quinine, Doris started supplying him with books and, occasionally, food. But, to Greenley's unspoken relief, her visits became less and less frequent as Hooker became healthier.

During the first week of November, Greenley, like most other bluecoats, voted to reelect Lincoln. The president won handily — thanks in part to Sherman's taking Atlanta and other Union victories within a few months before the election.

Lincoln, supposedly to celebrate the military, not political, victories, proclaimed the last Thursday of the month to be a national day of Thanksgiving.

Lincoln's proclamation formalizd an unofficial harvest festival that had been celebrated off and on in many states. New Englanders, including Greenley's troopers, were particularly fond of it. They usually tried to have a banquet sometime during November to commemorate the Pilgrims' success in colonizing the Northeast. Having the president set aside a specific day and give his personal approval for the celebration seemed to add zest to this year's festival.

Greenley helped his men plan the feast. He sent out patrols to hunt wild turkeys and ducks. The patrols came back with what obviously were honestly killed wild fowl. But many troopers also returned with what probably were the spoils from chicken coops and barnyards.

No matter where the birds came from, there was enough meat by the Tuesday before the celebration to give Greenley a turkey of his own. He brought it to Doris, who baked it along with a variety of side dishes.

After he arrived at Doris's, an idea came to him. "There's more here than we can ever eat. Why don't we take some to our Rebel friend in the fort?"

He didn't know what made him think of that. It was as if sympathy for the prisoner entered his brain as he breathed in the aroma of the food.

So, Greenley and Doris went to Tree's cell. They took two wicker baskets — one for the guard and one for the prisoner — with them.

"Thanksgivin'?" Tree sounded sarcastic and the left corner of his lips started to pull up in a sneer. He looked around the cell.

Suddenly, both his mouth and his voice softened. "Come to think of it, least I'm alive when I've got no call to be. Maybe that's somethin' to be thankful for. Surely, I'm thankful to ya'll for thinkin' 'bout me."

Something like a smile appeared between his moustache and the several days' growth of whiskers on his chin. He drew a blanket around his shoulders as Doris put the basket down on the cot. Tree sat down beside the basket and opened it. He made appropriately pleased and grateful comments about each bit of food as he ate. It was as if he were an invited table guest. Greenley waited for Tree to finish eating to ask, "Would you like to write your family and let them know what's happened? I'll do my best to see the letter gets through."

Another half-smile. "No. Thanks very kindly for the thought. Don't have any near relations 'round here. Word o' mouth should've let my friends know by now."

Tree steered the talk to other subjects, repeatedly thanking Doris for her nursing and asking for the loan of a needle and thread to sew up the slits in his trousers' and underdrawers' legs. He asked where Greenley was from, talked about the income and workload of milling, compared milling as a livelihood to cow hunting and farming, and predicted that another cold spell would hit before Christmas and sweeten the orange crop. All of it was like polite dinner conversation. And, strangely, that unnerved the major. The only thing close to war talk came when Tree, for the fourth or fifth time, complimented Doris on the turkey. She, for the fourth or fifth time, again credited Greenley with the idea of bringing the meal to the fort.

"We knew you'd be awful hungry in here," she said.

Tree shook his head. His smile twisted downward and to the right, into something like the snarl of a dog. "But this ain't been real hunger. I found out 'bout real hunger in Vicksburg."

That word struck Greenley like a fist in the chest.

Blood rushed to his head, making his face uncomfortably warm. "Oh, Christ," he breathed out the words. "You were there?"

Hooker nodded. He looked quizzically at the major. "From the way you look, you were too. I got out two days before ya'll came in. Wasn't pretty, was it?"

Greenley shook his head. "How'd you get out?"

The sneer straightened out, but the smile did not return. Tree's voice was like a teacher's explaining an arithmetic problem. "A few o' us were put on detached duty to start the Cattle Guard. Me 'n' a captain snuck out the night o' the second. Took us days to get out o' the Vicksburg area. Matter o' fact, we spent most o' the fourth in a briar thicket on a ridge watchin' ya'll march into town. Took most o' the next three months to travel east. Dodgin' ya'lls patrols 'bout every other mile."

A few minutes more of small talk and then Greenley and Doris left. When they walked out of the fort, the sun was a red line above the riverbank. Shadows darkened the streets. A private, his blue uniform blending into the shadows until all that could be seen were his hands and his head, lighted street lamps. He was the only person the pair met on their way back to the bakery. Neither of them talked as they walked into the house.

Dan's sleep that night was dreamless. But, before dawn, he was jerked awake as suddenly as if someone had blown reveille at the bedside. He sat up, slightly frightened, unsure of what had awakened him and unable to return to sleep. From somewhere outside a whippoorwill called. Peaceful. Maybe too peaceful. Guilt overwhelmed him.

Why should he feel at peace with the rest of the country going up in flames? Why should he eat his fill when there were places like Vicksburg? Why should he be in love and happy when hundreds of thousands of lovers were torn apart? Why should he be doing any of this — sleeping, eating, and falling in love — when about the only other satisfied creatures on earth seemed to be the buzzards that fed off the carrion of the battlefields?

No use trying to go back to sleep, Greenley decided. He dressed and walked through the predawn darkness to Doris's bakery. After her bout with ague, she had given him a key to the building. He used it to enter. The glow from embers in a potbellied stove near the oven guided him as he made a pot of coffee. Doris, wrapped in a blue robe, entered the building about the time the eastern horizon was turning pink from the rising sun.

"To what do I owe the honor of havin' coffee made for me? Nice change. For sure."

Reveille echoed through the streets from the direction of the barracks as Dan poured a cup and handed it to her. He sipped from his and waited for the sound of the bugle to die before replying.

"Couldn't sleep. Somethin's botherin' me and I just figured out what it was. Never mind that. Once this war is over, would you like to see Ohio?"

The dark eyes gleamed above the rim of the cup as Doris took her first swallow. "What's in Ohio? Mighty cold there."

"Oh, but it's a dry cold. Real easy to stay warm during the night. Just need to be a couple."

# 22 🌾

A FEW HOURS LATER, as he was mounting his horse to lead a squad in drills, Greenley discovered that he was, for the first time, a commanding officer. Holmes walked over to the stables and announced that he was going on furlough. He would be aboard a Boston-bound ship that was leaving the next high tide. The major was put in charge of the post until Holmes returned sometime after the New Year.

Assuming the colonel's duties actually did little to change Greenley's work schedule. However, it confirmed his suspicion that Holmes did virtually nothing. The work consisted of signing such papers as the post's log and the guard schedule. Greenley wondered whether Holmes had been a heavy drinker before getting command of St. Augustine. If he hadn't been, boredom probably drove him to the bottle.

Most of Greenley's time still was spent with either Doris or Mac. He also found himself frequently going to the fort and talking with the prisoner for an hour or so at a time.

"When do you figure to send me to a prison camp?" Tree asked during one session, abruptly ending the small talk between them.

The major shrugged his shoulders. "Probably after the New Year. Let you stay here and get your strength up a while longer. Then we'll take you to Fort Clinch and let them ship you north."

Hooker's half-smile, half-sneer twisted his lips. "Good idea to wait. Havin' people escort me to Clinch surely would spoil their holidays."

Greenley realized he was being challenged. "Oh? You think it'd be that hard a job?"

The right side of the prisoner's mouth curved upward, creating more of a smile. "Sixty miles 'tween here 'n' there. Hell o' a lot can happen in that distance. I like you, Major. Don't you or anybody you like try takin' me. I'm serious as the cholera."

Greenley let the threat pass and soon forgot it as he began to be infected by the Christmas spirit. Doris could take most of the credit. Her bakery continually smelled of gingerbread and cinnamon. The aroma wafted out into the yard and into her house. It was an incense that made Dan think of decorated trees and stockings on the mantle.

He took a buggy ride with Doris west into the woods to gather mistletoe. One large clump nestled in an oak at least 30 feet off the ground. Greenley climbed to it, his boots repeatedly slipping on the bark and causing him to hug the trunk. Eventually, he reached the clump, cut it loose with his saber, and returned to the ground, scraping the buttons off his uniform jacket when he slid down several feet. "A dozen battles and then I almost get killed by this," he said as he handed her the clump and his jacket flapped in the breeze.

It later proved to be worth the risk. Doris hung sprigs of the mistletoe above each doorway in her home and bakery. Greenley was hit with kisses — ranging from sisterly pecks in the bakery to long, passionate embraces outside the bedroom — anytime he moved around her.

Doris was spared the trauma of having to plan and execute a Christmas Eve dinner when Dan again accepted Mac's invitation to Miss Fatio's. But the news of the invitation didn't please Doris as much as Greenley had expected. Instead, it sent her off on a flurry of fabric hunting and sewing. She decided to tear up three other dresses, one white, one red, and one green, and use the scraps to create a party gown. When she wasn't putting something in or out of an oven or waiting on a customer, she was sitting in the bakery rocker, sewing together strips of fabric. The sewing was accompanied by constant grumbles about three weeks not being enough advance notice of the dinner party.

Then, five days before Christmas, Tree's prediction of another cold spell came true. Temperatures kept decreasing until Christmas Eve morning, when ice formed in the water trough outside the stables. It was a paper-thin covering over the water and had melted within a couple hours after sunrise. Still, it was the first ice Greenley had seen since arriving in Florida. As he poked his finger through it, he felt as if he were greeting an old friend from home.

Sunset brought a promise of more ice. Dan felt the cold pricking his cheeks as he walked Doris from her home to Miss Fatio's. The cold made the inside of the boardinghouse more than usually welcoming. Heat from the diningroom fireplace radiated out into the entrance hallway. Greenley unbuttoned his greatcoat and handed it to the younger servant. Doris had worn a black overcoat that covered her to her ankles. Her work over the last three weeks slowly was revealed as she unbuttoned the coat. First there was the tan of her neck and shoulders. Another button showed about four inches of white lace, pirated from the trim of an old tablecloth. The lace crossed her shoulders and chest, allowing only a slight glimpse of her cleavage. Two more buttons and the red bodice of the dress came into view. Then, as she undid the rest of the buttons and Greenley peeled the coat off her, the whole of the dress was unveiled. It flowed from her 18-inch waist out to at least four feet across at the hem. An old work dress of linsey-woolsey, a coarse weave of cotton and wool threads, was used for the bodice and red stripes. Two other dresses contributed the white and green stripes. Both of those dresses were made of bengaline, a weave of silk and wool that was twisted into cord. Red stripes were sewn between the green and white. The combination of the two fabrics made each stripe stand out in sharp contrast to its neighbor. It was a striking dress, but, considering its colors and the heavy, warm materials that went into it, Dan wondered if Doris ever would wear it to anything other than a Christmas party.

She gave the correct smiles and nods in returns for the polite compliments paid her and the dress as she glided from the entranceway to the sitting room, where the older servant poured steaming ladles of spiced rum and heated wine into mugs and glasses.

As the party guests finished their before-dinner drinks, a skiff on the river neared the docks. The riverfront was deserted except for two privates on sentry duty. They watched the skiff, its white sail gleaming in the bright moonlight. Such boats were common enough sights on the rivers and bays. Sometimes, they ventured out into the deep ocean. They were 12 to 15 feet long, with narrow, flat-bottomed hulls no more than four feet wide. Usually, they had only one sail and several pairs of oars. The skiffs were favored by oystermen, flounder fishermen, and others who needed to travel in shallow water or over barely submerged reefs and sandbars.

The sentries stood next to each other as the skiff approached. Dark shadows of three figures could be seen moving about the boat. Its sail lowered on the mast and oars splashed in the water, drawing the boat still closer to the docks. One of the sentries, taller than his companion and with yellow hair that hung limply down his neck, decided to yell out a challenge. But, before he could speak, a resonant bass voice shouted from somewhere beneath the mast. "Hello the pier. Ya'll want oysters with Christmas dinner? Got dozens o' 'em for a good price."

The taller sentry looked to his right and down at his shorter, dark-haired companion. They nodded at each other. "Come on in," the taller one called. "Let's see what you've got."

Oars splashed several more times and then the skiff glided up to the end of the dock, where both sentries were kneeling. Their rifles lay beside them, The taller one stuck an arm toward the skiff. He expected somebody in the boat to extend either an arm or an oar to him so he could help pull the skiff flush against the pier. Instead, something long and slender jumped out, like a cottonmouth striking at its prey, from the darkness in the boat. The thing wrapped around the tall sentry's arm. He tried to jerk away, but the thing only tightened its grip. It yanked him by his arm into the water. He felt a moment of numbing pain as the cold water engulfed his body and flowed into his mouth. Then arms hauled him out and into the skiff. He blinked the burning of the salty water from his eyes and saw the barrel of a revolver resting against his nose. Three clicks, which sounded so loud to him that they seemed to echo across the harbor, announced that the gun's hammer was cocked.

"Listen good, boy." It was the same bass voice that had called from the boat. It now came from behind the gun barrel. "You've got a rebel prisoner here?"

The sentry nodded.

"Where?"

After swallowing and choking down a mouthful of salty water, the sentry was able to say: "Room in the old fort."

A hand out of the darkness of the boat unwrapped the slender thing from the sentry's arm. He glanced down and saw that the thing was a leather whip. The gun barrel was removed from his nose, with three clicks telling him that the revolver had been uncocked. A bulky figure in front of him moved, rocking the boat. The sentry risked looking behind him. His companion still was kneeling at the end of the dock. The dark-haired sentry's arms were raised. Coils from another whip were wrapped around his neck. A short, reed-thin man in dark clothes stood by him. In one hand, the man held the handle to the whip that was coiled around the kneeling sentry's neck. The other hand held a revolver pointed at the coils of the whip.

The bass voice came from the bulky figure. "Skeeter. Room in the old fort. Can your man find it?"

A much higher-pitched voice came from the thin man. "Can you?" The kneeling sentry nodded.

Both the little man and the big man kept their voices slightly above whispers. "Okay," the bass voice spoke to the tall sentry. "You stay here. You'd catch your death walkin' in the cold air."

The big man moved, again rocking the boat. He picked something up from the bench on which he sat. He held the thing — a blanket — out to the sentry. "Get yourself as dry 'n' warm as you can. We'll let you go in a bit. Just think of yourself as passin' by all this. No real concern of yours. 'Member: 'He that passeth by, 'n' meddleth with strife belongin' not to him is like one that taketh a dog by the ears.' Proverbs, twenty-six: seventeen."

He looked behind him and spoke toward the stern of the boat. "Volusia, take him over to the island."

Another rocking of the skiff came as the big man leaned forward and reached above the tall sentry to grasp the end of the dock. His breath came in short groans and grunts as he pulled himself out of the boat. When he left, the tall sentry could see a third man in the stern, an arm on the boat's tiller. That man turned the tiller, pulled a lanyard rope to hoist the sail and then tugged at a pair of oars. The skiff headed south.

Looking behind him, the tall sentry saw his companion standing between the other two men. The big man had a gun belt around his neck and a long piece of gray cloth over one shoulder. The smaller man picked up the two sentries' rifles and pitched them into the water.

Smoke from the fireplace weighed on Tree's eyes and he began to doze as he lay on his cot. He was dimly aware of a guard outside the door giving the usual "Halt. Who goes there?" challenge. A mummer of more than two voices could be heard replying to the guard. The guard made a grunting noise. Tree thought little of the exchange outside the door until he heard the key turn in the lock. Then a booming sound, almost as loud and sharp as a gunshot, rang out when the door was kicked back on its hinges. That was followed by a shouted "Merry Christmas" from Heavy and Skeeter.

Something gray flew across the room, Tree caught it and saw it was his swallow-tailed coat.

"Put it on," Heavy said. "It's a cold night for a ride. But we're fixin' to go on one."

He took the gunbelt from around his neck and laid it on the cot. Tree picked up the belt and cinched it around his waist. The holster on the right side held the Colt .44 Army Model that he had stored along with the coat and most of his other possessions in Volusia's wagon. A Bowie knife was in a sheath on the left.

"Sorry 'bout your old Walker's Colt," Skeeter said. "It's still at the bottom of the creek."

He and Heavy both had their revolvers out and pointed at two soldiers. Hooker recognized one as the black private who had been guarding him. The other one was a short, dark-haired white man. Both looked scared. Heavy threw the guard's rifle into the room as Tree drew his own revolver. The three armed men and their two blue-coated companions then quietly walked across the fort grounds, over the drawbridge and out the gate. Tree covered his gray coat by draping the blanket from his cot over and around his shoulders. He took the black slouch hat off his guard and put it on his head.

It was only a few hundred yards from the fort gate to the stables, but it was the longest distance Tree had covered in nearly two months. A burning ache started in his knee and he could feel something moving inside the joint, behind the kneecap. He began limping as he tried to keep up with the rest.

The five didn't meet, let alone get challenged by, anyone until they came to the cavalry private guarding the stables. That trooper wasn't able to get the word "Halt" out of his mouth before a revolver poked him in the ribs. Skeeter held the gun while Tree undid the flap on the cavalryman's holster and lifted out the handgun. Another Colt Army .44. "Might as well start a collection of these," Hooker said as he stuck the revolver in his belt.

Skeeter appropriated the cavalryman's carbine. He put it in a scabbard as he collected the three least-worn saddles in the stable. Peering into each stall and checking the corral outside, he searched for the best horses.

Heavy kept his revolver trained on the three Yankees while Hooker cut a four-inch-wide strip down the length of his blanket. He divided the strip into six pieces. Slinging those pieces over his shoulders, he rummaged around the stable until he found a length of rope. At a wave of Tree's hand, Heavy brought the Yankees over to a line of stalls. Tree cut three pieces of the rope and used them to tie the hands of the Yankees to the frames of a stall. He stuffed a piece of blanket into each mouth and secured the gags with the other pieces.

"Try to be comfortable as possible," Tree told them. "Hope somebody comes along afore daylight 'n' finds you."

He and Heavy walked out to the corral, where Skeeter had three horses saddled.

"Before we leave, I'd like to look around town a bit," Tree said as he mounted. "Want to see if I can find some old friends."

"Brocktons?" Heavy asked.

"Yeah."

Greenley's half hour before dinner was spent mostly sipping a hot, spiced rum and listening to Captain Nathan Collier predict when and how the war would end.

"Gah-ant has Petersburg in his grip. If Shah-man isn't in Savannah now, he will be in days. The whole South is ours for the askeen," Collier whined in New Englandese identical to Holmes's accent. If the voice hadn't sounded younger, Greenley could have closed his eyes and believed that his commander had returned.

Collier came by the accent honestly. He was born in Salem, Massachusetts, near Holmes's Boston. Collier and witchcraft or, least, witchcraft trials, were the only things Greenley knew of that came from Salem. Didn't speak very well for the town.

The captain still was in his early 20s. Gold braid and brass gleamed on his uniform in the light from the lamps and the fireplace. He was the only officer at the party to come in the full dress uniform, complete with sword and holstered sidearm. Collier had a round, fresh face that apparently couldn't grow any whiskers. He made up for the lack of facial hair by allowing his light brown mane to grow down to his shoulders. It was a style becoming increasingly popular among junior officers. Federals were trying to imitate George Custer, a long-haired cavalry officer who figured prominently in the Battle of Gettysburg. Confederates were aping the hairstyle of George Pickett, whose name also was attached to the Gettysburg fight. Greenley frequently wondered what would happen to one of these hirsute fashion plates in a place like the trenches outside Vicksburg, where lice seemed to form a nation of their own and dedicated themselves to around-the-clock feasting.

Lice-infested trenches didn't seem to be in Collier's future. He had been a second lieutenant at a supply depot in his home town for about a year. Then, several months ago, the government offered promotions to junior officers and noncommissioned officers who volunteered to lead newly formed black regiments. Collier volunteered, became a captain, and immediately was sent to St. Augustine as part of the occupying force.

Every other officer in the sitting room had at least seen a battleground. And Greenley noticed that none of them seemed to be paying much attention to what Collier was saying. His discourse was particularly annoying since he said nothing that hadn't been repeatedly printed over the last month in every newspaper not published by a rabid secessionist. Anyone setting out to be a genuine pompous ass at least should be a pompous ass with his own, original ideas, the major thought. All parroting the ideas of others does is create an artificial pompous ass.

Still, Collier seemed to have a rapt audience. A young, willowy blond in a green silk dress hung on to the captain's arm and, judging from the way she stared up at his face, his every word. Most of the other women in the room also seemed intent upon watching him. Dan noticed with pride that Doris was not one of those. She sat on the fainting couch, her lips occasionally touching her wine glass, seldom even looking at the young captain. Her eyes scanned the room, taking in the furniture, the drapes and the dresses of the other women. Greenley noticed that Collier, as if in revenge for not getting Doris's attention, seldom looked at anyone or anything else but her.

Miss Fatio broke up Collier's lecture with the call "Ladies and gentlemen, dinner is served." Everybody filed into the dining room.

Mac was seated at the head of the table. Greenley was seated at the other end. Doris was at his right elbow. Mac had brought a rather plump woman with reddish brown hair who was seated beside him. Miss Fatio and her sister were seated in the first two chairs on the right side of the table. Their nieces and nephews were at a table in the far corner of the room. The rest of the officers were arranged down both sides of the table, each seated next to the woman he had escorted.

The older servant entered from the side door,

carrying a tray with the china tureen on it. She put it on a sideboard, a small table near Mac's right elbow. Mac lifted the lid. An unmistakable aroma of oyster stew, the briny tang of the oysters mixed with the homey scent of warm milk, wafted through the room. The servant laded the yellowish white stew into bowls, which then were passed down the table. Miss Fatio picked up her soup spoon, the signal for the rest of the party to start. Greenley was savoring the first spoonful. It wasn't quite hot enough to burn his tongue. Still, it was so warm that he forgot the chill of the night. It had enough black pepper in it to offset the blandness of the milk. He spooned up some more, making sure that this time he had an oyster in it.

Concentrating on the stew, he barely heard and paid no attention to the sound of footsteps on the porch. Boarders who had decided to eat elsewhere that night, he thought. His back was to the main door and he did not even sense that anyone was coming through it. Mac was the only person in the room to have a good view of the main door. Greenley thought of nothing except the taste of the stew until he heard Mac, in a hoarse, strained whisper, rasp out: "Oh my God."

The weird tone of the voice drew everybody's eyes to Mac, who was staring at the main door like a rabbit transfixed by a rattlesnake. Greenley turned his head and, instinctively, started to rise.

"Sorry to interrupt. Ya'll keep calm." Tree's voice had became familiar enough to Greenley that he identified it even before he turned. But then, something else entered the voice. An almost canine growl when it ordered: "No sudden moves."

A hissing sound filled the room — the collective gasps from everybody at the table. Greenley slowly got to his feet. There were three men in the doorway. All of them held revolvers just above their hips. The guns were pointed at no one in particular, but everybody in general.

Tree was in the middle, with a gun in each hand. He wore a black, wide-brimmed hat and a long gray coat. His companions each held one revolver. Both of them were dressed in dark clothes.

"We've got nothin' agin any o' ya'll," Tree said as his eyes shifted across the room. "Lookin' for some friends o' yours we thought might be 'round here."

One of his companions, who looked tiny and frail next to the height of Tree and the bulk of the third man, walked backward for two steps and turned into the guest sitting room. Greenley heard the hinge creak on the humidor. The small man returned with a fistful of cigars and one dangling from his mouth. "Christmas present from 'em to us," he said, putting all but one of the cigars into his coat pocket. He took the cigar that had been in his mouth and, reaching up, stuck it in Tree's. Then he bit off the ends of the other cigar and put that one into his own mouth. Greenley didn't need to look over to Miss Fatio to know that she winced as the small man spat the cigar ends on the floor.

The small man took a lamp from the table by the door. He used its flame to light his cigar and then Tree's. Burning tobacco outweighed the aroma of the stew in the room.

"Those that we're lookin' for ain't here," Tree said. "So, ya'll take care."

As he and his companions backed out of the room, Tree nodded in Doris's direction. "Lovely gown, ma'am. Thanks agin for everythin'."

Another nod, this time towards Greenley. "My compliments, Major. Thanks for your courtesies."

At that moment, Collier kicked back his chair. He shouted "What the hell is go-een on?" and fumbled with the clasp of his holster flap.

The roar of the gun was almost drowned out by the screams of the women and children. A cloud of black gunsmoke mixed with the blue wisps from the cigars. A shriller scream cut through the rest of the noise. It came from Collier. He thrashed on the floor, clasping his right knee with both hands.

Tree, smoke still rising from the barrel of the gun in his left hand, continued backing out of the room, moving in step with his two companions. Greenley, despite the ringing in his ears from the shot and the general tumult in the room, heard Hooker say "Knee for a knee."

Red liquid spurted between the fingers of Collier's hands as he held the knee to his chest. Miss Fatio, the pallor of her skin coming through the rouge on her cheeks, watched the captain for a moment. Then, her head jerked about on her shoulders as if she were being slapped by an invisible hand.

"Blood! Oh, heavens, he's bleeding!" Her scream drove out all the other sounds in the room. "Stop him! Stop him! He'll get it on the seat cushions! The table-cloth! The floor! Oh, somebody stop him!"

# 23 ✺

THE SHOOTING OF COLLIER WENT DOWN in the folklore of the St. Augustine garrison as "The Battle of Fatio's Soup Tureen." It went down in Greenley's mind as an extremely deep canyon in a military career that already had more valleys than hills. He felt the blood rising into his cheeks as he wrote the official report. The report told his superior officers how a couple of untrained farmers had penetrated the town's defenses, freed a prisoner from a fortress that had not been breached in the past 200 years, and wounded a captain while almost all the rest of the garrison's officers were trying to swallow oyster stew.

But, after writing the report, Greenley thought of how much more could have gone wrong. Even Collier turned out to be lucky. The bullet had gone through the front of the knee, chipping away some of the bone as it skipped across his kneecap, and then out the other side. A major artery could have been cut. If that had happened, the captain would have bled to death as the rest of the party watched. The bullet could have lodged in the kneecap, forcing, at best, painful surgery to extract it and, probably, amputation. As it happened, the wound was clean enough that the surgeon had little more to do than sew up the holes. Collier's leg would be stiff for the rest of his life, but it still would be attached to him. On top of everything else, the wound was considered serious enough for him to be invalided out of the service.

So, Collier departed in early February. He left on the ship that brought Holmes back to St. Augustine. The colonel reacted to the incident by waging a campaign to have Collier awarded a medal. To the surprise of everyone who knew anything about the shooting, the War Department quickly agreed. Apparently, the department's decision was hurried along by the fact that the captain's father was a judge and influential in Massachusetts Republican politics.

"Probably the first man ever commended for gallantry in defending oyster stew," Mac said when the news of the medal reached St. Augustine.

Even if nobody else got any medals, at least everybody else got away more or less unscathed. The three soldiers who were tied in the stables were freed within minutes. Greenley found them when he arrived at the stable to begin a pursuit of the fugitives. He ran to get guns and men as soon as Tree and his companions left the Fatio house. A search party of at least 20 rode out within minutes of the shooting. But the searchers found no trace of their quarry.

All they discovered was a strange light glowing on an island a few miles offshore. Greenley sent several of the search party back to town to get a boat and investigate the light. It turned out to be a bonfire. The tall, blond sentry was warming himself by it when the others arrived. He was dropped off at the island by the third rebel in the skiff and together they built the fire. There really were some oysters in the boat and the third rebel roasted them. He gave the tall sentry about a dozen of them before sailing off toward the south.

The censure that the major expected from his superiors never materialized. They, and most other people who ever talked about the incident with him, laughed and sympathized more than complained and criticized. Most, that is, except the Brocktons. Greenley couldn't blame them. Tree undoubtedly would make all of them — and particularly Eric — targets. Knowing that, Greenley tried to get word to them as soon as possible. The first night, after failing to find the fugitives by sunrise, he sent part of his patrol back for supplies. He and the others pushed on south. They reached Brockton's cabin by sunset the next day.

But word of the escape got to the Brocktons ahead of the patrol. Otto was hitching a yoke of oxen to a wagon when the searchers arrived.

"Ride with us," Greenley told Otto. "That's the safest thing. They'd have to come through us to get to you. Help us get him. The quicker we find him, the better off all of us will be."

Tobacco-browned saliva dripped out of Otto's mouth and hung in his beard as he yelled out a series of obscenities and curses. "Tree rode right through you the other night. He'll do it agin anytime he goddamn well feels like it. You're the idiot who was so tender-hearted toward the bastard. Ride 'round here 'n' give him somethin' to shoot at. If he wants me, he'll have to come lookin'. I sure as hell ain't goin' lookin' for him."

Otto finished attaching the harness to the yoke as his voice raised to a shriek. His sons rode in from the south and hitched their horses to one of the cypress fence rails of the corral.

"We're goin' cow huntin'," Martin spat out the words from the corner of his mouth as if they were quids of tobacco. "Probably ain't comin' back till we've got enough money to hire our own goddamn army 'n' fight a war our way."

In contrast to the screaming of his father and older brother, Corley sounded quiet and weary. "Just get the hell out o' here," he said, a note of resignation in his voice.

Eric said nothing. He stood by his horse, staring at the soldiers. His lips were almost white against the tan of his face. His legs trembled, and he leaned against the corral fence to steady himself.

Greenley didn't argue with the Brocktons. He couldn't, since he felt most of their anger was justified. With a wave of his hand, he had the patrol circle about and ride away from the cabin. Instead of continuing further south, he led his men north until they met the rest of the patrol returning with supplies. Then they all spent a week riding in circles between Pilatka and Enterprize. It was as fruitless as Greenley expected it to be. The palmetto scrub had reclaimed its own and would not give them up to strangers.

Despite their vows to disappear, the Brocktons were the only cow hunters that Greenley saw over the next two months. The ease of selling and shipping cattle in St. Augustine overcame their fears of being waylaid on the trail. At least the fears of Otto, Martin, and Corley. Nothing could ease, much less overcome, Eric's fear.

Every palmetto clump hid a rifleman. Someone was waiting to jump down from every oak branch. For two months, he shook every time he filled his canteen from a pool or stream. Filling a canteen required him to bend over and expose his back to the thick weeds on the shore. He kept expecting a bullet to come from those weeds.

Chole and the kids had left home and returned to her parents by the time he came back from selling the Cattle Guard's herd. He knew better than to face Heavy and try to collect her. Even if there was a prayer of getting forgiveness for the ambush, there was too good of a chance that his wife had talked about him. And even if she didn't talk, there might have been bruises that had not yet faded on her or one of the twins. And then Tree got loose.

Eric was toying with the idea of enlisting in either army. The hazards of military life paled when compared with the advantages of having thousands of armed men to hide among and to act as a shield. But he would not try to join any troops in central or northeast Florida. Too great a chance that word of the ambush had spread through the ranks. Confederates in particular could have heard of it and his part in it. If they didn't consider him a traitor and kill him themselves, somebody would spread the word to the Cattle Guard.

Tree's group also had too many friends and relatives among the civilian population for him to risk joining a Yankee unit in the occupation force. Odds favored somebody spotting him and informing. It would be too easy for a gunman to sneak up on him some night while he was on sentry duty.

Eric was beginning to believe his best chance was to start drifting up to the Tallahassee area and then west. If he was pressed into the service of either army, so be it, as long as he was far enough away from anyone who knew him.

He had spent the last two months in the palmetto scrub, hunting cattle and staying away from anybody except his father and brothers. When they drove cattle into St. Augustine, Eric would stop and camp by a freshwater creek about ten miles southwest of town. His father and brothers would finish the drive and bring him a share of the money. On the last trip, they also brought a gallon jug of corn liquor.

It had taken him three days of almost nothing but drinking and sleeping, but Eric had killed that jug. Then he started riding south, intending to join his father and brothers at the cabin and cowpen by Haw Creek. It should have been a perfect day for the ride. Sunny, but still cool enough to require a light jacket. But his hangover tormented him. The movement of the horse under him jarred his aching joints and started a rhythmic thumping in his head. His mouth and throat felt as if they were stuffed with cotton. Trying to clear them, he took long, frequent slugs from his canteen. That, in turn, forced him to stop frequently to urinate.

His canteen, which usually lasted all day in cool weather, was drained before noon. He stopped to refill it at an oak-shaded pond. It was in the middle of lowlands that would be marshes during the wet season. He climbed down from his horse and walked to the edge of the water. He cupped his hands, scooped up some of the water and sniffed it. There was a hint of sulfur, but the water did not seem to be briny or contaminated. It tasted fine when he sipped it, so he bent over and submerged his open canteen under the water.

There were rustlings in the weeds behind him and in the oak that extended a branch above his head. He thought little about the noises. Dozens, if not hundreds of birds and animals would be attracted to the pond during the dry season. But then, for a moment, the scrabbling in the oak became louder. Eric turned toward the noise in time to see something brown leap from the limb onto him.

He fell into the water and then was jerked up to the shore by the lapel of his jacket. The water cleared from his eyes and he saw the barrel of a revolver pointed at his forehead. Skeeter held the revolver.

"Get up," the little man hissed through his teeth.

Again using the jacket lapels, Skeeter yanked the taller man to his feet and then pushed to start him walking. They went on for several hundred yards. Whenever Eric tried to stop, Skeeter pushed him on, alternately using his left hand and the revolver barrel. They came to a stand of pines on a small rise of land. Tree was there, leaning against a pine, with a length of rope coiled about one shoulder. A dozen other cow hunters, all veterans of that last, aborted drive, were with him. Heavy sat on the ground with his back resting against a pine trunk.

"Didn't you figure it was gonna end this way?" Tree asked, staring at Eric.

Hooker took the rope from his shoulders flung it

at Skeeter, who drew his knife and cut a short length from it. Tying Eric's wrists behind his back, Skeeter pushed down on the prisoner, forcing him to sit on a fallen log. Tree again leaned backward on the pine trunk. His arms were folded across his chest. There was no expression in his eyes or on his face.

Eric didn't even try to keep his voice from wavering. "What are you goin' to do?" was all he managed to say.

With a shrug of his shoulders, Tree pushed himself away from the trunk. "What happens to you is gonna to be official 'n' legal. I want the whole damned world to know that. You're a traitor to the Confederate States of America. 'N' I'm the highest-rankin' Confederate hereabouts."

Heavy had kept his head down, concentrating on the toes of his boots. The position added a third chin and made him seem even bulkier and more wrinkled. His third chin disappeared as he snapped his head up and toward Tree.

"Hold it. We've taken him alive. Let's get him to the proper authorities 'n' be done with it."

A mockingbird, apparently with a nest on a limb somewhere above the group of men, shrieked a warning call that was a raspy parody of its usual song. Other birds of various kinds joined in with their own calls. Tree had to raise his voice to be heard over the chorus.

"The proper authority would be a general officer. Anybody know where one is? Tallahassee, maybe? Who feels like escortin' good ol' Eric two, three hundred miles to find somebody to set up a real court martial?"

Hooker looked around him, glaring at each hunter

in turn. Each one, except for Heavy, shook his head as Tree's gaze locked onto each pair of eyes. The preacher again looked down, burying his chin against his chest.

"I sure ain't in the mood to do that, either," Tree said. "'N' the law gives us a way out. There's somethin' called a drumhead court martial. It's 'posed to be for crimes that need punishin' when there's no time to get together officers for a regular court."

Heavy kept is head down as he replied. "Don't try teachin' me 'bout the Army. I was ridin' after Seminoles when your ma was weanin' you. 'N' I never saw a court martial, drumhead or otherwise, done without an officer. Let's try Lake City. That's no more'n a four-day ride. Maybe there's a detachment there we can hand him over to."

Mutterings, groans, and other sounds of disgust came from the group. Heavy looked up and then stood. It was his turn to lock eyes with the rest of the group. His voice grew louder and took on the sing-song cadence of his sermons.

"We're supposed to be a militia. A band o' soldiers dedicated to a cause. We ain't a lynch mob. A gang out for revenge. We seek justice. Let justice come in its own good time."

Most of the birds quieted. But the mockingbird kept up its warning shrieks. Another sound began. It was a series of pained gasps coming from Eric. The gasps increased in both volume and intensity until they sounded like retching. He was dry-eyed, but his face was wrinkled and red.

Heavy listened to the heaving and felt himself growing sick. He knew the others could accuse him of arguing just for the sake of keeping his son-in-law alive. Nobody else knew how much he wanted to see Eric die. Too much. So, he would argue against the killing for the sake of his own soul. If there was to be revenge today, he didn't want to be the one to take it.

"This ain't no court martial 'n' ya'll know it," he said. "But if ya'll are out for blood, let's get it done with."

Tree sighed. "Yeah. Might be you're right. But that really don't change things that much." He turned and looked at Eric, who had folded himself into a blubbering lump on the log.

"Damn. I'm pretty well regrettin' gettin' you alive," Tree said. His voice was flat, emotionless. He might as well have been talking about the chances of rain. "One shot 'n' we'd all be on our way by now. 'Stead, here we are arguin' over you."

Heavy decided to push the debate to its conclusion. "All right," he called out to the group. "Is anybody sidin' with me or am I wastin' my breath 'n' everybody's time?"

Nobody spoke or moved in reply. Heavy nodded and said, "Let's get it over with."

Volusia was wearing a black cotton neckerchief. He reached up, untied it and threw it to Tree. "Might as well have an official-lookin' blindfold."

Tree nodded. He went over to Eric and took hold of his right arm. Skeeter came and took the left. The two half dragged, half carried him to a patch of grass outside the shade.

"No. No. No," Eric chanted through the sobs and gasps. He started babbling incoherently after the sergeant draped the black neckerchief over his head. The neckerchief covered Eric from the crown of the head to just above his Adam's apple, which was bobbing up and down frantically. Hooker cut a bit of rope off the coil and used it to secure the neckerchief about Eric's throat

"Skeeter, Volusia, Lonesome, get your rifles." The three obeyed and went to stand by Tree, who paced off ten yards between himself and Eric. "Ya'll 'n' me are the firin' squad."

The neckerchief puffed out and deflated as Eric breathed. Sobs continued to come from under it. Then it started rolling about on his shoulders.

Everybody watched the neckerchief for what probably was seconds but seemed like an hour. Eventually, Skeeter spoke. His face had a greenish tinge, with a white outline around his lips. "You really expect us to take revenge on that?" he hissed through clenched teeth.

Tree breathed in deeply. "No. Not ya'll," he exhaled.

He drew the holstered gun with his left hand and held it at arm's length. A low moan came from the neckerchief as Tree sighted along the barrel. The explosion of the shot cut off the moaning. Screeching from dozens of birds rose above the shot's echo. Their wings flapped as they launched themselves into panicked flights. At that same instant, the neckerchief caved in above Eric's forehead.

# 24 🕮

News of Eric's death drifted northwards to St. Augustine. It took no more than three days for it to reach the streets. A fat matron brought the word into the bakery along with money and an order for two dozen rolls. Greenley was there, munching on a beef pie. He was in earshot of the woman as she told Doris that Eric's father-in-law delivered the body to Otto's cabin.

The pastry and meat stuck together into a gluey wad in Greenley's mouth. Unable to swallow, he ducked out the door and spat the wad out into the grass at the side of the shop. The woman was walking out the door as he reentered. Doris's eyes focused on his.

"Eric might as well've killed himself the minute he turned his coat," she said. "Tree gettin' out didn't make much difference. Some Rebel would've gunned him down sooner or later."

Dan knew she spoke the truth. He also had been expecting Eric's death since Tree's herd was ambushed.

The guilt that had seized him let go its hold. "Wonder if the rest of the Brocktons will feel that way," he said.

He had to wait two more weeks for an answer. Then, the Brocktons came to St. Augustine. Five strangers were with them. All five wore bits and pieces of uniforms — three Confederate and two Union. They all had the sweaty, oily faces, the matted hair, and the dirt and sun-darkened skin of men who have been out in the scrub for a long time. Deserters.

They rode past the headquarters. Greenley leaned against a column on the veranda and watched them. He thought about asking Mac to check wanted posters for the descriptions of the two wearing blue. Better not, he decided. No use making the bad blood with the Brocktons any worse.

Otto turned his horse from the rest of the group and steered it toward the headquarters. Greenley unbuttoned the flap on his holster, but the elder Brockton made no threatening gesture. He rode the horse through the open gate and stopped at the veranda steps.

"Word from the palmetto's that Tree's gettin' up a hell of a big herd," Otto said, his voice emotionless. He was reporting as usual, as if his youngest son still rode in the group on the street behind him.

"Otto, I'm sorry. . ."

The apology was cut off as it left Greenley's mouth. "Want to show me how sorry you are, get your men together 'n' let's go," Otto said. "Tree's hide 'n' Tree's herd. Those are what I want for Eric. Gonna help me?"

Greenley nodded. He went in and relayed the report to Holmes. "Those peckerwoods must be too stupid to quit," the colonel said.

He had a point. Reports from military dispatches and newspapers showed that there were no organized Confederate armies between Florida and North Carolina. Sherman had taken Savannah a few days before Christmas. A month later, he had marched north from what was left of that city. He now was turning South Carolina into a giant bonfire. Grant had Lee trapped in Virginia. Dispatches for the last month indicated that Lee's army was on the verge of being broken.

So, there was good reason to question why Hooker would again be preparing for a drive. He had no place to drive the cattle to. And, even if he did have somewhere to go and arrived, there was a good chance that the armies he was trying to feed would no longer exist.

Similar thoughts nagged Tree as he, Heavy, and Skeeter guided about 500 cattle into a pasture just east of what used to be the Spring Garden mill. The rest of his group had also been hunting through the scrub for weeks. They were going to have a huge herd, maybe the biggest they ever had driven. But none of them had any idea of who eventually would reap the benefits of their work.

Hundreds of other cattle already were grazing in the pasture. Tree had picked the old plantation as a meeting point.

Fifteen hunters were there before he arrived. Spring Garden's acreage was speckled with grazing cattle. The herd, mostly steers, dined contentedly on the foot-high grass that had grown around the blackened stumps of the groves and the ruins of the buildings.

Clouds darkened the sky as the newly arrived cattle mixed with the others. A drizzle began that soon turned into a rain heavy enough to make the hunters ride for shelter. The mill was the only building which provided refuge. Its timbers and stones were charred, but its roof had not completely collapsed. A portion of it remained, slanting at a steep angle like the roof of a lean-to. Raindrops tapped the roof's wooden shingles and ran down the slope with a sound like the scrabbling of tiny feet. Water running from the spring gurgled as it passed by the now-still water wheel. The occasional lowing of a steer or the bark of a dog were the only other sounds for several minutes. The men sat, stood, or leaned among the rubble and stared at each other in the dark shade of the building.

Then a blond teenager called Swede asked: "What're we gonna do now?"

Tree stepped from the darkness of a corner. He knew Swede was about to air the doubts that probably plagued everybody in the group.

"We're goin' north. Like always." Tree feared that his voice sounded as full of false confidence as it actually was.

Freckles that dotted Swede's nose and cheeks were hidden by a sneer. "Baldwin's gone. Savannah's gone. Hell, is there a railhead 'tween here 'n' Washington that ain't gone?"

Hooker listened to the rain for a moment. He sucked in breath between his teeth and then raised his voice to be heard above the sounds from the roof and the spring. "Don't know. But I signed an oath. I'm sworn to get cattle to the armies o' the Confederacy. Same oath ya'll took."

Somehow, as he talked, his doubts stopped nagging. "Maybe we won't find a railhead. Maybe we won't even find an army to feed. But we'll damn sure find hungry people. They're up there somewheres. My job's to feed people. Always has been. I reckon God intended me to do that all my life. I aim to get beef to hungry people. Right now, those people are up north. If I've gotta drive to Virginia. Hell, if I gotta drive to Canada, I'm gettin' beef through to those people."

Heavy's voice came from the darkness. "I'm jealous. You're getting good at sermonizin'."

Tree smiled. The others laughed, although some of their laughter came out more like nervous giggles.

Swede was among those who giggled. He joined in as the rest began talking about particulars of the drive. The talk covered such subjects as tallies of the herd, plans for river crossings, fears that the rainy season already was upon them, and dozens of other details. But nobody again questioned whether there was any point to making the drive in the first place.

Tallies put the herd at slightly less than 3,000, about 500 more than Tree ever before had tried to drive. It was going to be hard to move that many cattle without drawing the interest of rustlers, Yankees, or both. So, the smartest route would be to the north and east. Keep away from the St. Johns until the herd was about ten miles southeast of St. Augustine. Then, head west and cross the river at a bend where the water was no more than a few hundred yards wide. Ruins of a Seminole War stockade called Fort Hanson were on the west bank.

The route to Fort Hanson was twisting and round-about, adding a good two weeks to the time it would take to reach the state line. It also meant gambling with running into Greenley from St. Augustine or God-knows-who from Pilatka. But the route steered away from most swampy areas while paralleling enough creeks to ensure good water the entire way. It kept the herd away from the stretches of the river most traveled by gunboats and avoided most of the towns where rustlers and Yankees congregated.

Eventually, the rain stopped and allowed a few hours of dry daylight to move the herd into a tighter circle in preparation for the drive. Heavy and Swede had the last night shift and woke the rest of the camp long before dawn. The sky above a pine stand to the east was turning pink when the group finished a break-fast of grits, salt pork, and biscuits.

Volusia had the pots scrubbed and stowed and the oxen hitched to the yoke by the time the others were saddled. He was in the wagon, heading toward the sunrise, while the others were cracking their whips and shouting to the dogs to get the cattle moving.

Clouds already were casting their shadows over the herd when the rest of the hunters caught up to Volusia for lunch in a wide pasture bordered on the west by a small lake. Tree felt an ache in his hips and right knee as he climbed down from the horse. He saw that Volusia, Heavy, and Skeeter also moved stiffly — sure signs that the rainy season was upon them early.

"Damn," he said to the horse he had been riding. "Like we weren't moving slow enough to begin with."

Rain fell each day, usually in afternoon thunder-storms that quickly ended, but sometimes in constant, soaking streams that nagged the drive for hours. Mud pulled at the hooves of the cattle and horses, further slowing the pace. Thunder and lightning made the herd jittery. Twice there were small stampedes that caused no injuries but wasted hours in getting the herd circled and quieted. After two weeks, the herd was but 50 miles from Spring Garden, less than half the distance that a drive should have covered.

Mud churned up by the passing hooves made it easier than usual to track the herd. Even a group of Yankees without an experienced scout could tell where the drive was by the wide swath of black mud through the palmettos. The weather was taking its toll on the men, and not only in the physical pains of arthritic joints and ague attacks. Everybody was either soaked by the rain or steamy hot from wearing the heavy rubberized ponchos. Food often was soggy and cold, despite Volusia's best efforts to shield his work from the storms. The slow pace galled everybody. And the strain of keeping guard over the herd as it milled in frightened circles during frequent thunderstorms made the drovers as edgy as the cattle.

"'N' let us not be weary in well doing: for in due season we shall reap, if we faint not,'" Heavy said, almost groaning as he climbed back into the saddle after a quick meal of sodden biscuits. "Galatians, six: nine."

Tree listened as he tried to force a bite of biscuit down with a gulp of cold, especially bitter chicory. He knew the quotation was the closest to a complaint that he would hear from Heavy.

# 25 🔥

After a week of fruitless searching for Tree's herd, Greenley rode into Pilatka and into what looked like a combination of a Fourth of July celebration and a Greek bacchanal. Blue-clad soldiers, black and white, filled the street between the old judge's mansion and the church-turned-stable. Those who had guns fired into the air. Some sang "John Brown's Body." Others screamed incoherently. Most of them had giggling women at their sides who swayed with them as they weaved down the street. Almost all carried bottles or jugs from which they took long pulls between either screams or stanzas of song. A slight breeze fluttered Union flags that hung from every doorway and gatepost.

Navigating through the mob was difficult. Even combat-trained horses shied at the noise. Occasionally, one would kick out as the crowd pressed too closely, but the kicks didn't seem to faze anyone. Greenley and his troopers had to carefully thread their horses through the weaving mass. Eventually, they reached the front veranda of the mansion. There, in a rocking chair, sat a colonel. His gray-bearded face was split with a smile that belonged on a Halloween pumpkin. A large brown pottery jug rested on his lap. He cheerily waved in reply to the major's salute.

"Colonel, what the hell's goin' on?" Greenley asked as he walked up the veranda steps.

"Got the word today," the colonel's accent was undecipherable through the slurring of his words. "Lee surrendered last week."

Greenley had expected that news for months. For four years, he had hoped —sometimes prayed — to hear it. Yet, he now was shocked. He felt his face burn and, for a moment, his ears rang until he couldn't hear the tumult in the street. The colonel held out the jug toward the major, who took it and slugged down the liquid. Homebrew. But made by somebody who knew what he was doing. It was almost tasteless when he first put it in his mouth. And it went down like water when he swallowed. Then it hit his stomach and a warm, comforting glow spread through his body. He handed the jug back to the colonel and noticed that the ringing was gone from his ears.

"How'd you get the news?" he asked, trying to force himself to be military and businesslike.

"Dispatch on a gunboat," the colonel replied. "Still waiting for confirmation."

Greenley nodded. "How about Joe Johnston and Dick Taylor?"

The colonel offered the jug back to Greenley. "No word. It can't be too long, though."

Greenley took another drink, but his enthusiasm was draining away. One military dispatch announcing

Lee's surrender was little but a glorified rumor until confirmation arrived. And even if Lee surrendered in Virginia, the war still would continue in Florida until either — or probably both — General Johnston in the Carolinas and General Taylor in Alabama quit. Tallahassee still was held by the Confederates. A month earlier, federals attempted to take the city. Militia thrashed the attackers.

Still, there were reasons to celebrate. The chances were better than fifty-fifty that the dispatch was correct. Lee surrendering would also mean that Richmond was in Union hands. Capturing Richmond, in turn, would mean that the Confederate government was without a capital and disintegrating. Maybe the little war in Florida was not yet over, but the worst obviously was past for the rest of the nation. Reason enough for the street party. Greenley's troopers thought so. The word got to them from passersby. Gradually, the entire company, without orders, dismounted and melted into the crowd. The major watched them go and mulled over the idea of getting the company back together and camping outside of town. No. Let them go for the night. Reality will settle in with the hangovers in the morning. For now, let everybody pretend the war has ended. Greenley again accepted the jug from the colonel and took a long pull.

Some of the company sobered up long before the next morning. They were caught by the afternoon thunderstorm away from their gear and rain ponchos. Miserably soaked, they made their way back to the stable-church and their horses. Greenley, although feeling the effects of the whiskey himself, managed to get the troopers at the stable to put up a semblance of a camp on the riverbank just west of the mansion. The rest of the company had reassembled by the next morning. They rode out with most weaving in their saddles and many leaning to one side or another and retching about every half hour.

The company made a ragged line heading northwest over mostly vacant pastures. About two hours out of town, Greenley saw two black triangular specks ahead of the column. The specks became larger as he watched. Riders coming toward him. He halted the company and waited. Eventually, the specks took on the shapes of Martin Brockton and one of the five deserters. Ever since starting out, the Brocktons and their five companions had stayed away from the company. Greenley had suggested that he take the company in one set of circles, starting toward the northwest, while the others started toward the northeast. Whoever would first cut the trail of the herd would send outriders to get the other group. Otto had embraced the idea in hopes of reducing the time it took to find the cattle.

Maybe that would happen. But Greenley's main reason for coming up with the idea was to keep Otto's men apart from his. There was no need to remind his troopers that it was possible to successfully desert. And, Greenley admitted to himself, he simply did not want to be around those five. It was not fear, exactly. Something deeper. Akin to his feelings when he came across rattlesnakes. Instinctively, he knew that he could not coexist with either rattlers or these deserters. Before long, he would kill them or they would kill him. Actually, when he thought about it, rattlers were preferable; they would warn before striking. And, when looked at objectively, their skin was attractive.

To look at the five riding with the Brocktons was to know that they would not warn before striking. Backs would be their favorite targets. They all but advertised that fact by wearing pieces of different uniforms. They either took their clothing with them when they fled their respective armies or they scrounged from prisoners and the dead. Either way, they obviously were neither inspired by courage nor held in check by scruples. Months of living in the scrub had ground oil and dirt into their skins until all their complexions were a mottled, grayish brown. Their hair and beards were thick tangles that reminded Greenley of hairballs coughed up by cats. An odor came from them that repulsed even his nostrils, which had become used to the stench of trenches and of Vicksburg. Each of the five smelled more like rotting, dead flesh than anything else Greenley had encountered. The Brocktons were welcome to them all.

The one riding with Martin wore a blue kepi. It was his only vestige of a uniform. From a distance, the rest of his clothes appeared to be brown. But, when Greenley rode to within a few feet of the deserter, he saw that the clothes, denim trousers and shirt, actually should have been the off-white of unbleached cotton. Dirt dyed them a shade of brown.

Even after a bath and dressed in a freshly cleaned and pressed suit, the deserter would be repulsive. A thick mass of beard, so black it almost looked blue, cascaded from his chin down to the middle of his chest. Hair, equally as black and tangled, hung over his ears and down to his shoulders. His nose and eyes were the only facial features not covered by the hair and beard. Those were enough, though, to impress the deserter in Greenley's memory. The nose was a fat blob that looked as if someone had thrown a lump of red meat at the man that stuck in the middle of his face. His eyes bulged from the sockets. That weird, permanent stare, and the lack of either emotion or intelligence in the dark pupils and irises, made the deserter look like some huge lizard perched on the horse. Greenley would not have been surprised to see a scaly tail coming out from the seat of the trousers.

"Found the herd," Martin said as the major approached. "Maybe 20 miles southeast o' here. A big'n. Daddy 'n the others are trailin' 'em now."

That was enough conversation for Greenley. He wheeled his horse about, shouted commands to the company, and began following Martin and the deserter to the east, crossing the river just north of Pilatka. It took until noon of the next day before the company caught up to the rest of the Brocktons. Otto was leaning against the trunk of an oak, looking at the sky, when Greenley rode up to him.

"They're still headin' north," Otto said. "Bound to turn west 'n cross the river sometime soon. We don't need to be in no hurry, though. The weather'll keep 'em movin' slow."

Greenley followed Brockton's eyes up to the sky. More thunderheads were forming to the northwest.

"Any good ideas of where they'll cross?"

Otto shrugged his shoulders. "The way they keep goin' north, they must be figurin' to cross somewheres north of Pilatka. That way, they'd steer clear of any patrols from the town. There's a couple places downstream from Horse Landing where they might try it.

Places where it narrows. Places with sandbars 'n' such. Just can't figure out which one."

He snapped a twig from a branch above his head and then squatted on the ground. Using the twig, he traced a curving line in the sandy soil. "This here's the river." Then he drew a large circle to the right of the line and jabbed the twig into the ground several inches above the circle. "The twig's Picolata. It's a good bet Tree won't cross downstream o' there. Too good a chance o' runnin' into cavalry or river patrols from Jacksonville."

He pointed to the circle. "This here's the big swamp. Be a damned fool to try gettin' to the river through there."

Greenley nodded. He knew the swamp. It was a series of bayous, marshes, small lakes, and shallow creeks that went by several names. Long Swamp, Big Cypress, Hell Cat Bay. Whatever it was called, it was fifteen miles long and fifteen miles wide, mostly dark, sulfurous water and thick, black muck that could suck men or animals a dozen feet underground. Where there wasn't water or quicksand, a jumbled mess of briars and gnarled, ancient trees blocked out the sun. He had skirted the edges of the area several times. Once, he had been close enough to it at sundown to see dark clouds, like smoke rising from a burning pool of kerosene, coming up from the even darker shadows of the trees.

The clouds turned out to be millions of mosquitoes and yellow flies that viciously attacked him and the company. Netting did little good. Enough attacking insects pressed against the gauze to widen the holes and permit at least some of them to get at one's flesh.

Horses went mad from bites and from insects flying up their nostrils. Several of the company were thrown. Some frenzied horses, after throwing their riders, took off toward the blackness of the swamp and were never seen again.

Insects, alligators, cottonmouths, and snapping turtles might thrive within the shadows of that swamp, but nobody would try to keep horses, dogs, cattle, and people alive in it. Greenley knew that Brockton was outlining the only logical route for the cattle drive to take.

"They're goin' through high ground just east of the swamp now," Otto said, his finger tracing through the sand to the right of the circle. "Figure he's gotta turn west somewhere's 'tween the creek here —" he drew a line at the upper edge of the circle "— 'n' Picolata. Less'n ten miles 'tween 'em. All we gotta do is ride 'round that territory 'n' keep our eyes open. We're bound to find out where the crossin' is."

Greenley agreed and ordered the company to head for Picolata, about 15 miles to the north. It was an easy ride along a grassy ridge that ran just west of the riverbank and far enough away from the edge of the swamp and its insects. Even the afternoon thunderstorm did not create serious delays. Brockton's group rode slightly ahead of the company, as if Otto knew how the major felt about the deserters. During most of the trip, the only sounds came from snatches of conversations among the troopers and the occasional "Kee-Hi" from an osprey as it swooped down on some river fish.

Before noon the next day, Greenley could see wisps of smoke in the sky, apparently from the stacks of a boat docked in Picolata. Some civilians — fishermen, farmers and women heading to market — crossed paths with the company as it neared town. Greenley knew he had nothing to worry about from the passersby and paid them little attention. When he had almost reached the outskirts of town, he saw the speck of a horse and rider off in the distance. The speck turned and headed southeast as the company rode past.

Greenley thought no more about the rider than he did any of the other civilians he met, until Otto rode back and said: "That could be one o' Tree's boys. Want us to go after him? Last thing we need is somebody tellin' Tree we're visitin' here."

The speck already was out of sight. Greenley shook his head. "No. If it's one of Tree's, he's got too good of a horse to catch him now. Don't wear out any of our horses in a chase."

# 26

THE COMPANY ENTERED PICOLATA'S main
street — in fact, its only street — a little after noon.
Smoke from the twin stacks of a gunboat floated into
the sky like a signal guiding the company into the
town. The boat, a converted side-wheeled steamer,
was docked at the town's pier, about 100 feet of cypress boards and pilings that stuck out into the river.

Brockton's group veered off from the company
and hitched their horses to rails and posts by the row
of buildings that lined the east side of the street. The
eight disappeared among the shadows cast by the little
collection of false-fronted, plank-and-log shops.
Greenley brought the company to a halt by the pier.
He dismounted, handed his reins to a corporal, and
walked down the pier to the gangway of the boat.

Greenley expected to find a friendly boat in the
town. Union steamers had been using Picolata for re-
fueling stops during the 14 months since Jacksonville
was occupied. He half-expected the boat crew to have
confirmation of Lee's surrender and, possibly, news of

Johnston and Taylor. What he did not expect to find was the boat's flag hanging at half-mast.

A sentry, armed with a long single-shot rifle, challenged and then saluted him at the entry to the gangway. The black ribbon, a mourning band, tied around the sentry's arm stood out in sharp contrast from his white canvas uniform. An officer, dressed in the Navy's wool frock uniform coat despite the growing heat of the day, met Greenley at the other end of the gangway. The officer's mourning band was hard to see against the dark blue of the uniform.

Before his hand had returned to his side from saluting, the officer asked: "Have you got the word?"

For an instant, Greenley thought the officer was referring to Lee's surrender. No, not that. Nobody would be talking about the imminent end of the war while wearing a mourning band. Greenley shook his head.

"The president is dead."

Greenley heard the words but didn't understand them. Perhaps he had been stationed too long in the South, where "the president" usually meant Jeff Davis.

The officer repeated the sentence. "The president is dead." Then added, "Assassinated a week ago in Washington."

His voice was almost a squeak. He had the same wide-eyed, pained, expression and sickly, pale complexion that Greenley had often seen on men after their first battle.

"My God, Lincoln," Greenley whispered the words. The news came like a physical shock, as if an artillery shell had exploded nearby, knocking him half unconscious and almost smothering him with dirt.

The officer, who eventually identified himself as Lieutenant Commander Boyles, captain of the boat, had no more details. He had gotten the news the day before when a dispatch arrived in Jacksonville. Boyles and Greenley walked silently to the other side of the boat and stared across the water to the oak-shaded west bank. Eventually, they were able to talk about other matters. There was no confirmation on Lee's surrender. Nor was there any word of Johnston and Taylor. Greenley got a promise of help from the gunboat. Boyles said he was going upstream and, if he saw a herd of cattle crossing, he would fire his cannons. The cannon fire would alert Greenley's company while pinning down the herd at the crossing.

Talk from the boat's sailors spread the news of Lincoln's death to the company before the major could return and announce it. Few of the troopers said anything to him. Those who did mostly just echoed his shock. But Greenley could sense the mood of the company as it rode out of town. The elation the troopers had felt at the news of Lee's surrender evaporated. Now, they were sullen, hurt, and angry. In a way, Greenley mused, that might be better for the job awaiting them. Before arriving in Picolata, he believed, without anyone telling him, that nobody gave a damn any more if the Cow Cavalry was caught. Now, the troopers were out for vengeance. Targets for the vengeance were available where and when Tree made the river crossing.

The Brocktons and their companions emerged from the shadows and again rode ahead of the company. As they traveled south, Greenley looked around for more riders that could be scouting the company.

There were none the rest of that day.

❖             ❖             ❖

Skeeter had worried that he was pushing too far when he scouted clear to Picolata. It was at least 25 miles from the herd and a good six miles from the Fort Hanson crossing. But after seeing the long line of riders that could only mean a Yankee cavalry patrol, Skeeter knew he was right to travel to the town. He made a mental note to give thanks by attending the next services Heavy conducted.

Trying to cover as much ground as quickly as he and the horse could stand, Skeeter rode at a trot for most of the rest of the day. He traveled several hours in the dark until he was convinced to stop by the pain in his rump and the flecks of foam coming off his horse. After a few hours of rest, he was back in the saddle and riding in the cool of the before-dawn mist. The mist had not burned off by the time he reached the cook's wagon. Volusia turned around and drove in Skeeter's wake until they reached the rest of the herd. The outrider's report brought the herd to a stop and the men to a meeting by the bank of a water-filled sinkhole.

"Also saw smoke comin' up from town. More 'n' likely from the stacks of a gunboat," Skeeter finished with a tired sigh. "Bet that'll be on the lookout for us too."

Volusia put pine needles and cones under the pile of sticks he had made to begin the fire for lunch. "So, do we turn back 'n' cut across south of the swamp?" he asked as he worked.

Several in the group nodded their heads and

murmured. But Swede pointed toward the cattle. "Hell, it's taken us a good month to get this far. These critters'll be dead o' old age afore we get 'em to market."

A splash came from the sinkhole. Several of the group stood to look in the direction of the noise. They held their guns, waiting to to see if a gator was coming for their dogs. A heron wading in the water with a fish in its beak erased their fears.

"Doublin' back won't do us any good," Heavy said as he sat back down in the grass. "Once we get southwest o' the swamp, what'll we do then? We'll just be askin' for attention from that gunboat, the cavalry, 'n' whatever is in Pilatka. Might as well head to St. Augustine 'n' turn the cattle over to the Yankees now. Save us the trouble o' gettin' shot."

More murmurs from the rest of the group were followed by a variety of alternate routes to the river, each of which immediately was shot down by good arguments against it. Several of the men muttered curses. Swede turned his back on the rest and began chucking twigs into the water of the sinkhole.

Tree was silent. He sat on the grass in a ball, with his knees drawn up to his chin. His hat was pulled down until the brim touched his nose. Suddenly, he pushed up the brim.

"If you're damned if you say 'Yes' and damned if you say 'No,'" he said, "What happens if you say 'Maybe'?"

That was met by a chorus of "Huh?" from the rest.

"I'm sayin' we don't go north 'n' we don't turn back, least not all the ways." Tree unwound and stood up as he talked. "We go back maybe five miles 'n' cross the river at Old Man Compton's."

Compton owned a small farm between the swamp and the river. His cabin was perched on a bluff overlooking a bend where the river narrowed as much as it did at Fort Hanson. It was about halfway between Pilatka and Picolata. But the swamp was between the herd and Compton's.

"You figure to drain the swamp to get to Compton's?" a hunter asked sarcastically.

"I figure to find a way through the swamp," Tree said, sparking a round of groans. "No. It can be done. People snake logs out o' there sometimes. If you can run oxen in 'n' out to pull the logs, you can run cattle through."

His words started coming out more rapidly. His hands bobbed and weaved in front of his chest, as though he was trying to pull the others to him. "Keep the cattle strung out as tight as we can. Just like a river crossin'."

Heavy snorted through his nose like a winded horse. "'Cept this crossin' would be fifteen miles wide 'stead o' half a mile. You really figure we can keep the herd together that way for fifteen miles?"

Tree scratched the stubble on his chin. "It'll be a two-day trip. We won't be able to stop for food or rest. It won't be as much fun as a night in Baldwin used to be, but it's doable."

He looked at the faces that were staring at him. Most of them obviously were skeptical. But the sneers of derision were gone. He was winning them over to the plan.

"Sure, it's a gamble. But we'll hedge our bets. Split the herd. That way, we don't risk losin' everythin' at one shot. Heavy'll take half 'n' follow me south.

Skeeter, you stay here till one o' us comes back for you. Good water 'n' you can use the woods for cover if the Yankees come. Compton's a good place to make a stand if they hit us there. Once everybody's through the swamp, we can get back together for the river crossin'."

Heavy took on his bass sermon voice. "One of my favorite passages always was John, eleven: sixteen, where Thomas says, 'Let us also go, that we may die with him.' Maybe that applies here."

The wagon would be an encumbrance going through the swamp, and anyway, there would be no time for hot meals. So, the group decided to send Volusia with two hunters and the extra horses back south. He would go around the southern end of the swamp and meet the rest at Comptons. The others would camp and wait for the wagon's arrival.

Most of the next two days were spent cutting the herd into roughly equal halves. Six drovers got one half moving at dawn of the third day. Tree rode ahead of them. Nobody saw him until late in the afternoon. Then Heavy, who was riding in the lead, saw a figure sitting on a stump off to the southwest. A horse, with hobbles fixed to its front feet, grazed in a nearby meadow.

The stump was at the edge of what from a distance appeared to be a half-mile-wide lake. But when Heavy cantered nearer to the figure on the stump, he saw that the lake actually was just a sheet of water, no more than a few inches deep. Brown weeds stuck up three feet high from the water. The swamp itself, a dark tangle of thin trees and thick clumps of grass and vines, began on the other side of the water.

Tree sat on the stump, whittling with his Bowie knife at a long, thick branch from a nearby water oak. He looked up from the work as his friend approached.

"Watch out for the horse, will you?" Tree asked as he cut off a knobby piece of bark. "I better do this job afoot."

Heavy nodded as he dismounted and walked over to the water's edge. He could see the black soil, formed by centuries of decay from dead leaves, trees, and animals, under the water. He walked a few feet from the stump and stepped into water. The soil felt like a sponge under his feet. It had become soaked by the rains until it could hold no more. Water now sat on the surface and attracted egg-laying insects.

"Might as well make camp with us tonight 'n' start in the mornin'," Heavy said. "No need feedin' any more skeeters than you have to."

A wind from the west blew odors from the swamp over to the camp. Sulfur from the water mixed with a musty, unclean stench from rotting vegetation. Horses, cattle, and men all wrinkled their noses. Then came sundown and black clouds flew up from the water. The hunters had been expecting the attacks and had wrapped themselves in mosquito netting until they looked like mummies. Night herders got the worst of it. Their horses continually shied and kicked in efforts to dodge or strike flies and mosquitoes. Sometimes, a horse went into a snorting, bucking fit after insects flew up its nostrils. The cattle milled and bawled as they tried to fend off the attacks. Dogs snarled and howled. Nobody got much rest.

"'N' this is just the start of it," Tree muttered as he wound another swatch of gauze around his head. He walked off toward the swamp in the gray light that came a half hour before the sun actually rose. Using the oak limb as a staff, he prodded the ground and poked into the underbrush, hoping to scare away anything dangerous before he stepped on it. He wore his carbine on his back, using a piece of rope tied around the barrel and stock as a sling.

Heavy watched him walk around the south end of the pool of water. Tree drew his Bowie and hacked at the bramble bushes and scraggly pines at the margin of the swamp. He was cutting a trail for the herd. Within minutes, the shadows of the swamp closed over him. The preacher kept staring at the place where his friend had entered, hoping to see some movement. But he gave up and, turning to the rest, shouted: "Let's get 'em movin'. 'But he that shall endure unto the end, the same shall be saved.' Matthew, twenty-four: thirteen."

A week of circling between Picolata and the ruins of Fort Hanson produced nothing but saddlesores on Greenley and some of his troopers. Fears of being on a fool's errand began to nag as the company, for the third time that week, prepared to make camp on the east bank across from the pile of timbers that had been the fort. Boyles' gunboat had run its errand upriver and had returned. It had passed the company two days earlier. Standing on the deck and using a megaphone, the commander had shouted that there had been no sign of a large herd crossing.

Otto and two of his deserters had scouted ahead of the others. They rode into camp shortly before sundown. Blank, tired faces told Greenley all he needed to know before any of them started talking.

RICK TONYAN

"Nothin'," Otto said as he dismounted. He stretched by bending backwards, putting both hands in the small of his back. "Not even a cow pie that could belong to that herd 'tween here 'n' town."

Greenley watched the deserters climb off their horses. One was short, with the rounded face and belly that comes from too many beers and potatoes. His hair was a dull red. It looked like the loose ends of yarn in an unfinished piece of crochet as it stuck out from a low-crowned, brown slouch hat. The beard was curly and, because it was almost the same color as the sunburned skin, hard to see from a distance. He wore a torn, formerly white but now gray-brown undershirt above patched cotton trousers. The trousers, with the red stripes of the artillery down their sides, could have been faded Union issue, but probably began life as the sky blue of a Confederate uniform. There was no doubt about what uniform the other deserter wore. During rain and the cool of the night, the major had seen him in a short blue shell jacket. Its arms were decorated with the chevron of an infantry corporal, two light blue Vs. The jacket now was rolled up and tied behind the saddle on his horse. He wore an un-bleached cotton shirt and the trousers to match the jacket, dark blue with lighter blue stripes.

That deserter never came within ten feet of the rest of the company. Now, he held the reins of the three horses and led them away while his two companions squatted in the grass beside Greenley.

"Maybe we better head on south," the major said. "If they were crossin' here, we would've come on them by now."

Otto shook his head. "Wait. I've got Martin 'n'

336

Corley checkin' out from here to Pilatka. Tree might be enough of a lunatic to cross the swamp. If he does, I just hope he's got enough cattle left to make it worthwhile us grabbin' 'em."

A small dark gray shape, like a walking blemish, moved from under the chubby deserter's hat. It went down through his beard past his neck and into the undershirt. Greenley watched the speck's passage. A louse. The deserter remained squatting on his haunches with both hands gripping the barrel of his Sharps carbine. Probably too used to lice to bother swatting at one.

An hour passed before Corley and Martin rode into camp. They had the other three deserters with them. At least two, the black-bearded one and a beardless youth who wore a butternut uniform and kepi, undoubtedly were deserters. The third could have been a layout, professional outlaw, or anybody else with some kind of reason for living in the scrubland. That one wore nondescript pieces of cotton clothes topped off by a gray hat, with a wide brim and a crown about five inches high. The hat could have been part of a Confederate uniform, but just as well could have been picked up in any store. The hat's owner was slim, but not particularly skinny and about five feet, nine inches tall. His hair and beard were brown. Except for the smell and dirt, the man was so commonplace that he would disappear if he ever walked into a crowd. The thin, gawky one in butternut was no older than 20. His hair was a light blond, but, with dirt, it took on the tan color of old hay.

Otto walked up to the four and began talking to them before before they dismounted. Greenley followed and reached the group in time to hear the word "Comptons."

# 27 ✺

I<small>T WAS HARD TO TELL WHEN THE SUN ROSE</small> or set in the swamp. A canopy of closely packed cypress and other trees allowed very little light to filter to the bottom. Dusk meant that the darkness increased to the blackness of a cave. Dawn meant that the blackness lightened to the dull gray of open sky during a thunderstorm.

A thunderstorm hit the swamp during Tree's first day. The swamp turned as dark as a moonless night in the open. He heard the thunder, but never saw the lightning. Rain bounced off the cypress canopy and turned into a dense mist by the time it filtered through the branches to the ground. The water soaked his mosquito netting and clothing. A fine, choking spray came through the netting into his nose and mouth with each breath.

He wore his wool uniform trousers and bib-front shirt to protect him from insect bites and two-inch-long briars. He was sweating, and the heavy clothing already was soaked, long before the rain added its weight. By the time the storm ended, Tree felt as if 20 pounds of lead were tied to each arm and leg. His right knee stopped bending. He could feel something move behind his kneecap. The hot, stabbing pain, which occasionally had flared up ever since the injury, returned. His walk become a stiff-legged shuffle.

Weaving back and forth among the tree trunks, he poked the ground with the oak limb to find firm-enough footing for the herd. He used his Bowie on the trunks to gouge out chunks of wood. The gouges could be seen during the daylight and felt by riders during the night. There usually was enough firm ground and space between the trunks for a 15-foot-wide trail. But, occasionally, the trunks, some of which were so wide that a cow could hide behind them, grew too closely together. Other times, his staff found little firm ground. Twice, Tree almost lost the staff. He poked the limb into what he thought would be spongy-but-walkable ground only to find the staff being pulled downward from his grip by quicksand.

Night, as he expected, was the worst. It took only a few hours for mosquitoes to tear holes in the netting. And, from the beginning, the netting didn't stop the yellow flies. The flies were half-inch-long shapes among the smaller buzzing things that swarmed around him. He knew them from their bites. They felt like dull-pointed darts that stabbed through the gauze and even penetrated the thick material of his trousers and shirt.

Several times, Tree came to hammocks, islands of high land in the marsh. Thoughts of resting for a few hours plagued him each time he found a hammock. Exhaustion was becoming more noxious than the insects. It squeezed on his temples like a belt cinched around his head. But every time he started to give in and lie down on a hammock, he heard whips from the drive in the distance behind him. The hammocks were not large enough to hold the herd. Cattle and dogs would stray off and fall victim to gators, cottonmouths, and quicksand. He had to keep marking the trail and those following him had to keep driving the cattle.

Tree heard snakes slithering into briar patches and gators splashing and bellowing in the water. He never saw any of them. His staff and the noise he made going through the water and brush scared the reptiles from his path. But he knew that the temptation of dog meat and beef would overcome gators' fears when the herd passed.

He had become something of a swamp animal himself by mid-morning of the second day. No thinking, just acting. Cutting out undergrowth and gouging signs in cypress trunks. Poking the staff to find the firmest ground. Walking. And walking. And walking. He carried some salt pork and biscuits in a sack slung over his right shoulder. But he didn't think to stop and eat.

The swamp took over all his senses. Its darkness obscured his vision. All he could feel on his skin was pain where he had been scratched and cut by briars and bitten by mosquitoes and flies. The incessant croakings of frogs and the sing-song chirpings from insects rang in his ears and made him clench his teeth until they ached. He constantly tasted the salt from his own sweat, which dripped into his mouth from the mosquito netting and his moustache. And the stench of sulfur from the water overpowered any other smell. It was like walking through a cloud of gunsmoke that never dissipated.

Sometime in the afternoon, he suddenly realized that he was swinging his Bowie at nothing. There were no more trunks or thick growths of underbrush. Instead, palmetto fronds brushed against him. The staff was tapping at good, solid ground. He was walking on the upward slope of a ridge. A horse snorted as he reached the crest of the ridge, and a man's voice said, "Who the hell are you?" Then there were the unmistakable clicks of a gun being cocked.

Tree unwrapped the netting from his face. He saw a man on horseback holding a double-barreled shotgun. Sideburns as white as sunbleached linen protruded from the man's hat and down his cheeks. Old Man Compton.

"By God, I made it," Tree whispered as he slipped down to his knees and then fell backwards onto the grass.

Greenley had never heard of the Comptons until Otto told him: "Cattle pourin' out o' the swamp into the Comptons'. It's a place on the river 'bout five miles south o' here. Owner's got four sons. Two o' 'em with the Rebels in Virginia. So, Tree must've thought o' him 'n' decided to cross there. Right through the goddamned swamp. Son o' a bitch. He was crazy enough to go. 'N' lucky enough to make it."

The company broke camp and headed south. Otto rode beside Greenley. Both were silent for most of the trip, except for Otto occasionally muttering "Son o' a bitch."

Hooker woke up to the sight of cattle milling about a corral and pasture. He was lying on blankets. When he sat up, he realized he was under the roof of the dog trot of Compton's house. Most of the other drovers in the first group were snoring as they lay on their own blankets. Tree looked over to the corral and saw Compton and two of his sons. He got up and joined them.

"Hey there. Been out only four hours," the elder Compton greeted him. "Don't you need more? Me 'n' the boys can watch your cows."

Tree shook his head. "Got to get back 'n' tell the others we're here. Can I have a fresh horse? If it gets killed or lost, I'll trade you one from the herd. Owe you a lot already."

Compton ducked through two of the corral fence rails and grabbed a brown gelding by the rope wrapped around its head as a halter. Tree followed and held the horse while its owner got a blanket, saddle, and bridle from the stable within the corral.

When he reached the top of the ridge, Tree glanced back at the cattle grazing around Compton's home. Then he turned the horse toward the darkness of the swamp, found the trees where he had made the last cuts to mark the trail and entered. With a horse, the trip back wasn't as bad as the first. Many of the daylight hours were spent in a sleepy daze. He periodically nodded off in the saddle until jerked awake by the horse shying. Insect attacks gave him no chance to doze during the night. The horse bucked and reared its way through the darkness. By dawn, Tree was ready to surrender to exhaustion. He stopped on the first dry hammock he found and slept with the horse hobbled beside him. Rainfall from the afternoon thunderstorm awoke him. He was back on the trail within a few minutes and made it to Skeeter's camp before midnight. Another few hours' sleep and he was up at dawn helping the others get the second half of the herd in line for its journey.

Hooker believed he had become calloused to the swamp after two trips. He was wrong. The third was the worst. He thought it would be easier with companions. But traveling in a group didn't help. All it did was create more warm-blooded attractions for even more flies and mosquitoes. The insects breached the defenses of the gauze soon after sunset. Dogs whined and snarled continually as they scratched and bit at the attacking insects. Several dogs bolted from the herd. Sometimes, a fleeing dog would run a few feet into the black water and then, with a loud splash and an agonized yelp, it disappeared into the mouth of a gator. Several other dogs and straying cattle were shot after being mired in quicksand.

The borrowed horse shied and bucked for most of the first day and through the night. By the next sunrise, it was too tired to fight. Its legs kept folding under it, a sign of exhaustion. Tree gave up and started walking, leading the horse by the the reins. Eventually, the ground under his feet became firmer and he knew he was nearing the end of the swamp. He lifted his eyes. The canopy was getting thinner and he could see blue sky.

But he also saw a column of black smoke, like a vein running through the sky. Too much smoke for either a campfire or a passing riverboat. Weather was too warm for it to be from a chimney. Something was on fire about where the Comptons' farm should be.

"Christ no," Tree breathed the words to himself. He meant them as a prayer, not a curse. He jumped back into the saddle and spurred the snorting, balking horse toward the smoke. Hoofbeats from behind told him that several others also had seen the smoke. He turned and saw Skeeter and four other riders. "Damn it. Stay with the herd." Tree's voice came out in the caninelike snarl. The riders stopped.

His horse would do no more than a canter. It stumbled, almost throwing him over its head. Tree dug in the spurs, keeping his eyes on the smoke. Then he came to the first of the cattle from the other half of the herd. They wandered about Compton's pasture, grazing. Whatever happened, at least some of the cattle were untouched. Then he saw the source of the smoke. Several outbuildings on the farm were afire. But the house and the corral were safe. Men walked around the grounds. Hooker didn't stop to count them and gambled that everybody he saw was on his side. He rode on past the corral and reined in the horse. Compton, holding his shotgun, and one of his sons, carrying a long-barreled rifle, trotted over toward him.

"Yankees," Compton shouted out as he approached. "Hit us a couple o' hours ago."

Tree was about to ask if anyone was hurt when the elder Compton gestured with the shotgun toward the house. A man lay on the dog trot. He was long and broad, with the middle swelling up like a mountain rising from a plain.

Tree stumbled toward the dog trot. His vision blurred with a dark red haze. The haze had struck him once before in his life. Almost two years earlier. In Vicksburg. When he ran from a magnolia tree to a pile of smoking lumber and bricks.

Heavy was covered from his neck down with a multicolored quilt. A red stain darkened the white square of the quilt that covered his chest. The chest was moving up and down rapidly. Heavy's head turned toward Tree. He tried to sit up, but failed.

"We saved the herd." The words came out in a hiss with the breath escaping Heavy's lips.

Compton came up beside Tree. Both of them reached up to their heads and removed their hats.

"He was the only one hit. We saw 'em comin'," Compton said. "Caught 'em in a crossfire from the house 'n woods. Got at least those," He again gestured with the shotgun. This time, he pointed toward the pasture to the north of his house. Three blue-clad figures lay in the grass.

"Reckon several more were winged. They all took off fast."

Tree listened, but didn't pay much attention, as he watched Heavy. For some reason, the preacher's face didn't seem as lined as usual. His rapid breathing began to slow. Then his chest stopped moving. Heavy's right hand fell out from beneath the quilt. His Bible was in his grip. The book thumped against the planks of the dog trot as the hand fell.

# 28 ☀

I<small>T WAS THE FIRST REALLY HOT AFTERNOON</small> of the year. Hot even by Crackers' standards. The sun had heated the hilt of Greenley's saber until it was painful to touch. Foam came off his horse, although he never went faster than a walk. To keep the horses from heat exhaustion, the company dismounted and led the animals for one out of every three hours. Relief eventually came with the afternoon thunderstorm.

For most of the time, the company moved silently. Occasionally, one of the seven wounded, towed on stretchers tied behind their horses, cried out or moaned in pain. All the care they'd had so far was first aid by a surgeon's orderly who rode with the company. That was the main reason Greenley now was heading back to St. Augustine. The wounds appeared serious, but not necessarily fatal, if the seven could get to somebody who knew how to take out bullets and amputate limbs. There was nobody like that with the company. Letting the herd move along its way would kill nobody. Keeping up the fight at the Comptons' probably would have killed the seven. Also, the major wanted to replenish his food and ammunition and pick up as many more troopers as he could.

He had left the Brocktons and the deserters near the Comptons. "Just keep doggin' their trail," he told Otto. "There'll be plenty more river crossin's where we can get them."

It was about a day's ride from the Comptons to either Pilatka or St. Augustine. But Greenley had no idea who the doctor was in Pilatka, or even if there was one. He knew the seven would find help in St. Augustine, so he headed for that town. He told Otto to send runners to St. Augustine to let him know where the herd was moving.

Hoping to allow the seven some rest, Greenley camped early by a freshwater stream about six miles west of St. Augustine. He and four troopers rode into town to fetch the surgeon and some ambulances. They arrived after dark. The troopers went to the hospital. Greenley decided to see if Holmes was sober enough to hear a report.

As he approached headquarters, he saw the colonel with three other officers sitting on chairs on the veranda. Light from the windows reflected off the gold braid of their uniforms. One of them wore a uniform that was noticeably lighter in color than the others. By the time Greenley got to the fence, he could tell that officer was in Confederate gray. All four on the veranda rose as Greenley tied his horse to the fence. The gray-clad one walked over and met the major halfway across the lawn.

"Captain Ryan Moultrie, sir," the Confederate said with a salute. "Now a paroled prisoner of war."

Greenley returned the salute. Moultrie continued talking, as if he were reciting a memorized speech. "All troops o' the Confederacy in this state have been surrendered. I have been an organizer o' the Cattle Guard in the northeastern 'n' north-central areas."

The two walked up the veranda steps as Moultrie talked. He kept his voice quiet and flat, but still sounded as if the words were being forced out of his mouth. "I believe you are in pursuit o' one o' my units. Have you found them?"

Greenley sighed. "In a manner of speakin'. At least found their guns." He stood at the top of the steps and saluted Holmes and two other colonels. One was named Perkins and was stationed at Fort Clinch. Greenley didn't know the other.

That one identified himself as he returned the major's salute. "Colonel Arthur Springer of the Second Indiana Cavalry. I'm on the staff of General Edward McCook. He has received the surrender of Tallahassee and is in possession of the city."

A servant brought a fifth chair onto the veranda and ushered Greenley to it. "When was the surrender?" the major asked as he sat. "I've been out in the scrub so long that I've lost track of the days."

"We've been in Tallahassee since May tenth," Springer replied. "The official ceremonies were on the twentieth, five days ago."

Greenley swallowed rapidly several times to keep from gagging on the bile that churned up from his stomach. Three dead, seven wounded. At least some of the seven maimed. Perhaps some more will die. And the war they supposedly were fighting already had ended.

Springer gestured with his hand toward two decanters on the table. "Bourbon or gin?"

Greenley shook his head. "I'm here with a detail. We're goin' back as soon as we can line up some medical help for my wounded."

Perkins pointed to Springer, Moultrie, and himself. "We'll come with you. Our job is to round up any hostile detachments and give them the word. Have them surrender and parole them."

Springer rose from his chair and walked off the veranda. Perkins and Moultrie followed. Greenley watched them for a second. Both colonels seemed to march. They stepped in unison to beat of a drummer that only they could hear. It was a way of walking found in most career officers — the ones who left home at 17 for West Point. They fought in Mexico and against various Indian tribes. Springer, in particular, seemed like the model for the West Point career man. Tall, silver-haired, and slender, with a close-cropped beard. Perkins was a bit chunkier and shorter, with pepper-and-salt hair and a beard that flowed down to his chest. Moultrie, shorter and thinner than either of them, walked slowly behind the other two as they headed for the stables.

Greenley saw that his men were getting horses and ambulances ready for the trip back. Then he walked over to Doris's. He knocked and the door opened. She stepped back behind the door so that it blocked the sight of her from the doorway. Light from the oil lamp she carried flickered out into the street. Dan stepped into the room, but went no further than the doormat. She closed the door and stepped around to face him. The red dressing grown was cinched around her waist. Green and white checks from the calico wrapper could be seen between the folds of the gown.

"I didn't wake you?"

Dark ringlets obscured her face as she shook her head. "Just relaxin' afore turnin' in."

Greenley hurried his words. "I've just got a couple of minutes. Came over to make sure you heard the news."

A smile, the same one that appeared every time she teased him about something, parted her lips. "Sure I've heard. What are you rushin' off for? Want to get back to Iowa tonight?"

"Ohio. Ohio. Ohio." Greenley was becoming exasperated. He couldn't tell whether she honestly got all Midwestern states mixed up in her mind or if she was continually joking.

"Whatever. Still, what's your hurry to go anywheres?"

The exasperation left him as quickly as it came. He couldn't find it in him to stay irritated at her for more than fleeting moments. "I'm goin' back into the scrub. One more time. Job's not over yet. But it's about to be."

"Okay. Get along 'n' get it over with. Why'd you come by here?"

The words rushed out of his mouth: "I've got to know. When I go back to Ohio, will you come with me?"

Still the teasing smile. "Sure. But you've got to make an honest woman o' me first. If I've got to live in freezin' weather all winter, I want a ring to keep my finger warm."

He reached out to pull her toward him. But she still held the lamp and one of his hands touched the heated glass of the globe. The pain made him flinch. She giggled. Then she turned back to him and bent over to kiss the burned hand. Her head slowly rose up his arm from the hand until it reached his mouth. Her lips closed on his. After the kiss, they both had to take deep breaths before they could talk.

"Got to go." He walked out backwards so he could keep looking at her.

"For God's sake be careful, now. There's no sense gettin' shot up with the war over 'n' everythin'."

Of all the times he had left her to go on patrol, that was the first parting warning she ever had given. That thought bothered Greenley, although he did not know why, as he walked back to the stable.

Two ambulances and the rest of his detachment, including a surgeon and Springer, Perkins and Moultrie were waiting for him when he entered the stableyard. Greenley rode with the other officers at the head of the column. He looked at the headquarters building as they passed it. Holmes was still sitting on the veranda, rocking in a chair. A glass was in his hand.

"Must be thirsty work 'round here, judgin' by your commander," Moultrie, riding beside Greenley, leaned over in his saddle to whisper.

Greenley glanced at the Confederate and smiled. It was tempting to agree and spend the trip complaining about the habits and inabilities of higher ranking officers. But, with two other colonels in the group, it would be unwise. Also, he didn't know whether Moultrie was trying to be humorous and friendly or making a serious complaint. Although they were riding close enough for their stirrups to touch, Greenley could not tell if Moultrie was smiling. Indeed, it was hard to tell anything about his facial expressions or features. His beard, hair, and complexion were so dark that many of his physical characteristics blended into the night. All Greenley could see was that the Confederate and he were about the same height, although Moultrie's shoulders were narrower. Perhaps he was also a few years younger.

The group moved onto the dirt ruts that passed for the road leading west. Lanterns hung on the sides of the ambulances. They cast a feeble yellow light on the road and threw huge shadows of the riders out to the palmettos on either side of the ruts. Creaking springs on the ambulances and the clip-clop of the horses' hooves were drowned out by other sounds of the night: the chirping of crickets, the hooting of owls, and the croaking of frogs. Whippoorwills called out their names. Occasionally, the loud bass croaks of gators rolled over the other noises.

Greenley decided to break the monotony of the ride. He turned in his saddle and spoke to Moultrie. "The bunch I'm after is led by a sergeant named Hooker. Know him?"

"That's why I'm here," the Confederate replied. "He'll recognize me 'n' quit on my say-so. Worked with him off 'n' on since '62. Both of us were in cattle afore the war. When the government got the idea for the Cow Cavalry, we were detached from the army at the same time. Rode together from Mississippi. Before that, our company was on detached duty from Joe Johnston's army to scout 'round Vicksburg. The siege eventually trapped us in the city."

They reached the rest of the troopers after midnight. Sentries spread the word of the surrender and the camp awoke with cheering and singing. Everybody slept in fits and starts for the rest of the night. After breakfast, the officers agreed to let all but a handful go back to St. Augustine with the ambulances. After some cajoling by Greenley, including promises of a bottle for each when the job was done, and a half-hour-long speech by Springer, a sergeant and four privates volunteered to be the handful to stay. It was past noon before the company broke camp. Greenley, his five troopers, and the other officers took the path northwest toward Picolata.

They were still several hours from the town when two riders came down the path from the opposite direction. One rider held back while the other kept getting closer. Greenley recognized the second one as Corley Brockton. The one who was holding back probably was one of the deserters who realized that there were four officers in this group. Any of the Brocktons' deserters would have good reason to be wary of that many officers in one place.

"This your idea o' more help? Where the hell's the rest o' 'em?"

Greenley wondered if Corley ever spoke without sneering. But, he kept his own voice as pleasantly matter-of-fact as possible as he replied. "Won't be needin' them."

Corley didn't respond. "The herd's crossed the river at Comptons' all right. Headin' due north." His squinting eyes suddenly widened as they focused on Moultrie's gray uniform. Greenley introduced Corley to the other officers and then told him: "We're goin' over to Picolota and take a boat across. Have your Pa meet us."

Otto and his two sons arrived in town shortly after dusk. Greenley was waiting for them. He sat in a chair beside a wooden Indian in front of the largest building in town. It was a riverside dance hall. Inside, a piano player had begun. The music drifted from the other side of the swinging doors into the street. Apparently in recognition of the surrender and of the fact that a Confederate was at a table inside drinking beer with two Union colonels, the player was concentrating on nonpartisan songs of peace. First, a rousing "When Johnny Comes Marching Home," then a soft "Tenting Tonight." As the Brocktons rode up, the piano was playing and a variety of voices were singing the maudlin chorus of "The Vacant Chair":

"We shall meet, but we shall miss him,
There will be one vacant chair;
We shall linger to caress him
When we breathe our evening prayer."

The Brocktons tied their horses to hitching posts. "The rest are waitin' on the other side o' the river," Otto said. "What's gonna happen now?" Greenley replied by ushering them inside the building. Springer, Perkins, and Moultrie were sitting at a large round table. A pitcher of beer was in the center of the table and each officer held a stein. Four more steins were set out in front of four other places at the table. The Brocktons and Greenley sat. Around them, soldiers, sailors, and civilians sang:

"When a year ago we gathered,
Joy was in his mild blue eye
But a golden cord is severed,

And our hopes in ruin lie."

Several of the singers were women. Corley studied each of them as his eyes shifted to take in all of the room. Otto and Martin kept their eyes on the officers at the table.

"You really figure Tree's gonna come in without a fight?" Otto asked, half sarcastically.

"He's a soldier in my command. He's done his duty for the last four years. Now his duty is to surrender." The irritation in Moultrie's voice was obvious. "He'll do that like everythin' else he's done since takin' the oath to the Confederacy."

All three Brocktons shook their heads. "Can't see Tree or any o' 'em givin' up that many cattle," Martin said.

Springer leaned forward toward the Brocktons, as if to make sure they could hear his voice over the singing. "We'll worry about the cattle later. Under the terms of the surrender, any livestock temporarily becomes the property of the federal government. But any man who claims ownership of a horse or mule gets it returned. Cattle will be confiscated. The government may claim, or trade them. Or, probably, they will revert to their original owners. In this case, I guess that means the people who are driving them now."

The singing had stopped. Greenley was grateful for that for two reasons. One, he never liked songs that did nothing except remind him of the war dead. Two, there was nothing in the room to distract him from the full enjoyment of the Brocktons' reactions.

Otto had been sipping his beer as Springer talked. Suddenly, at the words "the people who are driving them now" he spat. The beer spewed in an arch that included Otto's sons, Greenley's left sleeve, and some of Springer's chest. Foam, like sweat coming off a horse, stuck in Otto's beard.

"The hell you say," followed the beer out of Otto's mouth. "What 'bout us?"

Springer, his eyes wide in surprise, took the yellow bandana from his neck and wiped it across the beer on his shirt. He kept his voice under control as he replied: "You'll get the usual civilian scout pay. Twenty-five cents per day for each of you."

Both sons made noises that sounded like combinations of belches and yelps of pain. "We've got a deal," Martin whined. With the back of his left hand, Otto slapped his son's arm. Martin clamped his lips together.

Perkins' voice took on the tone of an officer who was used to being obeyed. "The only deal we recognize here is the one laid out in the surrender terms agreed to by the United States government. We'll have to wait for final word on this, but I imagine the government will decide it needs the beef and will pay the current owners for the herd."

He got up from the table. The other officers followed his example. Greenley, biting his lip to keep from smiling, looked down at the Brocktons and asked, "Comin'?"

With the same back of the hand that he had used on Martin, Otto wiped the foam off his beard. "Not at least for now. Maybe we'll see you 'cross the river."

The officers left the room as the piano player coaxed the keys into producing the opening bars of "The Girl I Left Behind Me."

Otto held his breath as he watched the quartet of

uniforms go through the swinging doors. Then, he coughed and put his elbows on the table.

"You really expect us to have gone through all this for twenty-five damned cents a day?" Corley asked.

"Hell," his father replied. "Our deal's still good. We just ain't been talkin' to the right people. "Let Danny Boy 'n' the rest o' that bunch fetch Tree's herd for us."

Otto dug in his pocket and pulled out a doubloon. He handed it to Corley. "Get another pitcher. Might as well get some whiskey too. Then both of ya'll leave me to think a bit."

His sons disappeared among the dance hall crowd as Otto threw a shot of rye down his throat and then followed it with a sip of beer. True, he and Holmes were too tightly wound together for the colonel now to get untangled. Holmes might know about the surrender terms, but, combining his greed with fears of having his past cattle dealings revealed, he still could be forced to play a part. The other Yankee colonels would go back to wherever they came from as soon as Tree surrendered. There was nothing Otto could do about Tree. The blood was too bad between them now. Might as well fight it out with money and cattle involved than just go at it for the simple pleasure of watching the bastard die.

That left Danny Boy. Probably will have to kill the poor, stupid son of a bitch. It'd be easy to put a bullet into him any time. But he always had other soldiers around him. One major could vanish in the scrub. Somebody would come looking if more than one Yankee suddenly disappeared now that the war was finished. Otto needed to keep the good graces of Yankees since they were running the whole state. Killing several of them would not do at all. So, whatever else happens, Danny has got to get off by himself in the scrub.

Otto finished the glass of beer. He reached for the pitcher, but stopped before he poured out any. No use befuddling the mind now. Find a place to make a stand. There's that cypress cabin and cowpens where Haw Creek branches. Water on the west, north, and south would stop anybody sneaking up from those directions. There are woods to the east, but enough open pasture between the woods and the cabin to give clear shots at anybody coming from that direction. He would have seven men with him. Enough to drive the cattle there and to get whoever comes from the woods in a good, killing crossfire.

Carrying the whiskey bottle with him, Otto left the table and walked though the crowd. He disengaged his sons from two gaudily dressed, heavily perfumed women. Corley and Martin followed their father out the door.

"Get the fellas back from the other side," Otto said. "We're goin' to St. Augustine at first light."

Greenley and the rest camped at the outskirts of town. The next morning they took a ferry across the river and didn't bother waiting for the Brocktons. "With luck, you got them out of my life," Greenley told Springer as the detachment rode west.

"Hooker should be pretty easy to find," Moultrie said. "I've driven herds through this territory myself a couple o' times. Bet we cut 'cross his trail in two days."

Greenley believed the Confederate was overly confident, but fortunately, he didn't take the bet. During the morning of the second day, Greenley heard the crack of whips coming from the west. He, the colonels, Moultrie, and the sergeant rode toward the sound. The sergeant held a flagstaff, resting its base in his stirrup. The flag was rolled around the staff and covered by a tubelike piece of canvas. They stopped in a grassy field when they came within sight of the herd. The sergeant took off the covering and a white flag of truce fluttered in the breeze.

They saw a rider gallop from the herd across the field. It was Tree. He reined in his horse within a few feet of Moultrie. Greenley was surprised at Tree's appearance. He looked worse than he did when he was imprisoned. Large, angry red swellings dotted his face. Probably insect bites that had become infected. One on his right eyebrow had forced the lid halfway down his eye. The stubble on his face had almost grown into a full beard. He sat bolt upright in the saddle, squared his shoulders, and saluted. But instead of looking straight ahead as dictated by military training, his eyes shifted from the flag to Moultrie.

All four officers returned the salute. Tree dropped his hand and said, "It's over. Ain't it?" The voice sounded like someone heading for bed after working 12 hours in a hot sun. His shoulders slumped and the head dropped until the chin almost touched his chest. Without waiting for a reply, he turned his horse and slowly rode back toward the herd.

# 29 ⚡

THE OFFICERS HAD THE ENLISTED MEN build a lean-to. Two canvas tent skins were stretched over a limb of a huge oak at the border of the grassy area. The men staked down one end of the skins to the ground. That created a shelter under which Springer and Perkins sat on folding wooden camp chairs. Meanwhile, an outrider left Tree's camp and returned within an hour with the cow hunters' wagon. Then, one by one, starting with Hooker, the hunters came into the shade of the lean-to. Each one raised his right hand and repeated after Springer, who recited an oath of allegiance to the United States. The hunter then received a slip of paper, his parole, signed by Perkins. The process took only a few minutes for each man.

Most of the hunters also surrendered guns, which they put in a corner of the lean-to. Greenley supervised that part of the surrender. He became skeptical as soon as Tree handed in his weapons. The sergeant gave up one Colt revolver in a holster, although he had at least two on him when he rode up from the herd a few hours earlier. At that time, Greenley also had seen the stock of a carbine sticking out of a scabbard tied to Tree's saddle. But the only long-arm Hooker gave up was a worn double-barreled shotgun. Some of the cow hunters did not surrender anything. They said they lost their guns on the trail. The major was tempted to point out that somebody had enough guns to hold off his company at Comptons'. Several of those who surrendered guns turned in U.S.-issue Enfield rifle-muskets and other weapons that obviously had been captured from federal troops somewhere along the way. Greenley even recognized an old muzzle-loading Springfield carbine. It had been carried by one of his troopers, who dropped it after being wounded at Comptons'.

Not wanting to start a fight that probably would have wiped out his detachment, Greenley kept silent until after the paroles had been handed out and the cow hunters had returned to their camp. Then he asked the colonels if they wanted to search the camp — and especially the wagon — for more weapons.

"No," Springer replied. "Why start trouble? Do you seriously think these men" — he gestured toward the cow hunters' camp — "intend to continue the war on their own? If they were officers, the surrender terms would have allowed them to keep their sidearms anyhow."

Moultrie came into the lean-to. He apparently had heard Greenley's question and was smiling at Springer.

"Besides, ya'll might need those fellas 'n' their guns afore this is all over," the captain said. "Somebody's got to move these cattle from here. Don't see your scout 'n' his boys volunteerin' for that job.

Leastwise, they're not volunteerin' to do it for twenty-five cents a day. If we ever see your scouts again, it'll probably be through gunsmoke. Either that, or kiss these cows goodbye."

Perkins nodded. "On the subject of the herd, let's get over to their camp and start dealin' with the livestock."

The cow hunters claimed private ownership of the oxen and horses — all but one gelding, a large, dark chestnut that Tree led by its bridle to Perkins. The "U.S." brand on its flanks could be seen from several yards away.

"Damn good ridin' horse," Tree said. "Been with me since Vicksburg. Call him Yankee. Don't know his given name. Could I buy or trade for him?"

Perkins smiled. "Sorry. He's property of the U.S. government."

The other horses were divvied up among their owners within a few minutes. Deciding what to do about the cattle took hours. Tree's men rode among the herd, counting as the afternoon thunderstorm doused them and the cattle. Eventually, Hooker, riding a sorrel mare, came to the lean-to and handed Perkins a sheet of paper.

"Tally puts it at just under twenty-three hundred head," Tree said. "Lost 'bout five hundred along the way. Particularly in that swamp."

Perkins glanced at the paper. "This meadow's too small to keep that many cattle grazin' for very long."

Moultrie and Springer stood on either side of Perkins, who gestured to them as he kept looking at Tree. "We've got an idea. There's plenty of graze just to the west of St. Augustine. Turn the herd around, cross the river at Picolota and go east. Colonel Springer and I will give your men a safe conduct pass. Nobody in the Army will molest them. Any trouble, the Army will help. Maybe take five days, a week at the most, to finish the drive."

Tree shrugged his shoulders. "Sounds fine. 'Cept what happens once we get the cattle there?"

Springer answered. "We don't know exactly. Maybe you'll get paid for the herd. Maybe it'll be confiscated. That's ultimately up to our commander in Tallahassee. But, one way or another, the chances are that the government is goin' to need that beef. We've got a lot of hungry people to feed right now. Get the herd near St. Augustine and we can ship it out from the docks."

Moultrie took off his hat and fanned it toward the colonels. "This Army's all there is to care for the South right now. Not much left from Georgia to Virginia. No crops, no herds. Nothin' but what we can get to 'em through the Army. Your duty was to supply the South with beef. In a way, it still is."

Tree rubbed the mare's nose. "Yeah. Reckon so." He breathed out the words in a sigh, almost a whisper. "We'll start at first light."

Moultrie put the hat back on his head. He smiled, a slight upturn of the lips between the black moustache and beard. "No. They'll start. You'll stay with us. Just for a spell. Come with us to Jacksonville."

The right side of Tree's mouth began to pull into a sneer. Moultrie waved his hands downwards, trying to squelch any complaint. "No. No. It'll be all right. We might need you to help bring in any more of us who still are out there. We'll know in a week. 'N'

Jacksonville's the nearest place with a workin' telegraph. We'll get a message on what to do with the herd 'n' then you can get over to St. Augustine."

Neither Moultrie's gesture nor words changed Tree's sneer. But he said nothing. He nodded his head, climbed on the horse, and rode back to his camp.

Jacksonville was the largest city along the St. Johns. It sat at the river's mouth, where the water divided into dozens of channels and fingers that turned into a delta and then filtered into the Atlantic. The heart of the city was a warehouse district on the northwestern bank. Since the '20s, the city had been a center of the river trade, a major shipping point for cattle, lumber, turpentine, and citrus. It developed a more prosperous, settled look than most of the other river towns. Until the war, three-story brick buildings were common. The false-fronted log and plank shops, like those of Enterprise and Picolata, were confined to the back streets. Even the old judge's home in Pilatka would have been lost among the stately houses that sat back from oak-shaded lanes. As proof of its arrival into the upper crust of cities, Jacksonville even maintained a public library.

But, over the last four years, the city had been tossed between Union and Confederate hands like a ball thrown back and forth by boys playing catch. Yankees invaded, occupied, and then evacuated Jacksonville three times. They returned a fourth time in February of '64 and stayed. The large homes that had not been burned in the process had been occupied and vandalized.

By the time Tree arrived with the four officers,

most of the best residential areas looked like giant piles of charcoal sitting on either side of weed-choked sandy ruts. Some of the brick warehouses still lined the waterfront. Many of the hotels, bars, and bawdy houses were untouched. The library also remained, but it had been taken over as the staff headquarters for the occupation forces.

Within an hour after their arrival, Perkins and Springer found and paid for rooms for Greenley, Moultrie, and Tree at a hotel a few blocks from the riverfront. The hotel looked as if it had been made by attaching two adjoining whitewashed frame houses into one L-shaped building at the corner of two streets. One wing had a dining room, a parlor, and a bar on the first floor. The kitchen building was in back of one wing and a line of privies in back of the other. There were 25 guest rooms, each with a large four-poster bed, a small chair, a table and a chamber pot. Greenley settled comfortably into his room. It had a view of a nicely trimmed yard with several large magnolia trees, one of which spread its branches over to the roof of the red brick kitchen building.

Perkins and Springer had told him to stay near to the two Confederates, but not to seem to be spying upon them or guarding them. Other than that, Greenley had no orders. He went to the post headquarters the next morning to see what his duties were to be. Perkins arrived at headquarters in a carriage drawn by a mismatched pair of brown horses and driven by a black enlisted man.

"Come and check with us now and then. Other than that, just sit tight and enjoy yourself for awhile," Perkins said. "Keep your Rebel friends close at hand if we need to scour the countryside for more of them. That's about it. The nice thing about winnin' a war is the relaxin' you do afterwards."

Five days lazily passed. Greenley occasionally saw either Perkins or Springer being driven about the city. The colonels were staying in one of the larger homes that had survived, a three-story, red brick manor house that looked like it belonged in the middle of a large plantation instead of a city. It was the quarters for senior officers and was segregated from the street by a large, black, wrought-iron fence. From there, Perkins and Springer each morning rode in their carriages around a circuit that went to the post headquarters, to the telegraph office, and then back to the mansion. For three days, Greenley walked from the hotel to headquarters each morning and saw them on their circuit. One or both would wave at him, which he took as a signal that neither had any orders for him.

The only official business he conducted at headquarters was cashing in his last pay voucher from St. Augustine. He had not needed cash out in the scrub and the voucher had lain in the bottom of his saddlebag. Now, he had need of the money to do something he had wanted to do for months. Armed with $80, he began to patrol the streets in search of an engagement ring. He feared that anything he found would eat up all his pay. But he found that all mercantile and pawn shops had a variety for sale. With or without stones, in gold or silver, for $20 or less. The selection enticed him toward buying the wedding band while he was in the process. Still, the number of choices available kept him from making up his mind on which rings to buy.

He decided to think over his options and went to

the hotel saloon. It was tiny. Room for no more than six average-sized men to stand at the bar without bumping their shoulders. The bar itself, the floor, and the walls were all paneled in a dark oak. Light came from coal oil lamps in a chandelier. But the paneling seemed to absorb most of the light, giving the bar the atmosphere of a small cave. The hotel owner, a fat bald-headed man who wore a perpetual smile, presided over the bar. He was standing behind it as Greenley entered. Moultrie and Tree stood on the other side, each sipping white liquid from a wide-mouthed brandy snifter.

"Milk punch?" Moultrie asked, holding out his snifter toward Greenley. "They make a pretty good one here."

Greenley had tried a milk punch once. It was a mixture of cold milk, brandy, and spices that was popular in the Deep South during the summer. But the milk seemed to sour on his stomach when he tried it. He shook his head and ordered a beer.

Having nothing else to talk about, he told about his morning of ring shopping and the selection available. Moultrie, in a quiet, level voice, quickly drained off Greenley's pleasure by explaining: "Sure. A lot of new widows needin' cash. You'll find bargains in rings all over the South."

Greenley downed his beer in one long swallow. "Never thought of that. Damn. Seems like a mighty morbid way to start a new life. Usin' the leftovers of somebody else's misfortune."

In the darkness of the bar, Tree was a shadow looming over Moultrie. "Let me guess," the voice came from the shadow. "Doris Brava? I owe ya'll somethin'."

Two coins dropped on the bar. Tree pushed the coins and they slid along the polished surface to Greenley. The coins glimmered in the lamplight. One was gold and the other silver. The major picked them up, and saw that the inscriptions on them were Spanish.

"After ya'll kept me alive, I went 'n' ruined your Christmas party," Tree said. "So take these. Go to any good blacksmith 'n' he can melt one into an engagement ring 'n' the other into a weddin' band. Long as you got a good idea o' the size o' her finger."

Greenley held the coins in his hand. "Guess her ring finger's about the size of my little one. I can't take these. Lord, man, you're gonna need every coin you can get a hold of."

Tree drained the snifter. "Spanish money's as close as the nearest ship headin' to Cuba. Still plenty o' cows out in the palmettos. Cubans still need 'em. I'll be huntin' cows from now on. Go ahead 'n' try the coins."

Moultrie turned his head toward Hooker. "Never figured you for a romantic. There somebody 'round that you figure to melt some coins for?"

The room was too dark for Greenley to see Tree's expression. But he could hear a catch in the voice when it replied, "Not really. Please 'cuse me. Reckon the punch ain't settin' well with me today. I'm goin' to my room for a spell."

Greenley and Moultrie watched him walk out the door and then turned back to their glasses.

# 30 🖑

$T$REE BREATHED DEEPLY as he walked out of the hotel into the sunlight. A breeze out of the east brought a slight taste of salt from the ocean with it. He hoped the officers weren't offended, but he had to escape into open air. Ghosts from Vicksburg haunted that bar. It wasn't just Moultrie's question. The bar itself seemed too much like the hole dug into the hill near the Masons. Laura already was in his mind when the officers forced the memories out into the open.

Boredom partially was responsible for the melancholy. Too much time to think and remember. The same thing happened to him in the cell at Fort Marion. Except the cell had nothing to overtly remind him of Vicksburg. Jacksonville had many such things. The magnolias in back of the hotel seemed too much like those in the Masons' front yard. Too many of the houses seemed like those built on the hills above the Mississippi. Rows of burned-out buildings were too much like those leveled by the siege. He walked down to the riverfront. Steamboats docked at wharves. Black stevedores hauling freight to and from the boats into brown and red-brick warehouses. All of it way too much like Vicksburg. Tree found another bar, bought a bottle of rye and took it back to his hotel room. Within an hour, he had fallen into a nightmare-plagued sleep that continued off and on until the next morning.

A knock at his door woke him. He discovered a film like pond scum covering his eyes, but he reached the door, opened it, and dimly saw a smiling Greenley. "Feelin' better?" the figure in blue asked. "I think you will be after hearin' this."

The pond scum also seemed to have coated Tree's tongue and made it stick to the bottom of his mouth. He was unable to reply. The major didn't wait for an answer. "Just saw Colonel Perkins. He says it looks like all the Cattle Guard are accounted for. No need for you and Captain Moultrie to hang around any more."

Tree ran his tongue over the back of his teeth. That scraped off enough of the scum for him to ask: "What 'bout the herd?"

"Perkins is waitin' for a telegram from Tallahassee. Says he expects it any time. Get dressed. Get some breakfast and come with me to headquarters. Maybe he'll have word by then."

Two cups of coffee were all that Tree wanted for breakfast. They were enough to clear the scum out of his vision and mouth. A chaw of tobacco while he walked down the street with the major cured the rest of the hangover. He and the Yankee made a detour on their way to headquarters. They stopped by the stables, where Moultrie already had finished saddling a horse. They shook hands. Both the major and Tree promised to visit Moultrie's home near Mellonville. The captain got into his saddle, waved, and spurred the horse into a trot down the street. Greenley and Tree continued their walk to the headquarters building.

A crowd of civilians always hung around the steps leading to the veranda of the headquarters. It was a mixture of everyone who might want anything from the Yankees. Women in the black dresses of widowhood, holding the hands of small children and asking for food and shelter. Well-dressed, portly business-men looking for governmental contracts. Ragged newly freed slaves wondering where they should go and what they should do.

As he and Greenley neared the building, Tree noticed one man at the edge of the crowd. The man leaned against a horse, which was tied by its reins to the picket fence that surrounded the headquarters. Obviously a cow hunter, he wore a wide-brimmed, high-crowned brown palmetto-straw hat and had a whip looped over one shoulder. He was short and skinny. That drew Hooker's attention because the hunter looked so much like Skeeter. Tree walked a few steps closer. It was Skeeter.

A quick jog closed the remaining steps between the hunters. "What the hell are you doin' here?" Tree asked.

"Got in last night." Skeeter pushed the hat back to reveal his eyes. "Figured you'd show up here some-time."

Greenley came up behind Tree and was intro-duced to Skeeter. "We're goin' in right now to see what the disposition of your cattle will be."

Skeeter's eyes were bright, with angry red veins

spilling into gray irises. "They've already been disposed o'. Two days after we camped out west o' Augustine. The Brocktons come up with four or five other fellas 'n' a written Yankee order to seize the cattle."

Tree spat out his quid. He felt his bottom jaw thrust out until his upper teeth locked behind his lower ones. The chances of betrayal had preyed on his mind, particularly when he was told to leave the herd. But, somehow, perhaps because of his treatment by the major during his captivity, he had forced down his suspicions and kept his objections to himself. Bad mistake.

The low, doglike growl that he couldn't control started rising out of his throat. He reached with his right hand for the butt of the belt gun. Then he stopped the movement with a jerk of the hand when he realized he had neither the revolver nor the belt. He hadn't worn them since the surrender.

Greenley's voice sounded honestly surprised. "Who signed that order?" He held up a hand. "No, wait. Let me guess. Was the name Holmes?"

Skeeter nodded.

"He's got no more business signin' that than he does the Emancipation Proclamation," Greenley turned toward the steps and began shouldering his way through the crowd. "Come on, both of you. We're goin' to Perkins."

Tree heard Greenley, but he already had turned his back on the major and was walking toward the stables. Skeeter untied his horse and followed. Greenley turned, shouldered his way the opposite direction back through the crowd, and came after the other two, all but begging them to go back to headquarters.

Greenley's voice was drowned out by Skeeter's. "Only me, Volusia, Dinghy, Lonesome, 'n' Swede left. We've made camp a little ways south o' town. Rest took off after they had to give up the herd. Brocktons started drivin' south."

The major stopped talking, but he continued to trail after the other two until they reached the stables. There, Tree opened a corral gate and walked into a pen of milling horses. His sorrel mare was in the pen, but so was the dark chestnut gelding. Hooker did not find the gelding as much as it found him. Its whinny came out in a loud humming sound as it stared at Tree. He came over to it, grabbed the rope halter around its face and led it out of the corral. The soldiers loitering around the corral did nothing to stop him. His saddle and tack still were at the hotel.

Skeeter, leading his own horse, followed as Tree and the gelding walked down the street. Greenley watched them go and then turned back to headquarters. He again was pushing through the crowd before the thought stuck him that the horse was federal property and that he had allowed Hooker to walk away with it.

Perkins was sitting at a desk in what must have been the front parlor of the headquarters when it had been a home. Springer was with him. They both smiled as Greenley entered and Perkins held out a slip of paper. It was a transcript of a telegraph, authorizing the sale of the cattle to the government and their shipment from St. Augustine to South Carolina.

"This won't be doin' much good now," Greenley said. "For all I know, the cattle are bein' cut in some Havana butcher shop at this minute."

Springer's and Perkins' faces looked as if the major had slapped them. Surprise eventually gave way to indignation as Greenley relayed Skeeter's story. Perkins scribbled furiously with a quill pen at a piece of paper.

"Holmes is nothing more than another cow thief, like the rest of them," Perkins mumbled as he wrote. He showed the paper to Springer, who bent over the desk and signed it. Perkins slowly fanned the paper in the air to let the ink dry and then handed it to Greenley.

"You are hereby authorized — hell. You are ordered to arrest Colonel Holmes on charges of grand theft of government property. Go to St. Augustine and get the provost marshal. Clap Holmes in irons and await further orders from us. Want to take some more men with you?"

Greenley shook his head. "Don't want to wait to muster a detachment. I'm gettin' a horse and ridin'."

He started for the door, but then turned back to the colonels. "Oh, wait. The Rebel sergeant. When he lit out, he took that dark chestnut with him."

Perkins angrily waved a hand. "Well, clap him in irons too. If you come across him on the road. Just don't go out of your way looking for him."

Springer put a hand on Perkins' shoulder. "There's a better way to deal with that. What about the horse the sergeant rode here? The sorrel mare? Did he leave her at the stables?"

Greenley nodded. "Okay. I'll have a government brand slapped on her." Springer managed a tight-lipped smile. "Then I'll just change the list of surrendered items. Where there's 'chestnut gelding' I'll put 'sorrel mare.' If you ever see Hooker again, just tell him to change the brand on the horse."

Tree and Skeeter turned west off the road and into a pine forest about five miles south of the city. The horses threaded their way around the trees until they reached a clearing, where the rest of the hunters were gathered around the wagon.

"Enjoy yourself in the big city?" Dinghy asked sarcastically. "Otto Brockton sends his regards. Reckon he's sorry he missed you when he stopped by."

Hooker didn't reply. Without even looking at any of those who were watching him, he went to the back of the wagon and rummaged through the ropes, tools, and weapons. He drew out his carbine, Colt, and gunbelt. First he loaded the carbine and then the revolver. He returned to the wagon and emerged with a bundle wrapped in brown paper.

The bundle held a thick book, with a cover that appeared to have originally been black, but was now faded by use and the sun until there were streaks of reddish brown in it. A black holster, with a Remington .44 and gunbelt, also were in the bundle.

"Those're Heavy's, ain't they?" Swede asked.

"Yeah. Been savin' 'em for his family," Tree held up the Bible for a moment and then placed it back on the paper and rewrapped it. He unholstered the Remington, unhinged the loading lever, and took a handful of balls out of the belt's bullet pouch.

"Figured they'd want the Bible 'n' gun. But —" he held up the revolver "— I also figure they'd want this used for what I intend to do with it now."

Nobody replied. The only sounds around the wagon were the slight creaks made by the loading lever as Hooker moved it and the taps made by the lever as it hit the balls.

A wind came out of the northeast, pushing a sheet of clouds over the sky. By noon, a steady rain was falling, the sort of rain that would stay at least the rest of the day. It brought with it the scent of the pines as it dripped from the needles down on Tree and the others as they snaked the horses and wagon through the woods.

The rain also followed Greenley as he stayed on the road until he reached St. Augustine. It was after dark, and he knew Mac would not be working late. So, he rode up to Miss Fatio's gate, tied his horse there, and took off the saddlebags, in which he had stowed the arrest order to save it from the rain. He walked through the guest entrance. The smell of roast beef and the clatter of plates being passed guided him to the dining room. Gasps of dismay from Miss Fatio and the serving girls announced his arrival. He had not removed either his hat or poncho and both had dripped water in a trail from the entrance to the dining room door. Mac, who had been bent over the serving platter carving off a slice of beef, looked up and dropped the large knife and fork.

Greenley, who had not felt welcomed at Miss Fatio's ever since his prisoner caused the stain on the dining room carpet, realized his gaff. "Sorry, ma'am. But this is an emergency." He took off his hat, which caused more water to shower down, and bowed toward Miss Fatio, who was standing as if she was posing for a woodcut illustrating how to come to attention. Her face looked as if she were gargling quinine.

Mac was on his feet and moving even before

Greenley said "Come on" and gestured with a jerk of the head toward the door. He had the order out of the saddlebag and in the marshal's hands as they walked down the hallway.

They sprinted through the mud to the provost's office. Mac unlocked the door, went to the gun rack and removed a short, double-barreled 12-gauge shotgun. He began muttering as he loaded the gun. "Hell of a way to end a war. Haven't seen Holmes about the last couple of days. Can't believe he'd light out, though. Let's check his quarters first. Try to do this as quickly and cleanly as we can and not get too many more folks involved."

He took a poncho from the office's coat rack, put it on, and then held the gun underneath it. They walked back into the rain and over to headquarters. The sentry told them that Holmes was in his room. Mac let his breath out in a slow, very low-pitched whistle of relief.

The room's door was unlocked. It swung open, with a slight creak of the hinges, when Greenley gently pushed on it with one hand. Mac entered first, the shotgun outside the poncho, but pointed at the floor instead of the figure seated in a chair before a rolltop desk. The room smelled like a privy, with the ammonia reeking from an unemptied chamber pot beside the large four-poster bed. There also was the odor of soon-to-be-stale fish coming from the window beside the bed.

Greenley undid the flap of his holster, but hesitated to draw. During four years in the Army, he never imagined the situation that would have him advancing on one of his superior officers with a gun. Since he was doing that, nothing else that happened in the room should have surprised him. But Holmes' reaction did. Without a word, the colonel lurched to his feet with his hands in the air. No bluster. No protest. No challenge to the men who were coming at him. Not even a request to see the arrest order.

"Gawd, I'm sorry," Holmes whined. His arms came down, but he still made no gesture of resistance. He reached for a bottle on the desk and filled a glass. "Don't imagine either of you are in the mood for one last drink? Notheen like this was supposed to happen."

The major didn't listen to Mac going through ritual of reading the arrest warrant. Instead, he watched the shadows cast on the wall by the single candle in the room. Then one of those shadows moved from the sill of the bedside window. Greenley's hand went for the butt of the revolver. He stopped the draw when the shadow meowed and plopped with a thud onto the bed. Coacoochee.

"What the hell is he doin' here?" Greenley pointed at the cat, which had a half-eaten slice of mullet in its mouth.

"Don't know why I couldn't leave it. Took it in with me," Holmes said as he weaved from side to side. "Doesn't seem to like my company. But comes in for the smoked fish. It seemed so lonely. And it's my fault."

Holmes shook his head. His eyes widened as he stared at Greenley. He seemed to realize that the major had no idea of what he meant.

"Gawddamn. You don't know, do you?" The whining disappeared and the voice held a note of surprise. "This is just about the gawddamn cows?"

Holmes' tone again changed. It seemed sympathetic, as if the colonel was consoling a wounded soldier. "They took the woman along. Got her yesterday. Last I saw her, she was in a wagon with the oldest Brockton boy."

Greenley's hand again touched the revolver butt. "Doris?" The name exploded out of his mouth before his throat closed to the point he had difficulty breathing, much less talking. His head felt as if a steel band were being screwed ever tighter around his temples. A foglike curtain blurred the images in the room.

"Brocktons came into town and right into her shop. Led her out at gunpoint and put her in the wagon. Told me to tell you that she'll be all right. So long as we don't send troops after them. Said you can come and get her at the Haw Creek cowpens. But come alone. Gawd. Oh Gawd. I'm sorry."

Holmes was in a cell at the provost marshal's office before Greenley felt his throat clear and his jaw unclench enough for him to talk. "Those boys are in a spot where they could fight off all of this garrison. They'd be able to see us comin'. Doris'd be panther bait before any of us could get off a shot. Maybe I can sneak up alone and get her out."

Mac shook his head. "I've got my job. The government wants the Brocktons."

Greenley got a map and a pencil out of Mac's desk. He drew a circle around the area where the Haw Creek cabin was. "Here they'll be. Just give me a couple of days headstart. You can do your job, but give me some time. Two days. If I'm not back by then, somethin' around Haw Creek will be munchin' on my bones. Doris'll probably be gone too. Get the Brocktons then, but give me a chance first to get her out."

Mac studied the map. "All right. But start tomorrow morning. Get some rest now and get going at daylight."

Greenley headed for the door. "Forget it. I'm gettin' a fresh horse and headin' out. I can keep to the road at least until daylight. But I want my two days to start at dawn."

Mac took his watch out of his vest pocket and flipped open the cover. "Like hell. It's eight o'clock. Your two days ends forty-eight hours from right now."

He shouted the last sentence, so that Greenley, who was running through the rain toward the stable, would have a chance to hear it.

# 31

CLOUDS OBSCURED THE RISING SUN. Dawn was marked only by the sky changing from black to gray — a shade almost identical to the color of the smoke coming from the cabin's chimney. Instead of rising into the damp sky, the smoke circled around the chimney and became lost in the gloom of the morning. More smoke came from a small fire by the corral. A black rubberized canvas poncho, one end tied to a rail of the corral and the other end pegged to the ground, formed a lean-to over that fire to shelter it from the drizzle. The wood smoke should have made the morning smell pleasant and kitchenlike. But, mixed with the odor of damp manure from the corral, it was almost sickening.

Otto avoided the smell of the air by inhaling steam from his coffee cup as he reached for the cabin door. When the door opened, two hounds scampered off the dog trot and over to the corral. Otto stood in the doorway and watched them run to a clump of palmetto, where they sought shelter from the wet. He stepped onto the dog trot and stared out into the woods. There was no breeze, so the moss hung limply, like tattered gray curtains, from the oaks. The gloom kept him from seeing very deeply into the woods. That worried him. Too good of a chance for ambush if they tried moving the cattle. Better to stay put and wait for whoever was coming from the woods. Otto knew he still had the whip hand to force out from cover whoever came. Tree would come out for the cattle. Greenley for the girl.

The deserters were ready. A scrabbling noise, like that of a giant squirrel, on the back of the cabin roof proved that. The roof sloped backward, providing cover for someone lying on it. A rifleman on the roof would have a clear view and the first shot at anyone coming from the woods. So, before nightfall, Otto had divided guard duty chores. He and his sons took turns watching the cattle. The deserters took turns watching the woods from the rooftop. The slope was level enough to allow lying or walking on it, as long as whoever was there was careful. But it was steep enough that anyone who was careless and dozed off would slip and fall. That kept the sentries on their job.

Otto walked back into the cabin and poured some more coffee from the pot in the fireplace. He and his sons had developed a habit of drinking from one pot while the deserters drank from another. Officers and enlisted men drank from different pots in the Army. Why not carry that over to cow hunting with strangers? The deserters' pot sat on the campfire under the poncho. A constant tapping sound came from the poncho as the drizzle struck it. Otto could hear snatches of whispered conversation from the five who drank from the outside pot. Then, he heard the soft, rhythmical squishing sounds caused by a horse walking though mud. Corley was returning from watching the cattle. Time to wake up Martin.

Snores from the sleeping loft, above and behind Otto, showed that Martin still was asleep. Then came a moan, a soft whining sound underlying the ragged snoring. The girl was waking. Otto did not know whether she was awakening from sleep or from a pain-induced stupor. Either way, he was pleased. Conscious, she would be a better hole card in the game that would begin before too long. Otto reached up into the loft, felt a warm, thin arm and pulled on it. He jerked her by the arm to the dirt. The girl fell with a soft, fleshy thud and a sharp cry. She was naked, the skin a pale, creamy beige below the tanned face and neck. Her hair hung forward, covering her breasts and sweeping the floor as she rocked her head back and forth. The cry faded back into the moan.

Otto felt a slight knot in his stomach and a warmth spread through his body as if he'd just had a shot of whiskey. It was a pang of lust. He forced himself to ignore it. No time for that. Besides, he had his turn with the girl. He, Corley, and Martin had divided up riding time with her when they settled on the schedule for riding around the herd. Best now to concentrate on the job that awaited.

The noise of the fall awakened Martin. He sat up naked on the blankets and looked down at the girl. "Get dressed," Otto snapped at him. "'N' get her covered."

Martin reached beside him and picked up something white. He threw it at his father. It was Doris's linen chemise. Otto caught it in midair with his right hand while reaching for the girl with his left. He shook her by her shoulders. He stared into her eyes, trying to see if she was alert enough to understand anything. Her pupils had widened until there was no more brown left in her eyes. The black pupils were rimmed by what should have been narrow circles of white. Except now the whites were mostly red. Tears came from the sides, slipping over the quaking lower lids and down the cheeks, which already were lined by hours of earlier crying. Still, the eyes had not gone completely dull, like those of a dying animal. Enough sparkle remained in them to show that she wanted to live. She would be able to do her part.

"Put this on," Otto flung the chemise at her. For a moment, the ivory fabric covered her face. She took it and listlessly put it on over her head. By the time she was standing, with the chemise covering her from shoulders to ankles, Martin was clothed, with his gunbelt around his waist. He jumped to the floor and walked to the fireplace.

"Coffee?" Martin asked, smiling slightly, as if he and Doris had just finished a meal in a Savannah restaurant.

"She won't have time. You'll be damned lucky to finish a cup here yourself," Otto said. "We're goin' to be busy this mornin', or we'll be heatin' our next pot in hell."

A shadow further darkened the meager light from the doorway. Corley stood there, water dripping from his poncho and hat brim. "Get me a length o' rope afore comin' in," his father said to him.

Within seconds, Corley was back, throwing a piece

of hemp across the room as he walked in and over to the coffee pot. Otto caught the rope and sliced it in half with his Bowie. He turned to Doris. "Sugar, I want us all to live through today. Your chances o' doin' that get better the quieter you are. Just don't fight us 'n' you'll get by."

He looked past her shoulders, to where his sons stood watching. "Martin, come on 'n' bring her." Otto walked to the door and outside. Martin, holding Doris by her shoulders, followed. The girl barely moved her feet, so Martin half-dragged her through the mud to the corral gate. Otto then took one of her arms and tied it to the gate with a piece of the rope. He flung the other piece to Martin, who tied the other arm. "Sorry. Know it's uncomfortable," Otto said to her. "But whoever comes out o' those woods, I want them to be watchin' this corral, not us. If your Yankee friend comes, just keep him occupied for a moment or two 'n' we'll do the rest."

The drizzle had slackened to the point that Otto didn't feel the need for a poncho. But enough was falling to make Doris's chemise transparent within a few minutes. The deserters kept watching her, not the woods. Otto tried to put their minds on their work by having them repeatedly check to see that their powder was dry. He changed the sentry on the roof. Once on the trail, the deserter in the Confederate butternut brown had shown off by using his rifle to bring down an eagle soaring at least 200 yards above a lake. That was the kind of shooting Otto wanted from the roof. So, the blond youth replaced the deserter with the long, black beard and blue kepi.

Otto resumed his vigil on the dog trot, near the

cabin doorway. He cradled his Sharps in the crook of his right arm. Martin saddled a horse and began circling the cattle outside the corral. Corley was in the cabin loft, dozing. An hour passed. Doris slumped against the ropes. Her head hung down to her chest, with her hair dangling below her waist, hiding her face. Otto occasionally glanced at her as his eyes swept the open spaces between the cabin and the woods. Then, he saw one shadow move among the patches of shadows under the oaks. "Company's comin'," he yelled. Martin spurred his horse up to the cabin, taking his carbine from its scabbard as he hitched the horse to a fence post of the corral. Corley awoke at his father's call and stood in the doorway. Four of the deserters gathered their rifles from a stack near the campfire. They stood between the cabin and the corral. Otto heard the fifth deserter move on the roof, shifting his position. The shadow emerged from the oaks. A lone horseman. He dismounted, with a carbine in his right hand. His form became more distinct as he walked toward the cabin. When he reached the edge of the field, Otto could tell that he was clad in blue.

"Mornin' Major Greenley," Otto called as he shifted his carbine and cocked the hammer. "What brings you out in weather like this?"

Greenley feared that his voice would tremble, but he was able to reply clearly and loudly: "I'm here on business. You like deal makin'. Let me have the girl and you ride off with the cattle."

He advanced toward the cabin as he talked, trying to scout the land for cover. There was a slight rise in the ground a few yards from the corral. That would give some protection when the shooting began. All Greenley wanted to do was get Doris free before the fight. He sensed movement on the roof of the cabin. Before he could swing his Sharps toward the movement, he heard a shot.

Then he saw a brown figure tumble from the roof and land in a patch of mud. A voice, sounding strangely like the snarl of a dog, came from the woods behind him. "Cut her loose or we cut ya'll down."

Greenley glanced in the direction of the voice. Tree stood with his carbine trained toward the cabin. Skeeter was nearby, with smoke coming from the barrel of his rifle. Four other cow hunters either stood or kneeled among the oaks, guns ready.

Otto looked at the body in the mud. Its arms and legs stuck out at weird angles, like a marionette without strings. Piece of bad luck. Really bad. Things still could work out for the best, though.

He had planned on handling Danny Boy and Tree separately. Now, they'd shown up at the same time. Nobody's fault. Nothing he could do about it. Might as well play the cards that were dealt and trust that luck would change before the end of the game. He turned his head toward the corral, nodded to Martin, and pointed at the girl.

Martin drew his knife as he trotted toward Doris. Two quick slashes and she was free, standing, but motionless. "Doris, just walk to me," Greenley called. She lifted her head and began a slow walk, weaving drunkenly.

As she walked, Martin backed away, toward his horse. The deserter wearing the Union shell jacket edged toward the corral. The black-bearded one ducked through the corral fence.

"Come to me, Doris, Just keep walkin'." Greenley kept his eyes on her as he took a few more steps toward the corral.

Otto slowly moved from the cabin as Corley knelt in the doorway. The deserter with the gray slouch hat side-stepped toward the clump of palmettos, where the dogs stood silently watching.

"Keep walkin'." The only sounds were Greenley's voice and the clicking of gun hammers being cocked.

Doris weaved a few more steps while the short, chubby deserter knelt in the mud, training his rifle toward Tree's group. "Come to me. Everythin's goin' to be all right," Greenley kept his voice low, reassuring.

He took another step toward the girl. She tottered forward until she got to the top of the small rise. Greenley raised his voice and snapped out the command: "Now! Get down!"

She fell behind the rise. Then, the explosions of the first shots slugged Greenley's ears. The shots set off a chorus of panic-stricken bawling from the cattle and yelping from the dogs. Greenley sprinted to get between Doris and the corral. He knelt and shot at the chubby deserter. The black cloud of gunpowder obscured his vision for an instant. When it cleared, he saw his target curled in a ball in the mud.

The long-bearded deserter snapped off a shot from his rifle and dove for the cover of the cypress water trough in the corral. A bullet whistled from the edge of the woods and stopped the dive short of the trough. A dark stain appeared on the deserter's shirt, just above the rib cage.

Otto ran for the corral. Greenley reloaded his Sharps and fired a shot toward the runner, but missed. A bullet screamed by Greenley, close enough that he could feel its heat on his cheek. Instead of reloading the Sharps, he drew his revolver and aimed toward Corley in the cabin doorway. But before Greenley could shoot, Corley was knocked sideways and back, as if kicked by a huge, invisible animal. He disappeared into the darkness of the cabin.

Greenley searched for another target. Then, from behind him and to the left, he heard a voice scream "Glory to God." He turned and saw one of the cow hunters, with a youthful, freckled face, twist to the ground. A revolver seemed to jump from the youth's hands. It arched through the air and landed near Doris. Greenley looked behind her and saw another of Tree's men lying at the edge of the woods.

The rest of the cow hunters came toward the cabin, firing handguns. None of them ran. They walked carefully, deliberately, so that they could aim as they advanced. Greenley reached behind him with his left hand to touch Doris, fired a shot toward the cabin, got to his feet and joined the hunters. Targets became hard to find in the milling of the cattle and horses. Some of the animals were running in circles around the cabin, shielding the fighters from each other.

Trying to aim his revolver, the deserter with the gray hat stood up from the palmettos. He saw Volusia at the same instant that the hunter saw him. But Volusia already had the hammer cocked on his gun. His shot hit the deserter in the neck. His hat flew off as his head jerked back and his body collapsed into the mud.

Tree dove and landed belly first in mud near the

corral. He rolled to his right side to avoid the hooves of passing cattle. He saw the blue-jacketed deserter at the corner of the cabin. The deserter had his gun at his side. His eyes bulged and his head bobbed from side to side, looking for either a target or an escape route. Tree aimed the Colt at the middle button of his jacket, but, before he could fire, several bullets screamed from behind and flew past him. At least one of those bullets spun the deserter around to the back of the cabin. For an instant, the deserter seemed to be pinned to the wall, then he slid down into a sitting position, his legs spread out awkwardly, like a speared frog's.

Bullets came from the corral. Tree looked for a target, but could see nothing except legs of running cattle. Then, he heard a high-pitched horse whinny from the side of the corral. He spotted Martin, trying to get a foot in a stirrup as the horse bucked wildly. Tree fired twice, missing both shots. He reached for Heavy's Remington in the holster. Martin was in the saddle and riding off before Tree finished the draw.

Greenley also saw Martin. He knew he had emptied his revolver and didn't bother to aim it. Instead, he holstered the gun and ran toward the horseman. He reached for his scabbard and drew his saber as he ran.

A shape emerged from the doorway of the cabin — Corley, trying to run, but stumbling clumsily. His right shoulder slumped downward and his shirt was dark with blood. Still, he was escaping. Tree had the Remington out and tried to aim at Corley. A steer ran in front of the gunsight, destroying the chance for a shot. He again tried to aim, but other cattle kept getting between him and his target. "Damn. Bastard's gonna make it," Tree muttered as the stumbling figure got to the rise, near Swede's body.

But a puff of black smoke appeared from the other side of the rise and Corley leaped into the air. His mouth opened into a wide circle and, for a brief instant, a shriek came from him that could be heard above the other noises of the fight.

A smoldering hole appeared where the crotch of his trousers had been. Another black cloud came from the rise. Corley fell backwards. The smoke cleared and Tree saw Doris, kneeling on the other side of the rise. She held Swede's revolver in both hands.

Tree looked toward the corral. He saw Greenley, a saber raised in his right hand, leap at Martin. The major landed against the neck of the horse as it bucked. His weight sent the horse off balance and it crashed into the corral fence. Splinters flew from two rails as they gave way to the falling horse and men. The shock of the crash knocked the saber from Greenley's hand. Tree watched the blade arc through the air for an instant. Then the horse got back to its feet and ran, leaving the men grappling with each other and rolling between shattered rails.

Another bullet came from the corral. Tree crawled along the fence line, trying to see the last target. He came to the mud and blood-stained ball that had been the chubby deserter. A cattle whip was looped in the body's gunbelt. Tree had left his whip tied to his saddle on his horse in the woods. But he needed to move cattle now. So he jerked the coiled whip from the body and rolled under the bottom rail of the fence.

Martin and Greenley wrestled among the broken

rails near the fence gate. Greenley could not see. It was as if a red veil was tied over his eyes. He could feel his opponent's hands on his neck. But all he could see was a red mist. He punched with his right fist and felt Martin's stomach give way under the blow. The hands loosened for a moment and Greenley snapped his head backwards, breaking the choke hold.

Tree stood in the corral and caught a glimpse of Otto, squatting behind the water trough. Holding the whip in his left hand and the Remington in his right, Tree began walking through the pen. The cattle between him and the trough parted as he cracked the whip. With their instinct for finding the weakest spot in a fence, the cattle stampeded for the broken rails.

Greenley saw them coming through the red veil. He jumped sideways and then rolled along the fence rails. Martin's back was to the broken rails and the cattle. He took a step toward Greenley, reaching out, trying to regain the choke hold. Then the first steer to leap the unbroken bottom rail caught him in the back with a horn. Martin fell. He made a sound that might have been a scream, but it was muffled as the cattle's hooves ground his face into the mud.

As the cattle ran from the whip, Tree took his first shot at Otto. The Remington, lighter than the Colt and with the downward angle of the barrel, felt strange in his hand. The shot thunked into the side of the trough. Brockton crouched behind the trough and reloaded his Colt by switching cylinders.

The loaded cylinder was in place by the time Tree took his second shot. This one struck the upper right corner of the trough. Cypress splinters flew. Several struck Otto's cheek. He recoiled from the sting, jumping back slightly from the protection of the trough.

Tree braced for his chance at a clear shot. He trained the sights on Otto's chest and pulled the trigger.

The black, sulfurous cloud came between them. When it left, Otto was staggering and waving his revolver toward Tree. The gun never fired. It slipped from Otto's hand as his fingers slowly unwrapped themselves from the butt. Then Otto dropped to his knees, shook his head, and fell forward.

Tree walked toward Otto, with the Remington cocked. When he reached the head, he could tell there would be no need for another shot. He eased the hammer forward, took his finger off the trigger, and holstered the gun.

Greenley could hear nothing for several seconds after the cattle left the corral. His ears rang from gunshots. On top of that, there was a pounding noise. It sounded as if ocean surf was ebbing and flowing with the rapid beating of his heart. The red veil began to relax its hold from around his eyes and he began to focus on his surroundings. He saw Tree standing by the water trough. Two cow hunters were walking toward the oaks. Skeeter stood near the cabin door. Then Greenley's eyes focused on Doris, sitting in the mud behind the slight rise. She held a revolver in her right hand. Her left arm hugged her legs just below the knees.

It was Greenley's turn to lurch drunkenly from the fence to the rise. His vision had cleared by the time he reached Doris. Clear enough to see the red welts on her shoulders and arms. The angry red blotches, soon to become bruises, under her eyes and on her cheeks. The red slashes, outlined in purple, on her wrists. He knelt beside her and held out his arms. Fearing to hurt her, he did not touch her. But he took the revolver, its barrel still warm, from her grasp. As she surrendered the gun, she folded herself between his arms and put her head on his chest.

What should he say? "Are you alright?" or "It's all right," or any dozens of variations of such expressions seemed banal. So Greenley said nothing, tossed the gun on the other side of the rise, and dropped his head until his cheek rested on Doris's hair.

Something was laid across his right shoulder. It was a heavy piece of fabric that draped down from the shoulder to his bent knee. He looked at it. A Confederate gray, swallow-tailed coat. It was decorated with the yellow chevron of a master sergeant.

"Way too hot for this," Tree's voice came from behind and above Greenley. "But cover her with it for right now."

Greenley put the coat over her shoulders. Surrounded by the coat and his arms, Doris put her face against his chest and sobbed quietly. Greenley didn't know how long they sat like that. Sparse sunlight began to show through the clouds and he could feel himself gradually become warmer as he sat. Eventually, he again heard Tree's voice.

"Need help?" Tree stood in front of them and whispered, as if they had been sleeping and he didn't want to disturb them.

"We've got their horses 'n' wagon now 'sides our own," he said. "Plenty o' extras for y'all. Found most o' her clothes 'n' put 'em in the left-hand room o' the cabin."

Doris's voice was quavering, but she was able to answer first. "Thank you."

Greenley helped her to her feet. He started walking with her toward the cabin. "We'll take their wagon. Everythin' will be all right."

He looked over Tree's shoulder. The bodies of the Brocktons and the deserters were gone. A trench had been dug near the corral. The other three hunters were shoveling sand into the trench from a mound of freshly dug earth.

"We're just 'bout done here," Tree said. "Volusia 'n' Dinghy are gettin' Swede 'n' Lonesome back to their homes for buryin'. Skeeter 'n' me are goin' to get our dogs 'n' come back for the cattle."

Greenley remembered that Tree didn't know the final decision on the herd. "Army's ready to buy them as soon as you get them to St. Augustine."

Tree took a plug of tobacco from a pouch on his belt. "Ride with us." He bit into the plug. "Less ya'll want to get back straightaway by yourselves."

Greenley glanced down at Doris. The pupils of her eyes were retreating and the brown irises were returning. "Thanks. I better get her straight to St. Augustine," he said. Tree nodded. Behind him, the others had finished their work and stowed the shovels in their wagon.

Doris rested her head on his shoulder. "St. Augustine? Let's talk 'bout headin' elsewhere. I want away from here. Right now, Wisconsin sounds mighty good."

Gold flecks beamed for a moment in her eyes. Greenley looked at them, smiled and said: "Ohio."

Skeeter walked away from the cabin, leading both his and Tree's horses. Dinghy already was in his saddle.

Volusia climbed onto the seat of the wagon. Two horses were tied by their reins to the rear of the wagon. Each of those horses carried long, limp bundles wrapped in blankets and tied across the saddles.

"God, man," Greenley said. "I'm sorry. The war's over and you've still lost two men."

Tree chewed for a couple of seconds before replying. "All the end of the war means is we stop shootin' at blue uniforms. We were going to settle with the Brocktons no matter what happened with the war. We'll always be settlin' with people like the Brocktons. With us, wars don't end. Just the enemies change."

Volusia cracked his whip and the oxen strained at their yokes, pulling the wagon forward. Dinghy rode beside the wagon. They headed east, into the woods.

Tree walked back to his horse and mounted. Skeeter climbed into his own saddle. Both of them turned their horses toward the woods. Greenley shouted out, "Hey! Just remembered somethin'."

The sergeant turned in his saddle. "Colonel Springer says to make sure and change the brand on that horse."

Tree's smile was broad enough that Greenley, from several yards away, could see the teeth. The hunter lifted his right hand and started to salute. But, instead, he brought the hand up to his hat. He took off the hat, waved it, and put it back on, pulling the rim down over his eyes.

A whip cracked in the woods. Skeeter already must have found some cattle. Tree spurred the gelding as he turned it toward the noise. He ducked his head as the horse passed under a moss-laden branch. The moss parted as he rode through it. Then the gray wisps came back together, hiding Tree from view.

THE END

# Historical Notes

**Ague:** The disease that plagued Tree, Doris, and practically every other 19th-century Floridian was spread by mosquito bites. Nobody knew that for sure until the science of bacteriology was developed toward the end of the century. Before then, most people blamed the disease on "bad air" from swamps. Its other common name, malaria, is Italian for "bad air" *(mal aria)*. Strangely enough, malaria replaced ague in popular usage about the same time that scientists proved the disease really had nothing to do with bad air.

**Baldwin:** The town still exists off U.S. Highway 90 on the western edge of the Jacksonville-Duval County metropolitan area. At one time, it was as wild as any of the Western trail towns, but it never regained its full vigor after Yankees destroyed it in 1864. The story about its name being changed from Thigpen is true.

**Black powder:** A finely ground mixture of sulfur, saltpeter, and charcoal, black powder was invented in the late 1200s. It was used in firearms until the late 1880s, when modern "smokeless" gunpowder came on the market. Anyone who fires a black-powder weapon will notice two things hanging in the air: a strong smell from the burned sulfur and a black cloud from the charcoal dust. The cloud, as black and dense as a thunderhead on a July afternoon, usually is between the shooter and his target. This puts to lie many of the tales of rapid-fire sharp-shooting. For example, Wild Bill Hickok supposedly demonstrated his skill by throwing his hat in the air and, as it flew, shooting neatly spaced holes into his hatband. The fact is, Bill couldn't have seen his hat after his

399

first shot. The only way to accurately aim after the first shot of a black-powder weapon is to either wait until the cloud dissipates or move to get a clear view of the target.

**Cleaning guns:** Maybe the worst part of black-powder shooting is the requisite cleaning of virtually every part of the gun. The patch box on the side of the stock in most black-powder long-arms usually holds screws and other little tools used in cleaning. Water, preferably boiling, was used to flush out the powder residue. Then the gun was thoroughly dried. If any grease or oil was available, the lubricant was used on the metal parts to prevent rust. It would take an experienced gun owner about 30 minutes to clean a weapon.

**Coacoochee:** Perhaps no other Native American hero has been as unsung as Coacoochee, or Wildcat. He probably defeated more whites in face-to-face combat than Sitting Bull, Crazy Horse, Cochise, and Geronimo combined. Yet, he is all but unknown outside of Florida and the Eagle Pass area along the Texas-Mexican border, where he spent his last years. Even most people who know of him can't pronounce his name. The pronunciation given in this book comes from C. Randall Daniels-Sakim, an elder of the Muskogee Seminoles near Blountstown, Florida.

**Cow hunter:** The word cowboy wasn't used in Florida until recently. For most of the 19th century, they were called cow hunters. It was a fitting name, since the job was more like a hunt — tracking down animals through wilderness areas — than herding domesticated cattle on open pasture land. Today, the word cowboy is bandied about frequently by people both in and outside of the business. But cowboy can have a somewhat negative connotation. A cowboy usually doesn't own his stock and sometimes is an irresponsible drifter. Most of those in the business refer to themselves as ranchers or cattlemen.

**Dialect:** Most 19th-century residents of north and central Florida had Scotch-Irish roots and their dialect held traces of the accents of their ancestral homelands. This showed in such speech patterns as almost never pronouncing the "f" in "of." By the 1860s, the Cracker dialect would have been pervasive enough that even those not of Scotch-Irish descent, such as Doris, would have spoken it. Floridian accents have been homogenized over the last several decades with an influx of Yankees. The accent still exists, however, particularly among natives of north-central Florida who were born before the 1930s.

**Dickison, John J.:** Captain "Dixie" Dickison's exploits as a Confederate guerrilla leader are legendary. Dickison, from rural Marion County near Ocala, fought along the banks of the St. Johns, attacking Union outposts and gunboats. The pint-sized guerrilla was particularly successful at sinking or capturing gunboats. He probably is the only cavalry officer in history to have scored more victories against his enemy's navy than army.

**Enterprize-Enterprise:** Eventually, those who spelled the name "Enterprise" won. The town declined in importance after a railroad line was built. In 1882, the city of DeLand was founded along the tracks, about 15 miles north of Enterprise and two miles east of the St. Johns River. Six years later, the seat of Volusia County was moved from Enterprise to DeLand. Enterprise still exists, although it is no longer an incorporated municipality. The giant housing development of Deltona borders the community on three sides.

**Fatio Boarding House:** Both Miss Fatio and her boarding house are historical. The house still stands, open to the public, at 20 Aviles Street, St. Augustine. Built by Andres Ximenez in 1798, it is known as the Ximenez-Fatio House. The furniture and china described are on display at the house. Miss Fatio supposedly was so proud of her china and concerned for its safety that she would wash it herself rather than trust it to her servants.

**Fort Marion:** Castillo de San Marcos in St. Augustine was known as Fort Marion from 1825 to 1942. It was named in honor of Francis Marion, the "Swamp Fox," a guerrilla leader in South Carolina during the American Revolution. The fort saw little service during the War Between the States. Occupying Union forces were quartered in a former Franciscan monastery (across from what is billed as the Oldest House in the United States) at the corner of Charlotte and St. Francis streets. Headquarters (now part of the Trinity Episcopal Church parish hall) and the provost marshal's office (now the Government House) were across from each other at the corner of King and St. George streets. The fort and Government House are open to the public.

**Minorcans:** Although they were recruited from a variety of Mediterranean islands, all of the former indentured servants were called Minorcans. They were brought from their homelands in 1768 and set down on a plantation owned by Andrew Turnbull, near present-day New Smyrna Beach. There originally were about 1,400 laborers. No more than 750 still lived in 1777, when most of the survivors escaped to St. Augustine. There, the governor of British East Florida, Patrick Tonyn, sided with the runaways and imprisoned Turnbull.

**Muzzle-loaders:** A few firearms during the War Between the States fired self-contained metallic cartridges similar to those used today. But most soldiers, and particularly such militia units as the Cattle Guard, used muzzle-loading weapons like Tree's carbine. The lead bullet, either a round ball or a cone-shaped "Minié ball," frequently was wrapped with a charge of gunpowder in a paper cartridge. The shooter tore off one end of the cartridge with his teeth, poured in the powder, and wedged the ball tightly against the charge by shoving a ramrod down the barrel. A small copper cap, containing a tiny explosive charge, then was put on a nipple under the hammer of the gun. When the trigger was pulled, the hammer struck the cap, firing the explosive and sending a shower of sparks into the powder charge. Many shooters, particularly those like Tree, who used their own non-military-issue weapons, didn't bother with cartridges. They carried their powder in flasks and simply poured it down the barrel when loading. With or without a cartridge, muzzle-loaders could not be expected to fire more than three shots per minute.

**Olustee:** Much of the battlefield has been preserved and is open to the public. It lies between Lake City and Jacksonville off U.S. Highway 90 near Interstate 10.

Several militia groups and irregular cavalry units were stationed near the place where Tree and his group were located. Olustee was the biggest full-scale battle of the war in Florida. Out of slightly more than 5,000 Union troops involved, 26.5 percent were killed or wounded. That was the third-highest Yankee casualty rate of the war, behind the Wilderness-Spotsylvania campaign in Virginia and the Battle of Port Hudson in Louisiana.

**Pilatka-Palatka:** Eventually, the spelling was settled in favor of "Palatka." The old judge's home, known as the Bronson-Mulholland House, exists at 100 Mulholland Park and is open to the public. Standing nearby is St. Mark's Episcopal Church, which quickly regained its stature as a house of worship once the Yankees and their horses left. The story about the invaders taking down the bell and putting it in the middle of an aisle is true. When they left town, the Yankees also took the church's Bible and some prayer books. A Northern veteran had an attack of conscience in 1906 and returned the books.

**Revolvers:** During the 1860s, even fewer revolvers than long-arms fired metallic cartridges. Although revolvers could be fired very rapidly, each chamber had to be loaded separately, a process that took several minutes. Most of those using percussion revolvers either carried more than one gun or had spare cylinders.

Sometimes, the sparks from the cap on one chamber would fly into other chambers and set off every one in the gun. That usually resulted in more damage to the gun, the shooter, and innocent bystanders than to the intended target. As a safety precaution, most revolver owners put a pinch of cornmeal between the bullet and the powder charge. The cornmeal blocked stray sparks from hitting the gunpowder. Also, most shooters didn't load the chamber directly under the hammer when carrying the revolver in a holster. That prevented the gun from firing if it fell out of the holster or was jostled. Thus, most people who owned six-shooters usually had only five shots at their disposal.

**Saddles:** The saddle Tree brought back with him was called the McClellan, after Union Gen. George B. McClellan, who developed the split-seat design. It was standard issue for Yankees during the war and for the remainder of the U.S. Cavalry's life. Many Confederates appropriated the saddle during the war, and it became the most common saddle of Florida cattlemen. Until the introduction of the McClellan, most Floridians used what are now called English saddles. The large Mexican-Western saddles now used by virtually everybody in the cattle business came into vogue in the 1930s, when ropes began to replace whips as the main tools of the industry. Neither the McClellan nor the English styles had horns on which ropes could be secured.

**Salt pork:** Similar to heavily smoked bacon in taste and appearance, salt pork stored well and usually didn't spoil on long trips. Therefore, it was the meat of choice on cattle drives, wagon trains, ocean voyages, and military expeditions until better food preservation techniques came along in the late 1800s. Although they had plenty of beef on the hoof around them, Florida cattlemen usually preferred eating pork and saving the steers for monetary gain.

**Sharps:** Sharps were among the best and most popular of the breech-loading percussion long-arms. The breech is the portion of the gun that includes the firing chamber. Skeeter and other owners of breech-loading weapons could fire much more rapidly than those using muzzle-loaders. In the Sharps, the trigger guard was attached to a lever that, when moved forward, exposed the firing chamber. A shooter would move the trigger guard and put a paper cartridge into the chamber. Moving the guard back brought down a small razor that cut off the end of the cartridge. The shooter put a cap on the nipple under the hammer and the gun was ready to fire.

**Starke's Plantation:** The community of DeLeon Springs sits on part of what used to be the Starke family's Spring Garden Plantation. The main yard and the spring now are in DeLeon Springs State Recreational Area. Parts of the mill remain there and have been incorporated into a restaurant. Volusia was right when he observed that the sulfur odor was decreasing. It was so bad in 1831 that naturalist James Audubon, who visited the spring, described the smell as "highly nauseous." Yet, today there is no odor.

**Steer throwing on foot:** This practice grew out of Florida cow hunters' reliance on whips to drive and control their stock. Because they didn't use ropes, they developed other means of holding down cattle. Most modern cattlemen rope and tie their stock like their Western counterparts. But the practice of steer throwing on foot survives in rodeolike contests among Florida cattlemen.

**Tobacco:** Chewing tobacco was ubiquitous in Florida throughout most of the last 200 years. It still is favored over smoking products by farmers, cattlemen, and others working with their hands outdoors. Chewing on a quid frees both hands for tasks other than holding a cigar, cigarette, or pipe. And there is no fire danger — an important consideration when working around hay and other combustibles.

As Otto pointed out, the humidity of outdoors Florida also discouraged smoking. Cigarette, cigar, and pipe tobacco became soggy until the invention of foil packs. For years, Floridians preferred plugs, in which the tobacco was pressed into cakes that retained the freshness of the leaves. The introduction of resealable foil packs in the 1960s made looseleaf tobacco more popular.

The phrase "thirsty for tobacco" was the 19th-century equivalent of "nicotine fit" and was widely used by Confederates.

**Whips:** Most cow whips were 12 to 15 feet long. Although by now ropes are used for most tasks, whips left their legacy on the Florida ranges. Rural Georgians and Floridians still call themselves Crackers, a name that has come down over more than a century from the sound of the whips on drives and cow hunts.

If you enjoyed reading this book, here are some other fiction titles from Pineapple Press. For a complete catalogue or to place an order, write to Pineapple Press, P.O. Drawer 16008, Southside Station, Sarasota, FL 34239, or call (800) PINEAPL.

## Cracker Westerns:
*Thunder on the St. Johns* by Lee Gramling. Young Josh Carpenter and his family, homesteaders in 1850s Florida, join forces with an ex-gambler and a resourceful trapper's daughter to help settlers save their land from outlaws.

*Riders of the Suwannee* by Lee Gramling. Tate Barkley returns to 1870s Florida just in time to come to the aid of a young widow and her children as they fight to save their homestead from outlaws.

*Trail from St. Augustine* by Lee Gramling. A young trapper, a crusty ex-sailor, and an indentured servant girl fleeing a cruel master join forces to cross the Florida wilderness in search of buried treasure and a new life.

## Other Florida Fiction:
*Forever Island* and *Allapattah* by Patrick Smith. *Forever Island* has been called the classic novel of the Everglades. *Allapattah* is the story of a young Seminole in despair in the white man's world.

*The River is Home* and *Angel City* by Patrick Smith. *The River is Home* tells of a Louisiana family's struggle to cope with changes in their rural environment. *Angel City* is a powerful and moving exposé of migrant workers in Florida in the 1970s.

*A Land Remembered* by Patrick Smith. Three generations of the MacIveys, a Florida family battling the hardships of the frontier to rise from a dirt-poor cracker life to the wealth and standing of real estate tycoons.